Christmas Under the Stars

Karen Swan was previously a fashion editor and lives in East Sussex with her husband and three children.

Visit Karen's website at www.karenswan.com, or you can find her author page on Facebook or follow her on Twitter @KarenSwan1

Also by Karen Swan

Christmas
UNDER THE STARS

KAREN SWAN

PAN BOOKS

First published 2016 by Macmillan

This paperback edition published 2016 by Pan Books
an imprint of Pan Macmillan
20 New Wharf Road, London N1 9RR
Associated companies throughout the world
www.panmacmillan.com

ISBN 978-1-4472-8016-3

5 7 9 8 6

A CIP catalogue record for this book is available from the British Library.

Typeset by Ellipsis Digital Limited, Glasgow
Printed and bound by CPI Group (UK) Ltd, Croydon, CR0 4YY

Visit **www.panmacmillan.com** to read more about all our books
and to buy them. You will also find features, author interviews and
news of any author events, and you can sign up for e-newsletters
so that you're always first to hear about our new releases.

Prologue

Saturday 25 March 2017

Lucy pulled the bedcovers back up, smoothing out the wrinkles and re-plumping the pillows, the covered hot-water bottles already warming the sheets, the steam from the hot bath in the next room escaping round the door and misting the small mirror on the dressing table. The guests would be freezing when they got in.

Outside, the wind moaned again and the windows rattled in their frames. The storm was really gathering strength now, this afternoon's break in the blizzards but a brief hiatus as the eye passed over them, and she could see the snowflakes dancing in feverish patterns, tangoing with the flurrying gusts like a shaken-up snow globe.

She crossed the room to draw the curtains, glancing for a moment at her own home across the courtyard. From this four-star perspective, she saw how shabby the little bungalow was becoming – even aside from the industrial bins parked along her wall, the white paint was slowly blackening from rain and snow melt and moss and damp; the kitchen window was cracked in the bottom corner (from a thrown shoe, if she remembered rightly); and the planters either side of the door were depressingly neglected, with just a few skeletal twigs poking through the snow all that remained of the hydrangeas she'd planted last summer. She turned away, vowing to set Tuck onto it as soon as the snow went. A lick of paint, a trip to the nursery and her modest little home would look very different. Feel very different.

In here though – in here, all was perfect, as it always should be in a hotel (wasn't that the point of them, after all?) and with a final glance, she let herself back out into the hall. The door clicked shut behind her and she smiled at a Japanese couple coming out of their room further down the corridor. Room 28 – the electric towel rail was faulty in there.

'Hey there, is everything OK for you? Do you need any fresh towels, more water . . . ?' she asked as she passed, and they politely demurred, probably more on account of their limited English than anything else.

Crossing the carpet in brisk, silent steps, she used the service stairs, exiting into the kitchen where her mother was standing over a bubbling pan of soup, much to the surprise of the staff, who were only just arriving for their shift and couldn't have looked more astonished to see her with her shirtsleeves rolled up if she'd been standing there in stockings and suspenders. Barbara glanced up as she came over – her cheeks were pink with harried fluster but her eyes were bright and of course, not a platinum-bobbed hair was out of place. It never was. Not in a storm. Not in a crisis.

'All done?' she asked.

'Everything's sorted,' Lucy nodded.

'Good.' Barbara checked her watch, rubbing her hands together the way she always did when she was anxious. 'Well, they should be here any minute now . . .'

Lucy's phone rang and she glanced at the name on the

screen. 'Hi,' she said, turning away and walking over to the back door, a smile already on her lips, suddenly blind to the bleakness of her tired bungalow as she gazed through the window, across the courtyard again.

'Luce, it's me!' Tuck's voice sounded distant. The line was breaking up and she could tell he was outside from the way that it sounded as though sheets were being shaken out beside him.

'Where are you?' she called, hoping he could hear her over the wind.

'On my way back from Bill's.'

Lucy bit her lip. Of course he was. Every day ended with a beer or four with the boys. She guessed it was four tonight given that he was walking home in these conditions, no doubt having been forced to leave the truck keys behind the bar. The staff knew him too well.

'Listen,' he shouted. 'Have you spoken to Mitch or Meg?' He sounded out of breath, as though he was running or at least walking very fast.

'Not since this morning.'

'*Shit*,' he muttered.

'Why?'

'I can't get Mitch on his cell and I don't know where he is. I thought they were gonna come back down during the break in the weather this afternoon?'

'Well, not that I've seen. They must still be up at the cabin.' She frowned. 'Why? What's going on? What's wrong?'

'There's a couple of hikers missing in Wilson's Gully but Search and Rescue won't go out – no visibility and the avalanche risk's too high! Fucking pussies. Everyone's freakin' out. One's a twelve-year-old boy, for Chrissakes. *Twelve*.'

3

Lucy winced, knowing from his language it was definitely more than four beers. 'But Tuck—'

'Listen, I gotta go. I've gotta get hold of Mitch. He's a mile from there.'

She hesitated. 'You mean you want him to go after them? In this?'

'That's his call. But he'd want to know. I would.'

Lucy felt the pulse in her ear, her eyes on a racoon scratching around the recycling bin, seeing the way its fur was brushed to standing as another gust whipped the small courtyard and sent it scurrying for cover in the undergrowth again.

'Luce? You hear me?'

'Uh, yeah, yeah.'

'I'll be back in a bit, OK? But if they call in the meantime, you let him know I'm trying to get hold of him.'

'Sh-sure.'

'Bye, babe.'

'Bye,' she murmured, her voice a whisper, her heart pounding at double time, the phone like a burning coal in the palm of her hand.

Part I
BEFORE

Chapter One

Saturday 18 February 2017

The snow-lined gully curled and sliced before them, the tips of their boards overhanging the flat.

'I don't know, man, it's too much. Just look at those rocks,' Tuck murmured. 'We hit them at speed, they'll be like a fricking serrated knife.'

'I agree.'

Tuck turned, staring at his own reflection in the orange mirrored lenses of Mitch's polarized goggles. 'You do?'

Mitch nodded. 'So we better not hit 'em.'

Tuck swallowed as Mitch extended his arm and pointed out his line for their descent through the couloir. 'We keep to the shadow down this first drop here, then take the left side of the tower, 'cause you see the ice on the right? –' he indicated the six-metre-high finger of frozen granite smack bang in the middle of their path – 'Just a glimmer there? Slip or lose control on that and you'll hit the wall at a hundred twenty kph.' Mitch shook his head and tutted. 'So we keep left. It's gonna be tight.' He squinted as though calculating the mathematical ratios required to get round it, to survive, before looking back at Tuck and nodding with a smile. Tuck couldn't see his eyes behind the goggles but he didn't need to. He could read his friend like a book. 'It's doable.'

Tuck looked back down at their self-appointed mission, wishing he could feel so confident. 'Is that a crack?' he asked, slapping Mitch in the chest, his eyes up on the rocks above them.

'Where?'

Tuck pointed to a hair's-breadth line in the snowpack on the overhang, ten metres down, just past the tower. 'Jesus, man, that is loose as. It could come down at any time. It could dump straight on us as we're going past.'

Mitch grinned. 'Only if you're screaming like a little girl.'

Tuck slumped. Perhaps on the inside . . .

Mitch grabbed his shoulder and squeezed it. 'I hate to point out the obvious, buddy, but there's no other way down from here. We can either wait for that slab to slice, or we can zip this chute and get the hell out of here. The weather's closing in tomorrow and this is probably our only window to get the shot. I told you Meg made me promise this would be the last run before the wedding. She says she doesn't want me waiting up the aisle for her in traction.'

Tuck nodded but he still felt weak. He could best almost any other man on the mountain; but Mitch, his oldest adversary and best friend, was always first off and first down.

Beside them, Badger whined – not from fear but impatience. A cross of Bernese Mountain Dog and German Shepherd, his large frame but slim build made him the perfect back-country companion, running through the deep powder with impressive stamina, tongue lolling and ridiculously pink in the all-white terrain, ears up and tail aloft. Mitch had trained him since he was a pup and if the worst did happen and the snow cleaved – even if there was no one else around to pick up the transceiver signals in their backpacks – Badger would dig them out. He was their comrade and lifeline.

'You ready, huh, Badge?' Tuck asked, scratching him behind the ear with one bulky gloved-up finger. 'A'right, let's do this.' Pulling his glove off quickly, he reached up and turned on the camera on his helmet. 'You good?'

'The best, but then you already knew that, man,' Mitch grinned, wisecracking as ever. He stopped smiling suddenly. 'Woah! What the hell happened?'

'Huh?' Tuck glanced at his wrist, trying to see what Mitch could see. 'Oh. Nuthin'. Some branches caught me when I was doing the logs.' Tuck pulled his sleeve down and got the glove back on. It was minus twenty-five Celsius with wind chill today.

'Big fuckin' scratches.'

Tuck shook his head with a grin. 'They were big fuckin' logs, man.'

There was a pause as Mitch carried on staring at him.

'What?' Tuck laughed with a shrug.

'A'ight,' Mitch nodded. 'Well, see you at the bottom.'

And without a moment's hesitation, he tipped himself forward, accelerating with dizzying speed within seconds, keeping to the left side of the pass for as long as there was shadow before turning hard left round the tower and out of sight. Badger, knowing the drill, followed a few seconds after, pitching himself downwards without fear, his body in a rocking-horse motion as he plunged front paws first into the snow before leaping out with his hind legs, on and on, seemingly never tiring, never spooking.

'Shit,' Tuck muttered, feeling a swift kick of anger that he was now up here, alone. 'Goddam sonofa—' It was always a game to Mitch. Fear was an alien concept to the guy. Tuck tipped forwards before his brain could think about it again, his eyes immediately trained on his friend's tracks, the snow to the right side turfed up and crushed by Badger's exuberant descent.

He refused to look up at the perilous snow slab as he passed the tower – also the site of the narrowest turn – there was no point. If it came down now, he'd be crushed just from the sheer volume.

He held his breath and made it through, his eyes back on Mitch as he saw him take a nerve-shredding straight-line pass past the knife rocks. 'Must be crazy . . .' he muttered, still not believing that he'd allowed his friend to talk him into this, in awe that they were actually doing it; taking the line they'd talked about since they were kids, never thinking they'd have the expertise or balls, or equipment – *their boards, their design* – to someday go do it.

The granite walls whipped past at lightning speed – dagger-like icicles suspended in front of the exposed cliffs in a dazzling arctic blue, a membranous skin of ice swelling, magnifying, distorting the rock face – but there was no time to worry. Not now. This was instinct. There was only this moment and no other.

Mitch was already out in the sunshine, the gradient levelling off to a mere sixty-five degrees, arms punching the air as he slowed, knees bent as he idly swooped in lazy turns, the hard work over, the reward reaped as the endorphins flooded his body. '*Whooo-hooo!*' he hollered at the top of his voice, Badger barking in excitement as he caught up with his master.

Tuck was almost there himself – the walls of the couloir were about to splay open, drop away to open pasture, the mountain becoming a friend again – when he heard it, that low rumble like an old man's cough even as Mitch's victory whoops still echoed around them like bats.

Tuck couldn't turn back to see, not while he was still in the col, but then he didn't need to, to know that hundreds of tonnes of snow were falling and tumbling and gathering and sliding behind him. He saw Mitch hear it too, saw him look back and his body stiffen as he took in what Tuck could not.

'Fuck!!' Mitch hollered, turning the board ninety degrees and facing the end straight down the slope. 'Get out of there, Tuck!'

Tuck, listening to the sound of his own breathing against the growing roar of the avalanche, kept his eyes on his friend, following his every move as he cut left down the mountain face. It was a way steeper line than the one they'd planned but the trees were at a higher level there and they both knew the forest would slow the avalanche, though not necessarily stop it. If they could just get deep enough in . . .

But the noise was growing louder, the snow slide gathering volume and speed. They took lines that would ordinarily have made even Mitch pause, jumping big air without sight of what was below them or how far the drop, but what choice did they have? They had to take their skills past their limits or they wouldn't be getting out of this alive. Badger was barking but at full gallop, the snow more compacted on these exposed slopes from where the wind whipped it, so he didn't disappear up to his belly with every bound. He was keeping up.

Then the light dimmed and Tuck knew it was the avalanche spiriting ahead in a rolling, billowing airborne cloud, a sure sign the snow below it was snapping at his feet, gaining on him. He turned for more vertical pitch but the sudden flat light had robbed the snowy landscape of definition, texture, contrast, and at these speeds, on unknown terrain . . . He had to slow; he could be boarding straight towards a million-year-old rock wall for all he knew.

He couldn't see Mitch or the dog. The snow powder was showering down on him now like ash from a volcano, icy lumps battering his helmet like hail bullets, the sticky snow catching in his craw, his nose. He felt the back of his board nudged by the moving earth behind him, felt his balance wobble and put his weight on the front leg, trying to out-pace it when suddenly he saw the trees – their trunks like the legs of friendly giants, offering shelter. So close.

Too close.

Tuck braked hard, travelling too fast for the tiny turns he would have to make to wind through them – slamming into a tree would feel little different to the human body than slamming into a rock wall, or being pulverized by 500 tonnes of snow.

'*Yeah!*' he heard Mitch holler, just ahead but still out of sight.

'Where the fuck are you?' Tuck shouted, still not daring to look back as his legs – exhausted now, beginning to shake – manipulated the short board into tight chicane turns, the branches whipping past his face and body with stinging smacks.

'Over here!'

Tuck followed Mitch's voice, grateful for Badger's joyous bark telling him that wherever they were, it was out of danger. Tuck kept moving, zipping and weaving through the trees, not sure whether *he* was yet, before he noticed that the roar had become more distant and he could see shadows again. He strained his ears to hear, his eyes alighting on a faint lime glow fifty metres ahead. Mitch's jacket!

'Are we good?' Tuck shouted, his friend's jacket like a ship's beacon in the fog as he boarded straight up to him.

The two men hugged hard.

'Yeah, man! We're the freakin' best!' Mitch roared, thumping him mightily on the back so that Tuck knew he would be bruised the next day. Badges of honour.

They looked back through the trees together, the dimness of the snowscape telling them the avalanche was still in full spate, a snow tsunami – frothing and huge and devastating. And the best thing was – they had it all on film.

They whooped and faced up to the sky, both howling like wolves just as they had done when they were seven, and eleven, and fifteen, and twenty-one . . . Badger joined in, as though he too knew what they were celebrating – that they were young. They were free. They were alive.

Chapter Two

Saturday 18 March 2017

Meg could hear them from behind the curtain, the two older women disagreeing as per usual.

'You'll be saying we should just give them bibs, next,' Barbara huffed, sounding put out.

'Nonsense. I just don't see what's dignified about arranging them as swans, that's all,' Dolores rebuffed. 'Simplicity is best in my book.'

'Hmmph, well, we all know that's what you tell your hairdresser,' Barbara snipped. 'Besides, if it's good enough for the Japanese . . .'

Meg smiled, shaking her head at their toing and froing. They were more like a married couple than she and Mitch were going to be! She tipped her head to the side and held out the skirt again, taking in her reflection. She had never looked like this before. Princess dress, crown – well, '*ti-aaahra*' – it even sounded grand . . .

The hairdresser had tonged her long, chestnut hair into soft ringlets, pulling up tendrils at the side so that a half-ponytail tumbled from the crown of her head. The boutique had given her a bouquet of cream silk roses to hold; her actual flowers were going to be freesias – her mother's favourites – but they were out of season and therefore too expensive to get in especially for today so these would have to do. But other than that, this was it, she was good to go. The dress fit her perfectly now and this was all how it was going to be, two weeks today . . .

She whisked the curtain back and with her breath held, turned for Dolores and Barbara to see her.

Both women – knee to knee on the gold-thread sofa – stopped their bickering instantly, Barbara's hands flying to her mouth, speechless for once, as she took in the vision Meg presented to them – Meg, who was usually never to be found out of her beloved dungarees, hiking boots and Schoffel fleeces.

Dolores sat as still as if she'd been struck by the gods, but her orange-brown eyes were shining, her thin, weathered-brown face as softened as if she were butter in the sun.

'Oh, you precious child!' Barbara gasped, standing up and clapping her fingertips together. 'Where have you been hiding your light all this time?'

Meg smiled shyly. 'So you like it? You don't think it's too—?' She fiddled with the off-the-shoulder neckline that was delicately scooped and made a feature of her neck.

'Absolutely not. Give us a twirl,' Barbara ordered by circling her finger in the air.

Meg did as she was told, her face shining with delight as the sumptuous satin fabric billowed, Barbara fanning it outwards for extra effect. 'Oh, Meggy! You are the most beautiful bride I think I have ever seen!' she breathed.

'Hey!' Lucy protested loudly from behind her own curtain. 'What about me?'

'Well, of course alongside you, darling!' Barbara said, rolling her eyes at Meg, before tutting. 'What are you doing in there anyway? You can't take this long on the actual day, you know. It's bad form to keep your bride waiting.'

'I know that, Mom! But you try doing up all these buttons.'

'Honestly . . .' Barbara muttered, disappearing into the changing room to help.

Meg smiled, turning towards Dolores. She bit her lip. 'So?'

Dolores stood, her iron-grey, poker-straight 'schoolboy-cut' hair and leonine eyes a counterpoint to all the hyper-feminine froth and decoration in the boutique. 'If your mother could only see you now . . .' she said, taking Meg's hands in her own.

Meg looked down, feeling a rush of emotion, like a heat, rise through her. Both her parents were dead – her mother first from breast cancer when Meg was eighteen, her father three years later, slipping on a rock while out fishing and hitting his head as he went into the water – and there still wasn't a day that went by when she didn't find it profoundly shocking that she was an orphan now. Of course, she had Ronnie, her little sister by eighteen months; they had been close once, back when they'd still lived in England, Ronnie forever the practical joker leaving fart cushions under the seats or positioning fake dog poos on the carpets just as their mother welcomed guests at the front door . . . But that had all changed when they'd emigrated here, Ronnie struggling to make friends whilst Meg had found Lucy on the very first day. Something about Ronnie's clipped, frank manner and undeniable intellect hadn't travelled well and she had only become more isolated when their mother fell sick so soon afterwards. Perhaps if their father had lived, she might have hung around and stuck it out, but life hadn't panned out that way and she had fled for medical school the first chance she got, leaving Meg behind – though she would never see it like that. Now they communicated mainly via Likes on each other's Instagrams. Modern sisterhood.

Dolores squeezed her hands and she looked back up.

'Even though I was almost old enough to have been *her* mother, she and I were friends for a reason, Meg – we shared the same values, the same sense of humour. We both loved tacos. But more than any of that, we both saw you through the same prism – and I know she couldn't possibly have been prouder than I am right now. That old woman over there is right for once, you are *the* most beautiful bride—'

'Hey!' both Lucy and Barbara protested this time, albeit for different reasons, from behind the curtain.

'Less of the "old", thank you,' Barbara called. 'You've got a good decade on me.'

But Dolores didn't hear. Meg was the sole focus of her attention. 'What a wonderful young woman you've grown to be.'

Meg stepped forward and threw her arms around Dolores's neck. 'Thank you,' she whispered. Dolores might be her boss, but she was also the closest thing Meg had to a mother now.

'Although, did I see . . . ?' Dolores stepped back and lifted the netted skirt slightly to check her hunch. Brown leather-booted feet peeped back at her. 'Meg!'

Meg laughed. 'I will on the day, I promise, but those are so uncomfortable!' She frowned, glaring at the tossed-aside stilettoes on the dressing-room floor.

Dolores laughed too. 'You're not to wear thermals either,'

she chuckled, shaking her head in despair. 'Or Mitch is going to have *my* guts for garters!'

The other curtain was whisked back suddenly and Lucy came out, daintily holding up the front of the full skirt and high-stepping on her tiptoes like a bona-fide princess. 'Ta-da,' she smiled, dropping into a low curtsey.

'*Brava!*' Barbara cried, her blonde bob shining under the lights.

'Luce, you look stunning,' Meg sighed, watching as her bridesmaid did an extravagant twirl that suggested she had been practising in the mirror. Her blonde hair swung, the tonged ringlets keeping their hold better than in Meg's hair.

'So do you!' Lucy gushed, throwing her arms around her best friend's neck so that their netted skirts squashed together.

Meg had asked for the bridesmaid dresses to be made as echoes of her own – scoop-necked, three-quarter sleeves, full-skirted with a V-waist – the only differences being that hers had the embroidery and faux-seed pearls across the top, and the bridesmaids' versions were in a plum colour, not ivory, although if Meg could have had them identical, she would have done; she'd never liked to stand out.

'They've done such a good job,' Meg said admiringly, a small frown puckering her brow as she saw how Lucy's last few buttons hadn't been done up, the delicate fabric pulling at the seams.

'What? They won't have to take it out *that* much,' Lucy said defensively, seeing Meg's expression.

'Oh, no, I'm sure—'

'Ignore my daughter,' Barbara said, dismissing her with a haughty hand wave. 'She's just jealous because whatever weight you've lost, she's put on.' She looked at Lucy. 'I did tell you not to finish those Oreos. Honestly, when did you ever hear of a bridesmaid's dress having to be let *out*!'

Meg winced as she caught sight of Lucy's expression. Tact wasn't Barbara's forte. 'You look gorgeous,' she said quickly. 'And the colour's perfect on you.'

'Don't go swelling her head now,' Barbara tutted. 'No one will be looking at Lucy anyway. She's had her special day. This is all about you. You and Mitch.'

Meg smiled at the very mention of his name and turned to look in the mirror again. 'Yes,' she whispered. Would he like it? Would he even recognize her? She might have to tell him to look out for the girl in white, she looked so transformed.

'Well, at least I'm here. How are you going to know if Ronnie's dress still fits *her*?' Lucy asked peevishly, perching on the side of the sofa as she watched Meg preen and turn, just a peek of her boots visible as she swished her skirts side to side.

'Oh, that's OK, Ronnie's weight is pretty steady,' Meg said dismissively, rather liking the way her hair was relaxing into soft waves. It looked more natural, more 'her'.

'Still, it's a shame she couldn't be here. I mean, it is your final fitting. If she does fluctuate for any reason, it's going to be too late to do anything about it on the day.'

Meg sighed. She'd had exactly the same concern herself. 'I know, but you know what her job's like. I'll just be happy if she gets here for the actual wedding. I wouldn't be surprised if she's paged just as I'm halfway down the aisle.'

'Well, don't you worry, I'll sit on her if that happens,' Barbara said protectively, making everyone smile at the image. 'I'm not having you without your maid of honour on your big day. That wedding day shall be perfect or God help me, I'll die trying.'

'Thanks, Barbara,' Meg smiled gratefully, leaning over to kiss her on the cheek.

Linda, the boutique owner, walked back into the salon, carrying a selection of veils, some trailing behind her. Setting them down, she hurried over to inspect the latest alterations with her professional eye. 'It's not pulling anywhere, no creasing . . . ?' she murmured, pressing her fingers on the seams and checking the neckline didn't gape on Meg, frowning as she saw the two-centimetre gap along the top of Lucy's buttons. 'Sorry,' Lucy mumbled, her cheeks flaming. 'I'm a fluctuator.'

'Well, that's what fittings are for,' Linda replied with a diplomatic smile. 'We'll get this fixed by Wednesday if you can pop in again then.'

'Sure.'

'I hope that Mitchell Sullivan knows how lucky he is,' Dolores said, taking her seat on the sofa again and looking up at Meg with fiercely proud eyes as she continued to twirl in front of the mirror.

Meg stared at her reflection, transfixed. Exactly this time in two weeks . . .

'Now, are you *quite* sure you're not rushing into this?' Barbara asked, picking up a pearlescent hair comb from the accessories tray and examining it loosely. 'Because after all, it has only been ten years.'

Meg rolled her eyes and gave a groan as everyone chuckled. Together since they were seventeen, it had been the question on everyone's lips from the time they turned twenty, their forever-ness seemingly eagerly anticipated by all Banff. But they'd been in no rush, even if everyone else had. They'd had to save up for this wedding, for one thing, which had been no easy feat what with Mitch ploughing all his earnings into trying to get his and Tuck's snowboard business, Titch, off the ground; and all of her inheritance, when it had come several years later, had been eaten up by building the cabin and securing the Titch studio/shop in town.

'Well, now you say that like it's a joke,' Lucy said sombrely, wincing as Linda accidentally jabbed her in the back with a pin. 'But it's a serious point. Just because you guys have been together for like . . . an ice age, already . . . it doesn't necessarily figure that it's meant to be for the rest of your lives. You've got to give Meg the space to be honest about her relationship with Mitch – if it's *not* quite right, I mean. You hear all the time about people going through with it because it's what everyone else expects or because it seems like the next thing to do on the list. And meanwhile, they don't feel like they can put their hands up and say, "Actually, you know what? I'm not so sure . . ."'

Meg, Barbara, Dolores and Linda all looked back at her in astonished silence – before bursting into laughter.

'Lucy, *you* are what we used to call a card,' Dolores said, holding her glass up and toasting her.

'But—' Lucy protested.

'Oh, darling, you are a scream. Meg and Mitch not together? It's just perverse! They *look* right together, they *sound* right . . .' Barbara wrapped an arm round her daughter's waist and squeezed tightly. 'Besides, you are not the maid of honour, missy. If anyone's going to have that conversation with Meggy, it'll be her sister.'

'Why?' Lucy asked hotly. '*I* know Megs better than she does. Ronnie's never even here. She took off for Toronto the first chance she got, and look – surprise, surprise! She couldn't make it here tonight, she didn't make the bachelorette party . . .'

Meg cleared her throat and held up her glass, eager to stop Lucy from going on. 'Well, I'm happy to assure you all that I have no doubts whatsoever that Mitch *is* my perfect match. And I'm not saying that because it's a habit, or because I feel duty-bound in some way after so many years invested in him,' she said, smiling at Lucy, knowing she was only trying to be protective. 'I'm saying it because you are the most important people in my life and I want to share my happiness with you. You're my family and I love you all, and it means absolutely everything to me that you'll be there to see me marry the man I want to spend the rest of my life with.'

'Oh!' Barbara sobbed, a hand over her heart, head tilted as she held her glass up. 'We love you too, chicky.' And she embraced Meg in a cloud of Coco perfume and McCall's finest own-brand cashmere. Dolores stepped in too, layering her arms atop Barbara's.

Meg closed her eyes, feeling their warmth, their love.

Barbara lifted her head suddenly, as though feeling a draught. 'And you, Lucy! What on Earth are you doing, standing there like a salt pillar? If even Dolores can bring herself to show a little emotion—'

'Oh, hush, woman,' Dolores muttered, lightly slapping Barbara on the hand and making Meg giggle.

So Lucy stepped forward and added her arms to their overlapping, interweaving circle, like the outer petals of a flower. And in the middle stood Meg – feeling protected and safe from harm, ready for her Happy Ever After.

Chapter Three

The pine wood crackled, spitting out fiery embers every few minutes that glowed orange against the stove's hot glass doors before sizzling into black silence. Badger was unconcerned from his spot on the rug, one eyelid occasionally pulling up at the sudden noise before dropping closed again like a weighted screen. His furred belly was almost hot to the touch, Meg able to feel the fire's reflected warmth through her sock as she stroked his woolly black-and-white coat with her foot.

She rested her head back against the chair and looked out of the window again. Snowflakes pirouetted past the glass but it had long since stopped looking pretty. Snow was banked up along the sills in deep drifts, obscuring the lower panes and further reducing light. The storm had been sitting above them now for two days like a parked bus, the sky at knee height, the towering pine trees fatly padded with snow, Mitch's deep footsteps around the cabin marking every desperate dash to the log store. Neither one of them had been able to make it to work again today, and there was seemingly no end in sight yet. If anything, the blizzard was strengthening by the hour, the worst still to come.

She wondered if somewhere high overhead there was a spectacular sunset above the clouds this evening, a melange of coral oranges and pinks swirling in the sky like a painter's water. She remembered their friend Dave, a pilot, once saying the best thing about his job was that it was always a sunny day at his desk. He got to soar above the clouds for a living, chasing sunsets and racing for the horizon. She sighed, unable even to see to the far pole of the washing line, no birds tonight lined up in a row and swaying in the breeze.

Badger groaned, a deep, somnambulant sound that vibrated through her foot. Inactivity was exhausting for him. He wasn't used to this confinement either, although the harsh weather was making it easier to keep him in.

'You OK, old boy?' she asked him, setting aside her crossword and ruffling his fur with her hand. 'Are you bored?'

He groaned again, revelling in the sympathy.

'Mitch?' she called. 'You hungry yet?'

No reply.

'Mitch?'

There was another long silence and she was about to get up and check on him – it wasn't just the snow they had to worry about, living in the middle of a nature reserve; there was the wildlife, too – when Mitch walked into the room in his Canada Goose parka and Sorel boots, a scowl on his face and snow in his hair.

'Oh, no,' she sighed. 'What have you lost now?' She knew that look too well. It was always the precursor to a question that began with *Have you seen . . . ? Where have you put . . . ? What have you done with . . . ?*

'The monkey wrench?' The up-flick in his tone suggested she must know, that she must have used it last, although that was about as likely as him wearing her underwear.

'If it's not in the shed, then it's probably still in the loft from when you re-lagged the pipes last week. Why? What do you need it for?'

'The starter motor on the snowmobile's gone. I need to fix it up.'

'Well, not right now, surely?' she scoffed. 'You can't do anything in this. It's a blizzard out there. Are you mad?'

He looked scornfully at the white-out. 'Beginning to go that way and I will be for sure if I can't get into town any-time soon. We need supplies, Meg – the cupboard's damn near empty.'

Meg sighed. He'd been agitated for days now and she wasn't convinced it was all down to the weather, although he was never good on an empty stomach and it was true the larder was emptier than it usually would be. But it wasn't all her fault. With the Easter holidays beginning next week, she'd been working flat out with Dolores at the ski-rental store, fixing bindings, waxing skis and boards, sizing poles and helmets . . . She'd been starting at seven every morning and finishing as late as ten some nights and as a conse-quence, she and Mitch had eaten dinner in town every night – a few times ordering in pizzas with Lucy and Tuck at their bungalow behind the homestead, other times just getting a rib and fries at the steakhouse beside the studio. It had been the easy option at the time, meaning one of them (ergo, her) didn't have to do a shop and, worse, lug it up the mountain on the back of the snowmobile to the cabin.

But it wasn't proving so convenient now. By her own rec-ollection, there wasn't much more than some store-cupboard basics – tins of tomatoes, tuna and peaches, some pasta and rice noodles, half a stale loaf, eggs.

'Well, it's only been two days. I think we'll survive,' she smiled, trying to tease him out of his sulk.

'No. This is forecast for another *three days*, Meg.' His arm had swept across the room and was pointing towards the window and the unremitting whiteness beyond.

It was her turn to frown as she watched the wind whip up the snow, scarifying the deep ground cover. *Three more days?*

She smiled brightly and gave a lackadaisical shrug, determined not to be beaten. 'OK, so then this will be the week when we finally open those tins of peaches and butter beans that we put in the larder all those years ago. I'm sure I can find some recipe for putting them together that won't be toxic or inedible.'

Mitch didn't appear to find this prospect funny. 'We can't just sit here for days on end, waiting for it to pass till we can go out again, Meg.'

'Uh, yeah,' she contradicted with an arched eyebrow. 'That's exactly what we can do.' Her tone was light but she saw the thunder in his face and wondered again if it was just the weather giving him this cabin fever. Was it pre-wedding jitters? Or something more? Her stomach clenched at the thought – was he doubting them? Her?

'Look, let me just get the snowmobile fixed and then I'll race into town—'

'What is it with you needing to *race* all the time, Mitch?' she asked with a forced little laugh, feeling exasperated, worried it was her he was trying to get away from. 'Why can't you just sit still for once? You spent all weekend in the edit studio with Tuck. Wasn't that enough? When do

I get to have you? Isn't the whole point of having a cabin in the woods to be snowed in?' She arched an eyebrow suggestively but Mitch's return stare was brooding in all the wrong ways.

'You've been watching too many Doris Day films. You won't think it's so romantic if we run out of food.'

'Oh, I give up,' she sighed, turning away from him, his rejection stinging. 'You're determined to be grumpy. Fine then, go and pick on someone else. Badger and I are enjoying the peace.'

There was a tense silence and she knew Mitch was glaring at her – irked by her refusal to argue – before he irritably unzipped his coat and tossed it onto the back of the chair, where it promptly slid to the ground.

Badger gave a small whine as the zip clattered on the wooden floor.

'Fine. I'll speak to someone who actually *wants* to talk to me then.'

'Fine!' she called after him as he turned and walked towards the tiny spare bedroom that was only just big enough for a single bed, a desk and a wardrobe. 'Why spend time with me when you can spend time with them? Because they understand you, right?' she scoffed as the door slammed shut behind him. She stared at it, knowing that any second now she'd hear the familiar whine and crackle start up as he hit the frequencies of his beloved ham radio and chatted to these faceless, faraway friends that he would never meet. People that he seemingly felt more connected with than her, sitting in the next room.

She slumped back into the chair and looked out of the window again. The sky – having never achieved brightness anyway today – was already sinking into an indigo slumber, the drifts on the sills rapidly approaching the halfway mark. Hidden in the trees, muffled by rising snow, it felt as though their cabin was becoming smaller, as though the wilderness was swallowing them whole.

Friday 24 March 2017

'We have to move,' Meg snapped.

Mitch looked over at her standing by the window. Badger was lying on his feet in his customary place at the end of the bed, a much-needed heat blanket on these freezing nights. The embers in the small bedroom stove opposite were as faint as a sleeping dragon's heartbeat, the flames having long since died in the middle of the night.

'I mean, you agree this is ridiculous, right?' Meg asked, clutching her jumper closer to her body and motioning to the wall of white on the other side of the glass. Light speckled the surface, bending and refracting through microscopic air holes, the flakes which were pressed against the pane as prickly as cacti. 'It's the twenty-first century. We aren't even thirty. What are we *doing* living in the middle of nowhere like goddam hermits, unable to send an email or a text, completely cut off from civilization?'

'Not cut off. The snowmobile gets us into town in twenty-five minutes.'

'When it's working,' she muttered, padding across the floor in her thick hand-knitted socks, opening the stove door and throwing in some kindling sticks. 'Which it never is.'

Mitch smiled sleepily and shifted position to get a better view of her bending over. '"Never" is a bit harsh,' he murmured, graciously choosing not to state that it was her fault it hadn't yet been fixed. 'This is only the second time we've had trouble with it.'

'Well, it's pretty damned useless if it's broken down right when we're stuck in the worst polar storm anyone's seen for the last forty years.' She arranged some dried logs in a pyramid fashion, then closed the stove door and opened up the draught, watching as the heat swelled and ignited again. She straightened up. 'We've been stranded for three days now and if your forecast's right, it'll be another two before we can get into town,' she said despondently, looking out of the window again at the unremitting whiteness.

An unseasonal thaw a few weeks earlier meant that the fresh snowpack – all four metres of it – was now effectively gripping on to a glass surface and with all that new weight, it could go at any time. The avalanche risk was off the scale, unprecedented; and combined with the relentless blizzards and white-outs, the entire town was in lockdown. No one was allowed to leave their hotels or their homes.

Meg had lived here for eleven years, her family relocating to Canada for her father's work as a mathematician at the Banff International Research Station. As a result, Meg – a brown-haired choir girl with hazel-green eyes, from the Garden of England – had seen out the last years of her childhood in the snow and she knew just how playful and beautiful, capricious, belligerent and unpredictable it could be; she'd spent every winter weekend skiing and snowboarding, and it was how she'd met Mitch properly – sharing a chairlift with him one day, even though they'd been in the same English class for a year.

But she'd never seen anything like this before; at least, not on this scale. Overnight curfews, sure. But to be so many days holed up – trapped – in their cabin and the town quarantined, was another phenomenon entirely.

'Well, there's a brief hiatus tomorrow, supposedly,' Mitch said, clasping his hands behind his head and clearly liking the way the firelight glowed on her skin. 'Tuck says there's gonna be a few hours' respite before it closes in again.' Tuck's father had been mayor when they were growing up and the family, originally mountain pioneers, had lived in Banff for eight generations. There wasn't anything about Banff that Tuck didn't know and that included the state of the sky above it.

'So we could try to get down to town then?' Meg asked hopefully.

'*In theory* we could make a break for it, I guess.'

'In theory,' she repeated, ruffling Badger's velvety head and dropping down to plant a kiss between his eyes.

'Well, I'm kind of liking the idea of being holed up here with you.'

She glanced across at him, saw the smile playing on his lips, the dance in his eyes. 'You didn't yesterday.'

'Yesterday I was a fool. An idiot. I knew nothing.' A look she couldn't pin down came into his eyes. 'I don't deserve you.'

'No. You don't.' She grinned, sticking her chin in the air but feeling reassured by his attentions again. Yesterday had been a blip. Cabin fever. He'd had it then; she had it now.

He grinned back. 'And yet somehow, I do still have you.'

'Only because I can't escape. I'm trapped here.'

'Damn straight. You know we could never live anywhere but here.'

He was right. This was their home and for a moment, she saw its smallness and intimacy from an outsider's perspective – the caramel-coloured pine floor that had fallen out of favour in interiors circles but always felt so cosy to her; the vanilla-coloured walls that were bland to her eye (as a former art student, she lived for pattern and colour) but which Mitch had insisted on in case they ever did decide to go back to Plan A and rent the cabin out; the reindeer hides on the floor almost bald from wear; the blue-and-green knitted bedspread made by his mother, ragged from where Badger's nails kept catching it; the framed needlepoint of a heart on the wall which she had made in domestic-science class after they had got together and she knew he was the One.

'The neighbours wouldn't be tolerant of you pegging out the washing in the nude, for one thing. And I wouldn't be tolerant of them if they were.'

She bit her lip, knowing exactly where they were heading.

'Come back to bed.' He held his hand out to her, that sexy smile on his face. She still found him every bit as attractive as she had when they'd first got together, seventeen and ready to take on the world. She didn't mind that his nose was broken or that his eyebrows were effectively one. He still had the kindest eyes she'd ever seen and the sexiest bum. He suited his light brown hair both when it was long and shaggy – his winter look when he went into a sort of hibernating sympathy with the wildlife – and in its summer buzz cuts that felt furred in her palm. She liked it when he logged in his jeans and a shirt; she loved it when he closed the door on the world and wandered the cabin in just his hockey shirt and socks.

The little bedroom was bathed in an almost ethereal light thanks to the bright diffusion coming from the snowed-up window, the crackle of logs burning again in the stove, and she walked towards him, pulling her jumper over her head. Mitch fondly nudged Badger off the end of the bed and the dog slunk out of the room to curl up on the rug in front of the main fire.

It was a small life, she knew that.

But a big love.

Chapter Four

Saturday 25 March 2017, 6.15 p.m.

Creamed chicken and flageolet bean bake.

OK, so it wasn't a culinary masterpiece given that most of it was made from tins lurking under cobwebs in the furthest reaches of the larder, but she deserved points for sheer inventiveness, and over the last hour – as night had fallen and the wind blew itself inside out, howling around the cabin with ever-increasing ferocity – their little home had filled with a tempting aroma of sage (dried) and mushrooms (freeze-dried). She'd found some peas in the freezer and managed to make a creamy mash topping with a tin of condensed milk and a couple of clod-crusted potatoes, tubers shooting out at all angles, from a sack that had been kicked to the back of the larder and long forgotten.

'Mitch!' she called, her hands and arms swamped in the oven gloves patterned with red gingerbread men as she lifted the steaming dish from the oven and set it down carefully on the iron trivet. 'Dinner's ready!'

Pulling off the gloves, she turned to the hob, the saucepan lid rattling as the water roiled and steam billowed in plumes underneath. She grabbed it and poured away the boiling water, blanching the peas immediately and setting down the pan again.

Was he still on the phone? It had rung earlier when she'd been finishing the potatoes and she'd heard the murmur of his voice through the closed door – it was Tuck, no doubt, wanting to know why they hadn't made the dash into town during the storm's brief respite this afternoon, like they'd said they would. Little did he know they'd only just got out of bed. Storm? What storm? Baby, it's cold outside . . .

'Mitch! Hurry up! I'm serving!'

She bent down and pulled the dinner plates from the warming tray beneath the oven, wincing as she momentarily forgot about the silver rims around the edges and having to run her finger under the cold tap for a moment. She stood by the sink, looking out into the night, trying to see past this storm that seemed personally targeted, like a wolf trying to blow the house down; but the blackness was unremitting and all she saw was her own image reflected back at her in the small square panes.

Badger – knowing that if ever food was going to be dropped on the floor, it was now – was sitting in his usual spot by the bin, watching her intently, his head moving in time with her darting dashes from the oven to the sink and back to the hob again, like a spectator at a tennis match.

'Mitch?' she tried again.

No reply.

Meg cast Badger a look. 'Honestly, what's he *doing*? Go and get him, there's a good boy.'

Badger knitted his ginger eyebrows together in his black face, as though he couldn't imagine what was keeping Mitch either, and pattered across the kitchen.

Meg reached for the wine glasses in the cupboard and

retrieved the pinot noir she'd left to warm and breathe by the stove, having found it frozen almost solid that morning by the door in the shed. She hoped it would be passable.

She placed it on the small pine table which she'd decided to cover with a tablecloth for once and a small jug of holly branches dotted with berries snipped from the tree outside their bedroom window. Her view was that if they couldn't eat well, they should at least dine in style and that meant dressing the table and using proper glasses. Their day in bed together had left her feeling more connected to her fiancé than she had in weeks, his recent agitations soothed away, and she was now feeling strangely sad that the storm would soon, inevitably, break and their little mountainside bubble would burst.

She heard the front door slam, the wind propelling it with extra force so that the entire cabin seemed to shake for a moment and the curtains lifted in the draught like skirts. Running back to the open-plan kitchen area – at sixty square metres the cabin really was too small for unnecessary walls – she heaped the peas onto the warm plates and was spooning out the bake when Mitch appeared in the doorway, Badger jumping up and down excitedly the way he always did when he knew he was going out too.

Mitch didn't notice the dressed table or the steaming meal on plates in her hands. He was looking straight at her – apologetically, ruefully, but his brown eyes already had that brightness in them that always came when he was going out on one of his sorties.

'Oh, no,' she gasped, dropping the plate clumsily on the worktop so that a few peas rolled like marbles over the side and down the front of the unit. But even Badger didn't notice. His entire focus was on his master, recognizing the helmet in his hand and the harness already on over his waterproof trousers and parka, the small backpack on his shoulders, the length of rope coiled around his waist, his boots clipped shut and his skis no doubt already positioned outside the door with their skins on. He knew what it meant as well as she did. 'Mitch, no. You're not going—'

'Meg, that was Tuck. They've got two guests missing – a father and his twelve-year-old son. They went on a hike this afternoon, heading for Wilson's Gully.' His speech was low but hurried, urgency bubbling through.

'What?' she half-gasped, half-shrieked. 'Are they mad? *Who* would go out in these conditions? Don't they know there's a freaking lockdown?'

'I know. But apparently they set out thinking that the break in the weather this afternoon would hold.'

'How could anyone with half a brain think that? Haven't they heard of the eye of a storm? Didn't they see the forecasts?'

As if to prove the point, the wind gusted strongly again, making the timbers groan. Meg almost felt the wind was trying to wrap itself around the cabin and lift it straight off the ground.

Mitch shook his head. 'I don't know – they're tourists. Who knows what the hell they were thinking? But I do know that I have to do something. These people have been officially missing now for four hours already. The wife says they were due back at two p.m. and in these conditions, in the dark, Search and Rescue won't look now until first light. Their last known position is too far on foot from town and it's too treacherous to send out a team.' He sighed, looking directly down at her. 'They won't survive the night, Meg.'

'But it can't be down to *you* to save them!' Meg cried,

watching in mounting panic as he put on his helmet and fastened the straps beneath his chin. He checked the head-torch, a beam of dazzling, almost intergalactic white light dissecting the room in half. Satisfied, he turned it off again.

'Look, it's different setting out from here – I know the area better than anyone. The wife had a map of their route and where they were when she last spoke to them and it was Wilson's. If they're still there, then they're just over the ridge from here. Even in these conditions, I can be with them in the hour.'

'But what if they're not? What if they've moved on?' she demanded.

He glanced at her. Mitch didn't deal in what-ifs.

'Do Search and Rescue know you're going up there?' she asked, but his silence was all the reply she needed. They both knew perfectly well they'd forbid him to go out. 'So you're just going out *on your own*? With no backup?'

'I'll have Badger with me. He's better than anyone.' Badger's ears lifted at the sound of his own name, his head cocked enquiringly to the side, his paw held out in front of him like an invitation to dance.

'No!' Rushing past him into the hall, Meg pressed herself against the back of the door. 'You're not doing it. I won't let you.'

'Meg.'

'I said no! No.' She spread her arms wide so that they touched the walls.

Mitch walked up to her, his boots clunky on the floor, his technical, waterproof, windproof, thermally insulated clothes rustling as he moved. 'Meg, there's a twelve-year-old boy out there.' His voice was softer now. 'I can't just leave him out there all night. He'll be dead before dawn –

him and his father. There's no other way – I'm their only hope.'

She swallowed. She didn't like the idea of a child being out in these conditions any more than him but did that mean she had to offer up the man she loved, like a sacrifice to the gods?

'Look, I'll be fine. I'll take care, I promise. I'm not as crazy as you seem to think I am. Even I can see it's a bit breezy out there.'

She blinked at him, furious for doing the right thing, furious with herself. The snowmobile – that damned machine – if she had just let him repair it the other day, he could have travelled on that. The climb to Wilson's Gully was steep but on the snowmobile, he would have saved precious time. Getting to these hikers sooner. Coming back to her sooner.

'How long will it take?' They both knew perfectly well how long it took to hike to Wilson's Gully. As the crow flew, it was 1.5 km from here but the gradient was merciless and even in the summer when they picnicked there with Badger, it was a forty-minute exercise. But in these conditions, with this visibility? They both knew what she was really asking was, *What time should I start to worry?*

'Give me five hours.'

'*Five?* But you said you could be there within the hour.'

'It'll be slow going. I'll need a good margin of time for rests and orientation both ways, and I don't want you worrying unnecessarily. If I'm not back by' – he glanced at his watch – 'eleven-thirty, or you haven't heard from me, then you can raise the alarm in town.'

He cupped her face in his warm hands and kissed her sweetly on the lips, her hands holding onto his elbows, trying to keep him there with her, in this moment.

But he pulled away, resolute. She couldn't entice him this time. There was a man and his child running out of time on the mountain and no one was coming to look for them. No one but Mitch.

'I love you,' he murmured.

'I love *you*,' she replied fiercely, kissing him again.

Gently, he released her grip on his shoulders, reaching down to pat Badger, who was sitting patiently and looking up at him beseechingly.

'Ready, fella?' he asked, ruffling the dog's head.

Mitch opened the door just as a gust rushed at them, blowing Meg's hair clean off her neck and lifting the corners of the rug. Snow that had been blown onto the porch spilled in, great froths skimmed off the surface like the steamed milk on a latte, skittering a haphazard path into the cabin.

Meg gasped from the shock of it. Minus three temperatures with a wind-chill factor of minus twenty was not something you could ever adapt to, not even if you had lived in it your whole life.

Mitch bounded down the porch steps and unlocked the walking hinges in his boots, switching his bindings into tour mode before clipping into the skis. Meg closed her eyes at the sound of it, knowing he was unstoppable now. One small push and he'd be gliding away from her, faster than she could catch, heavier than she could slow. Badger was turning circles in the snow excitedly, his tail aloft, nose to the ground, trying to track a scent the way he always did – except it wasn't squirrels they'd be looking for tonight.

The carabiners jangled against each other on his harness and she tried not to whimper as he switched on the head-torch and the full brute force of the storm's strength was laid bare in that single strobe of light – trees were almost bent double beneath the wind's power, the air thick and dense like sifted flour as falling snow mixed with whipped-up snow so that flakes seemed to be defying gravity, whirling up, down and sideways.

Mitch secured the pole straps round his wrists and looked back at her, careful not to blind her with the light of his torch. 'Five hours,' he said.

And then, stabbing his poles into the snow, he pushed off, gliding away into the black.

Badger raced ahead, his joyous bark echoing like a gun-shot in the crystalline night, fading too soon. She stared into the silence, straining to hear anything that would tell her she wasn't alone.

But the night had claimed them.

They were gone.

10 p.m.

The world had become a negative of itself – the sky black, the land white, everything the wrong way round. Meg stood with her face pressed to the glass, her hands cupped round her face trying to spot the swing of a light beam somewhere in the trees or spiking into the night sky, but nothing inter-rupted the storm's rampage. Birds kept to the safety of the trees, bears – tricked out of hibernation by the rogue thaw a few weeks earlier – stayed in their caves, the people in town safe behind bricks and mortar. Only four living beings were pitching themselves against the elements tonight, and the storm – as though sensing their defiance – grew in intensity.

Meg's concern deepened as she watched. The storm felt

apocalyptic, end-of-the-world epic. Occasionally in the far-reaching dark, she heard the sharp crack of branches cleaved by the overwhelming weight of the drifts, the muffled rumble of snow shifting like tectonic plates on the mountainsides, and then worst of all, the return to silence afterwards, when her aloneness was amplified.

She checked the time: 10 p.m.

Ninety minutes left until she officially raised the alarm and told them Mitch was missing, that her fiancé had defied orders and logic and sense, that he had walked into a storm to save two strangers who might very well already be dead.

She paced the living room, wondered whether Lucy was still awake. The early starts at the hotel meant she was often in bed by now, but if she could just hear her friend's no-bull voice down the end of the line . . . She was good in a crisis, was Lucy.

Meg walked across the room and picked up the phone, dialling her friend's number automatically and then hesitating.

She frowned suddenly. Something was wrong . . .

There was another silence where there should be sound. She pressed the phone harder to her ear as though that would make a difference—

No dialling tone.

No!

With a gasp, she pressed down repeatedly on the connect button, her heart rate automatically shooting up. With no mobile or Wi-Fi connection up here, the landline was her only contact with the outside world. It couldn't be dead. It just couldn't. Mitch and Tuck had been talking on it just a few hours ago.

But it was. No familiar burr, no static or whine, even –

just the silence as complete as that filling up this cabin in the trees.

Her hands flew to her mouth as she straightened up, standing in the centre of the room and taking in the full implications of what it meant. It wasn't that Mitch would be trying to get through to her – mobile reception was almost non-existent up on the mountain. But if he didn't walk through that door ninety minutes from now, towing a very cold father and son and demanding a foot rub . . . if he didn't walk through that door ninety minutes from now, she had no way of raising the alarm.

If he didn't walk through that door ninety minutes from now, her world would end.

Midnight

The storm had worsened, if that was even possible. Meg had pulled on her boots, coat and gloves and headed out as far as the brook at the edge of their land, screaming his name into a wind that threw her own echoes back over her like a bucket of water. She had tried scrambling up the escarpment behind the cabin but the ragged handholds she could grab with childlike vigour in the summer months were now rounded and swollen with ice and snow, leaving no grip, no way up. She couldn't go further up the mountain and she couldn't go down it to town, not without the snowmobile – it would be impossible to ski through the forest in these conditions, in the dark.

Mitch was half an hour past his own deadline and all she could do was keep running outside, screaming his name into the maw of the storm, but the cold was dizzying, numbing her head, shredding her voice, and each time she was driven back into the glow of the cabin, feeling treacherous for seeking out its warmth when Mitch couldn't. Each time, she cried from the searing pain as blood returned to her extremities, filling the capillaries with painful progress, vital minutes dragging past before she could walk across the room to the phone and coordinate her hands sufficiently to try the line again.

But every time, nothing.

Nothing. Nothing. Nothing.

The minutes were passing, the night growing wilder, and she was doing nothing to help him, to save him.

She stoked the fire with trembling jabs – fear as well as the cold making her quake – knowing she had to keep the place warm for when Mitch returned. Because he would. He would.

She paced endlessly, her arms crossed and hands warming in her armpits as she tried to imagine what he was doing right now. She knew from her own failed forays that the winds were too strong to move through any more – he'd be blown off the mountain; that, or the mountain would move beneath his feet, deep slabs of snow finally losing their tentative grips as the wind bashed and whipped and scarred its surface. No, he wouldn't be walking now. He'd have dug a snow hole, that was it. If he'd caught up with them – and even if he hadn't – he'd be using his supplies and skills to keep warm and protected, knowing they wouldn't be able to venture back until first light. They'd be safer staying where they were now.

She dropped her head in her hands again. If only she'd let him repair the damned snowmobile . . . the blizzard he'd been working in back then had been but a shadow of this. It was their lifeline, the only thing connecting them to civilization and safe—

Her head snapped up.

She gasped and ran through to the spare bedroom, a single red power button winking back at her in the darkness.

Meg stopped and stared. This was Mitch's domain, his study; she only ever came in here to dust and she couldn't remember the last time anyone had stayed over as a guest. As much as everyone cooed over their views and the solitude and the night skies, they preferred to return to town and sleep in the safety of the valley floor.

She felt her breath come more quickly as she stared at the banks of black radio monitors stacked three, four high along the wall, the endless rows of buttons. There were so many. Why had she never listened when he'd tried to teach her how to work it, trying to share his interest with her? How many times had she run a cloth over these black machines, muttering about all those damned fiddly knobs and switches, things she didn't understand and had never bothered to try? It was Mitch's thing, that was what she'd always said, usually with a roll of her eyes as though it was a nerd's train set or a geek's Lego collection. But it wasn't. It was contact with the outside world. A lifeline. He'd actually told her she might need it one day if there was an emergency. And she'd always laughed it off, saying she didn't need anything so long as she had him. But now . . .

She sank into the chair, her hands pulling her hair at the roots, eyes scrunched tightly shut as she berated her own diffidence, her arrogance of always believing she was right.

She took a deep breath and opened her eyes again. No. She knew more than she thought she did. Because she had come in here on countless occasions, bringing him coffee and a doughnut, sitting on his lap and trying to distract him as he chatted with Pavel in Assam, or Guido in Santiago, or Derek in Maryland – all these far-flung people he'd never met but counted as friends as they chatted over the airwaves.

She tried to slow her thoughts, to cast her mind back. What had she seen without noticing it? She brought the image of him, in here, to her mind. He always held this in his right hand for a start, she knew, picking up the mic and feeling the 'speak' button under her thumb. And . . . she looked at the monitors . . . and when she called him for dinner, he always switched off this button last, she remembered, reaching furthest left and pressing it. The red light turned green. But was that . . . the transmitter? Or the receiver?

Her eyes skipped over the sleeping machines, her mind becoming sharper and clearer. She pressed what looked like a power button on another monitor and another green light blinked on; an LCD display flashed yellow, transmitting clusters of digits as unintelligible to her as lines of computer code.

She squeezed the button under her thumb and spoke quickly into the mic. 'Hello? Is anybody there?'

She let go of the button, knowing this at least would clear the channel for someone – anyone – to talk back to her.

Nothing. Nothing at all, in fact. There was none of the static noise, that electronic crackle that she always heard when Mitch operated it. Was it even on?

She checked the monitors again, pressing whatever looked like a power button and a couple of dials sprang into life, their needles swinging metronomically.

45

'Hello?' she tried again. 'Can anybody hear me?'

Still nothing.

She tried the biggest dial straight in front of her, turning it to the left and then the right. Immediately, that distinct static noise she recognized so well filled the room.

'Hello?' she cried again, her heart rate jumping up. 'Can anybody hear me? Please? Hello?'

She heard voices, or rather fragments of indistinct, tinny voices speaking in foreign languages. They sounded so far away, so out of reach. She slowed down her spinning of the dial, noticing the digital display that changed with her movements. 14.245.50 . . . 14.245.36 . . . 14.245.20 . . .

She realized the static lessened when she landed on an even number.

'I need help! Hello? . . . Please, can anybody hear me? . . . Mayday? . . .' She sobbed, battling to hold back her panic and desperation, as she picked up the voices of people casually shooting the breeze whilst her fiancé was lost in a storm, fighting for his – and others' – lives. 'Please help me . . . Can anybody hear me . . . ?'

Her fingers turned the dial slowly, her eyes on the digital display, trying to stop on round numbers, her thumb squeezing on and off the 'talk' button as she continued to call 'Mayday' into the void.

'Delta Echo Six Bravo Foxtrot, calling CQ, calling CQ, over . . .'

The voice filled the room, clear and distinct. Meg gasped, leaning in closer to the mic. 'Hello!' she cried. 'Can you hear me?'

She realized her thumb was off the button. She tried again. 'Hello? Can you hear me? Please, it's an emergency, I need help . . . Hello?'

'Bravo Foxtrot, calling CQ, over . . .' The man's voice was blurrier again. Had she gone too far on the dial? Her hand was shaking but she watched the numbers carefully as she scrolled back, trying to stop on the band that was clearest, willing her fingers not to let her down. She needed micro movements, not the big jerky, flailing movements the adrenalin in her body was calling for.

'Hello? Can you hear me? Please? It's an emergency. I need help.' She heard the tears in her voice. Why couldn't anyone hear her?

'This is November Alpha One Sierra Sierra, what is your call sign, over?' The man's voice burst into the room, as clear as if he were standing in the hallway.

'Hello? Can you hear me?' she yelled. 'Oh, my God, please say you can hear me!'

Silence.

'Hello?' she cried.

'This is November Alpha One Sierra Sierra, Commander Solberg, we can hear you loud and clear on the International Space Station. What is your call sign, over?'

Meg stared at the mic. The what? Had he . . . had he said the International Space Station? . . . Was she talking to an *astronaut*?

'I . . . I don't know!' she cried, forgetting to squeeze the button. She realized and did it again, squeezing the button so hard her thumb blanched. 'I don't know. I don't know what it is! But I need help! Please!'

Silence.

'This is NA1SS, Commander Jonas Solberg speaking. What is your name and location, over?'

'I . . .' She willed herself to stay calm. 'My name is Meg

Saunders and I'm in Cascade Creek, in Banff, Alberta, in Canada. Can you hear me? Did you get that?'

Silence. She closed her eyes and willed herself to wait for a moment.

Nothing.

She pressed the talk button again. If she just put the words out there, maybe someone would hear them, someone would help. 'Hello? There's a polar storm here. My fiancé Mitch Sullivan is lost in the mountains. Wilson's Gully. He went out to try to save some hikers but he hasn't come back . . . Please, we need help. Can you help me?'

'. . . One Sierra Sierra, copy that. Are you with him, Meg, over?'

Oh, thank God, he'd heard! 'No! No, I'm in our cabin. I'm on my own. I'm trapped and the phone line's down. I can't get down to town. He's going to die.'

Another pause, and then: 'Copy that. I need your call sign, Meg, over.'

'But I don't know it. I don't . . .' she panted, her panic beginning to overwhelm her again. 'I don't know how to use this. It's Mitch's. I don't know how . . .' she sobbed.

'NA1SS, copy that. Meg, I need you to take a breath. It's a collection of letters with a single number in the middle. Just take a moment, can you see it written down anywhere? Over.'

His voice was calm and it was enough to stem her desperation. She rubbed the tears from her eyes and desperately scanned the desk, speed-reading the papers on the top, but she couldn't see anything that looked like what she was searching for.

'No, I . . . I can't see anything. There's nothing here but old . . .' But just then, she caught sight of a small sticker stuck to the side of the black monitor with the big dial on it. 'Oh, wait!' she gasped, leaning out of the chair to get a better look. 'Uh . . . Oh, God, is this it? V for Victor, X for X-ray, Four, D for dog, D for dog, E for elephant? Could that be it? Hello? Over?'

Space crackled between them but a few moments later his voice came back, filling the room again.

'. . . is NA1SS to Victor, X Ra . . . ur, Delta, Delta, Echo. Is that corre . . . Do you copy, over?'

Static disrupted the line and it took her a moment to 'translate' the call signs back to the letters on the sticker in front of her. 'Yes. Yes, that's it,' she cried. 'VX4DDE.'

'. . . opy that . . . have the . . . sign . . . help is on its w . . . ust sit tight and don't go . . . side . . . the . . .'

His voice disappeared, his presence leaving the room and abandoning her to the storm's ferocity again.

'Hello? Commander? Can you hear me?' she cried. 'Please! Oh God, are you still there? Can you send help?'

But even as she said the words, she knew how ridiculous they sounded. What the hell could he do? The man was *in space*. She had got through to quite literally the only person in the world – no, he wasn't even in the world, he was off their planet – who categorically couldn't help her!

She threw the mic down in despair, collapsing onto the desk, her head in her arms as angry, bitter, furious sobs wracked her.

There was nothing, nothing she could do. Mitch was gone and she had failed him. There would be no help coming tonight. They had to wait for the sun to crack the night sky, for the snow cannons to blast away the loose slabs before Search and Rescue teams could be deployed, for the winds to drop before the helicopters could take off . . . So many conditions necessary before they could even start to look for the man she loved.

Three hundred kilometres above the Earth, Jonas Solberg looked back down at his own planet. The meniscus of light heralding the new day's dawn shone from behind the horizon like a halo, not yet visible from Earth. The airwaves were quiet, most of the residents of continental America now sleeping, even though the time aboard the ISS was – according to the GMT guidelines they worked to – currently half past seven in the morning. He had already orbited Earth five times since his own midnight.

He heard the woman's voice again in his mind – her panic, her tears, her desperation as she fought to keep her head above the emergency that was engulfing her. He pressed a hand to the window, the land mass of Canada almost out of sight now as they sped towards Greenland. But he had seen enough to understand her terror, for he could see what she could not – nature extended to her full might down there. He had done what he could to help, immediately radioing the SOS to his flight director in Houston, whilst trying to calm the woman: Meg Saunders in a cabin near Wilson's Gully, outside Banff in Alberta. But he had felt sick in his bones – the thick, swirling white cloud cover in the sky above her and below him had been a menacing sight. He hoped the best for her, that frightened, lone woman in the Canadian mountains, but it didn't look good: he couldn't envisage how anyone caught outside in a storm like that would survive.

Chapter Five

Sunday 26 March 2017

There were plenty of people now – now that the sun was in the sky and the snow had stopped, the wind had dropped, and the landscape simply looked pretty and puffed up in its fresh white padding. *Now* they were here.

And there were tens of them – Search and Rescue volunteers filling her tiny cabin, boiling her kettle to make rounds of coffee, tramping a slushy path outside the porch as they went back and forth with sombre expressions, the forest's beloved silence polluted by the synthetic crackle of two-way radios.

'So let's go over it again, Meg,' Martin Hughes, the S&R team leader, said, his knees splayed wide, his hands loosely clasped by interlaced fingers. 'He left at what time?'

'It was . . . uh, six-thirty. Maybe just before.'

'How can you be sure?'

'I was putting out dinner. We usually eat around then.'

Hughes nodded. 'OK. And he told you he'd be back at—'

'Half past eleven. He said to give him five hours.'

Five hours. The words echoed in her head. Five hours' margin for what, in ordinary conditions, wasn't even an hour's hike. It was too long to have been gone without raising the alarm. She never should have let him go.

'Has he ever done this before?'

'What? Gone to the gully?'

'Tried to launch a rescue mission on his own.'

Meg frowned, picking up on the undertone. What was he doing – trying to make Mitch out to be some crusading hero? 'No! N-never. It was only because it was so close to here and no one else was doing anything.' She directed a pointed stare at his boss, Robin Patterson, the station chief for the Search and Rescue unit. 'Plus he knows this back country better than anyone. He's an experienced skier and hiker, you know that. He said he couldn't just leave them – there was a twelve-year-old boy out there! He had to do something. That's the kind of man he is. He would never abandon someone in need.'

Hughes looked into the flames of the fire for a moment before bringing his gaze up to her. 'The thing is, Meg, those hikers he was looking for—'

She caught her breath. 'Oh, God. Have you found them?' Her hand covered her mouth, her eyes looking straight back to Patterson, his walkie-talkie silent in his hand. Tears welled. 'Oh, no . . . don't say they're—'

'They're fine,' Hughes interrupted. He paused. 'They always were.'

A stunned silence billowed out like a thrown sheet. 'What?' Meg croaked, her brain befuddled.

'The hiker and son got back to town. They were late but . . . not missing.'

'But . . .' The words wouldn't come out, stoppered by too many emotions. 'Mitch said Tuck—'

'We know. The man's wife had raised the alarm mid-afternoon and we got the call, but conditions were already too bad to go out in the chopper, the avalanche risk was too high to go on foot, and the light was already fading . . . There was nothing we could do until dawn,' Patterson explained with what Meg thought was a sheepish look. 'Then two hours later we got another call, telling us to stand down preparations, they'd made it back. Turns out they'd got lost when the weather closed in again. There was zero visibility but they made it down by following the river and then managed to hitchhike their way back to town. The boy's got frostbite on one hand and the father's suffering some mild effects of exposure but other than that – and a serious fright – they're OK.'

OK? Meg stared at him, barely able to process what she was being told. Lack of sleep, panic, worry, stress . . . they were making it hard for her to process facts, to think clearly, but she did understand the point he was trying to make: it had all been for nothing. Mitch had risked his life, walking into a storm – for absolutely no good reason.

'When . . . when did the call come? . . . To stand down,' she mumbled, feeling her panic rise again.

'Four-forty.'

'But that doesn't make sense.' Meg blinked, trying to comprehend. Mitch had set out almost two hours later. Even allowing for the time it would have taken him after Tuck's call to dress and get ready – maybe fifteen, twenty minutes – Tuck must have called at six-ish, at least an hour and twenty minutes *after* the good news call had come in. How could he have been so off the mark, making an SOS call to Mitch when everyone else was standing down?

But she knew exactly how. The doors to Bill's bar are

thick and heavy and very effective at locking out the world. News travels slowly over beer.

'. . . Does Tuck even know Mitch is missing?' Her voice sounded strange. Thickened, somehow.

'We've got an officer speaking to him and his wife, along with other guests in the hotel,' Hughes said. 'Tuck says he tried getting through as soon as he heard the hikers had made it back, but there was no connection.'

And at what time had that been? Meg wondered bitterly. Eight o'clock? Nine? She hadn't tried the line herself till ten.

'The air crew have sighted a pylon down in Blackwoods Gully,' Patterson interjected, holding his walkie-talkie up slightly. 'It knocked out all the phone lines on this side of the valley.'

Meg blinked. Bad luck mixing with horror again.

'What matters is establishing the route Mitch would have taken. It's imperative we find out which way he might have gone.'

'But surely you can see his tracks?' she asked, feeling another wave of fear. She looked over at Patterson. 'I told your team, just follow them out the door . . .'

'There are no tracks. Over a metre of snow fell last night, Meg, and what with the wind blowing so hard and all the avalanches—'

'Avalanches?'

'Thirty-three at last count,' Patterson said quietly. 'The choppers are still up, assessing the damage.'

'No.' She shook her head, knowing what they were implying. 'No. He's got a . . . a safety pack. A transceiver and a probe and those inflatable wings. He's a very experienced snowboarder. He's outskied avalanches before.'

'And he was wearing that when he left? You saw him in it?'

'Yes. Definitely.'

Patterson glanced at Hughes. 'That's good.'

'And Badger,' she said urgently, gabbling now, knowing what that look meant. 'He's got Badger and I can absolutely promise you, on my life, that dog would never let any harm befall either one of us.' She realized her hand was pressed against her heart, as though conviction alone would swing the balance.

Patterson's walkie-talkie crackled to life in his hand and he sprang up from the chair. 'Patterson.'

Meg watched him walk out of the room, appearing on the porch on the other side of the window a moment later, his gaze casting down the valley and then left, looking up the slopes.

'You're going to find him, right?' Meg asked, turning back and giving Hughes no corner to hide. She wanted him to look her straight in the eye.

'I promise you, we'll find him.'

She rubbed her hands together, one cupped around the other, then switched, feeling suddenly cold and shivery. 'He's . . . he's probably been in a snow hole, that's the thing. He'll have bunked down for the night and set out at first light again this morning. I mean, now with the conditions so much better and him not knowing those people are safe, he'll just keep going.'

Hughes nodded. 'I reckon so.'

'And he knows the terrain better than anyone. He and Tuck are forever going off on expeditions to do their filming. Sometimes they go for two, three nights and . . .' She shrugged. 'I don't worry. Not really.'

'He's a good guy. We're all real fond of Mitch. I assure you, we won't stop till we find him.'

A sudden commotion outside made them both look up – voices calling, doors slamming – and Meg was on her feet before Hughes, rushing to the window.

Patterson and a police officer were running, lurching down the slope towards the brook, the route Mitch had taken last night as he'd pushed himself off into the storm.

With a cry, Meg ran outside after them, oblivious to the fact that she hadn't got her shoes on until she sank into the snow up to her knees. But she didn't feel the stinging cold on her skin, didn't notice how her feet blanched and then blushed a strong, bright pink. She just ran, her arms flailing, trying to propel her onwards, faster. The clamour of voices round the other side of the escarpment told her people were coming. He'd been found!

Overhead she heard the heavy drone of a helicopter taking off not far away, the vibrations reverberating through her chest as its propeller blades sliced through a sky so frozen she half-expected shards to fall from it like daggers.

'Mitch!' she screamed, almost falling as she rounded the rocks, her mouth open as she gasped for breath.

But the sight that greeted her snatched it away in the next instant.

A man, his face all but obscured by the thick snow-encrusted fur trim of his jacket, was staggering down the embankment, his knees almost giving way from the effort of carrying something wrapped in a thick blanket.

'Mitch!' she screamed again, lumbering forwards as the other men turned, their arms outstretched to hold her back – or hold her up, she wasn't sure which; because she'd seen now what the man was carrying, Badger's dark mournful eyes peering back at her, his front leg supported with an emergency make-do splint.

'Badger,' she whispered, faltering to a standstill as Patterson lurched through the snow, back up the slope to her.

He didn't need to say the words. She knew it from the expression on his face, she knew it from the mere sight of her faithful dog being carried – limp, helpless and defeated. She knew it from the helicopter which had now moved clear of the mountains and was heading into the wide spread of the valley, a heavy, covered stretcher dangling from the winch below it and dragging in the breeze.

Part II
AFTERWARDS

Chapter Six

Saturday 1 April 2017

It was her wedding day but she was in black. There was no spring lamb but plates of sandwiches, the bottles of champagne switched for a mediocre white wine, the displays of photographs on boards around the large room which were supposed to have charted her and Mitch's lives up to this point where they were officially joined in matrimony until death would them part, now showing only Mitch, whose life wouldn't ever go past this point. Death had already parted them.

The guest list was largely the same and in some respects it could have passed for a wedding – the Homestead's beautiful reception room with its double-height ceiling and twin stone fireplaces at either end was crammed with people, and even the typed notice outside the door, *Closed for a private event*, was what would have been used had she been in white instead. But she wasn't dancing; she was sitting in a chair, staring at the flames that leapt and leaned and swayed like Arabian dancers, as all around her, people talked. They chatted, even smiled a little, the sombre silence of the church now beginning to dissipate as the wine's effects took hold and the tragedy of a life ended too soon was gradually replaced with more upbeat reminiscences of high-school pranks and daring back-country expeditions that had passed into the town's folklore. *He will be much missed.* That was the mantra that had been repeated over and over since his body had been found – tumbled and broken at the bottom of a couloir, a massive avalanche on top of him and poor Badger, the darling dog, sitting bereft on top, unable to dig that many metres deep with only one good paw.

Mitch hadn't been the only victim of the storm, she knew that. Old Mrs McClusky had slipped trying to clear snow from her path and broken her hip, dying of exposure within the hour when no one heard her cries over the howling winds; a car carrying six teenage boarders had hit black ice on the road out to Lake Louise, killing two, leaving three in hospital with 'life-changing' injuries and one in a coma; and some of the fifty-four avalanches that had struck in the Banff range overnight had completely engulfed seven remote (and thankfully empty) cabins just like hers. Meg supposed she was 'lucky' to have escaped one herself but it was hard to feel lucky just now. It was hard to feel anything at all.

A hand touched Meg's arm, lightly enough that it was several moments before she noticed. She jumped, startled, and Badger's hackles went up between his shoulder blades, fully alert to another threat to his owners.

'How're you doing, sweetheart?'

It was Barbara, doing one of her half-hourly rounds as though she was on a self-appointed suicide watch, checking Meg wasn't hot or cold, hungry or thirsty, tired or sleepless . . .

'Are you warm enough?' she asked, squeezing Meg's hand.

Meg nodded but Barbara tutted. 'You're frozen. Here, let's get that chair a bit closer to the fire.'

Meg went to protest but found she didn't have the energy and the chair she was sitting in was shuffled a few centimetres closer to the hearth, under the watchful eye of Badger.

'And you haven't touched your food.'

Meg looked down guiltily at the plate on her lap – or at least, aware she should feel guilty. But she didn't feel anything. She was in shock – deep shock that she had just buried her fiancé in the very church and on the very day where they were supposed to have been married. When they'd first been offered the date, Meg hadn't been sure. She didn't want to get married on April Fools' Day; she didn't want their day to be a joke. (And she could only imagine what Tuck, as best man, would do to mark it.) But Mitch had embraced the idea. 'We'll begin as we mean to go on – laughing.' But no one was laughing today.

Whilst the vicar had been shakily delivering her eulogy, praising Mitch's bravery, nobility, generosity, compassion and zest for life, Meg had stared open-mouthed at the altar where she had been practising to kneel in a long dress, listening to the organ that was supposed to be playing 'Here Comes the Bride' and not Handel's *Messiah*, formal displays of white lilies pouring forth at the pew ends instead of the bouquets of wild flowers she'd spent hours choosing.

Was he really gone? She'd stared at the coffin, its top adorned with hundreds of yellow roses, unable to believe he was in there, wearing the suit he'd bought to marry her in. They'd planned a small wedding – 'intimate' they'd said, although in truth they couldn't afford food and drink for a hundred people – but the church had been full to overflowing today. Mitch was one of the town's best-loved sons, a local boy who'd valued home and given his life in the service of others. There had been whispers he might make mayor one day or take over the Search and Rescue team or become the spokesman for the local tourist board. A local face, a name. But she'd just wanted him to be her husband. She'd have been happy for it to stop there. She didn't need him to be bigger or better than that.

'Tuck's getting ready to say a few words. Are you OK with that?' Barbara asked, rubbing her hand gently as though trying to warm it up.

Meg flinched at his name and looked into the flames. 'Of course.' But her voice was flat and her lips thin, the very mention of Tuck closing her down further. When she'd been standing at the lectern, reading 'Death is Nothing at All' in the monotone that was all her body could now produce, her eyes had met his briefly and she had been stopped in her tracks, feeling a fury explode in her as she took in his tear-streaked cheeks and swollen eyelids, as though his loss matched hers just because he and Mitch had been friends since kindergarten. According to Lucy, he had screamed like a child when they'd been given the news, dropping to the floor as though his bones had been snapped. Lucy was worried sick about him but Meg didn't care. *He* had made that phone call, *he* had sent Mitch to his death. Let him suffer, feel the guilt, live with the burden of what he'd done.

'I don't feel up to . . .' Her voice trailed off like a candle being blown out and Barbara patted her hand again.

'You just rest, honey. We'll look after it.'

Meg didn't notice her go. Badger had risen to a sitting position, his head perfectly positioned beneath her limp hand, and she automatically stroked his brow, seeing the way his eyes closed gratefully at her continued affection. It was just the two of them now. His spirits had been as low as hers and many times, she had wondered about *his* night up there in the storm, his distress as he must have dug and dug in the raging winds with only one good paw, the snow hole filling up again faster than he could clear it – until eventually even his hope had died and he was forced to keep watch instead over Mitch's still-warm body, far below in his snow tomb. Making sure his master was found was all he could offer in the end.

'Ladies and gentlemen.' Tuck's voice, as familiar to her ear as Mitch's, filled the room and a respectful hush descended almost immediately. Tuck was standing on a stool by the massive full-height windows, the spectacular panorama of the Canadian Rockies blushing in the sunset behind his right shoulder. His famously blue eyes were wide and fearful – Lucy had said his behaviour had been verging on the manic and Meg could see for herself that he had lost a lot of weight in just a matter of days – and his blond hair was sticking out at awkward angles just like when he and Mitch would come back from one of their filming-camping trips. But his ready, cocky smile that had won over most of the girls at school before he finally set his sights on Lucy, was nowhere to be seen. Meg couldn't decide if he looked like a little boy again or an old man.

'I want to thank you all for coming,' he mumbled, his eyes skipping over the crowd, as though trying to memorize the faces, or recognize them. 'Mitch would . . . he would have been very proud to know you all came out for him today.'

Meg watched as Tuck dropped his face down to his shoes for a moment and she tried to understand why he should have lived when Mitch had not.

He inhaled deeply and looked up again. 'Most of you here know what he was to me. My best friend in the world.' He nodded, his voice shaky. 'He's pretty much my first memory, actually . . . I remember him standing on our back porch. Red shorts, he was wearing. And he had, uh . . . this Hot Rod toy car that I just wanted so badly but didn't get for my birthday. And he offered for me to play with it, with him.' He shrugged. 'And that was that. Instant, lifelong friendship. We were brothers. Did everything together. Fished, learned to swim, learned to ski, to skate, play football . . . Of course, he was better at it all than me too – except poker. He couldn't lie as well as me, but that was all I had on him, the only thing.' He shook his head. 'And I never minded, no, I didn't. I was so proud of him. I was just so proud to call him my frien—' His voice rose up, like a corner being ripped off a sheet of paper, and he fell silent.

Everyone waited, heads cocked at sympathetic angles, brows furrowed with sadness and concern.

'We were so close, I think we both wondered if it could last, especially when we met our girls, Lucy and Meg. Most friendships can't maintain that balance when there's another relationship competing for your attention, but . . .' He looked out across the crowd. 'It wasn't like that for us. We just all blended. We became a family.'

Meg stared at her hands in her lap.

He swallowed, his bottom lip trembling from the effort of remaining stoic. His stop-start delivery reminded Meg of a heavyweight boxing match, just a few parries, one or two touches, and then heavy-breathing silence as the fighters leaned on each other, trying to get their breath back.

'And as much as Mitch was . . . like, this golden guy, Meg was the best thing that ever happened to him. She made him even better than before. He was so happy – you could just see it in him when they were together.' He looked over at her – broken, sorry – but she looked away, refusing to give him the forgiveness she knew, suddenly, that he wanted from her. It was a moment before he looked back over the sea of faces, another few moments before he could remember his place in the speech.

'He'd always had this . . . kind of edge, a reckless streak that could be sorta scary sometimes – like, things that should scare you, didn't scare him.' Tuck looked over at her again and she wondered what he saw of her there – pale and immobile in the chair, too grief-stricken even to stand. 'But when Meg came along, she smoothed the worst of that out of him. Don't get me wrong, he was still a freak in what he could do . . . but for the first time, she gave him someone to care about more than he cared about himself.' He gave a weak, lopsided smile. 'And Badger too. Christ, I mustn't forget him . . . Mitch adored that dog. If anyone took *my* place in his life, it was the damned dog.'

A spatter of laughter speckled the crowd, before everyone sifted into silence again.

'But now he's gone. Mitch has left us. He wasn't scared that night and he should've been. He wasn't selfish either and he *should've been*.' Tuck's voice cracked and he dropped his head, drawing in a shaky breath, perilously close to losing his composure.

Meg stared hard at him now. Was he going to say it, tell them all? *'It was my fault.'*

'He put other people first and he died for it – there is more honour in his death than there will be in my entire life. He was a giant among men and nothing will ever be the same again – not our family, not this town. We are diminished by his absence. We've lost the brightest star in our sky.' Tuck looked out at the faces staring back at him, his own eyes shining with tears. 'So it's up to us all, now, to find a way to carry on without him, to re-form our lives without him at the heart . . . And I guess we will, somehow. Life will go back to normal, perhaps sooner than some of us –' he looked straight at Meg, one tear sliding down his cheek, her own cheeks bone dry – 'sooner than some of us are ready for it to. But he would want that for us, I know he would . . . so we'll have to try.'

He reached into his inner jacket pocket and pulled from it a folded sheet of lined paper, his childish writing distinctive to Meg's eyes even glimpsed through the back. 'I'd like to finish by reading this to you.'

He took a deep breath and Meg felt her heart rate quicken as he began reading the famous Auden poem 'Stop All the Clocks', which most people had learnt from the film *Four Weddings and a Funeral*. The irony wasn't lost on her that a film of her life would be called *No Wedding and a Funeral*.

Someone sniffed. Others dabbed handkerchiefs to their eyes.

Meg stared back into the fire, feeling alone in the crowd, betrayed by her own desiccated grief and wondering when she would cry, when those first tears would come. Ever since she'd seen his body being flown across the sky, wrapped up in that red plastic stretcher, she'd felt mummified too.

Suddenly she was up on her feet and pushing against the door that led onto the deck outside. She needed the cold air to slap her, the punch of shock to bring her back to her full senses, to stop her from standing in there and screaming to them, 'No! He was *my* North! *My* South!'

The evening chill was at its finest and she began to shiver almost immediately as she did what everybody did upon walking out there: looked up at the crest of mountains crowding around and bringing the horizon to just a few kilometres' distance, like a belt that cinched in the Earth. The sky was the colour of a blood orange, casting a pink tint onto the snow below, the skiers' tracks above and through the pine trees indiscernible from here. It would have been a beautiful day for wedding photographs, a beautiful day to film his tracks in the snow, a perfect day to have set off on the rest of their lives . . . it almost made her head spin to think of how many better ways today could have been than this version.

'Hey.'

She twisted back to see Ronnie closing the door quietly behind her, a padded jacket in her hand. 'You OK?' she asked, wrapping the coat around Meg's shoulders. Meg gripped it gratefully and nodded, wondering if her sister could really comprehend the scale of her loss. She'd never really done the boyfriend thing, she hadn't yet lost her heart to anything other than her career – she'd known she wanted to be a doctor from the age of eight – and deep down, Meg knew her sister pitied her life choices, silently disapproving of her choice to forgo a university education for a cabin in the woods with her high-school boyfriend.

It hadn't really mattered back then, back when everything was normal. They had each made their choices and respected the other's but now as Meg's entire world lay in fragments at her feet, she felt a gulf separating her from her sister, for whom grief was a part of her day job. These words – 'I'm sorry for your loss,' 'How are you doing today?' – she repeated on a daily basis, the features on her face readily assembled to convey compassion and empathy before she walked out the door to repeat them to the next patient.

Meg looked back into the fire. Her sister's physical resemblance to her was sometimes unnerving – growing up, when their height differences had evened out, some people had thought they were twins. There was only a year and a half between them, after all, and they both shared the same slim build and long, thick, dark hair. The biggest and most obvious difference had been their eyes – Meg's were hazel-green, Ronnie's dark and rich and round, like chocolate buttons, emphasized by heavy black 'nerd' glasses that she somehow made look cool – and Meg couldn't bear to see this new vital departure between them: one happy, one sad; one successful, one broken.

'Can I get you anything? Another drink?' Ronnie asked, reaching for her hand, her fingers accidentally brushing against Meg's engagement ring and startling, as though aware of the wedding ring that hadn't quite made it.

Meg shook her head and turned to look back in on the wake through the picture window. Tuck had finished his speech now and everyone was clustered in groups again, heads shaking sadly as people no doubt reminisced on Mitch's short life. She saw his father standing at the other end of the room by the opposite fireplace, the skin on his face seeming to droop and fall off him. They had celebrated his sixtieth only three weeks before, Mitch remarking at the time that he hoped he aged as well as his father who could have easily passed for an early-fifty-something, with not a hint of grey in his dark hair – but he had aged significantly in that period. He had a glass of whiskey in one hand and was ostensibly listening as someone spoke to him, but Meg knew from that distant look in his eyes that he was as absent from the proceedings as she was. This wasn't how it was supposed to have gone. It was against the natural order of things. Wrong.

She turned away again and looked up at Mount Norquay, the local ski mountain, casting the longest, deepest shadow over the town. The lifts had stopped for the night now but it was almost perverse to think of all the people who'd been up there today, enjoying the views and seeking their thrills, sunbathing at lunch and making the most of this clement weather, blissfully unaware of the hole that had been blown in the centre of this town as surely as if an asteroid had hit Banff Avenue, the main street. They would have skied and boarded, drunk beer and hot chocolate and then shopped and eaten, and all the people serving them, looking after them – they would have been on autopilot, doing their jobs, feeling like frauds as they told their customers to 'have a nice day', knowing exactly how thin was the thread between thrill and terror, beauty and despair. This landscape was savage and merciless, relentless and unpredictable. You had a nice day if it let you. Meg didn't think she'd ever get on a snowboard or pair of skis again. She'd spent her late teenage years and early twenties out on the slopes every chance she got, sitting beside Lucy with a packed lunch by the half-pipe and watching as Mitch and Tuck worked on their jumps and tricks. It hadn't been so much a sport as a lifestyle, and then latterly a business – but there was no space in her head for that right now.

She caught sight of a bald eagle wheeling on a thermal high above the black run, knowing they liked to build their eyries in the crags there; she watched it glide, high and free, the black rooks in the sky's lower echelons taking care to keep their distance. That was how she felt – alone and unanchored. People had been coming up and hesitantly offering their condolences all day, anxious lest they upset her fragile balance, wary of her dry-eyed grief. They didn't recognize that the requisite for polite smiles and some sort of feedback from her was exhausting. They didn't understand that she barely heard their words or felt their sympathy; they didn't realize that just to breathe, to blink, was as much as she could manage, that all she could see through her open eyes were imagined images of Mitch twirling her in her white dress, of him whisking her upstairs to the bridal suite, in a hurry to officially make her his wife.

The bedroom in Lucy and Túck's bungalow had become her tomb; for the first three days after Mitch's death, she hadn't risen from bed at all, sleeping hard and constantly as though she could double-bluff death with her own unconsciousness. But it had disorientated her, waking at odd hours and finding herself in the strange, too-big bed. More than that, the moment after waking – when she remembered and the desolation rushed at her like baying wolves – was somehow worse than the numbing endurance that came from living and breathing through these first days.

'Well, you've got through today,' Ronnie said, watching the eagle too. 'They say that's the hardest part done.'

Was it? Was it *really*? She glanced across at her sister, wondering if she'd even heard the tactlessness in her voice. 'Yes . . . Just the small matter of the rest of my life to get through now,' Meg said quietly.

Ronnie looked pained. 'Meg, I didn't mean—'

'I know.' She sighed, looking away and feeling bad, and then instantly feeling angry that she now felt guilty on top of everything else. She and her sister didn't know how to communicate with each other any more. Ever since their mother's death, they had been like stars in the sky, pulled towards other planets and drifting out of each other's orbits, so that Meg wasn't sure she'd be able to call to her sister, even if she wanted to.

They fell quiet.

'Are you going to stay down here again tonight?' Ronnie asked, stuffing her hands deep into the pockets of her own coat. The clear sky meant the temperatures were icy.

Meg shrugged. 'I expect so. I seem to have very little say in the matter.' She hadn't returned to the cabin since Patterson and Hughes had brought her back to town to officially identify the body; no one would let her go and she didn't have the energy to fight them. She didn't know Patterson had told Barbara and Lucy and Tuck that she needed watching, that his years in the field meant he could read from a person's first response exactly how their grief would play out over the ensuing weeks. Those who wept and cried and shook their heads and pleaded – they coped, burning through the grief like a flame up paraffin rope. But those like Meg who became silent and calm, outwardly rational but emotionally unreachable – they were the ones to worry about; they'd seem reasonably fine, he warned, but that didn't mean there wasn't a time bomb ticking away inside them, it didn't mean the fuse wasn't lit.

'It's just because they're worried about you. We all are.'

'I'd feel better at home – it would make me feel closer to him.'

'Or it might make you feel worse.' Ronnie tilted her head, watching her. 'And you wouldn't eat or look after yourself. There'd be no one to keep an eye on you.'

'I don't need—'

'You *do*, Meg,' Ronnie said, cutting her off and wrapping an arm around her. 'We all would in this situation. You've just buried your fiancé.' She stopped short of adding, '*On your wedding day.*'

Meg squeezed her eyes shut, feeling the weak sun on her face.

'You need time to process it.'

Meg sighed, turning her face away and denying the truth; Ronnie's fingers on her shoulder slackened their grip.

'Besides, Badger needs to keep seeing the vet. It was a bad break.'

Suddenly the hum of conversation inside the reception increased sharply in volume and they both turned to see Lucy stepping out onto the deck, another coat in her hands.

'Hey, I've been looking for you. I thought you might want th—' She smiled. 'Oh, hi, Veronica.' Her smile faded, her body language becoming more closed. 'It was good of you to come.'

'Hi, Lucy,' Ronnie replied, nodding nervously, her arm dropping off Meg's shoulder altogether as Lucy leaned in to kiss her cheek. Meg looked away again – Ronnie and Lucy had never been close. Lucy used to moan that Ronnie looked down on them, '*like she's superior just because she's got a degree*'; Ronnie would complain that Lucy was too territorial about Meg: '*How can she be jealous of your sister?*'

It was true that Meg and Lucy's relationship was intense. They had been friends since Meg's first week at school when her hair had caught light over a Bunsen burner and the amount of hairspray in it meant she'd not only almost burned off her hair but almost burned down the school as well, earning her kudos from Lucy – no mean feat.

Lucy had a fearsome reputation as the don't-mess captain of the ice-hockey team and possessor of a withering sarcasm, and when Meg had started dating Mitch, both Tuck and Lucy had been forced into an uncomfortable foursome. If Lucy enjoyed a certain hard-core notoriety, Tuck was acknowledged as the school heart-throb and it was generally easier to count the girls he *hadn't* dated, than those he had; something which became more pointedly awkward the longer he went on seeing Lucy not as a 'target' (his phrase for the girls he wanted to date) but as collateral to Meg's presence, which was in turn collateral to Mitch's – a sort of necessary evil to endure. To Meg and Mitch, they were a clear match: Lucy was the only girl in school *not* falling at Tuck's feet, which had to be a good thing for keeping his ego in check; and Tuck was the only person with a smile sexy enough to be able to coax Lucy down from one of her rages when she felt the world was against her. But whether it was Lucy's quick wit that scared him off for so long, or whether Lucy was deterred by Tuck's bad-boy tag, when she'd walked in at Senior Prom with a game-changing haircut and body-con dress, Tuck had finally seen what had been under his nose all along and it had been fireworks ever after.

There hadn't been that same eureka moment for Meg's sister and her best friend. There had never been a bonding adventure or gradual understanding between them; if anything, they became more polarized as the years wore on, and when Meg had asked them both to be her bridesmaids, they had disagreed on everything from the colour of their dresses (Lucy liked lilac; Ronnie preferred navy or black), to how to celebrate Meg's bachelorette party (Lucy wanted strippers; Ronnie an expensive spa weekend at Chateau Louise), with the relationship hitting an even further low when Ronnie had had to miss it anyway on account of an emergency at the hospital. Meg could only wonder how they would have got on today if Mitch hadn't died, if this had been their wedding day after all, and it made her feel worse than ever to see them being nice to each other today.

'Do you need me?' Meg asked flatly.

'No, no, I was just checking up on you. Thought you might need this.' Lucy held up the jacket hanging limply in her hands. 'I hadn't seen you for a bit and got a little worried. I didn't realize you were having a sisterly chat.' She looked hesitant. 'But . . . I should go, I'll leave you to talk—'

'It's fine,' Meg murmured. 'Isn't it, Ron?'

'Sure, we just wanted to catch some air. It's getting stuffy in there. You've . . . you've done a fantastic job getting this organized.'

'I wanted to do it. He was my friend too,' Lucy said with rare understatement, even though she'd been run off her feet all day, preparing the food and getting everything ready for the reception, as well as having to man the usual front-of-house duties that came with keeping a hotel full of guests happy. Her father had left them when Lucy was sixteen, the same year she'd met Meg – following a divorcee guest back to Minnesota – leaving her and her mother to run the oldest hotel in town: sixty-four rooms, one hundred and forty-eight covers for breakfast and dinner each day, all year round, even over Christmas; skiers and boarders were replaced with hikers and bikers in the summer months.

Meg glanced across at her friend, hearing the protectiveness in Lucy's voice and loving her for it. Though they had had a slow start, what Tuck had said in there was true – their foursome had become as tight as a knot. 'What do you miss most about him?'

Lucy was silent for a few moments, her eyes too following the eagle in the sky. 'His laugh, weirdly. I mean, it's not like he was the biggest laugher.'

'No,' Meg agreed. Mitch's sense of humour had been dry and understated, and he preferred to be the one making people laugh, than doing the laughing himself. Meg had always thought it was a control thing – choosing to observe rather than partake, something she had put down to his mother dying when he was barely five and him losing trust in the world; but Lucy used to quip that it was a necessary result of his friendship with Tuck, who was always laughing, always at the centre of things. 'The town couldn't support two jokers,' she'd mutter.

'You?'

Meg felt her bones set at the question. How could she reduce her loss – him – down to one thing?

'His hands.' She looked at her own – petite and pale – as she said it. His had been the exact opposite: large and brown (even in the winter) from a life spent outdoors, always warm, the skin calloused and hard, the nails square and uncomfortably short. They had been hands that did things: grabbed rock overhangs on Sunday-morning climbs out back in the gullies, cut and planed the snowboards that were beginning to attract wide attention and big money; chopped the logs, built the cabin, tiled the roof, dug people to safety, held her at night . . . Those hands had shaped her world and now they were still and pale and cold.

They were all quiet together, watching the wind skim the mountaintops, the snow itself skiing off the cliffs and curling up into the sky in gossamer sheets. Was he up there – out there – somewhere?

'Well, it's too cold out here for me. I think I'll go and

warm up inside,' Ronnie said after a while as the silence lengthened, and Meg knew her sister felt as though she was intruding.

'Sure, we'll come and find you in a bit,' Lucy said, straightening up with a cheery smile, the chilly breeze lifting her fringe and parting her coat.

'Oh, Lucy, I'm sorry, I didn't know!' Ronnie exclaimed suddenly. 'Congratulations. When are you due?'

Lucy's mouth parted in surprise, her face frozen in horror. 'I . . .'

There was a stunned silence, eyes sliding from one to the other like skaters on the ice as Ronnie realized her slip-up too late. 'Sorry, I . . .' She bit her lip. 'I'll just go inside.'

Lucy watched her go, the background hum of conversation peaking sharply and then becoming muffled again as the door opened and closed behind her.

'You're pregnant?' Meg asked, her voice quiet, her eyes on the barely noticeable swell of her friend's belly as she felt the earth shift beneath her feet, the winds whip, the temperatures plunge. She felt as though she was falling, plummeting through a crevasse, away from the light. But when she blinked again, nothing had changed – and yet everything had.

'Meg—' Lucy said, her voice a croak. 'I wanted to . . . I didn't think—' Her shoulders slumped. 'I'm so sorry.'

'Why are you sorry?'

'Because it's not the right time.' Lucy stared at her, her eyes swimming with regret. 'It wasn't planned, you have to believe me.'

'Lucy, you don't need to explain yourself to me.'

'But I feel so guilty.'

'Why? Because something good has happened in your

life when something bad has happened in mine? That's crazy.'

Lucy lowered her eyes. 'Say you forgive me.'

'You don't *need* me to forgive you. There's nothing to forgive. I'm . . . I'm so pleased for you both. Come here.' Meg held her arms out and Lucy walked into her embrace. Meg hoped Lucy couldn't feel her shaking through the depths of her parka; she hoped her expression was backing up her words.

'How are you feeling?'

'Wiped out. And sick as the proverbial dog. Three times this morning.'

Meg tried to smile sympathetically. Just tried to smile. 'Oh, my God,' she mumbled. 'Tuck's going to be a father. What did he say?' She closed her eyes; just saying his name made her blood burn.

Lucy shook her head. 'He doesn't know yet. I only just found out myself . . .' Her voice trailed away. 'And anyway, he's been too upset. It's not the right time.'

Meg frowned. 'But how many weeks are you?' She looked down, taking another look at Lucy's small bump. There wasn't much to see, if anything. Meg probably would have mistaken it for a little extra weight herself, but she supposed Ronnie had a sharp eye as well as a professional one; nothing ever got past her.

'Five weeks.'

'Five weeks!' What did her sister have – X-ray vision?

'Part of me thinks it's the best thing I could do, telling him – it would give him something positive to focus on. The other part's frightened he'll hate the baby.'

'Why would he do that?'

'For making him feel guilty for being happy, when he

feels he should be sad.' She looked away again, swallowing hard. 'The timing's wrong. Everything's wrong, Meg.'

Meg put her hands on Lucy's shoulders and tried to summon a conviction she meant in theory but couldn't yet feel. 'No. It makes everything right. Tuck just stood up in front of all those people and told them we have to find a way to move on.' She took a steadying breath, trying to believe what she was saying. 'What could be more wonderful than this? Mitch would have been *so* delighted if he'd known. This is exactly what he'd want for you guys.'

Lucy stared back at her friend, her brown doe-eyes shining, her head shaking from side to side. 'It's too soon.'

Meg took another deep breath, like a swimmer in an underwater cave, breathing in an air pocket, trying to survive the waves. 'No. This is exactly what we need. You, Tuck, me – all of us. It's the first step on our new path. It's how we find the courage to move forwards.'

Lucy rolled her lips together, the tears sliding down her cheeks. Meg wasn't sure she'd ever seen her friend cry before. 'You really think so?'

'I know so,' Meg lied, gathering her into her arms again and feeling a single tear sliding down her cheek, Lucy sobbing into her shoulder. 'That baby's going to keep on growing and our world's going to keep on spinning, Lucy – whether we like it or not.'

Chapter Seven

Thursday 27 April 2017

Badger's ears drooped, watching from his spot on the front seat as she unlocked the padlock and pushed back the corrugated doors. He knew exactly where they were. He knew what it meant when she reversed the blue snowmobile out of the small concrete lock-up (Martin Hughes had had it towed down from the cabin and repaired for her whilst she'd been staying with Lucy and Tuck). He knew just where they were going.

Meg jumped back into the truck beside him and slowly drove it into the narrow parking space where the snowmobile had been. She pulled up on the handbrake with a tug and glanced down at him as she released the keys from the ignition.

'Hey, don't be so sad,' she said placidly, ruffling the top of his head. 'Come on.'

Badger whined and lay down in the seat, his muzzle between his front paws, the cast over the broken one now grubby and worn. Meg tutted impatiently and jumped down, loading the shopping from the truck into the sled attached to the back of the snowmobile. Moving fast, moving a lot, worked best. It didn't do to think too much –

that led to feeling, and burying her fiancé on their wedding day had been a horror she could barely stay conscious for.

It had taken its toll: she had dropped a ton of weight in the intervening weeks and her hair felt thinner when she brushed it; her eyes seemed to protrude from her face like globes; her lips were bloodless and thin. When she stood, very often her head buzzed and her vision pixelated, and voices sounded muffled and far away as though she was listening through walls.

That evening with Lucy on the deck nearly four weeks ago hadn't proved to be the turning point she'd hoped it would be. Learning about the baby as she watched the sun set on what was supposed to have been the greatest day of her life . . . she felt entombed, buried in emotions too dark and heavy to share. She wanted to feel happy for her friend but something in her couldn't quite reach that shore. No matter what she'd said to the contrary, it *was* too soon.

Not that there was any celebrating going on. Tuck still didn't know he was going to be a father – Lucy dithering and looking fretful every time Meg brought it up – and of course, he hadn't noticed that his wife was pale and puffy, alternately off her food or bingeing, and most conspicuously of all, not drinking. Most of the time he was too drunk to stand, the other times coming in so late, they'd already gone to bed. Several times Meg had been woken by what she'd thought was the sound of him crashing into the furniture in the room beside hers, his voice slurred and raised, Lucy shushing him desperately to keep the noise down.

Evening after evening, Lucy and Meg had made a sorry sight trying to eat their dinner, Tuck's chair empty, Meg struggling to swallow the food down, Lucy battling the severe nausea that was getting harder and harder to hide. But Tuck was never around to see it, sleeping late in the mornings, out all day, and the days slipped past, Lucy getting gradually bigger, Meg getting thinner and Tuck getting drunker.

Meg was convinced the three of them living together was toxic, her grief cancelling out their possibilities for happiness – how could they laugh when she couldn't even cry? – her presence fuelling their guilt. (Tuck had stopped trying to make eye contact with her since the funeral.) But Barbara – keeping an eye on them all from the hotel across the yard – was adamant Meg couldn't return to the cabin until she'd proved she was capable of looking after herself.

So Meg tried harder to hide her grief than Tuck, knowing everyone was watching her, waiting for signs that she was starting to 'get over it' and beginning to move on. She began faking it – the smiles, the conversation, the appetite. She had gone back to work almost immediately after the funeral, perfectly aware that Dolores was reporting her every move to Barbara; she stayed out in the workshop at the back, away from Joe Public, who didn't realize she was the walking wounded, her head bent over the skis as she adjusted the bindings with her box of tools. Occasionally, when they were really busy and it was unavoidable, she'd come out and wordlessly measure toddlers for ski heights and fit them for helmets, but several times she'd caught them watching her – big-eyed and still as she adjusted their chin straps – somehow knowing, sensing she was incomplete now.

Once in a while, the fakery had been interrupted with moments of genuine feeling – Dolores made her laugh till she almost cried when she accidentally put salt instead of sugar in her coffee and pulled a face of such shock and horror, Meg could now summon the image at will; a couple of times she had felt hungry from her long days at the shop and went for pancakes with Dolores at Melissa's Missteak after they locked up; she could sometimes sleep without dreaming, wake without gasping. Every tiny, incremental milestone felt epic.

Until she had woken up today and known it was time to move back to the cabin. Lucy had known it too – from the way Meg stood at the door, the very look in her eyes, the way she cleared her plate of food at breakfast and brushed her hair.

'Are you coming?' she asked now, holding open the truck door.

Badger sat up and whined again. Meg sighed and gathered her arms around him, lifting him gently to the floor and watching as he trotted out of the garage in his strange hobbling gait. Then she locked up, the padlock hanging heavily on the chain, and lifting him onto the saddle in front of her own seat, threw her leg over the snowmobile and strapped them both in.

Helmet on, the engine started first time, and she sat very still for a moment as the what-ifs of that night ran through her mind again. What if the starter motor hadn't broken? What if she'd let Mitch fix it in the blizzard after all? What if Mitch had been able to take it out in the storm? Might he have crossed the couloir before the snow slipped, taken a different route altogether?

She let the questions reverberate through her, knowing they wouldn't be denied anyway, before revving the throttle and leaving them scattered in her wake like toppled skittles in the snow as she sped away, too fast to catch.

She cut a line across the meadow, her tracks sharp and clean, heading straight for the innocuous, narrow pass between the trees where the steep incline up the mountain began, which she and Mitch always used as the private access to the cabin. There was that same familiar rush she always experienced as the snowmobile covered the ground quickly, eating up the hectares, the wind pinking her cheeks.

In the forest, sound altered as the view changed from clear sky to powdered trees. The throaty thrum of the engine was dampened, the slicing of snow clear to her ear as she turned a sharp left by the pylon, doubling the power for the short steep drag by the escarpment that could be icy on skis.

She glanced down at Badger, his ears flying back, eyes closed, comforted by the feel of her arms around him on the handlebars. He was more anxious about coming home than she was. He had none of the defiance that had driven her this past week, the burst of anger that was suddenly propelling her back to her own life and up this mountainside, as though by staring down the horrors that had claimed them she could somehow change them. He didn't have that to sustain him; he just missed his master, plain and simple.

Meg revved the throttle harder, feeling the gradient pitch up. She saw an elk in the distance, head nodding beneath the weight of its palmate antlers as it slowly picked a route along a narrow ridge, the tiny-footed tracks of hoary marmots criss-crossing a lattice in the thinning snow outside a cluster of rocks; red-hooded pine grosbeaks perched on fanned branches, sending down showers of snowflakes as they took flight with a flurry of wing flaps, ground squirrels scampering up and down trunks, fir cones safely clamped between their jaws.

And then quite suddenly, too soon, they were there, the snowmobile swinging round the pine tree with their initials carved in the base and which heralded the small clearing of their land.

Meg's hands flew off the handlebars, stalling the vehicle and sending her and Badger lurching forwards, her heart rate rocketing as she took in the tiny space she called home, robbed of speech at the very sight of it – not because she was assailed by the memories of the storm or of the years she and Mitch had spent there, but because of the years they hadn't – and now wouldn't.

The cabin was bedecked in flowers, the roof a carpet of roses, wreaths of berries and lisianthus at the window frames and door, garlands of buds twisted round the porch struts and the balustrades – and every single one of them dead, the once-bright colours bleached into powdery pigments as though an ash cloud had sieved itself over the plot.

Meg let out a cry, her fingers stumbling to release the seat belts, her knees buckling as she tried to stand, to walk towards the hut. Badger whined, jumping down awkwardly after her, trying to fathom the changes to his home.

Meg sank into the snow, panting as though she'd run up the mountain, her body trying to help her brain work harder to understand, dredging a vague memory of a promise of a surprise, Mitch teasing her – knowing full well she couldn't bear them keeping secrets from each other, even good ones – saying he'd got something planned for when they came back from honeymoon.

Honeymoon.

The very word was a shock, another jolt of remembrance. They were supposed to have gone boarding in Vail for a week but it hadn't once entered her head in all this time, unable to get past the wedding day itself. Had . . . had someone cancelled it for them? Barbara or Lucy or Ronnie? Or had everyone been too stunned, too busy organizing the funeral and it had slipped through, forgotten, the hotel baffled by their newlyweds' no-show and the unreturned calls to the cabin?

Her eyes lingered on the rosy roof, Mitch's grand romantic gesture now ghoulish and grotesque and pitiful. Who had done this? Which friend or favour had Mitch called in to do this for them? No one in Banff, that much was certain; everyone there knew what had happened. So then a specialist in Calgary, perhaps? How long had it taken to put up? How many people?

And how had he afforded it? All these questions ran through her head and she didn't have a single answer for reply and never would. Because he was dead. He was dead. He was dead.

She scrabbled to her knees and ran through the deep snow to the porch, grabbing at the garlands and pulling them away from the frame in a frenzy, clumps of leaves coming off in her hands. She screamed, furious, as the twine – finely knotted – held the greenery close, striating her palms with livid red marks as she pulled and tore and yanked it away, dead flowers littering the garden.

When the walls were bare, she ran to the shed and entered the padlock code, returning a moment later with the ladder and placing it against the side of the hut. A minute after that and she was standing on the roof, kicking the flowers off, tripping several times on the lengths of wire that held them in place. Petals scattered everywhere, the roses' heavy heads bursting under the swipe of her boots as she stomped and kicked and tore and screamed. And when the last rose finally fell, bloodless and dry onto the ground below, when wire sprang from the roof like an old man's stray hairs and she saw the pale ashes of a big, beautiful love scattered in the snow, she fell to her knees, exhausted and panting.

But still she didn't cry.

The cabin warmed quickly, the fire in the stove radiating a dry heat that pushed out the incipient damp that came from almost a month, unattended, in the snow. She unpacked the sled quickly – light was already failing – and restocked the larder shelves, refusing to notice how empty they'd been and the squabbles it had caused, refusing to remember that last desperate meal she'd cobbled together and which Mitch hadn't even seen as he buckled up and entered his last hours.

She threw together a basic soup – leeks, white beans, chicken stock and a dash of chilli oil – and ran a bath, ruffling Badger's head as she passed. He was sitting in his usual spot, on the rug before the fire, but he wouldn't rest, his eyes following her as she moved around the small area, his head lifting whenever she moved out of sight into the bedroom or bathroom.

She turned off the taps, the cabin filling with the competing aromas of soup and jasmine, stalling as she passed the phone. She stared at it, feeling a rush of hatred and knowing exactly what would happen now.

She lifted the receiver and – as expected – the dialling tone beeped in her ear.

She replaced it with a crash, marching towards the bathroom with a fury she couldn't quash, plunging herself into a bathful of water that was too hot. Of course she'd known the line was back up. Nearly four weeks had passed since the storm. The snowpack was steadily beginning to thaw as spring approached on hesitant tiptoes. There hadn't been a storm since, an area of high pressure settling over the national park, and Meg found it an insult, the clear skies mocking her, the wide panoramic view she had once loved now a jeer, reminding her in all its expanse of that one fateful night when the sky had fallen down and the walls of the world caved in.

She lay in the bath until the water was chilled, the soup forgotten, the fire almost out. Badger had settled himself outside the bathroom door, his occasional snuffles reminding her he was there, the odd whine a gentle reminder that he needed his dinner too.

The phone rang but she let it ring out, the noise abrupt and startling in the pervasive silence. But when it rang again, immediately afterwards, Meg knew she had to answer it. Barbara and Lucy would be dragging her back to the bungalow if she didn't show them she was OK to be alone up here.

'Hi.' She watched the water dripping heavily on the floorboards by her feet, her oversized sage-green towel wrapped twice around her. 'I'm OK. I was in the bath.'

'Oh, thank God for that,' Lucy said with evident relief. 'I thought I was going to have to come out and haul you back here.' Lucy's voice became muffled, as though she'd put a hand over the phone: '. . . in the bath.'

There was a pause as Meg waited for her to return.

'So, how is it up there?' Lucy asked.

Meg closed her eyes again as the memory of the cabin bedecked in dead flowers flashed in her mind. 'Fine, once I got the fire going.'

'Have you got enough logs for the week?'

'Yes, Mitch—' She stopped herself.

Lucy understood. 'Tuck can come up and chop some more for you at the weekend if you want.'

'That's not necessary.'

'But he'd like to.'

Meg rolled her lips together, knowing he wouldn't like anything of the sort; he'd be hungover to hell and besides, neither of them wanted to be alone with the other, the silent, unspoken accusation hanging like a chandelier between them.

'Have you told him yet?' she asked instead, holding the towel closer to her as a sliver of wind breached a gap in the timbers, rippling goose pimples over her skin. Before she had left, she had made Lucy promise she would tell Tuck tonight and Lucy had agreed – she was cooking him a special meal and had asked him to get home without stopping for beers with the boys first.

'Just about to. He's having a shower.'

Well, at least he was there. Lucy sounded so nervous, Meg half felt she should wish her luck. 'He'll be thrilled. You guys being a proper family is . . . it's the kind of good news he needs right now.'

'I hope so.'

Meg heard a clatter in the background. 'Everything OK?'

Lucy must have turned away momentarily because her voice sounded distant for a moment. 'Yes, he just knocked something over, is all. Clumsy as, is Tuck.'

Drunk, more likely. 'Well, good luck. I'm sure he'll be thrilled. You've been working yourself up over nothing about it.'

'I hope you're right.' But her voice sounded pale and

thin. In the background, Meg could make out the timbre of Tuck's voice.

'You should go.'

'OK,' Lucy agreed. 'But you remember what we agreed?'

'Yep. I'll call you if things get bad.'

'It doesn't matter how late. Even if you just want to cry. Or to breathe down the phone.'

'Like some dirty old pervert?'

'You know what I mean,' Lucy half scolded with a laugh.

'Yeah, I do . . . See you tomorrow, Luce.'

She hung up, feeling the silence rush around her like water again. She poked at the smouldering ashes and threw on a couple of logs, took the soup off the heat and went to get dressed.

As if it were that easy.

As if stepping back into the ruins of her life was as simple as keeping house – practising routine chores with a studied blankness, pretending she was just a normal person doing mundane things. Stocking shelves, setting a fire, running a bath, making a meal . . . But in the bedroom, which she had avoided going into thus far, she was hit with the full devastating force of her loss. His eternal death was nowhere more apparent than in the private space where they had loved as well as lived – his clothes, his scent making his presence as tangible in there as if he'd been lying in the bed, Badger on his feet.

His pyjamas were still folded – after a fashion – on the pillow beside hers, his favourite checked shirt in a heap in the corner of the room, ready for washing; balls of odd socks sticking out of shoes or from under the bed, the book he'd been reading still open and face down on the bedside table.

He might walk through that door at any moment.

He never would.

Meg turned abruptly and slammed the door shut behind her, her hand still on the handle lest it didn't catch and swung open again, letting the past trickle out. She stood motionless for a few moments, catching her breath, letting her heart settle – if it ever would – before digging a pair of grubby sweat pants and a hoody from the laundry basket in the bathroom.

She walked back into the kitchen and busied herself with preparing Badger's dinner. She would sleep in the spare room tonight.

Lucy dropped the hall phone onto the cradle, holding her breath as she watched Tuck walk naked back from the bathroom to the bedroom, towelling his hair and leaving splodgy wet footprints on the carpet behind him. His body was oddly marked with ski-bum tan lines at his wrist and neck, his face wind-burned, his lips chapped, his blond hair bleached even by the winter sun. He was still the most beautiful man she'd ever seen.

He didn't seem to notice her standing there, one hand clasped protectively over her belly, and she heard him hiccup, then belch, from the bedroom as he clattered open wardrobe doors, looking for clean clothes.

She was standing in the kitchen, doing the dishes, when he walked in a few minutes later. He sauntered over to the fridge and got himself a beer, popping off the cap and ducking a quick look under the blinds across the courtyard to see whether her mother was sitting by the window in her apartment in the hotel, watching them. He was neurotic to the point of paranoia about it, even though Lucy had reassured him a thousand times that her mother was simply watching TV, that she had no interest in watching the drudge of their domestic life from across the courtyard, but he remained convinced his mother-in-law was spying on them, adamant they had to move.

But to what? That was what Lucy wanted to know. Every cent he made went back into the business (or Bill's bar). At least here they didn't have to pay rent and it was central.

He took a swig of the beer (not his first of the evening, she was sure) and she felt his stare on her, sensed his resentment at having been called in early, the marital leash shortened for once.

'So, what's this thing you wanted to talk to me about?' His voice was surly.

Lucy bit her lip, feeling her nerves spike, as she slowly turned to face him. Would the words come?

He watched her, his cheeks flushed dark pink from the drink and she saw it again, that look that lurked in the furthest depths of his too-blue eyes now, whenever he looked at her.

She looked back at him, willing him to guess, understand, rejoice . . .

He straightened, mistaking her hesitation. 'Is it what we talked 'bout before? Have you reconsidered?'

Reconsidered? Lucy felt her stomach tighten and curl, repelled by the thought. The things he'd said that time – what, six weeks ago now? Yes, it had been a bad patch, even before everything with Mitch, but he'd been drunk; he hadn't meant the things he'd said. She knew he hadn't. She knew him better than he knew himself, that was the problem. 'Wha—? No!' she cried. 'How could . . . how could you think—?'

His face fell, desolation in his eyes again. 'Lucy, please. You know this isn't—'

'I'm pregnant.'

The words hit their mark. Tuck slumped as surely as if he'd been shot, the colour draining from his face, the beer bottle clattering loudly against the worktop as his arm dropped. 'What?'

The word was a whisper, as thin and friable as a winter's leaf.

'We're having a baby.' She tried to follow the words with a smile, to lead the way, to show him this was a happy thing, a good thing. But almost immediately, she felt the tears fill her eyes, her mouth twist into a grotesque rictus as the smile faltered and failed at the sight of his shock. His breathing was shallow, his face settling into that mask of despair he seemed to wear at all times now.

'Say something, please,' she whispered.

Tuck blinked and it was another minute before he could raise his gaze, as though it was something too heavy to be lifted, but she still felt that so-familiar jolt she always got when he looked straight at her.

'Fuck.'

The red eye stared back at her, unblinking in the dark. It didn't flicker, flash, pulse, beat. No light radiated from it. She couldn't see the monitors or the banks of buttons on the rigs, innocuous machines which, at one touch, turned the light green and the planet was shrunken and digitalized and brought into this little room like a cake on a tray. One wrist flick of the dial and she could speak to people in faraway lands the way Mitch had – all those far-flung friends he used to chat to. Were they wondering where he was? Did they assume he was busy at work or away on holiday? Perhaps he'd told them he was getting married and they thought he was on honeymoon?

The thought made her snap her face away to the opposite wall, a reflexive move that made Badger groan. She felt hot suddenly, the blankets too much, and she threw them to the ground with an irritable sweep of her arm. She lay there, staring into a darkness so complete she couldn't see her own hand in front of her. Someone – anyone – could have been waving a couple of centimetres from her nose and she wouldn't have known it. She was up here alone. She was totally alone—

What was that noise?

With a sudden rush, she sat bolt upright and turned on the bedside lamp, light showering the room like a spray of gold ink; Badger lifted his droopy lids to stare at her from bloodshot eyes before closing them again. Her heart was pounding but she knew she was over-reacting. It was probably just a racoon scratching for scraps, or that cougar Mitch had spotted climbing the escarpment a few weeks ago. She just wasn't used to being on her own up here, that was all. Her mind was playing tricks on her.

Meg stared around the room, taking in the unfamiliar-looking objects and furniture arrangement and wondering when exactly she had become a stranger in her own home. It was only nine years ago that Mitch had inherited the plot – and dream – from his grandfather and they had excitedly set to building the cabin. The idea had been to turn it into a holiday rental, utilizing its unique off-the-track location to appeal to experienced bikers and hikers, skiers and boarders who wanted a base from which to explore the back country. As Mitch had spent a whole spring and summer clearing trees, digging trenches and transporting timbers, she – and Lucy – had torn around town, bargain-hunting for bedcovers and lamps, curtains and rugs, always setting the fire each night and putting out jugs of fresh mountain flowers each breakfast. Mitch had laughed at her but he'd fallen for the dream as much as she had; they'd made themselves a home.

But time had passed – as it invariably must – and the new had become familiar and the familiar mundane, so that sitting here now, she couldn't remember the last time she'd actually looked at her own home. If she'd covered her eyes, there and then, would she have remembered that the picture on the wall was an Ansel Adams print of Drawbridge Peak or that the bed frame was brass?

Throwing back the covers, she walked over to the window and stared out. Stars prickled the sky but cast no light down here. She sat at the desk and stared at the one red eye.

This was a mistake. She shouldn't have come back. It was too soon.

She should call Lucy. She'd promised she would if she needed to talk . . .

It turned green, they all did, her fingers pressing each in turn, her eyes watching as the LCD displays came up and the dials swung into life. Static crackled and she picked up the mic, her thumb on the button.

'Hello? Is anybody there?' she asked quietly, before remembering: 'Over?'

White noise hissed and buzzed like angry insects.

'Hello? Can anyone hear me?'

Some voices came through, close enough for her to detect a Midwest accent, something Spanish . . .

'Hi! Hello?'

They crackled out of hearing again, out of range, the connection disintegrating. Perhaps she needed to change the frequency? She went to turn the knob left when a man seemingly stepped into the room – European, his English tinged with an accent she couldn't place, his voice calm, clear. In an instant, Badger was by her side, his head positioned under her hand, ears lifted quizzically at the disembodied sound.

'This is November Alpha One Sierra Sierra, calling Victor X-ray Four Delta Delta Echo, do you copy, over?'

Blood rushing through her head, her heart pounding, Meg stared at the digital display. 145.800 MhZ FM. The dial was still where she had left it that night. The exact point where her hope had died had its own reference number, like a map coordinate. X marks the spot.

'November Alpha One Sierra Sierra, calling Victor X-ray Four Delta Delta Echo, do you copy, over?'

Meg's eyes went to the sticker on the side of the monitor but she already knew the call sign. She would never forget it. The horror of that night was tattooed in her bones, every last detail, and now the sound of his voice was bringing it all back – that lone voice from the dark, the one lifeline they'd had.

She looked away and out of the window, up at the stars that did nothing but look pretty, the same stars that were nowhere to be seen during the storm when she'd had one wish that she desperately needed to come true.

'This is Commander Solberg of NA1SS, calling Meg Saunders. Do you copy, over?'

One star looked brighter than the rest. It was flashing, moving. Was it a plane? . . . Was it . . . was it him?

Her thumb pressed the button. 'I hear you.'

She watched the light flash in the sky, so far away. There was no way she could be talking to someone there – right?

'Copy that. It's good to get hold of you. I've been trying to re-establish contact for weeks, over.'

'I've been away.' Meg closed her eyes, her head in one hand as the memories continued to clamour like pawing children over an exhausted mother.

There was a pause.

'Copy that. I've just been concerned since our initial contact. I wanted to check you were OK, over.'

Meg inhaled slowly, pushing down the emotion that was billowing inside her, wanting to be let out, needing to be released. 'I'm fine . . . Over.'

Another pause. She watched the light blink in the sky.

'And your fiancé, Miss Saunders? Did they manage to send help in time, over?'

'No. He didn't make it. He died. He's dead.' The words shot out into the atmosphere like flares and she didn't need to close out with protocol this time; there wasn't anything that came after those words. She waited for whatever the technology was that allowed them to *chat* like this, to beam his sympathy back down to Earth.

'Copy that . . . Please accept my sincere condolences, Miss Saunders—'

'Thank you,' she said quickly, inadvertently speaking over him, his formality an echo of the official sentiments of the Search and Rescue team that had found Mitch, the coroner, the town . . . But they were words she didn't want to hear, words that only ever came with a fixed reality she didn't want to face . . .

'. . . see the storm from here. I knew it looked bad, over.'

She paused. He had *seen* the storm? From the safety of space, how small, how insignificant must her life-death emergency have seemed, her and Mitch scurrying like ants, invisible beneath the clouds? 'What, what did it look like from up there? Over.'

She could hear his intake of breath from Earth.

'I'm afraid it was large. Strong. Very severe. I was worried for you, over.'

She swallowed, her eyes dropping to the desk. If it had looked that bad all the way where he was . . . 'Do you think he stood a chance?'

Static peaked, some remote voices interfering at the fringes of the frequency, and it seemed an age before his voice beamed back down. 'No. I don't think he did. I'm sorry . . .' He didn't say 'over' but he didn't talk either. 'Have you got people looking after you, over?'

She paused, feeling the velvety smoothness of Badger's head beneath her fingers. 'I've got my dog.' Her words sounded hard, even to her ear.

The static spiked again and for a moment she thought she'd lost him. His voice became robotic and pixelated.

'. . . est companion. I miss mine. He's called Yuri, over.'

Meg frowned. It sounded Russian. 'Don't tell me. Named after an astronaut? Over.'

The sound of his laughter was surprising. '. . . ou are right. Yuri Malenchenko, the first cosmonaut to . . .' His voice broke up again.

'Hello?' she called, when he didn't come back again after the customary pause. 'Commander, are you still there? Can you hear me?' Damn, what was the call sign he kept using? 'Hello?'

'. . . copy? This is November Alpha One . . .' But his voice was indistinct now, other voices, closer ones, familiar accents, criss-crossing the airwaves and tuning him out.

She looked out of the window, her eyes searching the overarching blackness above.

But the star was no longer winking; the night was perfectly still.

Jonas stared down at the North American continent, heading towards the dawn in Europe. It had been several minutes and thousands of miles since he had lost contact with the woman but her thin, brittle voice still reverberated in his head – *'He didn't make it. He died. He's dead'* – saying the same thing in numerous different ways, as though that would make it more real, more believable.

The truth was, he had feared as much. Ever since he'd picked up her Mayday call thirty-two days ago now, the incident had stayed with him. He hadn't been able to forget it, to stop wondering about the man lost in that super-storm, the woman left behind and who was now lost without him.

For Jonas, it was her smallness that had haunted him. Every day he orbited his own planet, looking down on it from the view of the gods. Its scale and beauty were humbling, but even so, it was reduced to just a blue dot as he looked past it into the fathomless black beyond, humanity becoming microscopic, mere dust particles in the cosmos. When the Grand Canyon was nothing more than a pothole, the Great Wall of China but a yellow thread, it became almost easy to look back down and see the futility of mankind's ambitions – the merciless destruction of the rainforests, the steady pollution of the oceans, the relentless scourge of mineral resources, and all for what? On the individual scale, what did it bring? A bigger house? A designer wardrobe? A fast car? A new iPad?

But that lone voice calling out, carrying into space, had pierced the endless vastness of which he was now a part and anchored him back to his own planet again. Every pass they made of Canada, whenever work permitted he went to the viewing capsule and tried to look down, making futile attempts to see what he had only heard. But the mountains were no bigger than the ripples on his knuckles and he was denied the detail that could answer his questions. Who were they? Where were they? How exactly had things panned out that night?

Was there anything more he could have done from here? His relay of the SOS to his flight director had been almost instantaneous and they would have alerted Alberta Search and Rescue within moments. There probably wasn't anything *anyone* could have done, not down there, much less from up here – the guy could have been dead within five minutes of setting out; Jonas had orbited Earth sixteen times a day for fifty-three days now and he hadn't seen a weather system like that anywhere else, either before or since.

But that was scant consolation – he was the one who'd intercepted the call; he was the one who'd seen the almighty odds they were battling down there – and the echoes of her voice haunted him in the pervasive silence. He was an astronaut, a man of exceptional capabilities with an IQ of 157 and trained to deal with every possible technical, engineering, medical and meteorological possibility that space could throw at him. But as the world continued to turn outside his window, Jonas Solberg knew this frightened woman had done the one thing the European Space Agency had spent years trying to make impossible – she had made him feel helpless.

Chapter Eight

Friday 12 May 2017

The bell blared as the puck hit the back of the net, people cheering and drumming their feet on the bleachers as the display on the board changed from *Visitors 5 - Home 1*, to *Visitors 5 - Home 2*.

Tuck sucked on his teeth, seeing that there were three minutes left on the clock. 'Goddammit, they're playing tight,' he said to no one in particular and punching his fist into his gloved hand. 'What the hell's Tremblay playing at? It's clear they need to bring on Anderson and go wide . . .'

'Nacho?' Lucy offered, holding out the open bag towards him. Salt was her drug of choice right now. She couldn't get enough of it – a clear sign, her mother had told her, that she was deficient and would suffer bad cramps if she didn't improve her sodium levels quickly.

Tuck shook his head, looking irritated that she'd even asked, the expression on his face as she shrugged and helped herself to another telling her quite clearly that he didn't think she should be having them either.

Meg came back with the drinks, her fingers splayed wide around them as she shuffled sideways past the other spectators, apologizing as she trod on toes. Lucy watched her, feeling bad for being jealous of her friend's newly skinny figure; the heartbreak diet wasn't one that she'd recommend to anyone and it was perfectly clear that Meg wasn't controlling – wasn't even aware of – what she was eating at the moment. She was living at a subsistence level, her pallor wan, energy levels low; she spoke without tone, smiled without it ever reaching her eyes. Tomorrow, Mitch would have been buried for six weeks and although Meg never complained, never rang to talk in the middle of the night, never even cried, it was as though she was underground with him. She was alive but not living, conscious but not awake. Life was routine, every day the same – she got up, went to work in the rental store, went home and slept.

Lucy missed her friend almost as much as she missed Mitch. No one seemed to notice that she was heartbroken herself. She had known Mitch since fourth grade – albeit only from afar in those early years but in theory, he'd been in her life almost as long as he'd been in Tuck's. But her grief didn't count somehow; or at least, it couldn't compete with Meg and Tuck's – she was just the fiancé's best friend or the best friend's wife, always a step removed from the man himself.

A few times she had wondered how it would have been if it had been Tuck who'd died that night – she the widow, Mitch the bereft friend, Meg the coper keeping all the balls in the air and ballooning like a galleon in full sail. The same cast of characters playing different parts in the same play – would Mitch have hit the bottle to blank out the memories? Would she, Lucy, be drifting through her own life like a wraith? Would Meg be able to keep the secret that was burning her from the inside out?

'Here you go.' Meg handed over the beer to Tuck, the Fanta to her.

Lucy took a long slurp through the straw, grateful for the sugar hit. She was craving sugar too. 'You were gone a while. I was beginning to get worried.'

'Queues back to the hot-dog stand. What's the score?'

Lucy knew Meg didn't give a damn about the score one way or the other, even though a victory for the Calgary Flames tonight would send them through to the semis for the Stanley Cup. 'There's only three in it now. Oh, wait—' She caught sight of the scoreboard and realized she'd missed another goal, so absorbed was she in her own thoughts. That was another surprising thing about the pregnancy – not just the bodybuilder's gargantuan appetite, but the curious blankness that settled over her like a fog without warning, robbing her of the second part of a sentence or the punchline of a joke, or even why she'd walked into a particular room. It was one thing to be losing her waistline, but her mind too?

There were ninety seconds left on the clock; Tuck was sitting hunched forward on his seat, practically chewing on his knuckles. Lucy's eyes kept straying to the empty seat to his left. The tickets had been bought months ago, the four of them having always followed the League with messianic zeal. Not to have come tonight was unthinkable to Tuck. For him, coming here tonight was a way of honouring his friend's memory. '*It's what he would've wanted*,' Tuck had said as the girls stared at him, unconvinced.

Lucy felt a frisson of dread as the Maple Leafs – Toronto's finest – made another break, the winger dummying a quick one-two that put the keeper on the wrong foot, before swirling round the back of the goal and slicing the puck in neatly, nearside.

Dammit: 6–2. They were pulling away again.

She bit her lip, watching anxiously as the Flames tried to fight back but, for reasons that she missed, the game descended into a fracas between the Maple Leafs' enforcer and the Flames' power forward. The crowd roared as fists flew, the flash of blades ominous on the ice. Lucy hid her face, refusing to watch. She could never stomach the fights that broke out, she didn't find it 'entertaining' or part of the spectacle.

Twenty seconds later it was all over anyway, as the horn sounded and the Maple Leafs threw their sticks jubilantly in the air, the visiting fans on their feet. Lucy, Tuck and Meg didn't move as people got up from their seats; Lucy wasn't sure Meg was even aware the game was over. She was staring dead ahead, her drink clasped loosely and untouched between her laced fingers; she didn't even flinch when Tuck, in a sudden fury, threw his plastic cup against the back of the chair in front, sneering, 'Well, thank God he wasn't here to witness *that* fuck-up.'

Lucy touched her on the arm and Meg jumped, startled, falling back into her act as soon as she realized she'd been caught. 'Oh, hey, are we done?' She stopped short of asking the score. Tuck's black expression was all she needed to see to know they'd lost.

They filed out slowly in a line, one after the other, Lucy protectively keeping her arms bent at her waist, ready to keep at bay a stray elbow or stumbling drunk or anything else that might harm the baby as they pushed through the crowds. She was still at the stage where her bump was more of a lump, and it made her nervous that people couldn't see how fragile she really was. Then again, everyone had always mistaken her solidity for toughness.

They walked through the car park in a single line, Tuck leading them through the rows of pickups and jeeps. A few people were having tailgate parties, cracking open a few beers and letting the queues ease before heading out themselves. Two young couples were laughing about something as their forlorn trio trooped by, looking for the car. One of the girls, the prettier one, caught sight of Tuck and her eyes followed him.

Lucy, trailing behind him, was used to it – this always happened. It was the big downside of marrying a man who was more beautiful than she; he really could have been a model if he'd wanted. She hoped her swollen belly looked more like a baby bump in profile and she stretched her arm out, trying to take hold of his hand. It was her subtle way of signalling to these girls that he was taken, he was hers.

But Tuck, startled by the unexpected gesture, pulled his hand away instead with a bad-tempered sneer and a frown. His team had lost and he just wanted to get out of here. He wanted another beer – or ten – but it was a two-hour journey back to Banff.

Feeling stupid, stung by the rejection, Lucy glanced back at the girl to find her smirking. She had seen the failed attempt at 'ownership'; she could see that dumpy, pale Lucy had punched way above her weight landing a man like him. The girl didn't say a word, nor did she have to – the look in her eyes told Lucy it was open season; a man like that was up for grabs if a girl like her wanted him to be.

'Have I lost my waist?' Lucy asked, turning her back to Meg, who was sitting – gone again – at the table. 'From behind, I mean? You know how those skinny girls get when they're pregnant? No one can tell they're pregnant from behind 'cause they keep their waists. What about me? Be honest.' She lifted her shirt.

Meg had the decency to squint and at least try to look as though she was searching for her friend's lost waist. 'I think you look great.'

'That means yes,' Lucy scowled, planting her hands on her hips and looking down. Her feet were still visible – but she had big feet. 'Jeez, I'm only eleven weeks and it's all going to my ass. No wonder Tuck looks at me like I'm the Blob. Mom reckons I'm going to carry like her, "wide and low", she keeps saying, like I'm some sort of artic vehicle.'

Meg smiled. It didn't reach her eyes.

'So – that coffee I promised.' Lucy turned and busied herself with making their hot drinks. Meg was staying at the bungalow tonight; it was too late to go up to the cabin. She had wanted to go straight to bed – it was almost midnight by the time they'd parked up – but Lucy had managed to persuade her into having a 'nightcap'. 'It's not often you stay over these days,' she'd said with a beseeching smile, and Meg had relented. That was the thing about her – she was too generous.

Tuck hadn't hung around; his mood had barely improved from when they'd been leaving the stadium, and listening to them 'baby talk', as he'd put it, wasn't the thing to remedy it.

From her kitchen window, as the kettle boiled, she could see that almost all the lights were off in the bedrooms across the courtyard; their guests already asleep in preparation for the next day's activities. Her eyes rose to the sky. The moon was hanging low above the mountains tonight, as though it had snagged on a ridge and was tethered there, dark puffy clouds like floating bruises drifting past on a windy tide. But the nights were growing shorter already, the days longer. She had noticed mountain bluebells down by the meadow the other day; some of their guests had reported that Lake Louise was fully thawed again and the rivers were in full spate as the last of the mountain meltwater rushed through the valley in torrents, the mountains above soggy and bleached from a lightless season under the snow. All of it was beautiful; all of it was painful, proof that life was moving on, leaving their friend behind.

She set down the coffee mugs and sat opposite Meg, who immediately began warming her hands. For such old friends who'd never known a moment's silence between them, conversation had become sparse and strained these past weeks. Meg was doing her best but she was merely play-acting the person she used to be. The light had gone out and nothing caught her interest, not really.

'So, Tuck says he's getting loads of calls about the boards.' When Meg looked at her blankly, she continued: 'You know, ever since Brett Williams won bronze at Aspen.'

'Aspen . . .' Meg echoed.

'Yeah, you know, the X Games in January? Williams took third place on the "Slayer" Titch.'

'Oh, yeah,' Meg nodded. 'Well, that's great.'

Lucy sipped her coffee, watching her and feeling unnerved; it was obvious Meg didn't remember that night, or how monumental that win had been. It had put Titch Boards on the map and the four of them had celebrated all night. The crazy, dumb-ass sideline they'd set up in high school had become that rarest of phenomena: a hobby that had struck gold. They had come a long way from the days when the boys had sawed their own boards in half to see how they'd been put together, planing the rough edges and assembling their own, modified versions. And it had been a group collaboration – Lucy had come up with the name (a blend of the boys' but also a witty nod to their USP, the scaled-down size ideal for tricks) and Meg (who had turned down a place at art school to be with Mitch, much to the chagrin of her father, Ronnie and Dolores) had designed the graphics, pioneering the use of digital photography in a field that had hitherto followed the graffiti aesthetics of skateboarding or the Hawaiian influence of surf culture; the very small production runs meant they had quickly acquired collectible status.

But that wasn't to say it had been an overnight success story. Ten years in and they were only just beginning to reap the dividends, with Lucy and Meg both having to work – for Barbara and Dolores respectively – to cover the shortfall of their mutual monthly outgoings. But Williams taking a bronze medal whilst riding their board in one of the biggest snowboard events in the world had been the break they'd needed: online demand had quintupled overnight and they had boutiques all over the continent calling them up.

Mitch had been in his element, talking about setting up meetings with a manufacturer in Idaho who could deliver orders as quickly as they could place them. They already entered their own short snowboarding films annually to the Banff Mountain Film and Book Festival, with a view to making the cut for the worldwide tour that travelled to over forty countries globally, effectively marketing their product to their target audience with minimal financial outlay from them, but now he'd started talking about getting involved as sponsors at other smaller competitions as well.

He'd had big plans, a grand vision, but he didn't see what was coming for him. He could never have predicted that within a couple of months, he'd be dead and Tuck would be left to run the business on his own. Lucy was worried about her husband – he didn't have Mitch's vision, he wasn't a businessman and instead of dealing with suppliers and manufacturers, he was spending hours in the studio trying to finish editing the film for this year's festival, so that calls were going unreturned, emails piling up . . . The stress, the responsibility – it was too much.

Ditto Meg. Lucy could understand why she wasn't focused on the business right now. Beyond her artistic contributions, she had never been too involved in the day-to-day running of Titch anyway – but to have forgotten that night altogether, one of the greatest of their lives? It was almost as though she was a computer hard drive that had crashed, everything on it wiped clean. 'You do remember that, right?' Lucy asked, leaning in a little closer. 'The boys didn't go to bed till eight the next morning, they were so busy plotting and planning for world domination. They wrote their business proposal on the toilet tissue . . .'

Meg smiled, shaking her head. 'Crazy,' she said blankly.

Disappointed, Lucy sat back, patting her hand. 'You must be tired.'

'It's been another long day,' Meg nodded. 'Thank God the ski season's done. If I had to fit one more pair of skis . . .' She made a jokey strangled noise.

They lapsed into silence again. Meg seemed oblivious to it.

'So how are you sleeping now you're back home?' Lucy asked. 'You look pretty rested.'

'I am. I just put my head on the pillow each night and—'
She clicked her fingers.

'Any bad dreams?'

Meg shook her head – perhaps a little too hard – so that
her hair swung. 'None at all. Just . . . black.'

'Me too. I've never known exhaustion like it. Tuck's getting really fed up with me, 'cause I . . . you know.'

It was a moment before Meg did know. She straightened
up. 'Oh. Well, he needs to grow up and understand you're
growing a baby. *His* baby.'

'Yeah. I guess.'

'Is the sickness any better?'

'It is, actually. I'm down to only twice a day now which
is pretty good.'

'Pretty good,' Meg echoed, her eyes distant again. After a
pause, she added, 'You're so lucky.'

Lucy spluttered on her drink. 'Lucky? Me?'

'Of course.'

'Me with the swollen ankles and inability to keep a meal
down or stay awake past seven o'clock every night? Me?'

But she was up late tonight, wasn't she? And her husband was in the next room, not in the ground.

Meg stared at the cork noticeboard on the opposite wall.
'I'd do anything to have him back. A piece of him. A baby
would have . . . made it easier, somehow.'

Lucy felt her throat close up and the tears rush at her
eyes, guilt clawing at her. 'Oh, no, Meg, it would have been
worse, so much worse. You wouldn't wish a child without
its father, would you?'

Meg looked straight at her, her hazel-green eyes watery. 'I
wouldn't wish any of this.'

Lucy reached forward to clasp Meg's hand in her own. 'No.'

They sat in silence again, the clock on the wall ticking quietly above the fridge, the moon creeping along the mountaintops outside the window.

What was left of the coffee was cold now. From the sound of the snores coming through the walls, Tuck was asleep. It was safe for her to go to bed now. 'Time to sleep?' asked Lucy.

Meg nodded and got up, visibly grateful to be released from the strain of conversation.

'See you in the morning,' Lucy murmured, watching Meg go down the hall to the spare room that had become hers in the first weeks after Mitch's death and would soon become the nursery. She was trying her best to look after her, to be the friend Meg needed her to be. To be someone more than she knew she was.

Meg closed the door behind her with a click and leaned against it. Badger was already asleep on the bed thanks to Barbara, who'd been looking after him for the evening, and she walked straight over to him, nuzzling her face in his fur.

Tonight had been one of the hardest so far to endure. Mitch had passionately supported his team, always travelling whenever he could to support them, and he'd been so excited at the Flames' progress up the rankings this season. The score had suggested it had been a tight game, although she didn't recollect a single moment of play, but she knew he'd have loved tonight; he wouldn't even really have minded the defeat. Well, no, he'd have hated it, of course – his mood would have matched Tuck's – but to have been there, been part of the moment . . . That was what he loved.

'The journey's the destination, Meg, don't you know that?' he used to tease when she'd lose her temper sitting in traffic on the way out from Calgary or when she'd beg for mercy on a particularly gruelling hike, the picnic in his backpack and him fifty metres ahead.

Going to those games, the four of them talking and laughing all the way along the highway – the boys swapping facts and trivia in the front, her and Lucy gossiping in the back – it was what they did, what they'd always done, so when Tuck had first insisted they go to the game anyway, she'd thought he'd been joking at first. How could they possibly go to a game without Mitch? How could they sit there with his chair empty . . . ? How could they take it in turns to buy beers and hot dogs, but now just get three instead of four? Couldn't he see how diabolical that idea was to her?

But he'd been so adamant this was what Mitch would want, desperately trying to hold on to traditions made with his best friend and wanting life to be how it used to be, regardless of how anyone else might feel. His grief was total. His loss absolute. No one's could compete, not even hers – he wouldn't have seen that she'd thought she'd throw up when the guy in the seat one along had casually tossed his coat on Mitch's chair, how she'd turned away from the big screens whenever the kiss-cam came on, wouldn't have noticed that she'd had to hide in the toilets for fifteen minutes when getting the drinks because she thought she was having a panic attack. He didn't register that poor Lucy looked wiped out and nauseous and exhausted, he didn't see how driving home in a filthy mood muffled them with a soured silence.

He didn't see that his very presence repulsed her.

She squeezed her eyes shut, angry at this backwards step and feeling her pulse climb. She'd been doing so well too, working in the store every day and talking to people, remembering to eat lunch and managing not to feel too much. She was getting good at tuning out the world and turning down the volume.

She reached for her phone, setting the alarm. If she got in early in the morning and organized the dead rental stock for the clearance sale, she could clear some space for the Schoffel delivery they were expecting . . . She saw the email icon on the top of the screen and clicked on it, unused to being able to pick up Wi-Fi in the evenings; there was none at the cabin of course and she and Mitch shared a personal email address, so rare was any correspondence to them there. Almost everyone contacted them via their work addresses. So what came next was a velvet-gloved punch.

Oh! I have slipped the surly bonds of Earth,
And danced the skies on laughter-silvered wings;
Sunward I've climbed, and joined the tumbling mirth
Of sun-split clouds, – and done a hundred things
You have not dreamed of – Wheeled and soared and swung
High in the sunlit silence. Hov'ring there
I've chased the shouting wind along, and flung
My eager craft through footless halls of air . . .
Up, up, the long, delirious, burning blue
I've topped the wind-swept heights with easy grace
Where never lark, or even eagle flew –
And, while with silent, lifting mind I've trod
The high untrespassed sanctity of space,
Put out my hand, and touched the face of God.

The words were strong and soft, tender and brutal. With the lightest of touches, they pierced the membrane that had sealed her up and kept the world at bay; they broke the dam that had kept her dry, slow tears making a stately march down her hollow cheeks. But it wasn't just the poetry that her eyes kept returning to, it was the message at the bottom:

With deepest sympathies, Jonas Solberg.

Chapter Nine

'How d'you think he got it?' Lucy asked in amazement the next morning, flipping the pancakes onto the plate and drizzling them with maple syrup.

'I don't know. I just can't think. I mean, how many Meg Saunderses must there be in Canada, for God's sake? It's hardly an unusual name. My parents weren't exactly blessed with the originality gene.'

'And he's *actually* an astronaut?' Lucy asked, heaping blueberries on top of the waffles and bringing the plates over. 'Like, with a helmet and pet space chimp and everything?'

Meg smiled. Actually smiled! 'I'm not sure about the chimp but he does have a dog. He's called Yuri, although he's not with him up there. I know that, because he said he was missing him.'

Lucy held her cutlery in her hands, her momentary sugar craving forgotten as she gazed back at Meg in wonder. Her face was pale, her eyes swollen and puffy – had she . . . had she *cried*? – and it was clear she hadn't slept well, but she looked changed somehow. Not better, not happier, but definitely . . . present. 'How many times have you spoken to him?'

'Only twice. The first . . .' She swallowed, looking nervous, looking sick. 'That night, obviously. The landline was down and I couldn't get into town to raise an alarm so I tried Mitch's radio. I was just trying to get hold of someone, anyone, who could help. And it was him who answered.'

'On his spaceship?'

Meg cocked her head to the side, recognizing Lucy's trademark sarcasm. Her friend had hidden it away these past few months but if ever there was an occasion for it to rear its ugly head . . . 'I'm as baffled as you, remember. I couldn't work the thing—'

'Well, obviously you could! You made contact with outer space. Hey, have you given your details to NASA? Perhaps you could help them out. I hear they're working on some project with little green men on Mars.'

Meg laughed and it changed her face completely, boosting a pink flush in her cheeks and bringing a light to her eyes. She looked beautiful when she laughed although Lucy knew her friend had no idea of that fact. She had always been unaware of her looks, thinking she was just average – bemoaning when they were teenagers that she was just medium height, medium build, with medium-length dark brown hair and pale skin that didn't tan easily. But she didn't see what everyone else saw – how beguiling it was the way her top lip stayed full and straight when she smiled, the delicacy of her shoulders and arms, how wholesome she looked when her freckles came out in the summer. Little wonder Mitch had fallen so hard for her, or that Lucy sometimes saw Tuck looking.

Lucy smiled, taking the laugh as a small victory – a sign of progress – and began to eat. 'And the second time . . . ?' she prompted, her mouth full.

Meg's smiled disappeared, a flash of desolation in its

place. 'My first night back at the cabin. I couldn't sleep and . . . well, he was out there, trying to get hold of me.'

'Jeez, what is he? Some kind of stalker?' Lucy chewed quickly, laughing as she thought of another joke. 'Although, if he is, at least you don't need to get a restraining order. It's hardly like he's in the vicinity. He's not even in the same atmosphere.' She chuckled, pleased with herself.

Meg smiled too. 'No, it wasn't like that. He was just worried.' She paused, reflective. 'I guess from his point of view it must have been really . . . odd being all the way out there and . . . and hearing me.'

Lucy stopped chewing. She couldn't begin to imagine how terrible it must have been up there, all alone, that night. It had been bad enough down here, clinging to Tuck as the wind barrelled through the town, funnelled between the mountains. 'Shit.'

'Yeah,' Meg nodded, before taking a sharp intake. 'Still, it was nice of him to send the poem.'

'Nice of who to send what poem?'

They both looked up as Tuck wandered through in just his jeans, hands pressed back on his shoulders as he stretched long, the square muscles of his abs like stepping stones. His voice was still furred with sleep and Lucy didn't want to imagine what his breath must be like just now after all those beers last night, but he always looked good first thing. That tousled look suited him – surf-bum blond hair, snow tan, athletic physique, super-blue eyes ringed with long dark lashes . . . He still did it for her. Totally.

'Meg here's been talking to an astronaut. She used Mitch's radio the night of the storm and somehow made contact with—'

'The *International Space Station*? You're freaking kidding me?' If he'd been half-asleep moments before, he was wide awake now, pulling out the chair in front of Meg and straddling it. Meg seemed to recoil a little – from his breath no doubt, Lucy thought. 'Mitch had been trying for weeks to get hold of them.'

'He had?' Meg asked, surprised.

'Yeah. That's why he got that new super antenna.'

'Oh.' Meg looked stunned. 'I had no idea.'

'I can't believe you got hold of them,' Tuck said excitedly, shaking her lightly by the arm. 'You got any idea how many hams try to do that?'

Meg shook her head, taking her arm back from his grip.

'Thousands. And there's only like a five-, ten-minute window when you're in range.'

'Wow. I . . . I didn't know that.'

'And he called her back too,' Lucy said brightly, wondering if Tuck had even noticed her yet. Certainly he hadn't come over and planted a kiss on her lips the way he used to. 'When she got back to the cabin.'

'No shit!'

Meg nodded.

'And now he's sent her a poem, by *email* – which is lovely and all, but it's driving us crazy trying to work out how he got hold of her email address 'cause she didn't give it to him.'

'That's easy.' Tuck shrugged. 'He would have logged your call sign on your first contact and been able to trace it back to the personal details registered on that licence.'

The girls frowned at each other.

'Huh,' Lucy murmured. 'Is that legal? Aren't they supposed to be confidential or something?'

Tuck shrugged. 'He probably pleaded extraordinary circumstances? Or maybe astronauts get special privileges, I don't know.' He looked at the girls' plates – Meg's almost untouched, Lucy's cleared and practically polished clean. 'Are there any more of those pancakes going?'

Lucy pouted. 'Depends.'

Tuck leaned over, planting a kiss on her puckered lips.

'Sold,' she sighed, picking up her plate and walking back to the stove. 'To the only bidder.'

Tuck watched her go – she could see his reflection in the window but not the nuance of the expression on his face. Did he think she looked fat? Before she could see, he turned back to Meg, who had picked up her cutlery and was trying to summon the appetite to finish her breakfast.

'So, are you gonna write back to him?' Tuck asked her.

'Who?'

'Who? Whaddya mean, who? The astronaut! . . . Hey, what's his name anyway?'

'Commander Jonas Solberg,' Lucy answered for her, seeing that Meg had retreated into herself. 'We think he's European. He's got an accent, apparently.'

Meg looked nervous as she glanced her way. 'Do you think I should write back? I hadn't thought about it.'

'Well, you could say thanks at least,' Lucy called over the hiss of the batter hitting the pan. 'It was a kind thing to do and he must have gone to some trouble to get your details.'

'I guess.' Meg bit her lip. 'I can't believe he's got *email* up there. How come he can get it in outer space and I can't even get it at the cabin?'

'I think their tech system's a bit more geared than yours,' Tuck drawled.

'Hey, if you do write to him, can you ask him a question from me?' Lucy said, shaking the pan lightly. 'How do they go to the bathroom up there? I always wanted to know.'

'I'm not asking him that!' Meg said, looking mortified.

'Ask him what's been his best view then,' Tuck said. 'I bet he's seen some incredible sights.'

'I wonder if he can see the Great Wall of China? They say you can,' Lucy said, flipping the pancake expertly and sliding it onto the plate.

She brought it over and set it down in front of Tuck a few moments later, heaped with the last remaining blueberries and a ladle of syrup. Her reward was a squeeze on the bottom.

She smiled, bending down and kissing him again, grateful that his disappointment over last night's defeat had passed.

'So what have you got lined up for today then?' she asked, sitting in the chair opposite.

'Well, I'm heading over to Edmonton just as soon as I'm done eating this. I'm meeting with the organizers of the Ski and Snow Show – they're over from Toronto and they're the biggest forum to get.'

Lucy watched his eyes dart up to Meg – seeking approval, acknowledgement, her blessing, *something* – but she was still looking at her phone, the way her eyes were flickering left to right suggesting she was reading the poem again.

Tuck looked back over at her and arched an eyebrow but Lucy just shook her head. Meg had gone again.

'You should definitely write back,' she said in a louder voice.

Meg looked up. 'Really? You think so?'

'I do. He was kind. It's the polite thing to do.' Lucy chortled. 'Hell, there are worse pen pals to get than a rocket man.'

Three jeeps, two SUVs and a Pontiac – that was Meg's view outside the store window. The bus from Jasper had pulled in to the stop opposite, disgorging the latest stream of visitors, all of them blinking beneath caps and from behind sunglasses as they emerged into the spring air, looking left and right, wondering which way to go first, before invariably heading towards the pizza bar and grill.

The town had switched gear and the crowds in snow-boots and goggles had been switched over for those in trainers and backpacks. The sun had a bright, silky quality to it today – good for photographs – as though still warming up from the winter's hibernation, still testing its power, and not just the tourists but the locals too, moved with a sense of excitement. The temperatures were climbing and blossom peppered the trees, mannequins in the boutique windows wore shorts and pastel colours, and all the ski and board shops had their sale signs up, trying to clear old stock. It felt more like the true new year than that celebrated on 31 December – out with the old, in with the new.

But then, she'd already been watching it for weeks. Up at the cabin, the shift into full spring was even more dramatic and every night after work, she'd sit on the porch and look out until the sun dropped behind the ridge and the lights came on in the valley, like stars that had dropped to the floor. Her cliff-side perch gave her the eagle's eye privilege: she had watched the Bow river gradually replenish its signature mineral-rich turquoise colour now that the pale torrents of meltwater had raced themselves back to the ocean; the trees, after a winter of weight, hummed with the forest animals scampering through the bushy branches, the grass was threaded and dotted with bunchberry, common harebells and rock jasmine flowers. But it was the air – always the mountain air – that marked the calendar so precisely, and right now it was as sweet and dewy as sucking on a stalk of grass.

A door out back swung shut in the breeze and she heard Dolores drop another box on the pile in the storeroom.

'Hey. All done?' she asked as the older woman came in, rubbing the dust off her hands onto her dungarees. Her hair, cut in a schoolboy's short back and sides, had flopped forwards; her bosom was low but her arms were toned and strong in her T-shirt. No one who mistook her for an old woman had seen her hike the Sundance trail.

'Sure am. I couldn't be doing with all those boxes piling up out there like that.'

'You should have let me do it.'

'We needed someone on the shop floor.'

'No one's come in the whole time you've been out there.'

'But they could have done. Besides, you need to take it easy. You've been pushing yourself too hard these past weeks. You look tired.'

Meg arched an eyebrow. 'Have Barbara or Lucy been talking to you?'

'They've done nothing of the sort,' Dolores said, sticking her nose in the air. 'You know perfectly well I never take heed of what anyone else has to say.'

Meg smiled. 'Well, it still should have been me lugging those boxes around.'

'Why? Are you saying I'm too old?'

'Are you saying I'm too broken?'

Dolores patted her on the arm, as if to say 'exactly.' They were the two widows, both of them. Dolores and her husband Jed had opened the store forty-three years ago and Dolores had continued running it on her own after his death in 1997. Meg had been working for her ever since a Saturday job stint in school led to a full-time offer after graduation. It wasn't as though there had been much more she could take anyway; she could have gone to art college – she'd got the grades – but she hadn't wanted to be apart from Mitch and the steady success of the Titch boards meant he'd pretty much had to stay rooted here with Tuck. She'd often thought they were like a daisy chain, the four of them: one led on to the other, keeping them together, keeping them here.

'Now, coffee?' said Dolores.

'I'll g—'

'You'll do nothing of the sort. We need someone on the shop floor, remember?' Dolores said with a smile over her shoulder.

Meg sighed as the bell tinkled above the door and her boss disappeared past the Pontiac and out of sight. She looked at her laptop and tabbed back into emails again. The draft winked back, demanding her attention. She had spent most of this morning trying to get it right.

Dear Commander Solberg, thank you for sending the poem. It's really beautiful. It was very thoughtful of you to send it to me, I had never come across it before—

She pulled a face, looking away. It was too . . . too . . . ? Too formal. Too stuffy.

She pressed delete and tried again. *Hi, Commander, thanks for the poem. It's beautiful. I'm touched you went to such efforts to send it to me, you must have so many other more important things to do.*

She stalled again, watching the cursor flash. It reminded her of the flashing star she'd seen in the sky, her first night back at the cabin.

By the way, I think I saw you. When we spoke the other week, there was something moving really fast, with a flashing light, across the sky. Was it you? Or maybe it's impossible to see where you are, I don't know. It was strange to think you might be in there and we were talking on the radio at the same time. As you've probably guessed by now, I don't know how to work those machines. It was just a fluke that you picked up my call that first time but my friend Tuck is really impressed. He says that Mitch – my fiancé – had been trying to get in touch with you for weeks; he even bought a special antenna just so he could contact you. I keep thinking what a shame it is that I got to speak to you and he didn't. (I don't mean that rudely. I hope you get my point.) Anyway, Tuck asked me to ask you what your best view has been up there, but please don't feel like you need to reply. I bet you're really busy.

I hope you don't mind me using this email address to come back to you. I just really wanted to say thank you – for the poem, but also for what you did that night, picking up. I know it didn't make any difference in the end but being able to speak to another person – even if you were in outer space! – I guess it made me feel like I had tried and done what I could. It means I can sleep at night and not hate myself too much.

You're a really good person.

Meg.

She read it, then reread it. Was it too informal now? He was a commander, after all. He probably had people bowing to him, or saluting at the very least. She bit her lip, her finger hovering over the return button. Maybe she should try another draft, try to get the tone right . . .

The doorbell jingled suddenly and Meg looked up in surprise.

'Hi,' a woman said brightly, a small baby strapped into a baby carrier on her chest. 'Do you have any sunhats for little kids? It's way warmer out there than I realized and I didn't bring anything to cover this little guy's head.'

Meg smiled. 'Sure. We've just taken a new delivery, actually. I'll bring them through for you – they're out back.' She glanced at the screen one more time.

And pressed 'send'.

Lucy rapped on the door of Room 32, already knowing no one would answer – she'd seen the two twenty-something girls booked in here leaving with the rest of their group half an hour ago. They were travelling up to the Basin and Cave, if she remembered correctly, part of a college geology trip, her mother had said, and due to check out the day after tomorrow.

She pulled the laundry trolley to the door and opened the curtains. The day fell in, illuminating the cherry-wood repro furniture and blue damask furnishings which could tolerate years of use – abuse – and hid more than just the light. She opened the windows to let the aroma of Marc Jacobs Daisy percolate in the parking lot instead and checked the bathroom to see if any towels had been left in the bath, her eyes expertly, routinely, tripping over the room en route, looking for signs of damage or theft. But apart from the contents of a make-up bag spilling out over the dressing table, they seemed like just her kind of guests: reusing the same towels for the duration of the stay thanks to the water-conservation signs she'd had put up in all the bathrooms, and going heavy on the minibar which was always good for bumping up the bill. She made a note of what had been eaten or drunk and replenished it from her cart, before turning her attention to the rest of the room.

Clothes were strewn in messy heaps but at least they were on the chairs; various shoes were lying on their sides by the bags, a particularly nice-looking pair of lizard-effect high-heeled sandals perched on a shoebox. She could see from the sticker on it that they were her size.

Looking away with a sigh – not wanting to even glance at the comfort-first sneakers on her own feet – Lucy began folding the clothes individually, occasionally stopping to check a label on a top or examine a dress more closely. A couple of times, she held something against her in front of the mirror, feeling her spirits sink even lower. These girls weren't so much younger than her – only a few years maybe – but they had more money and broader horizons; they also had flat stomachs and small behinds.

Lucy's hands dropped to her sides as she stared at herself in the mirror. Again. She didn't care what Meg said, she didn't look great at all. She looked as disgusting as she felt – shapeless and lumpen like an old mattress. Where was the small, tight, high bump she always saw on celebrities in magazines? Why did she just look like she'd eaten a curry? Or a cow? And when was she going to get that glow people always talked about? When was her hair going to grow lustrous and shiny, instead of hanging lank as though she'd been caught in the rain?

A tear slid down her cheek as she saw the way the buttons strained on her shirt, knew that if she lifted it, she'd see the unsightly home-made waist-extender she'd made for her jeans from a bra strap. Was it any wonder Tuck had stopped looking at her, and whenever he did, it was always with this shadow in his eyes?

She raised the top she was holding up in front of her again. Cobalt blue and silky, it had a plunging V-neck and floaty, butterfly-style sleeves. Surely she could wear something like that and look OK? It was her usual size but she wasn't, at the moment, though it looked like it would stretch; the sleeve detail would detract from her torso and the V-neck would make the most of her cleavage, which was about the only positive thing to come from this pregnancy so far.

She went to the door and looked up and down the corridor. No one was around; Sharon and Jenna, the other chambermaids, were working on the floors above and most of the guests had now left for the day.

She put the *Do Not Disturb* sign on the door and closed it. With her fingers hurriedly unfastening the buttons of her shirt, she used her feet to push off the trainers and slip on the lizard sandals. Instantly, as she had to rebalance, her body looked better. She was forced to stand upright and throw her shoulders back, bringing some definition back to her waist.

Feeling encouraged, she unzipped the blue top, pulling it down over her head and wriggling as her hands grappled at the opposite shoulders, trying to tug it down. She managed to get it down to her chest – but there it stuck fast, the fabric strained to tearing point over her breasts, flattening and distorting them, her shoulders bunched up, not even enough room for her shoulder blades to move.

'Shit!' she hissed.

She staggered back, trying to look in the mirror and see

what she should do now – pull it back up or tug it all the way down? But if she did that . . . she really wasn't sure she'd be able to get it off again and what would she say to the guest then? How could Lucy possibly explain to this girl that her beautiful, expensive top had had to be cut, without coming clean about what she'd done?

'Oh,' Lucy wailed, stuck and already imagining the reviews on TripAdvisor. *The maid wore my clothes.* Or worse: *The owner cut up my blouse!*

She turned a circle as she began tugging the top back up, inching it painfully slowly towards her head – this had all been a mistake, a terrible, horrible mistake – when a sudden crunching noise underfoot made her freeze. Something had cracked.

'Oh, my God!' she wailed, feeling tears threaten. 'Are you kidding me? What was *that*? What was—?'

She was panicking now, becoming so flustered that she didn't hear the click of the door, didn't even know that Tuck was standing there until she heard him gasp with horror.

'What the fuck are you doing?' he cried, quickly shutting the door behind him.

'Oh, my God, Tuck, thank God, thank God!' she sobbed, hobbling towards him but losing one shoe – they ran large, it appeared! – and falling heavily, awkwardly across the bed.

'Jesus, Lucy!' he shouted, running over to her. 'Are you OK? Is the baby . . . is the baby OK?'

He rolled her over. She couldn't see a thing, completely wedged in the blouse, her hands flapping helplessly out of the top.

'Just get me out of this thing!' she wailed, drumming her feet against the side of the bed in despair. What the hell did she look like – belly out, jeans held up by a bra strap, one shoe on, trapped in another, thinner and younger, girl's blouse? 'Don't look at me! Don't look at me!'

'I'm . . . I'm not,' he said, his voice flustered as he began pulling carefully on the fabric. 'Can you squeeze your shoulders together more?'

'Does it look like I can do anything?' she cried.

'Don't worry. I'll get you out.'

'What will I say to her?'

'It won't come to that. She won't ever know . . . Just a bit more.'

With another tug, she was free, the top releasing with sudden ease and the bedroom basking in the gentle sunlight filling her vision again.

Tuck was looking at her exactly as she feared, the top limp in his hands.

'I was trying to see if I could look nice, OK? Just for a minute, I wanted to look better than *this*,' she cried, jumping off the bed and grabbing her shirt, buttoning it up so quickly, she didn't realize until she was almost done that she was one button out. Of course she was! She couldn't even wear a shirt properly. Crying, she grabbed her trainers and stuffed her feet back into them. 'And before you ask, no, I don't make a habit of doing this. I've never done it before.'

'Lucy—'

'Don't, Tuck!' she sobbed, hiding her face in her hands. 'Just go. I don't want you to even look at me.'

There was a long silence.

'Why are you even in here anyway?' he asked. 'Where's Janice? You shouldn't be doing this.'

'She's sick, we're short.'

His expression changed. 'She's always sick, that woman. I don't know why you keep her on.'

'Because she's damn good when she is here,' she snapped. What did he know about the staff? The most he ever came to helping out in the hotel was inventorying the bourbon.

Tuck sighed. 'Look, you're exhausted. You shouldn't be doing this. I'll sort it out in here. Just go and rest.'

'I can't—' she hiccupped.

'You can. I'm ordering you. I'll sort it out.' He got up from the bed and put his hands on her shoulders, planting a kiss between her eyebrows. 'Go on. Lie down and I'll come and find you in a bit.'

She stared back at him, puzzled by this rare kindness. 'But I thought you were going to Edmonton?'

'I'll reschedule, it's fine. The show's not till November, there's plenty of time.'

She looked up at him, those super-blue eyes gazing down at her. She still couldn't believe he was hers. Or she was his. Whichever. Or both. She still couldn't believe it.

Chapter Ten

Friday 19 May 2017

Meg was sitting in her favourite spot on the porch, her legs tucked up on the swing seat so that her chin could almost rest on her knees, a mole-coloured soft blanket wrapped tightly around her and her wet hair twisted into a towel turban. On the ground was a half-drunk beer and a snoring dog with a newly mended leg, but she couldn't take her eyes off the sunset, which was oozing fiery tendrils into the sky like long grasses swaying underwater. *Footless halls of air* . . .

She didn't know how long she'd been sitting there for. A few hours, certainly. It was a quarter to nine now but the sky was still bright, the fingernail crescent moon looking incongruous as it hung there, paled by the sun. In the valley below, the first lights had started to come on and the occasional red tail lights of vehicles on the highway glowed in the distance.

Summer was on the way. She could feel it on the breeze, closing her eyes every few moments and presenting her face up to the sky like a dog sniffing the wind. Mitch had been dead for almost two months and this would be the world's first summer in twenty-six years without him.

Twenty-six years. That was all the time he had had on this planet and of that, only ten years had been shared with her. Just ten.

She stared into the fathomless blue again, the words from the poem tiptoeing through her mind once more. *Oh! I have slipped the surly bonds of Earth, and danced the skies on laughter-silvered wings* . . . The thought of him up there – free . . . That poem had brought her more comfort than any words in a card, touched her more deeply than any hugs, and she had read it over and over until she knew it by heart and this had become her most treasured ritual, the best part of her day – coming in from work and sitting on the porch, swinging gently and watching the sunset as she imagined him dancing the skies—

The phone rang in the cabin behind, jolting her from her thoughts, and she stirred, her limbs stiff from sitting immobile for so long.

'Hello?'

'It's me.' Ronnie's voice was crisp and clear, the faint hollow sound of echoing corridors telling Meg her sister was still at work.

'Hey. How are you?'

'Fine. I just got off a shift and thought I'd try to catch you. Sorry I've been off radar. Work's been crazy.'

'It's OK.' They hadn't spoken since the funeral and they knew that, in part, it would have been because she'd been staying with Lucy.

There was a short pause. 'No. No, it's not.'

'Ron, it's fine. Your work is important – people need you and I know the kind of hours you work. It's not like I've been feeling especially chatty recently anyway. A phone call with me is like making small talk with Putin at the moment.'

Ronnie tried to chuckle at the attempted joke, knowing that Meg was still trying to occupy the role of big sister, the strong one. 'So how *have* you been?'

'I'm better, honestly. I'm definitely . . . definitely improving.'

'Have you lost any more weight?'

'No. And I'm washing my hair every night. And wearing clean clothes. The cupboard's full of food,' Meg said quickly, anticipating all the other questions that Barbara also fired at her on a daily basis.

'You're not just saying that? If I was to tell you I was actually standing outside your door and about to step in—?'

'I'd say come on in. Hand on heart.' Well, hand on broken heart, she thought to herself. 'Really, time's the healer. I'm doing great.' Meg was surprised by the sound of her own voice; she was almost convincing herself.

'So then . . .' There was a small pause and Meg could tell Ronnie was working up to something.

'What? What is it?'

'Do you think you'd be up to a trip? You could come and visit me.'

'What? In Toronto?' Meg asked, losing her composure and sounding shocked.

'Why not? I've been here six years and you haven't made it over yet. I've got some holiday I've got to take and I thought . . . well, I thought we could hook up and do something together.' There was a silence. 'Although it doesn't have to be here if you don't want – we could meet somewhere else if you'd prefer . . . Honolulu? Paris? Auckland?'

Meg burst out laughing. 'Oh, my God, you have to be kidding!'

'Why?'

'*Why?*' she shrieked. 'I can't . . . I can't go to those places.'

'Why not?'

Meg felt her hilarity segue into something more fearful, anxiety prickling up her skin. 'Because I can't. I have responsibilities here. Dolores needs me—'

'Dolores is perfectly capable of running that place without you, especially at this time of year.'

'That's not true!' Meg huffed indignantly.

'You work in a ski-rental shop, Meg, and it's May!'

'Yes, so now we've got hikers and bike—'

'There are only so many hiking boots and pop-up tents you can sell,' Ronnie laughed, but there was no amusement in her tone either. They both knew they were skidding into unspoken territory – Meg afraid to leave their home town, Ronnie afraid to come back. 'She can totally spare you.'

'Well, why don't you come here?' Meg asked, turning the tables on her little sister. 'If you've got time to kill, come back here and we can . . . I don't know, go camping for a few nights, maybe do that spa package at Chateau Louise that you're always talking about.'

Ronnie sighed, exasperated. 'Why are you so dead against going somewhere new? Seeking out new horizons? There's a big world out there, Meg. Come and see some of it with me. Let's have an adventure. There's more to life than that poky little cab—' She fell silent.

'Poky?'

'I didn't mean to say that! I meant small. It's small.'

'You said poky.'

Ronnie sighed, and Meg could tell from the muffling of her voice that she had her head in her hands. 'I knew this was a bad idea. I called up wanting us to do something together, something new, and instead all I've done is upset you.'

'I'm not upset.' But even to her own ear, Meg's voice sounded brittle and ready to crack.

There was a long silence between them and when Ronnie's voice came back on the line, it sounded weary. 'I don't know what's happened to us, Meg. We used to be so close. You were my best friend.'

Meg instinctively closed her eyes, knowing Ronnie was right and that she was going to drag Lucy into the conversation, as though it was Lucy's fault that the two sisters had grown apart. But it wasn't. Yes, it didn't help that her sister and her best friend didn't get on but the simple fact was, she and Ronnie were vastly different people – that wasn't to say they didn't love one another, but their parents' deaths had had a polarizing effect and instead of being brought closer together, they had been forced apart, having to identify and choose where their homes would be now. For Meg, that had been with Mitch in Banff. For Ronnie, a high-octane career in which she didn't have time to feel, or grieve. The river they had swum in had forked and they were on entirely different paths for the moment; but wouldn't they both end up in the sea, some day?

'Listen, forget it,' Ronnie said, her voice sounding defeated. 'It's too soon. I just thought a change would be as good as a rest. That was all.'

'I know, and I appreciate it. Maybe soon.'

'Does that mean you'll think about what I said?' Hope tinged her voice like blood in the water.

'Absolutely.' Not.

There was another silence. 'You know I love you, Meg? I know we don't see each other enough but . . . you're my sister. You're always in my mind.'

'I know, and I love you too . . .' They lapsed into silence again. 'Look, I'd better run. I was just on my way out to walk Badge before it gets dark.'

'Oh, OK, sure.'

'But we'll speak soon, OK?'

'OK—'

'OK, bye.' Meg hung up, grateful to have got the words out before her voice had betrayed her, tears already streaking down her cheeks. It was easy for Ronnie. Change was a good thing in her world – she'd had a dream to follow, a horizon to stake, and a seat on a plane would get her there. But for Meg, this place was her home, even if Mitch and her parents and Ronnie – all her reasons for being here – were now gone. She couldn't *leave*. It wasn't just that there was no place like home; for her, there was no place but home.

Chapter Eleven

Saturday 20 May

The bell over the door tinkled as Lucy opened it, Meg looking up and giving a pleased smile as she walked in. She was kneeling, fitting an old guy in a Lake Tahoe T-shirt and fliplens sunglasses with a pair of hiking boots. Badger was curled up asleep in his bed by the till.

'Morning,' Lucy sang, breezing through the store, stopping only to ruffle the dog's ears before heading straight to the small kitchen out back. She put the kettle on and checked the milk in the fridge as she waited for Meg to finish up with the customer, overhearing her a few minutes later giving him a free tube of SPF lipblock and telling him to watch out for bears. They were awake and hungry at this time of year.

'No wonder Dolores loves you,' she grinned as Meg wandered through. 'You're more like the tourist bureau than an overpriced rental boutique selling Chapstick. I bet he'll be back tomorrow to show you his photos. Where is she anyway?'

'Hiking.' Meg reached up into one of the wall cupboards. 'Cookie?'

'Rhetorical, right?' Lucy smiled, stirring their drinks and

tossing the spoon into the sink, where it clattered noisily. 'So, what was so important you couldn't wait till lunch?'

Meg bit her lip. 'He's written back.'

Lucy was puzzled, wondering what she'd missed. 'Who?'

'The astronaut!'

Lucy missed a beat. 'Oh.' She couldn't help but feel disappointed. She'd thought, when she'd got the text – *Big news! Coffee, here, now* – that it might be something more exciting than an email from a poetry-loving spaceman. Was it really that big of a deal? 'Well, what'd he say?'

'Shall I read it?'

'By all means.' Lucy pulled out a chair from the narrow half-table and took her seat, trying not to look more interested in the cookie than the email.

'*Hi, Meg, how are you?*' Meg read, giving a shrug and rolling her eyes. 'Well, does he want the long answer or the short?' she quipped, a deflective use of humour that she'd been relying on a lot recently. '*Sorry not to have responded sooner. It's been pretty busy recently—*' Meg squinted her eyes. 'What *does* he do up there, do you think?'

Lucy shrugged, breaking off a large chewy chunk of cookie. Today was a bad sugar day. It had taken three ginger biscuits just to get out of bed without throwing up. 'Tests whether the moon really is made of cheese? Checks for black holes? Who knows? Ask him.'

'You think?' Meg wrinkled her nose, then shook her head. 'No. No . . .' She inhaled deeply and began reading again. 'Umm . . . oh, yes . . . *Added to which we had some tech issues for email – happily all resolved now! I'm really pleased you liked the poem, I thought it might resonate for you. I hope you are doing OK.*

'*I'm afraid it wasn't the ISS that you saw that night as there are no flashing lights on board. Most likely it was a plane but you can see us at certain points in the day if you know where to look. We actually orbit Earth sixteen times every twenty-four hours but you can only really spot us early morning or at dusk when the angle of the sun reflects off us. If you're interested, we'll be tracking above you today at 19h11, travelling west to east at 42-degrees elevation. In normal speak, just look west to the horizon and put your arm straight out in front of you, then lift it by four fists' depth and that should get you looking in the right area. I'll wave just in case!* Smiley face.' Meg looked up. 'He's actually put a smiley face! Can you believe that? A smiley face from space?'

Lucy watched, bemused by her friend's geeky excitement. 'Who knew?'

'*Also – and I hope this doesn't read like a lecture – we're not in outer space but inner space. We're only 312 km above the Earth, unlike the moon, for example, which is 365,000 km away, so perhaps it's not so unusual that we should have made radio contact – that distance along a road would barely get you out of Alberta.*' Meg shook her head in amazement. 'Isn't that incredible? When he puts it like that . . . He must be so clever. I bet he knows lots of stuff about everything. Ronnie would love him.'

Lucy nodded. 'Uh-huh.'

Meg went back to the email. '*But I am pleased we've "met". We're busy most of the time but when it's quiet, it's really quiet so it's nice to get on the radio channels and chat to different people wherever we are. I've tried contacting you a few times when we've passed over but I seem to keep missing you. Or perhaps you're not using the radio any more? If you want, you can log onto this website, which shows our orbital path and when we'll be in communications range, www.*blah-blah-blah,' Meg said, skipping over it. *'By the way, tell your friend Tuck that my best sighting so far has been seeing the aurora borealis over Finland. It was freaky and magical all at the same time with these incredible colours flickering below us. I'm Norwegian, so I've grown up with these technicolour skies, but I never thought I'd see it from above! I'm taking lots of photos but I'll try and get one of your patch next time we pass over and I'll send it on to you.*

'Got to go now. We're preparing for a spacewalk tomorrow so it's all hands on deck here. Take care, Jonas.' Meg finished reading, her eyes bright. 'So how about *that*, huh? An email from a guy about to take a freaking *spacewalk*. That's pretty damn cool, you've got to admit.'

'Jonas?' Lucy repeated.

Meg looked confused. 'Huh?'

'He didn't sign off as Lieutenant or . . . or whatever his title is?'

'Commander. No, why?'

'First-name terms with an astronaut.' Lucy shrugged. 'That is cool.'

'Well, I guess we've spoken a few times now. He's somehow found himself caught up in my . . . mess, and he's been kind. He's gone above and beyond the call of duty.'

Lucy sipped her coffee. 'Well, good for you. There are stranger ways to make friends.'

Meg paused, her eyebrows all but knitted together. 'No, there aren't.'

Lucy spluttered on her drink. 'No, there really aren't,' she agreed, dabbing coffee from her chin. 'So are you going to wave to him this evening?'

'If I remember. I'm usually out walking Badger at that time.'

'Well, that's the good thing about the sky,' Lucy quipped. 'It's pretty big. You can see it wherever you are.'

Their eyes met, that shared humour of old pushing to the fore, and they laughed like they used to do, their hands clasping on the table and the sorrows of the past couple of months receding. At least for a moment or two.

But too soon, Meg's laughter died, that familiar distraction clouding her eyes again.

'What is it?' Lucy asked, sipping her coffee and wondering if there were any more of those cookies.

'Oh, nothing.'

Lucy arched an eyebrow, knowing her too well. 'Spill.'

Meg inhaled deeply. 'It's just that Ronnie rang last night and we had a bit of a . . . disagreement.'

Lucy blew out through her lips. 'Why am I not surprised? Let me guess, she was berating you for not being a judge? Or a brain surgeon?'

'No . . . well, yes . . . no, not exactly.'

Lucy tutted. Meg was so protective of her sister, even when Ronnie didn't deserve it. 'Which is it?'

'She was ringing to ask me to go and see her.'

'In Toronto?' Lucy curled her lip. 'Why would you want to go there?'

'Well, not just there. She said we could meet up somewhere else if I preferred. Honolulu, for instance.'

Lucy choked on her coffee, utterly incredulous. '*Hono*—?' she spluttered. 'Is she mad?'

'That was what I said.'

Lucy put down her mug. 'Well, obviously you realize she wasn't inviting you on holiday at all? She was trying to shine a spotlight on how small she thinks your life is, compared to hers. "Hey, let's just swan off to Honolulu!" She thinks this place is too small. It wasn't good enough for her so it can't possibly be good enough for you.'

'I know, I know. But I think her intentions were in the right place. I don't think she was trying to belittle me.'

Lucy was unconvinced. 'Listen, we can't all be game changers, Meg. We can't all save the world. There's nothing wrong with your life – you've got friends who love you, a steady job, that beautiful cabin. What's so wrong with that? What exactly is so wrong with small? Hasn't she heard that bigger is not always better?'

'Mmm,' Meg murmured, her hands clasped around the mug as she looked out from the kitchen, through the store onto the street beyond. 'I just keep wondering whether she has a point? I mean, maybe . . . maybe I should embrace *some* change. Think about getting a new job, perhaps?'

'Why? You love working here.' Lucy motioned to the tiny, two-metre-square kitchen, with just a pull-down table in the wall, a kettle, some coffee-stained mugs and a stack of Oakley sunglasses boxes in the corner.

'*Love*'s probably overstating it,' Meg said, pulling a face. 'I love Dolores but let's face it, it's not exactly scintillating selling walking socks and camping kettles.'

'Listen, Dolores would be lost without you. She's getting on. She needs you.'

Meg nodded but her gaze was still elsewhere. 'I know, you're right.'

'Besides, what would you do?' Lucy continued. 'Waitress? Hand out the shoes at the bowling alley? Why is that any better than this? And at least the hours are good and you get to have Badger with you.'

Meg bit her lip. 'Well, I've always liked the idea of having my own little business.'

'Doing . . . ?'

'I could set up a graphic-design consultancy. It was what I always thought I'd do, you know, back when I was applying to art schools. I kind of had all these plans and ideas. But then Mitch proposesd and . . .'

Lucy arched an eyebrow. 'Are you saying Mitch got in the way of your ambitions?'

'No! Not . . . in the way,' Meg stammered. 'I just . . . had to choose, that was all. I could stay here with him or go to art school and follow my own dreams. And I chose him. I never resented him for it – it was my choice, I knew what I was doing. I was *happy* to do it. I loved him. But now that he's gone . . .' She shrugged. 'Hey, Titch could be my first client.' She gave an awkward little smile.

'But you already do graphic design for Titch.'

'I know, and I love designing for the boards but there's other things I could be doing too. I have so many ideas but nothing I can really do with them. Titch is great but two collections a year mean it's just a sideline. I want to do more. I really think I could make a good go of it.'

Lucy stared at her, not sure whether she was successfully hiding the fact that she thought her friend's idea was mad. She sighed, feeling weary.

'Look, I get where you're coming from, I do. But you have to bear in mind you've just suffered a major trauma. It's natural that you're feeling unsettled – there's been a lot of change in your life recently. But what you really need at the moment is stability.'

Meg looked directly at her, apprehension in her hazel-green eyes. 'You think so?'

'I know so. You need to let the wounds heal. Setting up a

business would be so majorly stressful, it's the very last thing you should be doing. Be kind to yourself. Just eat, sleep, repeat.'

'Eat, sleep, repeat,' Meg echoed.

Repeated.

Lucy walked back down Banff Avenue feeling lighter, which was ironic because given what the scales had said this morning, she was now heavier than she'd been at any point in her life. But she was feeling better in herself. Ever since that wardrobe malfunction in Room 32 last week, things with Tuck had improved. It was almost as though, having seen her so wretched and despairing, tangled and trapped in another woman's clothes like a whale in a net, he'd finally seen past his own grief, seen that he'd left her to cope all alone, and he'd made more of an effort. He'd started coming home earlier in the evenings, he'd cut down on his drinking (a bit) and when his hands had wandered at night, she hadn't pushed them away.

Things were better than they'd been for a long time. He even seemed to be getting a little excited about the baby now that he'd got over that first thunderbolt of shock. She knew how daunted he felt at the prospect of becoming a father and her instincts had been right – the timing was wrong. Her growing bump was inexorable proof that his life was transitioning away from the one he'd known and loved with Mitch – young, carefree, careless. She knew he was just scared; he was being forced to grow up.

But they all were. Life wouldn't stay the same no matter how much they wanted it to. Poor Meg knew that better than any of them, although Lucy was bothered by her friend's sudden, out-of-the-blue urge to *force* more change. Then again, she mused, Ronnie always did that, making her sister feel inadequate, like she wasn't good enough.

The town was busy, the hotel full and Lucy smiled as she passed a small group of her own guests – a Portuguese party – that she'd checked in herself earlier. 'Hi there, finding your way about OK?' she asked as she passed them.

They all nodded appreciatively, smiling brightly, cameras in their hands.

'Just let me know if you need any further information or some recommendations for dinner,' she said cheerily, leaving them with a wave.

She looked in the windows as she walked, checking her reflection, and was pleased to see how her profile was now definitely beginning to look 'officially pregnant', if she pushed her tummy out. After the utter shock of that little blue line coming up and everything with Mitch, the fear of telling Tuck, and then the morning sickness that seemingly only cookies could cure, finally, *finally* things were turning around for her: the bump was becoming a proper bump – not a lump – her skin would start to glow, her hair would get thick like Meg's and at the end of it all, she'd have a baby, a beautiful baby that would make her and Tuck a proper family.

She stopped outside a boutique, her eyes on the tall, slender mannequins, but she didn't feel jealous; she didn't wish she was still like them now. She had something they didn't.

. . . Although that top was lovely.

She tipped her head to the side, lips pursed consideringly – if she went up a size, or three . . . ? – when a sudden flash of light caught her eye in the window's reflection. Across the road, the door to La Senza, the lingerie boutique, had opened. Tuck . . . !

She went to turn, to call out to him, but then she saw the bag in his hand and realized he had bought something. And from the size of the bag it was something small. Small and lacy?

She gasped and smiled, watching in the reflection of the window as he sauntered up the street, back towards the Titch shop. She didn't dare move; she didn't want him to notice her lest she ruin his surprise.

Instead she pushed open the door to the boutique and enquired after the top in the window. She wanted to look pretty tonight.

Chapter Twelve

His lungs felt as though they were bleeding but he wouldn't stop. He had to keep going, to make it back down to the parking lot in this one run. The light was fading – there wasn't time to go back to the top and do it again – and besides, Mitch had done it in one; he'd done it that day last fall when Tuck had gone to the factory to sign off on the new Titch prototypes. Mitch – who'd been more involved with the retail and networking side of the business – had taken advantage of the quiet phones and good weather to sneak a 'recce' of the route they could take for the short mountain film they were planning on shooting this summer, and he'd been flying high by the time Tuck had got back, a six-pack of beers on the desk in readiness for pressing the 'play' button and showing his old friend what he'd achieved.

Tuck had felt his stomach drop several times as he'd watched the video – impressed as Mitch had bunny-hopped the bike up two-metre-high boulders, springing on the back wheel like a pogo stick, using one fallen tree as a bridge to traverse a deep narrow crevasse, another as a barrier to stop the front wheel, flip the bike over in a somersault before landing on both wheels and continuing down the trail as though nothing much had happened.

And now it was his turn . . .

Tuck knew the first tree was coming up. His thighs were burning from the lactic acid build-up as he pedalled and bounced and hopped and balanced the bike from the top of the mountain to the bottom, but he refused to ever once let his foot touch the ground. He'd gone over the trick so many times in his head, watched Mitch's clip over and over so that the neural pathways in his brain knew exactly what he had to do and when. He knew the question wasn't *could* he do it, but did he *dare* . . . ?

The path was springy with fallen pine needles but the bike's suspension was beginning to creak, a sure sign he was at the limits of its – and his – capabilities. He knew that a hundred metres or so from now, he would take a sharp left and the forest floor would drop sharply, a sudden chasm three – maybe four – metres wide, ripping open the stone bedrock. That fallen tree was his only way across to the rocks on the other side.

He slowed as he approached, coming out of the seat and momentarily forgetting the pain in his legs as his eyes took in what, until now, had been only a dare behind a screen. The tree was huge, the base covered in a dark, slippy-looking moss, the blond bark stippled with rough psoriatic patches. He couldn't see to the bottom of the narrow gorge – not without getting off the bike – and he balanced for a few moments, hopping lightly in place as he worked out how to get the bike onto the tree. Mitch had come in from the left but the snowmelt had riven a channel that eroded the level. He looked at it from the right, where the land level was higher.

Barely giving himself time to think about it, he coiled his body tight and with a burst of power, pulled up on the handlebars, bringing the bike under him as he landed, hopping in place wildly for a few more moments as he tried to get his balance, now fully able to see the drop into the gorge from this vantage point.

A jet of adrenalin and anger shot through him as he stayed up on the pedals, weight forwards, and began inching over the 'bridge'. The trunk was rutted and uneven but he took it slowly, keeping his eyes on a spot perpetually five centimetres ahead of the front wheel, not once looking down on either side. He felt a visceral sense of relief as he crossed it within moments, the pine floor carpeting the ground beneath the tree again, and he hopped down with joyous ease.

Allowing himself to sit back in the seat, he followed gravity's pull down the mountain and the miles rolled beneath his wheels; he felt the silence like a weight on his back, his aloneness amplified beneath these thousands of hectares of giant pines, the whirr of the air slicing through the wheel spokes his only companion. He felt scooped-out and hollow. His friend was never coming back. Never again would he hear him whoop or yell, 'Hell, yeah!' down a mountain, never again would he have someone to share this love, this crazy, wild streak that made them seek out adventures on the mountains and in return, feel so wedded to this – their – patch of the planet. It was what had made this home, but everything felt different now he was on his own.

He'd tried to keep life the same – like doing this, right now. Like going to the ice-hockey qualifier the other week with the girls, so determined was he to make things feel normal. But it hadn't been. Lucy had been bitching all night about her jeans feeling tight, even while she chowed down on buckets of junk; and Meg had looked drugged and spectral, like a hologram of herself. And neither one of them had made a sensible comment about the match or the team, gossiping between themselves about God knows what as he had sat there, feeling more empty than at any time since Mitch had died, feeling like a ghost in his own life, the black shadow trailing him everywhere, joined to his heels, stitched to his soul.

There was no new normal. He kept his routines the same. He hit the studio to work on the films every Tuesday and Thursday nights, but the sight and sound of his friend, alive still on the screen, was almost more than he could bear. He still went to Bill's for drinks with the guys on Mondays and Wednesdays and Fridays but they all talked shit and he didn't care what a single one of them had to say. As for Lucy and the baby . . . this baby they had never planned, never even talked about; she'd just gone and done it, like it wasn't anything to do with him anyway, like it was going to make everything better. A Band-Aid baby.

He was so angry with her, most of the time he couldn't bear to look at her; and his anger only grew that she clearly didn't get it. He felt like she'd trapped him, played a trick and now she was falling apart, letting herself go, always looking at him with anxious eyes, wanting to know where he'd been on the one hand, pushing him away in bed on the other.

He knew he had to get his head straight. He was drinking too much and Barbara – always eagle-eyed anyway – was even more alert at the moment. Several times he'd caught sight of her watching him from her apartment window when he'd come home late. What was she doing? Logging his movements? He shook his head, feeling angry again – he was trapped, watched, monitored, assessed . . . and always found wanting.

He hopped down three stepped boulders, the bike landing with a groan on the last jump. The back wheel skidded out and he almost – almost – had to put a foot down to save himself from falling and he felt another spike of adrenalin in his hands, knowing he'd have to go back to the top and start again, failing light or not. His pride would demand it.

But he was so close now. Another 300 metres' descent and he'd have done it. It would be another thing he could share with his friend, the only way he had to be close to him any more. Pushing Lucy to the back of his mind, he focused on the final hurdle – quite literally. He knew exactly where the tree was going to be. He would be able to see a waterfall just to the right of it, the path forking beyond it, taking the left back to the parking lot.

And so it was. The vista unfolded exactly as he'd seen it on Mitch's Go-Pro and he readied himself, knowing that this was it – the *pièce de résistance*. Mitch had aced it, heading straight for the barrier as though it was a foam pit, not an immovable object that would catapult him into the air and hurl him, quite possibly, towards a broken back.

He gulped down air, his limbs fizzy with anticipation as he headed straight for the toppled tree, knowing he had to keep his nerve, just let the physics do the work – if he hit the tree dead on, he could somersault over it. Momentum was all he needed; that and self-belief.

Mitch had done it. He could too. He could! This was his homage to his friend, his apology.

He pedalled faster, eyes on the massive trunk that blocked the path. 'Just believe,' he told himself, only metres away, his fingers straining to squeeze the brakes, his will stopping them, knowing if he braked he'd still go over the tree anyway, but just leave the bike behind him.

But logic and instinct are two different things and as he saw the bulk of the tree – the weight of it, the utter immovability – his courage failed and his fingers automatically squeezed, the bike slowing dramatically and suddenly in that final stretch, so that when the front wheel nudged the trunk, momentum indeed carried him over, but somersaulting him alone through the air, the bike toppling back down on the wrong side of the tree.

He landed heavily, arm first, his body ringing with pain. He would have yelled profanities into the dusk but he had no breath with which to do so, for he was winded too and for several long moments he lay convulsed on the ground, his body twisted as his chest heaved, trying to get air back into his lungs.

By the time he did, the pain in his wrist and elbow were hitting a crescendo and he blinked his eyes shut, trying to control the deep throb in his bones. Was his arm broken?

He wiggled the fingers, just, and knew it wasn't, but he was badly bruised, his joints sprained. He fell back and lay there in the pines, his skin badly grazed, his body wrenched and wretched.

He had failed. Again.

It had all been for nothing.

Mitch could still beat him, even in death.

Meg stood on the porch, wrapped in her blanket, Badger sitting at the top of the steps by her feet, his ears up and watching a stag tread lightly just inside the treeline. She was lucky. At her elevation, the skies were clear, the sun at a low slant behind the ridgeline and the shy-peeping moon a sliver of its fullest self. Below her, Banff was in cloud, thick white plumes like a steaming, rolling sea on the valley floor, only the jagged peaks of Mount Rundle piercing through like mermaids' rocks.

It was cooler up here than in town too, at least three degrees, and she clutched the blanket tighter, her eyes falling every few seconds to the digital alarm clock she had brought through from the bedroom. Seven ten.

She looked west towards the brighter skies, her eye line falling to where she had practised with an outstretched arm and closed fist. How accurate was his alleged fly-by, she wondered? A few minutes—?

Spot on.

Suddenly, her gaze hit on a diamond in the sky. At first she wasn't sure – was it just a star? A normal, common-garden star? But no, it was travelling, moving fast, a tail of light streaming behind it.

She gasped as it sped through the air, knowing that was it – the International Space Station.

And Jonas was up there. She actually knew someone in that thing!

She laughed, the impulse surprising her as much as it did Badger as she shot her arm out, waving madly, knowing it was ridiculous, knowing he couldn't see. But he'd sent her a smiley face, he'd said he'd be waving. Wasn't it just too insane to think he was waving back to her right now?

She pressed her hands in a steeple to her mouth as she watched it draw closer. She couldn't believe how fast it was covering distance, nor how brightly it shone, the sun demonstrating its almighty power with one last dazzling burst on the Space Station's reflective panels before it sank below the horizon for another day.

She watched for another minute, feeling overwhelmed, as though she'd been part of something more – something bigger, cosmic – even if it was only as a spectator. It never would have occurred to her to look up, beyond her own world, her own life, that she might know someone whose world vision was so big, he'd needed to get off the planet to realize it.

Suddenly she ran inside and pressed all the buttons she knew to press, red lights turning green, dials flickering into life, that crackly static bringing the world into the bedroom. If she could see him, surely she could speak to him too?

'Hello?' Her eyes went to the sticker on the side of the rig. 'This is uh, Volcano X-ray Four, uh, Dog, Dog, uh, Elephant, over. Calling Jonas Solberg. Can you hear me, over?'

She pressed the button on the receiver and waited but it sounded different from before – noisier, 'dirtier' somehow with lots of interference, too many voices leaping in and out of reception.

She looked at the frequency coming up on the digital display: 145.800 . . . where she had left it from the first and second times she'd spoken to him. Should she move it? When she'd moved it that first night, it had seemed to move through the airwaves, finding empty pockets, rather like tuning the TV in the days before digital.

No. Surely it was better to stick with what she knew? That was little enough! She tried again.

'Volcano X-ray Four Dog Dog Elephant calling the International Space Station. Jonas, can you hear me, over?'

Still nothing. She stood up and leaned over the desk, her face turned up as she stared out of the window. She could still see him, the bright shooting star almost directly in front of the cabin – albeit hundreds of kilometres away.

'Jonas, can you hear me? It's Meg Saunders! Volcano X-ray Four Dog—'

'I can hear you all right,' he said suddenly, his voice as loud and clear as if he'd been in the next room. He appeared to be laughing.

'Jonas? Is that you?'

'Copy that. This is November Alpha One Sierra Sierra calling Volcano X-ray—' He broke off laughing again.

'Why are you laughing?' she chuckled, bemused by his own amusement. 'Over.'

Pause. 'Your call sign—'

More laughter.

Oh, God. 'Aren't I doing it right? Over.'

A few seconds passed and he was back again. 'You're doing it perfectly,' he said, but she could tell – somehow – that he was still smiling. It's funny, she thought, how you can hear a smile in a voice. 'It's good to speak to you, over.'

'And you. And guess what? I can see you! I'm watching you right now! Over.'

Silence.

'Can you see me waving?' he replied.

It was her turn to laugh. 'No, but I waved to you anyway . . .' She could hear him laughing again. 'Thanks for your email. Are you nervous about your airwalk? Over.'

Another pause. Another chuckle. 'The spacewalk today? I am nervous, yes. It's always a big deal. We have a Japanese cargo ship docking next week so we have to check everything's OK. Over.'

Meg waited for the words to transmit to her, a bubble of static making her eyes dart to the display. She looked back out the window. She could still see the speeding bright dot, like a silver bullet, but it was moving away from her again, too soon, too fast. 'It's today? But I thought you said it was tomorrow? Over.'

'Yes, it was when I wrote the email. Sorry, I'm already in tomorrow . . . We follow Greenwich Mean Time so it's quarter past three in the morning on board here, over.'

Meg gasped. 'Oh, my goodness, why are you still awake then? Shouldn't you be sleeping? Over.'

'Yes.' His voice sounded distorted, someone else cutting over them. '. . . cause of the emai . . . ondered if you might make contact. It's nice chatting with a familiar voice . . . ver.'

Meg's mouth opened in surprise. *He* liked chatting to *her*? 'I . . .' Interference spiked again, buying her time. She changed the subject. 'Have you done spacewalks before? Are they scary?'

She waited for his reply.

'. . . veral times . . . airy moments. Once there was a meteor show . . . a bit close but it was fine . . . the end, over.'

And to think that she'd spent her day doing a stock inventory! 'Do you have to do them regularly? Over.'

She chewed on her thumbnail as she waited for his response, her eyes tracking the bright dot, which was ever more distant in the sky now. A few minutes and he'd be out of range. Interference was picking up again.

'. . . ot so much but we do general maintenance and any repairs that need doing, over.'

Meg chuckled. 'You must be handy around the house then!'

She waited.

And waited.

'Hello, Commander. Jonas? Can you hear me? Over.'

'. . . Sierra Sierra . . . osing you. It's the busiest time . . . py me? . . .'

Voices interrupted them like a crossed line on the phone: nameless, faceless people, some of them trying to speak to him themselves, saying his call sign – she knew it by heart now – others just chatting, yet more still calling out to the ether, reciting obscure codes she couldn't understand.

She pressed her left cheek to the window glass, her eyes raking the dusk for the bright amulet, only just finding it as it sped away, growing fainter and fainter until finally it was out of sight again, chasing the sun.

'Hey.' Lucy turned from her spot at the stove and smiled as Tuck came in, his jeans muddied on the knee, his bike helmet in one hand. 'Good ride?'

He nodded but the movement was brusque and she felt a pip of anxiety at the surly expression on his face.

'I made fish pie. Thought we hadn't had it for a while. It takes so long to prepare I usually don't—'

'Don't bother on my account,' he said, tossing the helmet onto the table and walking over to the fridge. He pulled out a beer, opening it with a fluid, unthinking motion of his hand on the cap as he positioned it at the edge of the counter. She had found it sexy when they first got together.

'Oh, but I wanted to,' she said quickly. 'It's your favourite and I thought we both deserved a treat.'

He looked perplexed by the sentiment. 'Why?'

'Well, the last couple of months have been hard, obviously and—'

Her voice trailed off as she saw his eyes flick over her – was that disgust she saw in them? – before he put the bottle to his lips and swigged.

'I'm not that hungry,' he said, wiping his mouth with the back of his hand and sinking against the formica worktop.

Lucy opened her mouth to say something but stopped herself and went back to stirring the white sauce. He'd be hungry when she set this down in front of him, she thought to herself. He often said he wasn't hungry when he was. He just didn't know himself as well as she did, that was all.

The kitchen filled with a silence that wrapped around them both like a cat curling around their legs. She glanced over at him and gave a small smile.

'I'm going to have a shower,' he muttered a moment later, putting the almost-empty beer bottle down and walking out.

Lucy stopped stirring as she heard the water come on, the sound of his belt buckle hitting the floor. She looked up into the sky, trying not to cry. It was a cloudy night, no moon to see by, and she felt upset that he hadn't noticed her new top or seen that she'd done her hair and put on some make-up for once. Sometimes she felt he didn't even see her, except to criticize.

But then she remembered the day in Room 32, the way he'd taken charge and looked after her and she shook her head, trying to banish her negativity. No. Didn't he often cheer up after his shower? He was like most men coming in after a long day, needing some time to himself when he came in from work to recalibrate to family life.

The pie now browning in the oven, she was sitting at the kitchen table fifteen minutes later flicking through a gossip magazine when he walked in again, his wet hair slicked back, a grey waffle-knit jumper thrown over some checked baggies. She felt her spirits dive further. He looked sexy as hell, of course – he always did – but couldn't he *see* that she'd made an effort tonight? What was she doing, dolled up and cooking his favourite meal, when he just sloped in effectively in his pyjamas? This wasn't how she'd envisaged tonight going. And where was her little present?

'Smells good,' he said, coming over and planting a kiss on her forehead.

Lucy brightened, looking up at him in surprise. 'It'll be ready in about twenty minutes.'

'I'm starved,' he said, wandering over to the fridge again and pulling out another beer. She didn't frown. Instead, her smile widened. She knew him so well.

'So tell me about your day,' she sighed, leaning one arm on the table and resting her chin in her cupped hand, all the better for watching him.

'Not much to tell. I took a few calls about the Toronto Snow Show, spoke to a supplier about a polycarbon material I'm interested in.'

'Oh, yeah?'

'It's got more flex.'

'Great,' she said brightly. 'Mitch was always saying the one you had was too . . .' Her voice faded out. She hated saying his name in front of Tuck now. It had a visceral effect on him, closing him up, folding him down like an origami square repeatedly made into a smaller version of itself. She changed the subject. 'I saw Meg earlier. She was talking about starting up her own graphic-design business.'

'Really?' A sneer curled his lip.

'I know, that's what I said. A whole lot of aggro and for what? I tried telling her she doesn't need the stress.'

But Tuck wasn't listening; he was leaning back against the counter in his favoured spot, one ankle crossed over the other, his expression distant.

'What are you thinking?' she asked.

He glanced at her, as if realizing she was still there, then sighed. It was almost as though talking with her, just being with her, was wearying. 'Nuthin'. I got a prelim layout today for Toronto and I'm not happy with where they've put us. I want a better spot. No one else has got anything like Titch in the market and thanks to Aspen, we're flavour of the month.'

'Well, you're always *my* flavour of the month,' she smiled, making sure to squeeze her elbows in and inject her already-impressive cleavage with even more oomph.

It worked and she marvelled that it really was like training a dog. Tuck's eyes travelled over her as if for the first time this evening, noticing the new tenor of their dinner. 'Is that new?' he asked, his gaze on her décolletage but referring, she knew, to the more general vicinity of her blouse.

'Perhaps,' she said coyly, sitting back now and pulling away. He also loved it when she played hard to get.

'It's nice,' he replied, always at his most handsome when his eyes began to shine like that. It had been the thing she'd never been able to resist – even when she'd wanted to. It had been such a cliché to fall for him. All the girls at school had and – stuck with her best friend dating his – Lucy had seen it as a badge of merit to remain impervious to his charms. To bemoan his immaturity had been the only way she had been able to think of undermining his cocksure arrogance, to deflect attention away from the humiliating fact that he'd never tried it on with her, and she'd made it a point of honour that she would never make a move on him. But that didn't mean she hadn't made her moves – he'd been the one she'd worn that dress for to the Prom, and that moment when she'd seen him notice her *like that*, had been the best of her life, better even than standing at the altar with him and saying, 'I do.' She'd felt like she'd really achieved something, getting him to fall for her.

'I thought you'd like it. I felt like something new.'

She waited, pleased with herself for having teed up the perfect opportunity for him to reveal his purchase. *'Yeah? I got you something new too,'* he'd say and then he'd scoop her up (well, no, maybe he wouldn't pick her up at the moment, he'd need a winch) and they'd fall into the bedroom—

The kitchen timer beeped suddenly, making Tuck jump and shattering the moment.

'Oh,' she said, getting up to turn it off. 'Is it that time already?'

'What time?'

'Seven eleven. Apparently—' And she leaned forward, craning her neck to see out the window. 'We should be able to see the International Space Station flying over now.' She wrinkled her nose. 'But I can't see a thing with these damned clouds.'

'Space Station?'

'Yeah, you remember that astronaut sent Meg the poem? Well, they're quite the pen pals now and he said they'd be doing a fly-past tonight.' She shrugged, giving up on the blanketed sky and peering through the glass oven door to see how the pie was browning instead.

'Ten more minutes,' she murmured, casting her husband a sultry look that was intended to convey how they could fill the time, but he wasn't looking at her. He was examining his right hand.

'Oh, what's happened?' she frowned, catching sight of it and holding it up for a better look – there was a nasty graze to the side of the hand and his wrist seemed swollen.

'Nothing. I just fell earlier on the trail.'

She nodded but didn't say anything – she *knew* it had been a bad ride. 'Let me put some ice on it.'

'It's fine.'

'Tuck, it looks nasty. It must have been a bad fall.' She knew he hated her mothering him but she was right about this. 'What were you *doing?*'

'I said it's fine. Leave it,' he snapped.

Silence dripped down the walls like condensation and Lucy realized she was holding her breath. She had his hand in hers but it wasn't the bruising and the swelling that had caught her eye. It was what was missing that held her attention.

She stepped back, heart jack-hammering as she turned and slid her hands into the oven gloves. The pie needed another few minutes to get a really good golden colour but she had to busy herself, to think through what she'd seen. Because if she was wrong . . .

He stepped out of the way as she lowered the oven door and lifted it out, the potato topping still blond but the aroma curling appealingly around the kitchen.

'Where's your watch?' she asked lightly, glancing down at his left wrist in case he should be in doubt about what she was referring to.

But he missed the cue. 'What?'

'Your watch, you're not wearing it. I know it's not in the bedroom because I was in there earlier, tidying u—'

As she'd thought. An innocuous comment was nothing of the sort when he was in this mood, when he was guilty.

'What is this, a freaking inquisition?' he yelled. 'Do I have to run everything past you? Do I need permission to take my own watch off? I just had a shower, for Chrissakes! I took it off, OK?'

'OK,' she said quickly. 'I wasn't accusing you.'

He double-blinked. 'You weren't *accusing* me? *What* exactly weren't you accusing me of?'

She swallowed, the pie feeling heavy on her arms now as she stood there, the heat from the dish beginning to radiate through the gloves and burn her hands.

'I wasn't accusing you of losing the watch,' she said carefully.

But she couldn't help herself. Although she said nothing, she couldn't hide that she knew what she knew, and she saw him realize that he had said too much; he had dropped himself in it and now she knew what had happened as surely as if she'd seen it with her own eyes – because that watch was waterproof; she'd bought it for him.

She remembered the crunch of glass underfoot by the bed, the fact that he'd found her in the room even though the door was shut with a *Do Not Disturb* sign on it. It had never occurred to her to ask why he'd gone there. But now, as the pie went careering into the wall and down the fridge, they both knew exactly what had happened in Room 32.

Chapter Thirteen

Monday 22 May 2017

Hi Jonas,

It was so exciting to see you pass overhead the other day! I felt like I was in a sci-fi movie. I really hope your spacewalk went well. It sounds terrifying to me – one mistake and you could drift off into the galaxy? No, thanks!

I keep wondering what the stars must look like up there. We spend so much time down here, gazing up at them and pinning our wishes onto them – wouldn't it be terrible if they were utterly unremarkable up close? Like meeting a beautiful actress and discovering she's really very plain and it's all down to the make-up.

I keep rereading the poem you sent through – 'High Flight'? I googled the poet, John Magee. Did you know that he flew for the Royal Canadian Air Force and he died in a mid-air collision? The definition of irony surely, but I think it makes it feel even more poignant that he should have died in the air – as though, in his death, he got to live what he wrote in his poem: 'I have slipped the surly bonds of Earth . . .' I like to think that Mitch is living the poem too; that he's 'dancing the skies'. I imagine that's why you sent it to me?

Much of it must apply to you too, though – being out there, in the sky, dancing above the clouds. What's the line? 'The high, untrespassed sanctity of space . . .' I guess that must be why you knew it?

Anyway, maybe I'm reading too much into it. I probably am. But it's helped me, that poem, more than you could possibly know, so thanks again.

On a lighter note, I heard a joke the other day that made me think of you, so here goes.

Q: Where do astronauts park their spaceships?

A: On a parking meteor!

Sorry, I know it's quite bad!

Write if you get a chance, but you're really busy so if you can't, that's OK too.

Best wishes

Meg

PS But actually, if you could just answer me this – why were you laughing so much when we spoke on the radio the other day? Am I doing something wrong?

Tuesday 23 May 2017

Hi Meg (or rather, Dog-Dog-Elephant),

Bad? That joke was truly terrible! I tested it out on the crew at dinner last night and they all agreed it was the worst astronaut joke they ever heard. Now this is an astronaut joke:

Q: How do you get an astronaut baby to sleep?

A: Rocket.

See? Funny!

Talking of funny, the reason I was laughing at your call

sign on our last radio contact was because your adaptation of the Nato Phonetic Alphabet, which we commonly use for radio transmissions, is somewhat . . . unique. But very sweet too, so don't feel you need to change it. For one thing, it makes it a lot easier for me to find you in the airwaves!

How's the weather down there? It's looking very green from here; almost all the snow's gone now, even from the mountaintops? Make the most of the sun. We passed over a big typhoon in the Pacific heading towards the west coast. It'll lose power when it hits land but I imagine you'll still get a few days of heavy wind and rain, which sounds great to me – missing running water so much has been one of the biggest surprises up here. I'd love nothing more than to have a hot shower or to stand in the rain right now. Simple pleasures.

Write back,

J

Wednesday 24 May 2017

J,

On the contrary, I think <u>your</u> joke was appalling – far, far worse than mine, which I had tested specially on my friend Lucy before sending it out to space for you and she doesn't smile for just anything, you know. It sounds to me like you've all been in space for far too long and lost perspective on what's funny any more. It wouldn't be a surprise – after all, who would want to willingly stand out in the rain? You must have all gone mad.

Yes, the weather's glorious down here now. It's always a bit of a relief when the snow goes, everything becomes so much easier. Just keeping warm in my house requires so much effort – old trees need to be identified, felled, chopped, stacked, stored, brought in, fires set . . . It's so great to be able to get out of bed in the morning and not have to pull on twenty layers first. Plus I'm always grateful for the longer days. My cabin is in a nature reserve up a mountain so it gets really dark and quiet here. I don't feel frightened because I've got Badger, my dog, with me but a bright sky stops it feeling quite so isolated.

How much longer are you going to be up there for? Do you ever get bored with it, or would admitting that go against the Astronaut Code? I think I'd miss Earth too much to leave for any period of time. Ha! I can barely leave Alberta as it is. My sister wants me to visit her in Toronto but even that's too far for me!

Meg (aka Dog-Dog-Elephant)

PS

Q: What is an astronaut's favourite computer key?

A: The space bar!

Thursday 25 May 2017

Dog-Dog-Ellie,

It's your sanity I'm worried for if you think that joke was an improvement on the last. I couldn't even bring myself to read it out to the crew last night in case they staged an intervention and had you sent off to the Funny Farm (*).

In spite of your worrying taste in jokes, I do completely get what you mean about the snow and short days being hard work. I'm Norwegian and although my village – Stavanger – is in the south of the country, we're still significantly north of you and temperatures regularly stay below minus 20.

Further north, near Tromsö, they have two months of the year in Polar Night, when the sun doesn't rise above the horizon at all, and in the summer, they have Polar Summer, when it never sets. Funnily enough, it's the 24-hour days that are harder for most people to endure than the endless nights. And up here, we have sixteen dawns and sunsets a day, so it's like walking through the rooms of a house and turning the lights on and off. Sometimes I look up from a task only to find I've gone from mid-day in India to midnight in Hawaii in half an hour.

Why aren't you going to visit your sister in Toronto? You absolutely should. Your cabin in the woods sounds great but if there's one thing I've learned being up here, it's that there's more beauty and adventure in our world than we could ever hope to see in one lifetime. Go play!

I've got just over another two months up here; in fact, I'm well over halfway through the expedition now. We launched at the beginning of February and we're coming home via a Kazakhstani desert in late July. I'm nervous, I'll admit – not particularly at the prospect of us all being burned up as we re-enter the atmosphere, but because it's tradition and pro-tocol to do a press conference in Kazakh traditional dress immediately afterwards. Given your skewed sense of humour, I should imagine that will prove very amusing for you and a ripe opportunity for you to make jokes at my expense.

Talking of which . . .

Q: Why did the astronaut leave the restaurant on the moon?

A: There wasn't much atmosphere.

J

(*) Get it?

Friday 26 May 2017

I'm sorry, I didn't realize this was a competition. You may be further north where it's colder and darker but we still win on the dangerous wilderness scale.(*) We have bears. And wolves. And elks that could break your foot if they trod on you!

So – you were only up there a month when we first 'met'?

Meg / D-D-E.

PS

Q: Did you hear the one about the astronaut in a bullet-proof vest?

A: He was protecting himself from shooting stars.

(*) I'm not actually Canadian by birth. I'm English but my family emigrated here when I was sixteen.

Saturday 27 May 2017

Yes. I'd been up here six weeks and it was the first time I wished I wasn't up here.

J

PS We have polar bears.

Sunday 28 May 2017

The first time? So there have been other times when you wished you weren't up there?

M

PS I'll give you the polar bears. But my jokes still trump yours.

Monday 29 May 2017

Yes. And increasingly so.
   J

Chapter Fourteen

Sunday 23 July 2017

'You know, if there was more of a view, I think I'd find this easier,' Lucy puffed, lagging ever further behind their little group.

Dolores, Barbara and Meg stopped and waited again.

'It's just all these . . . trees, you know?' she panted, waving her hands around distractedly at the towering pines around them. 'There's nothing to see but trees. So . . . so . . . *boring*. No impetus to really . . . get going . . . you know?'

She reached the others and put her hands on her knees, trying to get her breath back.

'Come and sit for a moment,' Meg said, taking her by the elbow and guiding her to a boulder by the side of the trail. 'You're carrying two up this hill, remember.'

'Yeah, right . . . 'cause it's so easy for . . . Mom and Dolores.'

'Excuse me! What's your point?' Dolores asked, hands on hips and elbows pointed like arrows. She was wearing tan hiking shorts and a khaki vest, her skinny arms and legs nut brown from a spring and now summer being spent outdoors, her floppy sunhat secured with a string under the chin.

Barbara looked as though she was off to the country club, a tinted visor keeping back her champagne-white bob and her tennis trainers on, an ice-blue gilet folded over one arm. She didn't ever break out in a sweat unnecessarily, preferring to look the part, but even she was faring better than her daughter and to add insult to injury, as Meg handed Lucy the bottle of water, she lit up a cigarette. She wouldn't have looked at all out of place if she'd been holding a glass of wine either.

'When are you going to quit those things?' Dolores scolded, as she always did, taking advantage of the pit stop to reapply sunblock to her T-zone. 'They'll kill you.'

'Something's got to,' Barbara shrugged. 'I don't want to outstay my welcome.' She wrinkled her nose. 'There's nothing worse than not knowing when to leave the party.'

'Nonsense. I've got seventeen years on you and I'm nowhere near done.'

Meg smiled as they bickered, looking waifish in short denim dungarees, proper hiking boots – as if Dolores would have let her walk in anything less! – and a green V-neck T-shirt. 'Think this'll be us in thirty years?' she murmured to Lucy.

'Ha, we wish!'

Meg looked up and then down the path, wishing she'd been able to bring Badger – he'd have loved darting up and down the forest but no dogs were allowed in the springs. They had been going now for forty-five minutes but it felt longer with all these breaks. It was just an easy hike to the hot springs, they could usually do it in less, but Lucy had slowed down a lot since her bump had popped out with Porsche acceleration, going from zero to sixty in the past couple of weeks, even though the baby wasn't due until the very end of November, still a good four months away.

It was true there was nothing to see but trees, the sparkling sun rays unable to penetrate the dense canopies and illuminate the forest floor, but then Meg had always rather liked that – the mossy rocks and star-shaped lichen ground cover had been the land of fairies to her girlhood self and her imagination had always been attuned to the idea of underworld adventures springing from those shaded glades. Then again, she lived with a view – she was spoilt on a daily, hourly basis with vistas of stunning sunrises and sunsets; perhaps if she was living in a courtyard bungalow with a view up to the back of a hotel, she might crave an open aspect too.

'Come on, you'll feel better when you're in the springs,' Meg said, standing up and tightening the straps on the backpack that contained their brunch.

'No, I won't, they're far too hot – my doctor's said I can't go in,' Lucy moaned, getting up anyway.

'But you can still put your feet in,' Meg shushed her, knowing how much Lucy had begun to suffer with swollen ankles. Linking her arm through her friend's, she led her up the trail again, pulling slightly.

They walked for a few minutes in silence, Barbara finishing her cigarette, Dolores setting a steady pace and jabbing her Nordic walking pole into the ground every few seconds.

'Did you hear about the grizzly spotted down by the Cave?' Dolores asked over her shoulder.

'I know,' Meg said. 'They've set up an exclusion zone all the way to the Cascade trail.'

'You'll never believe this but I had a man come back yesterday saying he went down especially trying to find it,'

Barbara tutted. 'Damned fool. I think half these people confuse 'em with teddy bears. What do they think is gonna happen if they come across one?'

'I came across a bear once,' Lucy said, already panting again.

'You never told me,' Barbara scolded, whipping round to face her daughter.

Meg was surprised too. She didn't know about it either and she thought she knew all of her friend's stories and secrets.

'It was a couple of years ago. Me and Tuck went over to Vermilion Lakes for an evening walk and it was making its way down to the water.'

'Well, what happened?' Barbara asked, concern in her voice.

Lucy shrugged. 'We just . . . stayed in the car till it was . . . gone.'

Everyone groaned.

'Honestly, Lucy,' Barbara tutted, turning back.

'That is hardly what I'd call a bear tale!' Dolores said, shaking her head and picking up the pace.

They walked along, passing through shadows and cooing at the view in every break in the trees.

'By the way, Meg, when exactly is your flight?' Dolores asked. 'Because Amelia can't cover until Wednesday.'

'Uh, next Friday,' Meg replied, shooting Dolores a cross look, and then Lucy a nervous one. Dolores knew perfectly well she was worried about telling her friend she was going to Toronto after all. This was no innocent slip-up.

'Oh good, that—'

Lucy stopped walking. '*Where* are you going? And why haven't you told me about it?'

Meg took a deep breath. 'I'm going to Toronto for a long weekend next week.'

'To see Ronnie?'

Meg nodded. Why else would she go there?

'Even though all she ever does is upset you?'

Meg smiled, holding her hands out appeasingly. 'She's my sister, Lucy. That's . . . what sisters do. It doesn't change the fact.'

'Fact?'

Meg shrugged. 'That I love her. She's the only family I've got left.'

'Oh, thanks, thanks very much.' Lucy began walking again, with rather more vigour than she had hitherto mustered on the hike.

'Luce, you know what I mean!' Meg called after her.

'Do I? And where's *she* been for the past few months then, whilst I've been scraping you up off the floor and trying to put you together again?'

'I . . .' Meg gawped, losing her stride. Had she really been that bad? She thought she'd been doing OK. Not great, admittedly, but it had only been four months since she'd buried Mitch. She resumed walking. 'Lucy, listen, it's just for a few days, not even a week. I'm coming back! It's no big deal, I'm just seeing my sister.' What was so wrong with that? she wondered as she watched Lucy's retreating back.

With the new pace, they reached the springs a quarter of an hour later; were it not for the plumes of steam rising from the water, it would have looked just like a regular swimming pool. There were a dozen or so people there but it was far from crowded, precisely why they'd come now. The lunch visitors usually liked to take in the views on

Sulphur Mountain first and then stop here later when they stepped off the gondola.

Meg shrugged off the backpack, rolling her shoulders to ease the tension and slipping out of her clothes. Barbara, looking regal in a floral underwired swimsuit with a criss-cross detail across the front, was first in, using the stairs and careful not to get her hair wet. Dolores was in her black Speedo costume with the light blue trim, the same style she'd been wearing since the seventies. Lucy, wearing navy Bermuda shorts, had to make do with sitting on the side, dangling her legs in and looking sulkier than ever.

Meg felt sorry for her as she slipped into the hot waters. It couldn't be easy being pregnant in this heat and she increasingly suspected there wasn't going to be a 'blooming' stage in this pregnancy, just alternating symptoms and discomforts that had to be endured as the weeks counted down.

She gave a small shiver as she walked through the water. It was a hot day but the pool was hotter still and her body reacted almost instantly to the mineral-rich water, the tight muscles slackening. She had visited infrequently as a teenager, but Dolores had been coming several times a week ever since Jed had developed early-onset arthritis in his forties, and the habit had stuck even after he died. Since Mitch's death, Meg had begun to accompany her more and more too. She couldn't say exactly why it appealed to her now but it soothed her at a level that went further than skin deep. Lying with her arms stretched back on the stone wall, her body floating and her eyes on the mountains opposite . . . perhaps it was the closest thing she felt to being held.

Meg closed her eyes and felt the steam cleanse her skin, her cheeks flushing as her body grew warmer and heavier.

'Heavens, girl, you are far too thin!' Barbara said with a

gasp and Meg was shocked, as she opened her eyes, to find that the comment was directed at her. 'I had no idea you'd lost so much. When did you last eat?'

Meg's mouth parted in surprise. The only mirror at the cabin was at head height in the bathroom and although she knew her clothes were too big at the moment, she hadn't particularly thought about her weight loss. 'This morning,' she relied defensively, crossing her hands over herself and ducking a little lower in the water.

'Don't worry, Babs, I've been keeping an eye on her,' Dolores said, as she swam past in a neat backstroke, droplets splashing Barbara's hair. 'She is eating – it's just the nervous energy burning everything off. She's as nervy as an antelope in the pride lands. You don't trust the world not to hurt you again, do you, chicken?'

'Well, you're to have seconds of my banana bread,' Barbara said cluckily. 'With a bit of luck, it'll still be warm. Nothing better.' She glanced at her daughter. 'Although not for you, madam – you need to keep an eye on your sugar levels. I had gestational diabetes carrying you and the way you're shaping up, I wouldn't be surprised if you get the same.'

'Mom!' Lucy scowled, kicking her leg in the water so that it splashed up.

'Hey, that's a nasty bruise,' Meg said, noticing a dark mark on Lucy's thigh, just peeping through at the bottom of her shorts. 'How'd you get that?'

'What?' Lucy asked sharply. 'Oh, I don't know. It's nothing.' She tugged down on the hem.

'It doesn't look nothing. It looks sore.'

'It's fine. I didn't even know it was there.'

'How could you not know about it? It's huge! What did you do – take on a car?'

Lucy rolled her eyes. 'Look, I don't know, all right? I must have knocked into something. What does it matter? Don't make such a big deal of it. You're just trying to get the attention off of you and onto me.'

'I'm not!' Meg said, laughing and gasping at the same time. 'I was just—'

'Well, don't,' Lucy snapped, her eyes glittering dangerously as she glowered at her. Meg bent her legs, ducking so low that her chin skimmed the top of the water. 'I'm going for a swim,' she muttered, hurt that her concern had been twisted into something selfish and untrue.

She swam away, Barbara's hushed, annoyed tones drifting to her ear. '. . . what you've done . . . nly being kind . . .'

She let herself drift to the far end, her eyes sliding from the hazy mountains on the other side of the valley to the airy clouds that stretched and spun in the sky, Mitch walking through her thoughts every few minutes like a casual rambler who'd taken residence in her mind.

Barbara and Lucy were sitting together by the plunge pool but Dolores had moved off to chat with a group of friends who were also regulars, their baggy arms, white-haired chests and atrophied legs belying the fact that theirs were the most frequent and infectious laughs. Meg floated past on her back without interrupting, smiling as she heard Dolores deliver the punchline on her latest joke, which she herself must have heard fifty times. Meg was proud of her friendship with the older woman – loved her strength and defiance and determination to live life on her terms. Dolores had known hard times – unable to have children, Jed's premature death leaving her a young widow – but Meg had never known her to complain or bemoan her lot. Dolores was strictly of the view that adversity was good for you, that struggle was a requisite for happiness and as such, problems were merely opportunities in disguise. It made her uplifting to be around and it was perhaps no coincidence that Meg had been so ready to go straight back to work, just to be near her.

When she finally swam back to the others, Lucy splashed water in her face – a token of affection, she knew, and Meg smiled, her hurt feelings smoothed again. They might bicker but they could never stay mad with each other for long. Besides, Meg knew it wasn't her Lucy was annoyed with but her mother; Barbara was a kind-hearted woman and a loving mother but she could be heavy-handed in her comments to her daughter and had always seemed oblivious to Lucy's sensitivity about her size – warning Lucy off the cake, just now, would have hurt.

Shrivelled like dates, they climbed out and dried off, eating their brunch in the picnic area. The banana bread, thankfully, was still warm and the four of them ate the entire thing there – Lucy didn't have seconds – along with a plate of peaches and a flask of coffee.

'Think we should get moving?' Barbara asked, adjusting the position of her visor as Meg repacked the empties in the food bag and Lucy borrowed some of Dolores's sunblock. 'I've got a coach party booked in for after lunch and I don't want Nancy checking them in. Last time I left her alone, the dratted girl put a woman in a wheelchair on the fourth floor and oversold two rooms.'

Meg chuckled and stood up. 'Come on then. I've got some calls to make, anyway.'

'Have you heard from Jonas?' Dolores asked, tapping her walking pole against the soles of her boots.

Meg smiled. 'This morning, actually.'

'Yes? And what's he got to say for himself?' Dolores asked, throwing a wink to Barbara.

'He said he saw the bush fires in Australia.'

'Oh, my Lord,' Dolores tutted. 'They've been so bad. Have you seen them on the news, Babs?'

Barbara didn't appear to hear her; she was watching Lucy, who was trying – rather gracelessly – to stand, the shadowy bruise on her thigh clearly visible as her shorts rode up.

Dolores looked back to Meg with a tut. 'Did he take any pictures?'

'I don't know. Probably.'

'Well, ask him to send them if he did. I'd be intrigued to see it from that vantage point.'

Lucy, now standing, slapped the grass off her shorts and they began to walk, the steam from the spring rising behind their backs as they headed back towards the forest trail.

'Is this that astronaut man Lucy was telling me about?' Barbara enquired curiously, joining the conversation now.

'Yep,' Lucy replied, looking visibly more comfortable now that they were out of the direct sun and back in the shade of the forest. 'And he's not an astronaut man, Mom. He's just an astronaut.'

'But he's a man, isn't he?'

'Yes, but you don't . . . you don't say both, Mom!' Lucy said, rolling her eyes. 'You just say astronaut.'

'Well, that's what I did say. Honestly, I don't get why you're splitting hairs?'

Lucy groaned, making Meg and Dolores laugh.

'Well, anyway, he also did another spacewalk yesterday,' Meg continued. 'He gets really nervous about those. One wrong move and . . . hello, eternity!'

Lucy gave a shudder. 'And to think I can barely do a forest walk.'

'Did it all go OK?' Barbara asked.

'I don't know yet. Hopefully he'll have emailed by the time I get back.' She checked her watch, counting forward eight hours. 'It's . . . quarter to nine at night up there. He's usually got some free time in the evenings. His days are so busy.'

'Really? What do astronauts *do*, exactly?'

'Well, he says he's effectively a glorified lab assistant, but I think he's being modest. The ISS is basically just a giant laboratory, doing all its testing without the effects of gravity. They've got over a hundred and twenty experiments on board right now, all of which require monitoring and reporting, plus he and his colleagues have to test the effects on themselves too.'

'Sounds brainy,' Lucy said.

'I think he must be. But they also have to maintain the station and make repairs where necessary, so he's like a mechanical engineer too.'

'Brains *and* brawn? He sounds like my ideal man,' Barbara chuckled.

'A man orbiting space and getting out from under my feet is definitely my ideal,' Dolores quipped. 'More men should be put out there, if you ask me.'

Barbara cried with laughter, throwing her head back, and Lucy and Meg chuckled at the sight of them.

'*Plus*,' Meg continued. 'On top of all that work, he has to do two hours' exercise every day or else he'll suffer bone-density loss. Osteoporosis is a real problem in micro-gravity.'

'Oh, good Lord, don't let me apply for the space pro-gramme then,' said Dolores. 'I work hard enough for my bones as it is. Although you'd love it, Barbara. All that anti-gravity? Instant facelift!'

'Oooh,' Barbara cooed with wide eyes, bringing her hands to her cheeks and gently pushing up.

'Well, it's a wonder he has time to write,' Dolores said. 'He must really enjoy chatting with you.'

Meg shrugged. 'It must get lonely up there. I mean, as much as there's all this incredible beauty in space, he must be longing to be a part of things down here again. I think that's why he likes hearing my news. It's just . . . normal.'

'You should ask him what he misses about Earth,' Bar-bara said, puffing slightly. 'Although then again, don't. He's still a man. He'll probably say something completely banal like . . . Oreos! Or the Super Bowl.'

Meg didn't think he would say that – for one thing, he was Norwegian and Oreos and the Super Bowl were irrele-vant there. 'It's just a shame I can't get Wi-Fi at the cabin or we could have more of a conversation. As it is, we just end up writing these sort of monologues to each other, almost like diary entries. I write in the day when I'm in town and he replies at night.'

Dolores gasped. 'They're like postcards from space!'

Meg grinned. She liked that description. 'Yeah.'

'Don't you still talk on the radio?' Lucy asked. 'I mean, that's how you first made contact.'

'Occasionally. It's easier late at night when there's fewer people on the channels but it doesn't always work – the channels can get really crowded and noisy. You wouldn't believe how many people are trying to get hold of him – the ISS, I mean. It's a proper *thing*. Sometimes I can't get through at all, other times I can hear him talking to someone else, but it's really, really faint.'

'He talks to other people?' Lucy echoed. 'So then, do you think he's got other people he's writing to, too?'

Meg paused, not liking how the thought of that made her feel – and then not liking the fact that she didn't like it. She tried to shake the feelings off. 'I don't know. Maybe . . . Probably. He says once he's off-duty, there's not much else to do apart from look out the window, take some photos. Although they watch films on their iPads too and there's lots of books.'

She had never considered before whether or not their correspondence was 'exclusive' – after all, it wasn't like she was talking to any other astronauts! But in all reality, he probably did have other friendships just like hers; maybe someone for when he was passing over New Zealand? Or South Africa? Or Germany?

Dolores stopped walking, turning her face to the sky. 'What must it be like to be him, all the way up there and looking down on this planet? Imagine how it must expand the mind, the spirit! I can't think of anything more wonderful.' She turned to face them all. 'They should make a space trip compulsory for every person on the planet. There'd be a lot less war and pollution as a result, I can tell you that for nothing.'

Barbara laughed. 'I certainly agree with the principle, dear.'

'How long has he been up there, did you say?' Dolores asked, resuming walking again.

'Over five months now . . . He comes back next week, actually.'

'Oh, my goodness, how strange that will be for him!' Barbara gasped. 'Coming back down to Earth after all that time?'

'I know. He says assuming they have a good re-entry, it takes about three to six weeks before they feel "normal" again.'

'And if they don't have a good re-entry?' Lucy asked.

'Then he won't be feeling anything – they'll have burned up on re-entry into the Earth's atmosphere,' Meg quipped, laughing nervously, not finding it at all funny.

Lucy's eyes bulged. 'Ohmigod, are you serious?'

Meg nodded. 'If they come in too fast. *Or*, if they hit the atmosphere at the wrong angle, they can actually bounce off it like a skimming stone and be bounced back out into deep space.'

'Freaking hell! That's so intense.'

'Language, Lucy!' Barbara scolded.

Lucy rolled her eyes.

'So are you going to meet him when he comes back down?' Barbara asked.

'No!' Meg scoffed.

'But why ever not? If you've spent all this time corresponding with each other . . . aren't you curious to meet him in the flesh?' Dolores asked.

'Of course I am, but . . .' Meg faltered, not sure what to say next. 'Well it's easier said than done, that's all.'

'Why?'

'Because he lands all the way in Kazakhstan for a start—'

'Assuming he doesn't get fried or boinged into deep space first, of course,' Lucy quipped.

Meg jogged her with her elbow. 'Thank you. And then he's got to re-acclimatize – he says the ESA have to do all sorts of tests to see how his body has coped with being in micro-gravity.'

'ESA?' Barbara frowned.

'European Space Agency,' Meg clarified. 'And then he has to go on this, like, promotional tour for three months afterwards, going into school and colleges, tech and medical conferences. I don't see him making a detour to li'l old Banff, Alberta, do you? He's an important man.'

'Well, you could always go see him. Fly to London or Berlin or wherever the heck he's doing his tour,' Dolores said, as though it was the easiest thing in the world when she could barely cope with visiting her own sister in Toronto.

Meg just shook her head. 'Look, things will change. He'll pick up his old life and be super-busy . . . It'll be different for him then.' She smiled as she saw their expressions. 'What? It's OK. I know perfectly well that I'm only interesting to him while he's floating in space. I give him an outlet to communicate. But once he's back, with his family and friends and colleagues—'

'How old is he, this astro man?' Barbara asked.

Meg shrugged.

'Married? Girlfriend? Kids?'

'I don't know,' Meg replied, laughing lightly.

'Why not? He obviously knows about you and Mitch, doesn't he?' Dolores asked.

Meg felt her chest tighten. 'Well, yes but—'

'But what?'

Meg shrugged. 'We just have general chats, that's all. We don't get personal.' But that was a lie. They'd been nothing but personal. He'd sent her a poem that had felt like a hug, wrapping around her and holding her together on the darkest nights when she thought she might fall apart; and as their correspondence had gone from daily to several messages daily, she had confided secrets in him that she hadn't told anyone – not Lucy, not Ronnie, not even Mitch. Knowing she'd never meet him, not having to be face to face, had allowed an almost confessional freedom in their messages that would never have been possible had they been conducted in the flesh.

Barbara gave a little gasp, as though something had shocked her.

'What?' Lucy asked, jumping in alarm.

'Have you seen a picture of him?'

'Oh, Mom!' Lucy said irritably. 'I thought something bad had happened!'

'Have you?' Barbara asked, ignoring her daughter's complaint.

Meg hesitated, before nodding, self-consciously fidgeting with the straps of the backpack. 'Well, I did google him.'

'And? Surely that tells you how old he is?'

Meg remembered the shock she'd had when she'd seen his face for the first time. It had been an official ESA/NASA release, Jonas looking straight to camera with a wary smile, wearing his white spacesuit, his helmet on his lap and the Norwegian flag draped in the background. He was far younger than she'd anticipated – his strict observance of radio protocols had made him seem older – with fine features but deep-set eyes, pale skin and light brown hair. She'd found another image of him speaking at a press conference, wearing a badged boilersuit like a jet pilot, and that had been more surprising still as he'd been smiling in that one and the animation had lit up his face, changing him completely. He looked lean and athletic, confident and composed, wearing his accomplishments lightly. She'd spent a lot of time looking at that particular photo, trying to mesh the face to the voice, the astronaut to her friend. It still felt hard to believe she was talking to *him* and it had inhibited her responses so much the next few times they'd written, that she'd had to stop herself from looking at it at all. It didn't make her feel as though she knew him better; it made her want to run.

'He's definitely younger than I'd thought. Mid-thirties? White, clever-looking.'

Barbara gasped again and stopped walking.

'Oh, what now, Mom?' Lucy asked, before she too did exactly the same.

The sound was unmistakable – a snort, followed by massive paws pounding the earth and then a roar that made their bones quake.

Meg felt her stomach drop to her feet as she saw the bear move out of the trees, its shoulder blades rolling beneath a heavy fur hide, its eyes beady in a massive head and trained solely on them.

Lucy screamed – she was closest to it at the edge of the path – her hands flying to her vulnerable, protruding belly as she began walking backwards, trying to cluster for safety in their little group.

Barbara screamed and froze.

Meg did the opposite, sucking in frantic gulps of air, her hands reaching round the back of the backpack and groping, fumbling for the pepper spray she'd put in the mesh pocket at the side, never once thinking, not really, that she'd need to use it.

The bear rose onto its hind legs standing three metres tall, its paler-furred stomach extending past their heads, its sharp, thick claws visible now, every single one as sharp as a butcher's knife. It swiped, the rush of air blowing past Meg's face as it reached for Lucy.

Dolores roared, 'No!' and suddenly pushed Lucy as hard as she could. Lucy flew off the path, landing heavily on her side and rolling onto the grassy bank, her head missing a rock by mere centimetres.

The bear, having fallen back onto all four paws, turned towards her and reared again, its sights still on Lucy. She was closest, she was on the ground . . .

'No!' Barbara screamed, a blood-curdling sound that Meg knew, if they survived this, she would never forget. She picked up a stone, throwing it helplessly at the bear's back. Did it even feel it?

'Here!' Dolores roared, waving her arms frantically above her head. 'Look at me! Come here!' she screamed, her voice thunderous. 'Come after *me*!'

The bear turned as another stone hit it – a large one this time, striking it on the head.

Meg felt her stomach drop again as those unblinking eyes met hers for a moment, her hands still scrabbling to find the spray as the bear sized up every one of them.

'Yes!' Dolores hollered. 'That's it! Over here!' She was waving her arms above her head to keep the bear's attention, walking backwards now to draw it away from Lucy.

The bear came towards them in a swaying, lumbering walk, its weight vibrating the ground beneath their feet, its mouth hanging open, muzzle dropped. And always, its eyes unflinching upon them.

Behind it, Meg could see Lucy scrambling backwards

towards the trees, pine needles pressed into her skin and hair, her eyes wide, a look of sheer, stricken horror on her face.

The bear reared again, its distinctive damp, musky smell enveloping them and catching in the back of their throats; the spittle dripping from its black jaws, the yellow teeth glistening with saliva, the roof of its mouth ridged and speckled black. It was so close . . . Meg's fingers found the aerosol and she gave a cry of relief as she tugged it free, her hands shaking violently as she tried to remove the cap, to face it towards the bear.

She saw the paw swipe past her again towards the others, its power immense, and she screamed as she pressed on the aerosol, all her fear, all her anger released along with the spray. She kept on screaming, her finger white as she pressed hard, never stopping, sure her lungs were bleeding as pepper gas mushroomed in the air like a toxic cloud. Almost immediately the bear fell back on all fours, shaking its head agitatedly, pounding its paws into the ground, unwilling to retreat, here to fight.

Meg advanced, just one step. Two. But the bear moved back, away from her, its attacking roar changing to sounds of distress, whimpers, as the spray kept coming.

'Hey! Hey!' someone shouted. A man.

Other voices – lots of them – drifted down the track and then a crowd was running towards them, dust clouds at their feet as they ran. A few had sticks. They waved their arms as Dolores had done.

'Help us!' Barbara screamed. 'My daughter!'

The bear, hearing the commotion, seeing it was outnumbered, jostled backwards towards the trees, shuffling straight past Lucy, before turning and lumbering back into the forest from whence it had come, out of sight within ten seconds. Before the crowd even got to them.

Voices clamoured.

'Are you all right?'

'Call nine one one!'

'She's down! We need paramedics here!'

'Oh, my God, Lucy! Are you hurt?'

'Mom!'

Meg, shaking, couldn't take her eyes off the trees. Would it come back? Her arm was still outstretched, her finger still pressing on the button, but there was nothing left in the canister. It was empty.

'It's OK, honey, you're safe now.' Meg felt hands on her shoulders, arms around her. A woman's face came into her peripheral vision, kind brown eyes. 'You can put that down now. He's gone. You're safe.' A hand gently pushed her arm down and Meg let the woman slowly turn her to face the crowd. They'd been rescued? 'You're OK. It's over.'

But Meg's eyes had fallen to the sight of two people crouched over someone on the ground, nut-brown legs outstretched and motionless, a trickle of dark red blood seeping into the pine needles.

No.

It wasn't over.

Chapter Fifteen

Meg came back with the coffees, both Barbara and Tuck oblivious until her feet appeared in their frames of vision on the floor. Barbara straightened up and took hers with a weak smile.

'Thank you, dear,' she murmured, the cup resting in her hands like a heat aid for a moment before standing. 'I think I'll have this outside. Call me if anyone comes . . . ?'

Meg nodded, knowing Barbara was going out for a cigarette; her hands were still trembling, she was pale and Meg wondered whether she should be checked over by a nurse too. It was bad enough for her heart being confronted with a bear, let alone seeing it go to attack her pregnant daughter.

Tuck didn't move as his mother-in-law shakily walked off.

'Tuck? Take this. I've added some sugar. It's good for the shock.'

Tuck looked up at her, his famously blue eyes now blank. He didn't notice the coffee she was holding out to him. 'What if she loses it?'

Meg sank into the chair beside him, still holding his cup. Tuck had made it to the hospital before them, his expression wild and body language frantic as Meg and Barbara had run in after Dolores and Lucy, both being attended to on gurneys. 'She won't.'

'You don't know that.'

'No,' she sighed. 'But I do know Lucy's a fighter. And she loves that baby so much already. She won't let it go, Tuck. All she wants is for you guys to be a family.'

He stared back at her, his eyes roaming her face as though looking for answers or tricks there and for a moment – without the veil of anger that had fallen every time she'd looked at him since Mitch's death – she was reminded of the cocky, happy-go-lucky friend he'd been before: she could hear his easy laugh, see his ready smile, feel his straightforward love for her fiancé whom he had failed so catastrophically.

He must have read it on her face, for his expression changed completely in the next moment – like a cloudburst disgorging rain, his features crumpled and fell in on themselves, his handsome face distorted and lost in grief as he saw all that they'd lost. He dropped his head, his hands clasped around the back of it, as huge sobs wracked his body.

'It's my fault. I've ruined it all.'

Meg was silent for a moment, not sure whether he was referring to Mitch or Lucy.

'It's no one's fault – it was a bear attack,' Meg said quietly, defaulting to the present. It was easier; she couldn't forgive him yet – not even here, in a new emergency. 'We were just unlucky. Wrong place, wrong time.' The park rangers had been on the scene only minutes after the paramedics, shotguns slung over their shoulders as they studied the ground for bear tracks and followed its path into the trees.

He pulled away, standing up and beginning to pace. 'No. No. This is . . . what's that thing? Karma.'

Meg held her breath, not ready to have this conversation with him. Not here.

But she'd overestimated his emotional intelligence. 'I . . . I wasn't sure about the baby. I didn't think I was ready. I didn't want to be a dad and so now, I won't be.'

Meg swallowed, suppressing her own feelings of rage. 'Those feelings aren't unusual. It doesn't mean you deserve this.' Her voice was small and tight, as if it had been sewn up.

He raked his fingers in his hair, pulling it tight at the temples. 'She kept trying to get me to *bond* with it – wanting me to sing to it and stuff. But I'm not . . .' His face pleated again. 'I can't do that new-age shit. It makes me squeamish, her tummy, I don't *want* to touch it or feel for a kick but she won't listen.' He flashed her an apprehensive look. 'And she keeps saying it's fine when . . . you know. But I'm constantly worried I'm gonna hurt it somehow.'

'Look, you are not the first man in the world to have these feelings, nor will you be the last,' she said flatly. 'When the baby's born, you'll feel differently.'

But he shook his head, not believing her. 'No, I brought this on us. *I* did. I've been . . . I've been such a bad husband to her. I don't deserve her.'

True. 'That's not true – you are all Lucy's ever wanted. You're her world.'

Tears began streaking down his cheeks again and in spite of her contempt for what he'd done to Mitch – and he had done it, she was unequivocal about that – she felt an ache in her heart for him. He looked like a child, standing there, helpless, beating himself up. He suddenly inhaled deeply, roughly wiping his cheeks dry with the heel of his hand. 'I just miss him so much, you know?'

Her heart skipped a beat at the sudden mention of Mitch but she didn't stir, she didn't speak. It was the first time Tuck had dared to approach the subject with her since the funeral.

'Nothing's the same. I feel like . . . like part of me's gone too.'

Meg felt herself begin to shake. This wasn't the time. He didn't get to lump his concern about Lucy with his guilt about Mitch; he didn't get to sidestep what he'd done because of pity. But she was saved from having the conversation as Barbara came back, the coffee cup no longer in her hands, her complexion as pale as before.

'Anything?' she asked them anxiously.

Meg shook her head. 'Not yet.'

'Oh, I thought I saw . . . What can be taking so long?' she fretted, wringing her hands.

'I'm sure they're just playing it safe and running tests.'

Barbara nodded, but her gaze was fixed on the door that separated her from her daughter.

'Someone should be in there with her,' she muttered quietly. 'Don't you think? She must be so frightened.'

'It's probably best for the doctors if we're not. They need to get on with their jobs.' Meg patted the empty seat beside her. 'Come and sit down, Barbara – you look really pale. Are you sure you don't want someone to check you over? You've had a terrible shock.'

Barbara shook her head as she sat down, but her eyes were still on the door.

Another one further up the corridor opened instead and a doctor came out, speaking in hushed tones to a nurse by her side. She looked up and saw their little group huddled miserably in the reception area. She walked over and Meg automatically stood up, holding her breath. Dolores had suffered a cardiac arrest as they waited for the first responders and it was only the presence of a doctor in the crowd, who had given her heart massage until they arrived, that had kept her alive.

'Dolores has been very lucky – it could have been a lot, lot worse. The bear only just clipped her but she still suffered a deep laceration to the neck, missing the carotid artery by a couple of millimetres. We've stitched her up and started her on a course of antibiotics for the risk of infection.'

'When can we take her home?' Meg asked quickly.

'I'm afraid not for a few days. We need to keep her in to monitor her vitals. Even though she's in great shape for her age, the fact remains she's an elderly lady and the trauma of the attack has put her body under enormous strain.'

'Oh, my Lord,' Barbara whimpered, pressing her hands in a steeple to her mouth.

'Can we see her?' Meg pressed.

'She's sedated at the moment but one of you can sit with her.'

'Me,' Meg said quickly and stepping forwards, before feeling guilty – Barbara and Dolores had been close friends for thirty or more years. 'Lucy will need you two,' she added to Barbara and Tuck.

'Is there any word yet on my daughter?' Barbara asked anxiously. 'She's pregnant. Twenty-one weeks. We should be in there with her. She needs us.'

The doctor nodded. 'I'll go and check for you.'

She walked away and Meg turned to Barbara and Tuck. 'I'll go and sit with Dolores. Let me know as soon as you know about Lucy?'

They nodded and she hurried away, her hiking boots clumpy on the polished floor.

She pushed the door open and stopped there, halted by the sight of her fearsome, fearless friend hooked up to wires in the bed. Her athletic figure – always put to use stacking boxes or climbing ladders or hiking with the town's senior rambling group – looked suddenly frail and small when it was inert, her skin crêpey on the upper arms, her face slack from the anaesthetic. Meg bit her lip, feeling the tears start, as she finally saw that Dolores's body was what her spirit was not: old.

She closed the door behind her and walked up to the bed, pulling a chair to the side and lightly clasping Dolores's hand.

A large dressing had been wrapped around Dolores's neck like a scarf, her face untouched, so that there was nothing really to show the horror of what they had lived through, fighting for their lives against an animal that could have killed each and every one of them with just a few lazy moves.

But it so nearly had killed Dolores, and Meg felt a shiver of cold ripple through her at the prospect of losing her tough-on-the-outside ally and friend. She'd lost so many of her family already; she didn't know how she would survive losing Dolores too.

'I'm here, Dolores,' Meg whispered, gripping her fingers tighter as though holding her up. 'You just rest. I'm here.'

Lucy stared upwards, her eyes following the criss-cross tracks of the ceiling tiles, a blanket draped over her. It was warm in the room but she couldn't stop shivering, her mind on a loop, replaying that moment when the bear had reared and lunged, over and over again. Every time she closed her eyes, she recalled the size of it, the smell . . . She gagged again, leaning over the side of the bed, head hanging over the bucket the nurses had brought in for her.

She fell back on the bed, her arms draped over her bump, a single tear sliding down her cheek. The baby wasn't even born and she had failed it. She had done nothing to protect herself, just frozen on the spot. If it hadn't been for Dolores roaring and jumping about, demanding the bear came after *her*, Meg screaming in terror as she advanced with her arm outstretched . . . they had saved her, both of them – *they* had saved the baby and she, the mother, had done nothing, she'd just lain on the ground and waited.

Who was she kidding? She couldn't do this, she couldn't be a mother! She wasn't fit to look after this child, she didn't deserve to. Because this wasn't the only time she'd endangered it – every slap or punch, every kick or shove . . . And every time it happened, it got a little worse. She and Tuck were heading down a path from which there was no good outcome, she knew that, and yet— She rubbed the tear away angrily, hating herself, despising her own weakness, knowing he was a drug she needed, a man she could not leave.

The nurse walked back in with some fresh water and anti-sickness pills, Tuck barrelling in after her, his eyes as wide as if the bear were chasing *him*.

'Oh, baby, thank Christ,' he cried, rushing to her and enveloping her into his chest, his hands cradling her head against his heart, his lips in her hair. 'I thought I'd lost you. Both of you.'

She wrapped her arms around him, feeling him pinning her to him as fresh tears skidded down her cheeks.

'I'm going to make everything right between us,' he whispered urgently as she sobbed, his breath hot against her scalp. 'I'm going to change. Things will be how they used to be. I'll be the man you both deserve, you'll see. This is our second chance.'

She pulled away, knowing his apologies were groundless. He wasn't the one who had to change; it was all *her* fault – she pushed too hard, wanting too much from him, wanting it to be perfect. He wiped away her tears and she sank back against the mattress, for once wishing he wouldn't touch her; she had been poked and prodded all afternoon, the nurses taking blood tests and urine samples to check for foetal distress, wheeling her off for scans to check for internal trauma, everyone wanting something from her. She had sprained her wrist as she landed on the ground and she felt bruised and stiff, marked out as a failure.

'They said the baby's OK?' Tuck said, pressing the back of his hand to her cheek the way her father used to do when she'd been a little girl, running a temperature.

She could only nod. It was down to no credit of her own that either she or this child had survived.

His eyes took in her silence, her tears, her rare frailty and he reached a hand towards her, tenderly. 'Baby, I . . . I know I've let you down. I've been distant and . . . and angry,' he said, watching as she stared at the wall, clutching her hand and pressing it to his lips, trying to get her to look at him. 'I haven't known how to deal with . . . all these feelings. It's like there's just been too much, you know? I got confused. Everything that happened that night . . . it was such a goddam mess. I . . . I've been so angry, I know, acting like it was your fault –' she gasped, looking up at him finally. 'But of course it wasn't, you couldn't have known. I just . . . needed someone else to blame. I couldn't face up to what I'd done.' He kissed her fingers again, desperation in the gesture, his cheeks wet against her hand. 'But I've learned, Lucy. This has been my wake-up call. I miss my friend but I don't know what I'd do if I lost you and the baby. You're my wife. We're going to be a family.' He clasped her head in both his hands, gazing down into her eyes, no shadows there today. 'This is our turning point. We can make things good again, I know we can.'

She blinked back at him, feeling as though she was in a tunnel, his voice sounding far, far away. She wanted to believe him but she was running out of faith—

'How's Dolores?' she asked, in barely more than a croak. The screaming had shredded her voice.

'Dolores?' Tuck looked baffled that she should ask. 'I don't know. All I could think about was you. You two.'

'Where's my mom and Meg?' she asked, so quietly that Tuck had to lean in to hear.

'Your mom's outside. Meg's in with Dolores.'

'So then . . . that must be a good sign, right?' she whispered, another wave of tears overwhelming her as she thought again of what the older woman had done for her – selflessly, bravely, without a moment's hesitation, saved her when she'd been unable to save herself, just a coward lying on the ground . . . 'If . . . if it was bad, they wouldn't let anyone in, would they?'

'They said the claw missed her artery by a couple of millimetres but she's gonna be fine.'

'A couple of . . . ? Oh my God,' Lucy sobbed. She went to pull the blanket off her, to get up. 'I've got to see her.'

'You can't!' Tuck cried, holding the blanket down and

pinning her in place. 'You gotta rest. They're still monitoring the baby. Please Luce – just do what the doctors say. For
the baby's sake.'

She stopped resisting, her body falling slack, and he
relaxed again. 'Anyway, they've got her drugged up at the
moment. I don't think she's awake.'

Reluctantly, she let him push her back against the mattress, lying still as he fussed with her pillows, pulling the
blanket up tight and tucking her in. He kissed the top of her
head, marvelling over her as though she was divinely sent,
this loving cameo a counterpoint to their relationship acted
out behind closed doors.

It was a dynamic she knew too well, a story she'd already
lived through once before in her short lifetime. At what
point, she wondered, had they tipped from the light into the
dark? Long before Mitch had died, that was for sure. For the
first few years, it had felt like they were living the dream –
she was dating the school's bad boy/pretty boy, the town's
local hero. But as the magic dimmed and frustrations set in,
things began to change – just small triggers at first, like irritation if dinner wasn't ready. But it had steadily grown, the
tenor of the relationship changing, the catalysts for the vio-
lence becoming not bigger but smaller, until she'd realized
one day that actually, no reason was needed at all, that their
light couldn't exist *without* the dark – they could only make
love after the hate, laugh after the tears . . .

'Say something, baby,' he entreated, his voice a whisper
as he watched her profile, wondering where she'd gone.
'Tell me you believe me. Things are going to be better. We'll
get back to the old days. I know things have been bad but
we're through the worst now, we can get past this. I know
we can.'

Lucy looked at him, a solitary tear tracking its way down her cheek. Did he really believe that? Were his words true to him? Weren't their natures now fixed?

She turned her head, her gaze falling to the window that looked out onto the nurses' station. The blind was pulled down but the slats were flat, allowing a striated view through, and she felt her tear halt its march as her mother blinked back at her. Seeing it all. Understanding it all.

After all, it took one to know one.

Chapter Sixteen

Wednesday 26 July 2017

'You are to go. None of this nonsense.' Dolores's voice was firm.

'But, Dolores—'

'Don't you "But, Dolores" me. It's ridiculous that they're keeping me in this long as it is. I feel perfectly fine. I'm not having you miss your holiday on my account.'

'It's only Toronto. I can rebook. I can go any time.'

'Yes, you can. But do you?' Dolores arched an eyebrow. 'When was the last time you left the state?'

Meg opened her mouth to reply, but as she realized the answer, closed it again.

'And besides, you know perfectly well your sister probably won't take another break until the next leap year. She is to rest what you are to travel.' Dolores chuckled, shaking her head from side to side in amusement. 'Honestly, what a pair you are.'

Meg sighed, her coffee cup now cooling in her hands. 'Dolores, you were attacked by a bear.'

'Oh, trust me, I remember.'

Meg smiled, the smile turning into a giggle. 'I can't believe you were actually *drawing* it towards you. I mean, are you insane? "Here, bear, chase me, chase me!"'

'Says the girl who walked straight towards it.' Dolores shrugged. 'Anyway, better me dead than you girls. I've had my time.'

'No, you haven't!' Meg cried. 'You'd told Barbara only that morning that you had no plans to shuffle off this mortal coil just yet.'

'And I don't, but if it's an either/or situation . . .' Her eyes softened as she looked at Meg. 'You haven't got started yet. Your whole life is ahead of you. You need to start living it.'

'I am.'

'I mean properly.' She smiled but her eyes were sad. 'You're just sleepwalking at the moment, Meg. It's time to wake up and see the world. Really see it.'

Meg didn't reply. She didn't want to argue – Dolores was nowhere near as strong as she'd like to pretend – but why did everyone insist on making out as though she was only living half a life? Dolores, Ronnie . . . ? Her fiancé was dead. The life she was supposed to be living had been snatched away at the eleventh hour. Was it really so surprising if she didn't quite know her next step?

Dolores closed her eyes, looking tired again. It had been three days since the accident and although the wound was healing nicely, the doctors still weren't happy with her stats, her blood pressure erratically peaking at dangerously high levels. 'Promise me you'll go.'

Meg stayed silent.

Dolores opened one eye. 'Promise me. Or I'll die here just to spite you.'

'Fine,' Meg replied with a groan. 'But I'm going to be

calling daily and if they say you've so much as sneezed, I'll be on the first plane back.'

Dolores chuckled. 'You're stubborn, you know that?'

'Ha! Pot. Kettle. Black!' Meg laughed, holding her hand and squeezing it tightly.

Dolores sank her head back into the pillow. 'How's Jonas?'

Meg smiled. Jonas appeared to be Dolores's new favourite topic. 'He's fine.'

'Heard from him?'

'Yes, he emailed last night.'

'And what's he got to say for himself this time? You know, for a man stuck on a spaceship, he sure is talkative.'

'Shall I read it to you?'

'Well, there's nothing better to do in this godforsaken place . . . A postcard from space will have to do.'

Meg chuckled, pulling out her smartphone and finding the message. Dolores loved Jonas's galactic perspective almost as much as Meg.

'*Hi Dog-Dog-Ellie.*' Meg paused, eyebrows cocked. 'He's taken to greeting me like this now. He thinks it's hilarious that I don't know the proper thingies for call signs.'

'So do I,' Dolores grinned. 'I shall have to teach you. Go on.'

'*Sorry I haven't been able to write before now. Things are mad here with getting ready for our return on Friday. I feel more like a cleaner than an astronaut, wrapping and packing away all the waste that we need to bring with us back to Earth. We've even had to stop playing our bubble-wrap game because it's all stowed now—*' Meg looked back at Dolores. 'Did I tell you about that? The bubble wrap's stored in the Japanese module, out of the way, and they have timed races after dinner for who can take a piece there and get back in the shortest amount of time?'

'Such children,' Dolores groaned, clearly loving the sound of it.

Meg went back to reading again. *'Although Sergei still plays his guitar any chance he gets and most of us just go to the cupola every time we've got a few minutes, to take more pictures. It's hard to believe that after six months, we've now got less than two days left to enjoy this view. I'm not sure any of the pictures I've taken will ever convey what it actually feels like to be up here; words aren't enough either. I think it's because space is so beyond the human experience, we just aren't equipped to convey it. We talk about the physicality of it – weightlessness, lack of oxygen . . . but every time I look out and see the huge curve of the Earth, that thin disc of gold as another dawn breaks just over the horizon, it's my spirit that is stirred. I think it's not just scientists they should bring up here but priests and rabbis and imams, philosophers, politicians, world leaders . . . The world is ruled by money and divided by religion but when you see the planet from out here, you understand there's more to humanity than "just" physics and the physical.*

'Hey, listen to me! Quite the philosopher, huh?

'*But as much as I'll be sad to leave, I can't wait to get back. Fresh fruit and vegetables! Running water! The thought of a shower is almost more than I can handle—*'

Meg looked at Dolores again. 'Because remember, water just floats up there. It doesn't hit your skin,' she explained.

Dolores gave a look of distaste. 'Ghastly.'

'*The wind, trees, flowers, grass. The weather – rain, snow, sunshine. And smells! Colours. Noise. Even taste. Everything tastes bland up here. I can't wait to have some pickled mackerels. I can't wait to see my dog Yuri and go for a run with him on the beach and go out sailing. Before I came up, I was most excited about floating all the time but now my feet miss contact with the Earth. It's going to be good to be grounded again.*

'How are things with you? Did you go on the walk to the hot springs in the end? I hope Lucy got on OK, it sounds like she's having a tough time—'

'Didn't you tell him about the bear attack?' Dolores interrupted.

Meg shook her head. 'No. I wrote before it happened.'

'And not since?'

'Well someone's got to sit with you – to stop you from snoring if nothing else.'

Dolores cracked a smile – laughing wasn't allowed yet. 'He'll be wondering where you've gone.'

'I'm not the one on a galactic walkabout. It's pretty obvious I don't go anywhere.'

'And are you going to tell him about this?'

'No!' Meg protested, wrinkling her nose.

'But why not?'

'He'll think I'm a walking disaster.'

'*Why?*'

'Well, you know – first Mitch, now . . .' Her voice trailed off.

'Oh, I see. Calamity is your middle name.' Dolores arched an eyebrow. 'But did you bait the bear? Did you run off with its cubs? Did you drizzle yourself in honey?'

Meg laughed. 'No!'

'Exactly. It just happened. Shit happens – isn't that the phrase?'

'I know, but this isn't something I just want to . . . gossip about. It's not some story to bandy about in an email as entertainment.'

'Why not? Everyone's OK,' Dolores scoffed.

'You could have died, Dolores.'

'But I didn't. Listen to me, I'm seventy-three years old and I survived a bear attack! *I* intend to tell anyone who'll listen! Maybe it's different for you – you're still young – but once you get to my age, people spend their time looking back and telling their old stories.' She shook her head. 'No. This is the best thing to happen to me in years. I've got a new story to tell! *This* will liven up my craps nights no end.'

Meg chuckled, squeezing Dolores's hand again. 'Fine. I'll tell him about it then.' She looked back at the email, trying to pick up her place again. 'Ummm . . . Oh, yeah. Lucy. *It sounds like she's having a tough time. Tell her she's like me – on a countdown too! It won't last for ever. As a clever man once said, "This too shall pass."*

'Enjoy Toronto. Go to Soho House for cocktails if you get a chance. I went last year when I was visiting for an International Astronautical Conference – yes, it really was as fascinating as it sounds! – and loved the place.

'You'll have a great time. I know you're nervous about leaving home but if nothing else, one of the best things about travelling is getting to go home again. You have to leave in order to be able to come back, right?'

'He's wise. I like him,' Dolores muttered. 'How old did you say he is again?'

'Going by his photo, I'm guessing mid-thirties. Could be wrong though.'

Dolores tutted, at her evasiveness, Meg knew.

'I won't be able to write now till after we land and things are going to get pretty crazy for the next few days, so don't worry if I'm radio silent for a few days – assuming I don't get turned into a crisp, of course.

'In the event that I <u>am</u> frazzled – and that really would suck – I want you to know I've loved our talks. Our friendship has become one of the defining experiences of this expedition, which isn't something I anticipated when we blasted off in February. The rest of the crew have been jealous as hell of my bad-joke-telling, airwaves-hijacking pen pal in the Canadian Rockies. You're a really great girl, Meg Saunders.

'Over, but not out (I hope),

'Jonas x

'PS. Assuming you're going to try to tune in and have a laugh at my best Kazakh impression, I will try to wave if I can lift my arms.

'PPS Heard the one about the Englishman and the Irishman in Vegas sitting on a bench? The Englishman turns to the Irishman and asks, "Which do you think is further? Florida or the moon?"

'The Irishman turns to his friend and says, "Hello? Can you see Florida from here?"'

'On behalf of my Irish grandmother, that's a terrible joke,' Dolores muttered.

'I know. He's full of them,' Meg said, giving a careless shrug as she closed the email, but her heart was pounding again from the emotions it had stirred – every time she read it (and she'd read it a lot, whilst Dolores slept) she felt profound shock that he thought she was a great girl, surprise that he'd signed off with a kiss, but mainly fear.

Fear that he was going to die.

Fear that he was going to land.

Chapter Seventeen

Friday 28 July 2017

Ronnie was hard to miss as Meg walked out into the arrivals hall and it wasn't just on account of the banner. Or the balloons. (Anyone would think *she* was coming from space, not Banff.)

'Oh, my God,' Meg grinned, embarrassed, as her little sister ran towards her, arms out and squealing excitedly. 'A bear suit? *Really?*'

Ronnie took the head off with a 'Ta-da!' flourish. 'Hey, I've barely taken this thing off. I've done rounds in it – paeds only, obviously. Don't want to finish off the old dears on the geriatric ward. I've been dining out on your adventure all week. My sister, the bear hunter!'

'Hardly that. I cried like a baby.'

Ronnie grinned, enveloping her in a hug. 'I'm just so glad you're OK.'

'Well, clearly being greeted by you dressed as a bear is going to help me confront my demons.'

'Right? That's what I thought! We've got to face our fears!' Ronnie laughed, giving Meg her bear head to hold and taking Meg's wheelie bag from her grasp instead, leading them towards the car park, their arms linked.

Meg tilted her face to the sky as they walked outside, the tenor and palette of the urban landscape entirely different from the one she'd left barely four hours earlier – the emerald waters of the mineral-rich Rocky lakes now switched for the sea-like mass of Lake Ontario disappearing over the horizon; the busy chatter of seagulls replacing the singular cries of the high-flying bald eagles; and the ring of granite mountain ranges that hemmed in and preserved her little home town superseded by a bar graph of skyscrapers, the galactically inspired CN Tower standing tallest, sharpest and proudest of all. It wasn't her first time to the big city, obviously not, but it had been so long since she'd been here, she felt daunted by the sheer density of Toronto.

Ronnie moved out into the traffic with practised ease, carelessly glancing over her shoulder as she pulled into a six-lane highway, overtaking on this side and that in a kind of waltz, her fingers tapping on the wheel as Chum FM played on the radio.

Meg looked out the window at the buildings whizzing past, recognizing the splashy boutiques of designer names that she only usually heard about in magazines, sensing an energy in the walks of all those people hurrying up and down the pavements.

'Here we are,' Ronnie said forty minutes later, pulling up outside a tall white L-shaped tower block. 'Home Sweet Home.'

'You live in *there*?' Meg asked in astonishment, looking up.

'Yep.' Ronnie jumped out of the car and popped open the boot, oblivious to the enquiring looks of passers-by as she pulled out the wheelie bag wearing a headless bear suit. If nothing else, it was almost six in the evening and still eighty-seven degrees.

'But how can you afford it? It looks so expensive!'

Ronnie groaned. 'Wait till you see the inside before you make assumptions. This is what a junior doctor's salary gets you in the city.'

'Well, I bet it's a palace compared to my little cabin . . .' Meg sighed, those feelings of inadequacy which Lucy had warned her about beginning to spring up.

Four minutes later, Meg was blowing out through her cheeks, head nodding and hands on her hips as she looked around at the forty-seven-square-metre space where the sofa doubled as the spare bed and the main bed was a mattress on the floor of the mezzanine which had been slotted into the cavity above the bathroom; the kitchen itself was a metre-long worktop with an oven and fridge beneath and a shelf above, just a leg length away from the sofa. 'Well,' Meg grinned. 'I can see now why you're never in when I call.'

'Exactly,' Ronnie laughed, stepping out of the bear suit and letting it collapse in a heap on the floor, instantly cluttering the flat. 'Damn, that thing was hot. It's no time to be wearing fur,' she said, fanning herself lightly. 'Talking of which, who's got Badge while you're here?' she asked, reaching up to her shelf and bringing down two chunky wine glasses.

'Lucy and Tuck.'

Ronnie splashily poured almost the entire contents of a bottle of Chianti into them. 'And how is Lucy? She getting on OK?'

'Yeah, they kept her in for the first night just to observe the baby. It was showing some signs of distress when she first came in but everything seems to be fine now.' Meg watched her. 'Tell me something, though – how did you know Lucy was pregnant that day? She was only just over a month gone!'

Ronnie paused with the pouring as she thought back. 'Her breasts were bigger, she kept running to the loo, she wasn't drinking wine, she looked pale . . .'

'Yes, but a *month*? How is that possible?'

Ronnie gave a sheepish look. 'Fine. I may have slightly overheard her throwing up in the loos.'

'She could have just been drunk. Or eaten a dodgy clam.'

'Well, I may have caught a glimpse of a pregnancy kit in her bag in church too,' she said, handing Meg an almost-full wine glass and curling up on the poppy-red sofa beside her.

'So you mean you guessed?'

'Something like that.'

'And dropped her in it, before she'd told another living soul?'

Ronnie bit her lip. 'Possibly.'

'It was hardly the day for it,' Meg said quietly.

Ronnie swallowed. 'I know, and I felt like such a bitch as soon as I'd done it. I'm so sorry, Meg, really I am. She just . . . she just needles me all the time; little sub-radar comments that I can't call her on without looking petty or hysterical – or both. Not that that's any excuse, I know. I'm *honestly* really sorry, hand on heart. I promise never to rise to her provocations again.'

Meg sighed, shaking her head. *Never the twain shall meet.*

'Anyway, let's not dwell on that horridness. Let's only think positive thoughts this weekend. Chin-chin,' Ronnie said, changing the subject swiftly and holding up her goblet for a toast. 'I can't actually believe you made it.'

'Cheers!' Meg smiled, clearing her mind and coming back to the present. 'I'm so happy to be here.'

'Well, it's only taken six years! I guess it could have been worse.'

Meg gave a guilty look, taking a sip of her wine, but the glass was so full some of it spilled over the sides, splashing her Patagonia T-shirt.

'And you're still shopping where you work, I see. Clearly you've never heard of the Internet?' Ronnie quipped.

Meg stuck out her tongue. 'Ha-ha! You know perfectly well Dolores gives me a seventy per cent discount. It's not worth going anywhere else.'

'Oh, trust me, it so is. In fact, that's something we can do while you're here. I know some shops that would have great stuff for you – especially now you're *so* skinny.' She playfully squeezed Meg's knee. 'Although don't get any skinnier, okay?'

'Don't you start,' Meg groaned. 'I just found out Dolores has been putting baby formula in my coffee to fatten me up!' She grimaced. 'I thought it tasted strange.'

Ronnie chuckled. 'Good old Dolly.'

'She'd kill you if she overheard you calling her that. And you don't mess with Dolores – she bullies bears!' Meg laughed at her own joke but there was an edge to her laughter every time she tried to make light of the incident. Dolores might be dining out on the story but the truth was, Meg saw that pale furred belly, the glistening teeth, the gruesome claws, most nights when she closed her eyes.

'I'm glad she's getting better.'

'Me too. I've been so worried about her. I don't think I've ever seen Dolores stay in one place for so long before.'

'I'll bet she's driving the doctors nuts. She's probably

trying to harass her way out of there – get them so fed up of her, they discharge her just for the peace and quiet. It happens, you know.'

Meg chuckled. 'It wouldn't surprise me.' She was sitting with her left arm outstretched on the back of the sofa and her gaze fell to the view outside the window.

'Now you can see why I don't miss the views back home,' Ronnie said as she saw what Meg saw: row upon row of block windows, not a bird or a plant or a cloud to be seen.

'Do you know many of your neighbours?' Meg asked, looking upwards, the tower block rising to an eighty-degree angle before she could see sky.

'Many? Try any?' Ronnie shook her head. 'It's not like that here. People in this block are mainly young professionals like me – up early, home late, socializing elsewhere. We only really come back here to sleep.'

'And that's OK?'

'It is what it is.'

Meg looked back around the apartment. Apart from the red blocky sofa-bed, there was a tufted multicoloured replica of a Moroccan Aziz rug on the floor and some black-and-white framed Steven Meisel prints on the walls, along with an anatomical poster showing a dissected brain. A pair of running trainers peeped out of a rattan shoe-storage box by the bin beside the fridge, and the blue duvet for the mezzanine bed bulged slightly through the wooden balustrades.

'You should at least get a plant.'

'What? To remind me of home?'

'No, for company!' Meg was beginning to giggle.

'Best not – it wouldn't do much for my professional reputation. I hear people don't like their doctors to be unable to keep things alive.'

They laughed again.

'You know, it's been so long since we've had any proper time, just the two of us, I'd almost forgotten how much we laugh together,' Ronnie sighed, resting her head in her hand.

Meg wrinkled her nose. 'Sorry. That's my fault.'

'No, it isn't.'

'Come on, I've hardly been fun to be around these past four months.'

'It would have been creepy if you were,' Ronnie said, squeezing her knee. 'I just meant, I always seem to say the wrong thing when I'm back home. And that's not on you, it's me – it's like I don't fit there any more. I feel like I've got all these sharp edges and hard angles when I'm back. And yet, when I'm here in the city, I feel like a country girl, never quite hip enough, always turning up to the cool bar a month too late.'

'*You?* But you're so cool! Lucy and I always dissect your hairstyle and your shoes for at least a fortnight after you've gone.'

Ronnie glanced up from lowered eyes but looked away again. 'Oh, I don't think that Lucy would be seen dead in something I've worn.'

'That's where you're wrong! She's always asking after you, wanting to know if we've spoken and what you're up to out here.' Meg gave a big shrug. 'What can I say? We're living vicariously through you.'

'Huh,' Ronnie snorted. 'Well, if working nineteen-hour shifts and living in a box does it for you, go ahead, be my guest.'

'Are you still seeing that guy?' Meg asked, tucking her knees in tighter.

'Which one?'

'The trainee fishmonger.'

'Oh. No. Turns out our skill with a knife was about the only thing we had in common.' Ronnie gave a laugh, dismissing the subject as she always did. 'So what do you fancy doing tonight? Are you tired from the journey? We could do film and a takeout here. There's a great Vietnamese place down the block. Or we could go out somewhere—'

'"In" sounds perfect,' Meg said quickly. 'I'm not used to travelling so . . .'

'Great. I'm pretty wiped myself. A night on the couch with my big sis is just the tonic. You find us a film whilst I –' she leaned forward and poured the remains of the wine into their glasses, before padding over to the kitchen – 'get us some more drinks.'

Meg picked up the TV remote and switched it on. Naturally, it was set to the news channel. Her sister had never watched a soap opera or reality TV show in her life. 'What do you feel like?' Meg asked, staring at the remote and trying to find the programmes button. Was she holding it upside down?

'Not a horror! I know what you're like but I see enough blood in my day job, thanks,' Ronnie called, struggling with the wine opener.

'Ewww, no, why would you think I'd watch something like that?'

'Well, you always used to. Every weekend, the four of you would hide out in the den and delight in terrifying yourselves. I could hear you and Lucy screaming from my room – and I was in the roof!'

Meg smiled at the memory as she began flicking through the channels. 'God, I'd forgotten about that,' she murmured, remembering how Mitch used to blow on her neck just at the very worst moments, making her jump even higher. They'd been – what? Seventeen then? Eighteen? 'Well, happily I have outgrown those. How about a thriller? Or do you want a romance?'

'Ha, do I!' Ronnie finally pulled out the cork and brought the bottle over. 'Hey, did I see they're running—?' She stopped as she caught sight of Meg's face. 'What is it?'

'Jonas.'

'Who?' Ronnie looked across at the screen, sinking slowly onto the red sofa and trying to make out who Meg was referring to. All she could see was a picture of a space station, which then cut to old footage of a group of astronauts walking in their orange spacesuits, presumably towards the shuttle; which then cut to dramatic footage of a rocket taking off, huge engines blasting it away from the Earth. Then the presenters were talking in a studio, lots of men in suits looking serious; and then another shot of stressed-looking people in shirtsleeves all looking up at a big screen. The word *LIVE* was printed on the top corner of that grab.

'Jonas. He's on board.'

'Uh – who's Jonas?' Ronnie asked, refilling their glasses.

'My friend,' Meg murmured, her eyes reading the ticker tape that ran along the bottom of the screen. She gasped suddenly, her hands to her mouth. 'Oh, God, no!' It had been on her mind all day but . . . but she'd never thought anything might go wrong. Not really. This was NASA, the ESA!

'What?' Ronnie asked again in alarm, handing over the glass and trying to catch up with the story. 'What's a ballistic re-entry?'

Meg looked at her. 'It's the very worst thing that could

happen! It means they're coming in too fast or at the wrong angle.'

They watched in silence as more old footage was played, grainy and faded, showing a metal object dangling below a parachute and coming to rest, bumpily, in a desert. Ronnie glanced over at her. 'Sorry – how do you know an *astronaut*?'

Meg paused, her eyes fixed on the screen. 'He's the guy who answered my Mayday call the night Mitch was killed.'

Ronnie looked at Meg in utter amazement. 'An *astronaut*? Seriously?'

'Mitch's radio was the only way I could contact anyone and they . . . well, they were in range.' She inhaled deeply as the memories came flooding back. 'He relayed the message to his control centre and they alerted Search and Rescue. The team got to me before just dawn when the weather broke.'

'And now you and he are friends?'

Meg didn't appear to hear, her concentration focused solely on the television. 'Uh . . . we email, chat on the radio if we can get through.' She glanced at Ronnie. 'It felt like he understood, because he'd been part of it, you know? He was easy to talk to.'

Ronnie shifted onto her knees, eyes bright with excitement and indignation. 'And how come this is the first I've heard of it? You've never even mentioned him.'

Meg's eyes were back on the screen again. What was happening up there, out there? 'It wasn't a secret.' But only Dolores had been particularly interested – Lucy's eyes glazed over whenever Meg mentioned him – and even with her, Meg hadn't wanted to read out all their correspondence; some she had wanted to keep just for herself.

Her hands flew to her mouth again. 'Oh, my God, what are they saying? What's that?'

She pointed. The cameras had cut to a new shot, LIVE printed in the top corner again. It was of a desert, nine-tenths of the image taken up by sky and in the middle of it, a tiny black dot.

'Christ, it's fast,' Ronnie muttered.

'This is where they need to execute de-orbit burn,' Meg said with a frantic tone. Her heart was pounding. How could this be *entertainment*? 'It's what makes them decrease speed and land on the correct re-entry path. Get it wrong and they'll burn up or be bounced into deeper space.'

'. . . *travelling at 120 miles per second right now . . .*' the TV presenter said.

'It'll drop to 800 km an hour when they get to 10.5 km altitude,' Meg murmured, as though speaking to the presenter.

'I can't believe you know all this,' Ronnie murmured, agog.

'I told you. We talked.' Meg was chewing on her nails, both hands clasped in front of her.

'So how do they de-orbit burn, then?'

'There's an engine that fires for exactly four minutes forty-five seconds, venting excess fuel and weight – that helps, but the atmosphere basically acts as a brake. The Soyuz capsule will break up into three parts – the orbital module, the descent module and the instrument compartment. They're in the descent module – the other parts burn up. When they're coming through the atmosphere, they're travelling at the speed of sound but by the time the parachute deploys, they'll be down to twenty-two km an hour.'

'Jesus! You sound like an astrophysicist!' Ronnie laughed. 'Did you get a PhD off him?'

Meg pointed at the screen. 'Look! Do you see that? Those fiery sparks? They're the parts that aren't needed for landing. They're disintegrating, just like he said they would.'

'Well, that must be good then, right? If it's doing what he said.'

Meg chewed a fingernail. 'As long as the speed is right.'

'Can he see what's going on?'

'I don't know. I don't think so.'

'How long does it take them to land?'

'Once they're back in the atmosphere, just under an hour. Fifty-five minutes, I think he said.'

They watched the tiny black dot grow larger, moving so, so fast. It was almost incomprehensible that anyone could be in it.

Meg chewed another nail, feeling sick. In spite of Jonas's self-deprecating comments about wearing the Kazakh costumes, she'd thought he'd been joking – or exaggerating. It had never occurred to her that this would be televised, that she could sit on a sofa and just *watch* it.

The cameras cut again, this time bringing up head shots of the astronauts. There were three of them. The first was Sergei Taganovsky, the Russian cosmonaut and expedition leader. Jonas had mentioned him in a couple of emails (always playing the guitar and reigning champion of the bubblewrap races) and he looked almost exactly as she had pictured him – short, stocky, bald, with tiny eyes and a ready smile, he looked like the man who had grown up to live his boyhood dream. Miriam Goldenberg, the American, had a dark thick bob, warm brown eyes, olive skin, early forties? She looked probing and intelligent and insightful, but Jonas had told her she was badly missing her two kids. And then Jonas . . . her back straightened as his image came up.

'That's him? That's Jonas?' Ronnie spluttered, even though it quite clearly said *Jonas Solberg* at the bottom of his picture.

'That's him,' Meg murmured, pretending it was no big deal as she took in again his green eyes and fine nose, chiselled bone structure and military-style buzz cut.

'Yeah, 'cause you'd want to keep *him* a secret,' Ronnie laughed sarcastically. 'What a moose.'

They drank, Meg oblivious to the fact that she was sipping as the minutes ticked past, that tiny black dot growing larger and larger until, steadily, its shape became recognizable, the cameras able to zoom in, the heat on the outer surfaces creating a haze as it ripped through the sky.

'Oh, my God,' Ronnie murmured, in awe. 'How do they land that thing? I mean, how do you slow it down enough not to break every bone in their bodies?'

'That's the thing, you can't guarantee against it. They're in reclining seats which have been moulded especially around them, and there are shock absorbers that fire up on impact – sort of like airbags – pushing them back up again at the exact moment they touch Earth, but the force is still immense. Jonas said it feels like a head-on collision, even with all those safeguards in place.'

'Where even are they?' Ronnie asked, staring at the desert scenes and hiccupping slightly, pressing the back of her hand to her mouth and looking surprised.

'Kazakhstan.'

Ronnie arched an eyebrow. 'Why there?'

'Because it's big and flat and empty.'

'But how will they know where to find them?'

'They won't now. They'll have to use helicopters, Search and Rescue . . .'

The cameras had lost sight of the capsule. Having come in at the wrong angle or wrong speed, whatever it was, it wasn't going to land where it had been scheduled to, which meant that not only were there no cameras, but also no guarantees that there wouldn't be any obstacles in its path; there wouldn't be any emergency vehicles to get to them immediately and help them out; there'd be no one to cut the parachute ropes in case windy conditions dragged them off again . . .

Meg bit her lip, feeling sick as the television channel cut back to stock footage, the studio presenters all looking tense and sombre.

'What now?' Ronnie asked.

Meg shrugged. 'We wait. Once they land, the ground teams will be trying to get to them asap.'

They watched, silent and sipping wine, the Vietnamese dinner forgotten – at least for the moment, the menu unopened on the sofa as they listened to expert after expert offer an opinion as to what had gone wrong.

'Well, at least they didn't burn up or bounce onto Mars,' Ronnie said earnestly, slurring her words ever so slightly. ''Cause that would *suck*. Majorly.'

Meg looked sidelong at her. 'It's good to have you looking on the bright side,' she said. 'I can see your bedside manner is probably a thing to behold.'

Ronnie sat back and laughed. Meg chuckled too but her eyes were on the screen, waiting. The worst of the damage had passed. So long as their landing was good and he was OK . . . This was entertainment to everyone else, to Ronnie, but for Meg . . . he was her friend, her voice in the sky, her orbiting angel – the one radioing Mission Control in Houston for her, or warning of incoming storms . . .

After half an hour or more of waiting – another bottle opened – the *LIVE* box appeared on the screen again.

'Oh! Look!' Ronnie slurred, pointing to it as the cameras cut to the Soyuz capsule, now grounded, a huge orange parachute tangled and torn on the ground behind it. There were all sorts of vehicles clustered around it – fire engines, ambulances, jeeps – lights flashing . . . Some men in military uniform had placed a ladder against the side and were opening the hatch on the top.

They watched with bated breath as it was swung back and Meg thought of Jonas enjoying that very moment – fresh oxygen and sunlight flooding the cavity, the wind stirring the thick, still air they'd brought back with them from space. It felt like an age before anything happened, but then a hand appeared, and then a head – a bald one.

Ronnie started singing David Bowie's 'Starman', a wicked smile on her lips, but Meg was oblivious. She pressed her hands to her mouth as she saw the effects of gravity imposing itself on these bodies, which had lived without it for six months. Sergei came out first, pulled under the arms by the ground crew and carried to a waiting wheelchair, where he was covered with a blanket and some sort of crown. His legs didn't seem to work and his head appeared to be too heavy for his neck to support, lolling slightly as he tried to wave to the small assembled ground crew, all cheering. He was pale and couldn't seem to move his head in any direction – Meg knew, from what Jonas had told her, that that was the nausea kicking in.

Miriam came out second and it was the same for her, so Meg knew what to expect when Jonas finally emerged, limp and lean and very still. He looked different from his official photograph, the one she'd scrutinized, because of course his hair had grown in the time he'd been up there so that now it was shaggy and darker than she remembered, framing his face and making even more of a feature of his eyes. Or so it seemed to her, anyway.

She leaned in closer to the screen as she watched him being settled onto the chair, his head immobile but his eyes swivelling, taking in the vast, barren landscape, the scale of the distant hills, the denseness of the rocks, the colours of the desert, the feel of the wind on his face, the heat on his skin . . . And then, slowly, so slowly, he looked back up – up into the sky from which he had just fallen. *'The long, delirious, burning blue . . .'*

It was as though he was moving through water, every movement tiny and exhausting. He had told her about this – the extreme nausea that was induced as gravity immediately took hold of their bodies, the fluid in their brains still spinning from weightlessness. It would be several days before he would feel 'normal' again.

She watched, rapt, as he slowly looked back at the earthly panorama, at the assembled dignitaries and ground crews rushing about, his gaze finding the cameras trained upon him.

And as his hand raised in super-slow motion, just for her, Meg felt a sudden lurch in the pit of her stomach. Her rocket man was back on Earth.

Chapter Eighteen

Saturday 29 July 2017

It wasn't the strobe of light peeking from underneath the curtain and pooling on her face that woke her. Nor was it the traffic – sirens and car horns punctuating a background soundtrack of idling engines as they stopped at the lights below. It was the coffee machine, gurgling and frothing on an automatic timer, that made her wake with a start.

'Morning.' Ronnie's voice from on high was still thick with sleep, the word coming with visible effort as she struggled to sit up, before coming into view with hair that looked as though it had been carded by Russian weavers in her sleep.

Meg blinked up at her sister through the bars of the mezzanine, the duvet on her bed half off the mattress and inching towards the ladder.

'I think you look how I feel,' Meg mumbled, bringing a hand to her temple. 'Oh. I don't feel so good.'

'How do you think I feel?' Ronnie groaned. 'I've got to get down that ladder and right now, I can't even coordinate my eyes to blink.'

Meg smiled, falling back on the bed and curling into a foetal position, pulling the duvet tighter round her. But what the apartment lacked in size, it made up for in warmth and a second later she kicked it off again. 'Oh, my God, it's so hot in here,' she moaned. 'Why don't you sleep with the windows open?'

'I usually do. But I figured the traffic would wake you.'

Dozily, Meg gave a sort of grunt of appreciation, her mind slowly remembering last night's events. He was back. He was safe. He was gone.

The coffee machine continued to bubble.

'You couldn't get up and pour the coffee, could you?' Ronnie mumbled.

Meg made a strange close-to-death sound. Couldn't her sister tell she wasn't used to being hungover? That she'd lived the life of a nun for the past four months? 'Why me? I don't even know how to work that thing.'

'Because you're the closest.'

'Ugh,' Meg moaned. 'But you're the hostess.'

'I know, but you're the eldest.'

Meg smiled into her pillow and reluctantly got up. Some things never changed.

'God, I feel amazing,' Meg sighed, stretching out long in her chair, her face angled to the sun as the waiter took their menus away. The café was already full; they'd had to wait a quarter of an hour for a table and the queue was beginning to tail down the block now that brunchtime was seguing towards lunchtime. All around them were people *just like them* – twenty-somethings with ponytails and wearing exercise kit, rewarding themselves after a morning run or yoga class, Apple watches and Fitbits on their wrists, ear bud leads dangling down their chests, iPods strapped to arm wallets, as they laughed and chatted, meeting up with friends or lovers, and all the while, the queue shuffling slowly forwards in the midsummer sunshine. If that 'Saturday morning feeling' was a place, then that place was here.

Meg watched it all keenly, feeling the vibe buzz her bones as though a cable had been plugged into her and was charging her up. After their slow, somewhat broken start this morning, her hangover hadn't stood a chance against the refreshing waters of Lake Ontario – stand-up paddleboarding was harder than it looked and she had fallen in several times – and she wore the small damp patch blooming on her vest between her shoulder blades from where her wet hair dripped, as a sort of badge of honour, proof that she was like the rest of them – out there, *doing stuff*.

She had the same flushed complexion too, her muscles pleasantly heavy and wearied, and with Ronnie's kit on, Lululemon leggings and a boyfriend tee – her sister had flat-out refused to let her put on the shiny black Lycra cycling shorts she had packed – no one passing them would know she was an interloper from another world, just passing through. 'I never knew that would be so hard.'

'The SUP boarding? Best thing I know for getting rid of a hangover,' Ronnie said, pleased. 'Well, if you can't get a saline IV, obviously.'

'Do doctors really do that?'

'Of course,' Ronnie shrugged.

Meg looked around them again. They were sitting outside in the heart of Toronto's Mink Mile, so named in honour of the big-money designer boutiques that flanked this strip. The café's seating area was demarcated by neat box hedging trimmed to hip height, and calico awnings that rolled out from the wall cast a soothing shade over all the diners. On the windowsills were dense planters filled with herbs, and pinch-pots of Himalayan pink salt were placed on every teak-slatted table. Everything was so chic, Meg mused, taking in her surroundings with the eye of an outsider. It was casual and low-key – there was clearly no dress code – and yet, it had a level of sophistication that even the swankiest restaurant back home couldn't match. In Banff, quality of this level necessitated a suit, tie and small mortgage, but Ronnie just came here for brunch. She had ordered poached eggs and smashed avocado on rye, a green juice and a black coffee, and Meg had ordered exactly the same, not quite sure what a matcha crêpe or kimchi were. It was hard to believe she'd only come into the city from the mountains and not from another country altogether.

'I can't believe you've never tried SUP boarding – it's so much fun,' Ronnie said, crossing her legs and looking cute in her Nike aerosol-splash running tights and cobalt-blue vest. 'You've got the lakes right there.'

'You know me – I ski in winter and hike in the summer.'

'Yes, and you were doing that ten years ago! Expand your repertoire. You were good. A natural!' Ronnie said, smiling up at the waiter as he came back with a jug of water and a small bowl of dried-looking red berries. Meg stared at them, wondering what they were.

She tried one and instantly pulled a face at their sourness.

'Gojis,' Ronnie chuckled. 'They're an acquired taste.'

Meg quickly drank some water to get rid of the taste. 'I might give it a go when I get back. I bet Lucy would be great at it – we could do it together. All her years doing hockey mean she's got great balance.' Meg folded one hand over the other.

Ronnie arched an eyebrow. 'Aren't you forgetting something?'

'What?' She rolled her eyes. 'Oh, God, yes, of course. How could I have forgotten?'

'Actually, she'd be fine to do it as long as she was careful.'

But Meg wrinkled her nose. After Lucy's fall last week, she wasn't going to be taking any more chances. They'd all been badly shaken up.

'Or take Badger,' Ronnie said, watching her.

'Really?'

'Sure, as long as you get him to sit.' Ronnie giggled at a scenario clearly playing out in her mind. 'That would be so funny, him wandering up and down the board. You'd be in pronto.'

Meg chuckled too, amused by the thought of herself and Badger wobbling into the water. 'I'll investigate as soon as I get back.'

'Well, send me photos. I'll need proof.'

'Deal—'

'Ron?' The man's voice made them both look up. He was clutching a coffee, a newspaper folded under one arm and a small spaniel pulling on the other end of the lead. 'Hey, how are you? I thought it was you.'

'Hi, Jack!' Ronnie said brightly. 'I didn't know you had a dog?'

'Oh, I don't. But my elderly neighbour's just had a hip operation so I said I'd walk Pooky when I could.'

Ronnie arched an eyebrow. 'Pooky? The dog's called Pooky?'

'I know! It's terrible. Put it this way, I don't let her off the lead. No way am I calling out *that* name in public,' Jack laughed, his eyes falling to Meg as he noticed her sitting there. 'Oh, hey, sorry for interrupting.'

'Jack, this is my sister Meg. She's visiting from Alberta,' Ronnie said, motioning towards her. 'Meg, this is Jack Burrows – we work together at St Michael's. Jack's a trauma specialist.'

'Sounds alarming,' Meg said, holding out her hand. 'Pleased to meet you.'

'And you, Meg. Are you in town for long?' The dog strained on the lead, pulling his arm up, and he had to correct his balance.

'Just a few days. I'm leaving on Tuesday morning.'

'Where do you live in Alberta?'

'Banff.'

'Oh, wow,' he replied, his eyebrows up. 'Bear country.'

Meg paused and looked at Ronnie, who shook her head as if to say, '*Not me.*' She forced a smile as she looked back at him again. 'Exactly.'

Jack looked down at the dog, still pulling on the lead. 'Huh. So this must be a culture shock then. I don't suppose you get many men there walking miniature dogs called Pooky, do you?' He pulled his eyebrows down as though they were a cap on his brow. 'They're *men's* men over there, probably all have pet wolves.'

'Coyotes, actually – but yes,' Meg quipped, and they all laughed.

'Say, do you want to join us?' Ronnie asked, shooting an enquiring glance Meg's way.

Meg placidly shrugged her agreement but Jack was already looking regretful. 'Sadly I'm on my way back to drop this little princess home and then I'm meeting a friend for rackets. He's an out-of-towner too. Just here for the weekend.'

'Oh, that's a shame. Well, another time perhaps,' Ronnie smiled.

'Yes?' Jack asked, a note of surprise in his voice.

'It was a pleasure meeting you, Jack,' Meg smiled, looking up at him from behind shaded eyes.

Jack had to tear his eyes off her sister. 'And you, Meg. Enjoy Toronto. Especially enjoy the fact that you've got your sister to be your tour guide. I've never known her to leave that hospital.'

'Oh, right, 'cause you can talk,' came Ronnie's riposte as he allowed Pooky to lead him off, grinning.

Ronnie was grinning too.

Meg leaned in on her elbows and watched her sister watch him go. 'Well, he was *nice*.'

If Ronnie noticed her sister's heavy irony, she didn't show it. 'I know, isn't he?'

Their food arrived and both sat back in their seats to make room for the plates to be set down.

'And how long have you known him?' Meg asked, wondering what the orange powder was that had been sprinkled on her eggs.

Ronnie looked thoughtful. 'Seven months? Maybe a bit longer? He came from TGH . . . Toronto General,' she specified when Meg looked back at her blankly.

'He's nice.'

Ronnie, who had been sprinkling the pink salt on her eggs, looked up at her. 'You've said that already.' She flicked her eyes towards the eggs. 'That's paprika, by the way.'

'Oh, yeah,' Meg said quickly. 'I knew that.' She began to eat – it was heavenly! The best thing she'd tasted in months, although the Vietnamese takeout they'd finally had last night had been a winner too; her appetite, it appeared, had woken up. 'So . . .' She dragged the word out suggestively.

'What?'

'What? *Really?*' Meg teased. 'You obviously get on well together and he's super-cute. He's clearly into you.'

Ronnie studied her breakfast with rare interest. 'Don't be daft.'

'Daft? He didn't even notice I was sitting here at first.' She pulled a teasing face. 'He only had eyes for you, sister dearest. Has anything ever, you know . . . ?'

'Of course not.' Ronnie tutted, but a small blush was beginning to creep up her neck.

'Why "of course"?'

'Because he's a resident, for one thing. And because . . .' Her voice trailed off. There were no more becauses.

'You should call him.'

'Don't be ridiculous. I'm not asking him out.'

Meg chuckled. 'And you call me a small-town girl? Of course you can ask him out!'

'He's senior at work. There's no way—' Just then, Ronnie's phone beeped. She picked it up and read the text, her expression changing to one of surprise. 'Crap, I don't believe it. It's him.'

'And?' Meg asked, eyes bright.

Ronnie looked up at her in amazement. 'He's asking if we want to meet him and his friend at Soho House tonight?'

It was Meg's turn to look surprised, the smile fading from her lips. 'What, you mean like a . . . double date?'

'No!' Ronnie pooh-poohed quickly. 'This isn't a date.'

'Yes, it is. You like him, he clearly likes you. It's totally a date.'

Ronnie bit her lip. 'Well, will you come?'

'No. Because it's a date. And *I'm* not doing dating.' Her tone was light but Mitch's face was flashing through her mind like a beacon, the warning sirens in her brain louder than those of the ambulance going past on Yonge Street.

'Well, I'm not going without you,' Ronnie sighed, giving a careless little shrug.

'Ron!' Meg scolded.

'What?'

'You have to go!'

'I can't. The invitation was to us both. He's meeting his friend. I can hardly very well turn up on my own, now, can I?'

'But—'

'It's fine. You're not doing dating. I get it.'

Meg stared at her sister, not fooled for one second by this nonplussed routine; on the other hand, there was no way Ronnie *could* turn up on her own. She slumped, knowing that she – and she alone – stood in the way of her sister's potential happiness. 'Well, there has to be a code word for if I want to split,' she said reluctantly.

Ronnie hooked an eyebrow, eyes glinting with mischief. 'Code word? I like it. What though?'

'Ummm . . .' They both looked around, searching for inspiration.

'Got it!' Ronnie squealed, her eyes alighting on the menu. '"Chorizo"!'

'"Chorizo"? How am I supposed to casually drop that into conversation?' Meg cried. She put on a voice. '"Oh, I see, Jack's friend, you're a tree surgeon? Oh, oh, specializing in conifers, you say? And tell me, do you like chorizo? Because personally I prefer a chipolata myself."'

Ronnie laughed, throwing her head back and attracting

an admiring glance from the guy at the next table. Didn't her sister realize how gorgeous she was? Meg wondered as she grinned back. 'All right, all right, point taken. It's too obscure. It needs to be an everyday word.'

'But not one that might naturally come up in the course of a conversation.'

'So, everyday but not common.' Ronnie bit her lip. 'So not "table"? . . . Or "broom"? . . . "Feather"? . . . "Swing"?'

'"Swing"! *"Swing"*? I didn't realize "chorizo" was the high point!' Meg spluttered.

Ronnie laughed harder. 'I've got it,' she grinned as a yellow cab trawled past. '"Budgie".'

'*"Budgie"*?' Meg echoed, budgie-fashion.

'Why not? You weren't planning on talking about the secret lives of budgies tonight, were you?'

'It's not in my small-talk repertoire, no,' Meg deadpanned.

Ronnie smiled. 'Good. If nothing else, it'll be amusing to find a context in which you can use it.'

'Oh, good. Brain-teasers whilst I'm dying on my feet.'

'It'll be fun,' Ronnie said, shooting Meg a glance as she texted back their reply.

Meg smiled but didn't answer. She didn't want to admit out loud that it already was.

Chapter Nineteen

'You know we're going to get back here later and think we've been robbed,' Meg said as Ronnie pulled the door shut behind them and locked it. There were clothes everywhere, on every surface, which would have been easy enough to achieve in the tiny apartment, even without two panicking sisters going on a double date.

They had been relaxed to begin with, wandering over to Allen Park and sunbathing on the grass for a few hours, before wandering down to the harbourfront to catch the scene there – people lounging in deck chairs at the water's edge, boarders and bladers rolling past, families playing on the undulating wave-decks of the famous Conundrum Route . . . And all the while they'd been chatting, talking in a way that hadn't seemed easy or even, somehow, possible for so many years. For once, there was no Mitch or Lucy to distract Meg; no exams or clinics for Ronnie.

It was only when they'd got back home and cast their minds to the evening's plans that the worries had set in – trousers or dress? Heels or sneakers? Hair up or down?

Meg hadn't packed for a date, '*obviously*'. And Ronnie never went on them – who had the time? Nonetheless, she had an efficient (what else?) capsule wardrobe packed with multiple variations of jeans – blue, indigo, white and black, boyfriend, skinny, cut-offs, dungarees, torn, distressed, faded, bleached . . .

'How can one person have so many pairs?' Meg had cried in wonder as Ronnie opened up her wardrobe.

Ronnie had wrinkled her nose. 'I know. I do try to buy other things but any time I go to the shops, I get so—'

'Bored?' Meg had asked. Shopping bored her senseless, always had. It was Mitch who used to buy her new stuff, which usually meant technical clothing like a fleece gilet or new base layer for camping trips at the weekend.

'Overwhelmed. I just buy something denim and come home.'

'I think you've got a problem,' Meg had said, trying to count them all.

'Probably,' Ronnie had agreed, staring in at the stash with her hands on her hips. 'But everyone's got something, right? For some people it's shoes. For others it's bags. For you it's hiking boots. For me, jeans,' she had shrugged.

They came out onto the street just as the sun was peeping playfully from behind an 1870s house and throwing long shadows down the street. Ronnie's arm was outstretched to hail a passing cab.

Meg caught sight of their reflection as they climbed in – their long hair glistening, eyes painted in a smoky palette (Meg hadn't known three coats of mascara was a thing), the red sequins on her black Rolling Stones T-shirt catching the light. Ronnie had given over her favourite pair of jeans for the night – matt black stovepipes, rolled at the ankle and worn with a heeled boot – on account of the fact that they were her skinniest ones and didn't fit at the moment. Ronnie herself was in a pair of white boot-legs, gold strappy sandals and a white linen T-shirt with a gold-thread stripe.

Meg thought they didn't look like themselves, or at least, not the version she kept in her head where the two of them had tangled hair that frizzed at the temples, scraped knees and wore hand-knitted jumpers made by their great-aunt.

'Do you think I should have worn my hair down?' Ronnie fretted as the cab pulled into the traffic, patting at her high ponytail.

'Definitely up,' Meg replied, finding it hard to have an opinion either way – her sister would be gorgeous bald. 'So, have you ever been there before?'

'Soho House? Only once. A friend of a friend who's a member had her birthday there.' Ronnie glanced over and saw her face. 'What? What's wrong?'

'No, nothing.'

'Not nothing. You look like you're about to throw up. What's the matter? You know I was joking, don't you? You don't have to say "budgie" if you don't want to. We can split any time you want.'

'It's not that. It . . .'

'What?'

'I mean, *Soho House*. Even just the sound of it is cool. It's not the kind of place where I fit in.' She was remembering Jonas's email, his recommendation that she visit there.

'Hello? Have you looked in the mirror today? If you told people you were a model, they'd totally believe you.' She pulled a face. 'Yesterday? Patagonia T-shirt and Kmart jeans? Not so much.'

Meg gave a nervous laugh, smoothing out the non-existent wrinkles on her narrow thighs.

She looked out of the windows as the driver navigated the city streets, lackadaisically jumping a light at one junction and almost giving Meg a heart attack. The sky – glimpsed in long, narrow strips – was blushing into sunset, peach tints uplighting the powder-blue, west-facing windows glowing gold, and she saw that the city had a beauty all of its own. It wasn't Banff, of course. Nowhere was. Her home was special; remarkable; rare. Rocky Mountains and emerald lakes – what got better than that? But that didn't mean the urban landscape didn't have its merits.

Ten minutes later, they pulled up outside a beautiful brownstone building on the end of a block, black windows breaking away from its Georgian heritage towards a more industrial edge, a double door cut into the outside corner.

'Don't look so worried,' Ronnie smiled, paying for the cab before Meg could think to argue and leading her into the club. The reception area was panelled and painted in a Hague blue, a staircase rising away at the back, and after giving their names, they were shown where to meet their friends at the rooftop bar. 'Just keep going up.'

Meg peered in the various rooms on each floor as they climbed the stairs, glimpsing sofas covered in thick jewel-coloured velvet, panelled walls, oversized chandeliers, even a giant elk head mounted above a fireplace. But that wasn't to say the look was old-school colonial – there was too much 'loft style' exposed brick and metal for that, the wooden floors aged and weathered as though they'd been shipped in from old mountain huts.

Meg felt her pulse quicken again, the city's vibe beginning to throb through her bones once more as they stepped out onto the roof terrace. A sloping glass roof and glass balconies which only came to waist height, made it feel open to the elements; small round bistro tables, partnered with green metal chairs, were set out randomly on the slate floor. There was a soft seating area at the far end and squat planters filled with feathery-headed ferns introduced a naturalistic edge.

Jack rose as he saw them, his smile growing as they came closer. The guy he was sitting with rose too – sandy blond and lightly built, he was wearing stone-coloured jeans and a relaxed, unlined chambray jacket, the trousers rolled up slightly at the ankles; he wasn't wearing socks with his suede driving shoes. Everything about him screamed 'metropolitan male'; he was about as far from Mitch – dark, hulking, athletic, practical – as it was possible to get, which instantly put her at ease. There was no threat here. She was as attracted to him as she was to the chair – less so, in fact, as the boots were already killing her feet and she was desperate to sit down.

'Hey,' Ronnie said, leading the charge.

'I'm so glad you could come,' Jack said, kissing her and then Meg once on the cheek, before introducing his friend. 'This is Logan Hazard.'

'But everyone calls me Hap,' the man smiled, extending his hand to them both.

Ronnie got the joke immediately but it took Meg another moment to catch on; she was so nervous, her brain hadn't yet attuned to small talk and banter.

'Oh!' she laughed, a full four seconds late.

'Come and sit,' Jack said, pulling out their chairs. 'I ordered some wine. A white burgundy. Does that suit?'

'Great,' Ronnie grinned, taking the chair nearest to Jack.

'Lovely,' Meg echoed.

'To be honest, I wouldn't have ordered a burgundy as an aperitif if it hadn't been for Hap here, but grapes are his business so when he makes a recommendation, I act on it. What was it you said about this one? Dry and jaunty.'

'Something like that,' Hap demurred, giving a non-committal smile.

'Oh. Are you a wine critic?' Ronnie asked him, smiling up sweetly at Jack as he handed her a glass.

'I'm the president of sales for a vineyard in BC. We specialize in ice wines.'

Meg gulped, keeping quiet. Ice wine? Was that like frozen vodka?

'Ooh! I love the Inniskillin,' Ronnie enthused.

'Yes, that's a very good Riesling ice wine – we specialize more in Pinot Noirs – but they're actually just down the way from us.'

'And where's that?'

'The Okanagan Valley?'

'Wow. So what brings you all the way over here then?'

'The Toronto Food and Wine Show.'

'Sounds like my kinda gig,' Ronnie smiled. 'I bet the crowds, though . . . ?'

'Like you wouldn't believe,' Hap said with a roll of his eyes. 'And you're a doctor? Jack said you work together.'

'That's right. I'm in my second year,' Ronnie said, looking suddenly nervous as her junior status was flagged up. There was no doubt this – if it became a 'this' – could get tricky at work for them both. But Meg saw the way Jack was looking at her sister. 'Jack's the guy keeping everything together when the proverbial hits the fan,' Ronnie said, with a nod towards him.

'You guys pull the most insane hours,' Hap said, looking between them both.

'Well, the only reason Ronnie's here now and not in scrubs is because she was pretty much forced to take her annual leave,' Jack said with a wry smile.

'Which was, thankfully, the perfect opportunity to force my sister to come and see me,' Ronnie added quickly, bringing her into the conversation.

Hap smiled and looked at Meg. 'How about you, Meg? What do you do? Crazy hours too?'

'Oh, no. I work in a ski-rental store in Banff,' she said quickly, before taking a large gulp of her drink, predicting the small silence that followed as her lack of career, her complete absence of ambition, stalled the evening before it had even got going.

'What do you . . . uh, do in the summer then? There's no glacier over there, is there, for summer skiing?'

'No. We switch over to selling hiking and climbing equipment,' she nodded.

There was another pause.

'I'm guessing you must get to meet people from all over,' Jack said optimistically.

'That's right,' she nodded, taking another glug of wine and wondering how she could introduce a conversation about budgies. She shot Ronnie a desperate look. She was bombing, failing, embarrassing them both . . .

'But that's not Meg's overriding focus, is it, Meg?' Ronnie stared back at her with wide, prompting eyes.

Meg blinked. It wasn't?

'Titch . . .' Ronnie prompted.

'Oh.' She frowned. 'Well, I don't think—'

'Titch? Titch snowboards?' Hap asked.

'That's right.'

'What do you . . . ?' he enquired, clearly interested.

But Meg couldn't say the words. *My fiancé set it up. My dead fiancé.*

'Meg's a part-owner in the company,' Ronnie said instead,

her brown eyes shining proudly. 'She helped set it up with some friends in high school.'

'Well, *I* didn't really have anything to do with the running of the busi—' Meg protested, but Ronnie squeezed her knee.

'Nonsense. You gave them the deposit for the shop, didn't you? And it's your designs on the boards. They're a major part of the brand's USP.'

'*You* did those graphics?' Hap asked, looking astonished.

Meg was suspicious of his interest. 'Yes,' she said in a quiet voice.

'I'm always telling Meg she should set up her own graphic-design consultancy. She's got such a fresh take and a really unique look,' Ronnie said. It was true, the idea for running her own business was Ronnie's; she'd been saying it for years but Meg had always shrugged it off, seeing only the implied insult – that her present life was not enough – rather than the implicit compliment.

Hap leaned in, interestedly. 'I got one of the Crush limited editions last year.'

'You board?' she asked, mildly surprised. Somehow, she didn't take him for a tricks rider.

'No,' he said slowly, looking bashful. 'To be honest, I put it on the wall in my apartment.'

'Hap's into his *design statements*, God help us,' Jack said with a groan.

'Hey, you're just jealous because one of us can rock a trilby.' Hap pulled a face. 'I fully admit I'm the classic case of "all the gear, no idea".'

Both men laughed and Meg did too. Mitch and Tuck would have despised him on the spot but she liked his honesty. Most men would rather have pretended they were pro-shredders than risk losing face and admit they'd bought a snowboard because they liked the colours and patterns on it!

'Well,' Hap said, reaching for the wine bottle and refreshing everyone's glasses. 'If you did those designs, then frankly you have a moral responsibility to step up and get your work *out there*. It needs to be seen.' He looked straight at her and she felt a jolt at the sudden connection; it had been so long since she'd looked anyone in the eye, she realized. All these months, she'd bluffed her way through with vague smiles and saying exactly what people wanted to hear, keeping all but Dolores and Lucy at arm's length. Even Jonas, her unlikely confidant, had been bodily removed from the equation, so that he was more of a disembodied sounding board than a living, breathing person, much less a living, breathing man. But this guy, though he was foreign to her socially and culturally, though he was completely not 'her type', he somehow cut through her act. He didn't know her past or her present, her tragedies and sorrows. He just saw the girl in front of him in black jeans with a nervous smile. It felt liberating.

Hap sat back in the chair but still watching her.

A sudden change made her look up – the sky had quickly dropped into darkness but it wasn't stars she saw above her but strings of fairy lights flickering on, strung up between the glass-roof rafters – a *pretend* starry sky.

'So what did you two do today?' Jack asked, directing the question to Ronnie. 'CN Tower?'

'Obvs,' she concurred. 'And we'd gone SUP boarding this morning before we saw you, so we felt pretty entitled to slob for the rest of the day. We just sunbathed in the park and then hung out by the harbourfront.'

'Hey, it's a shame we didn't see you – we were down there this afternoon, tinkering about,' Hap said. 'We were getting ready for taking Jack's boat out tomorrow.'

'You've got a boat?' Ronnie asked with an envious tone.

'Well, it's no gin palace but . . .' Jack shrugged. 'It's my Sunday routine – pager turned off, picnic and a day on the water. Couldn't be without it.'

'Living the dream,' Ronnie quipped.

'Well, you wouldn't have said that if you'd seen my living quarters in the cabin. When I first moved to the city, I spent all my down-payment for a condo on the boat instead. I had to live on it for eighteen months.' He wrinkled his nose. 'It was a bit cramped.'

'Or cosy,' Ronnie shrugged, shooting him a coy look. 'Depending on how you look at it.'

'Or cosy.' Jack grinned and Meg felt suddenly embarrassed as the hitherto-unspoken attraction between Ronnie and Jack spilled onto the terrace, joining their group like a fifth presence. 'You know, you should join us tomorrow, if you're free. We'd love to have you.'

'Yeah, Jack could show off his knot-tying prowess to you,' Hap teased. 'Ask him to do his bosun, that's the hardest one.'

Meg tuned out, looking up at the pretend stars again, unable to see the real thing in the sky thanks to the city's lights. Unlike at home, where night settled over the valley like a velvet cloak – pure and absolute in its darkness – here it was more of a gauze, a reddish haze from the city percolating upwards and dimming the stars. She wondered what it must be like to live in a place where they were invisible, a notion rather than a fact – where you had to be content with merely believing they were there, though they couldn't be seen.

She thought of Jonas, only yesterday speeding up there amongst them like a pinball in a machine, taking in the Gobi desert, the Taj Mahal, Ayers Rock, the Amazon, and she smiled to think how much more epic his scale of sight-seeing was, taking in the world's great wonders in less time than it took her to visit this one city. She wondered how he was feeling having returned to Earth, putting boots back on the ground and becoming like everyone else again. Just a man. He would walk through crowds and do his shopping and buy socks and no one would be able to tell that he was one of that tiny elite who had stepped off this planet and seen the bigger picture.

'So are you going to go for it?' Hap asked, watching her stare at the fairy lights. Though they were no substitute, they were certainly pretty, throwing dappled shadows down upon the terrace.

'Go for what?'

'Setting up your own business like Ronnie says. You've clearly got the talent.'

'Oh, well, it's not that simple,' she demurred.

'Why not?'

Meg hesitated, trying to remember what Lucy had told her when she'd dared to voice the thought ... Dolores needed her. She wouldn't cope with the stress.

'I mean, I can see it would be tricky if you couldn't draw,' he added, grinning. 'But . . .'

'I have other commitments that would make it impossi-ble. I work closely with a friend and she needs me.'

'You mean the ski-rental thing?'

'Yes. She's much older. She doesn't have anyone else.'

'Don't believe a word of it,' Ronnie said, with a roll of her eyes. 'Dolores is tough as old boots. She'd be fine if Meg left. Meg just doesn't want to take a chance.'

'She's seventy-three years old,' Meg replied defensively.

'Exactly. A seventy-three-year-old pair of boots. Imagine the hide on them. You wouldn't mess.'

The guys chuckled but Meg felt angry, angry that Ronnie – after a day in which they'd been closer than they had in years – had chosen now to pick on her again.

'I'm amazed she's still working if she's that age,' Jack said politely, clocking Meg's expression.

'Well, she may not now, that's the thing,' Meg said hotly, shooting her sister a furious look. Dolores's recovery was going to be slow – certainly slower than Dolores would be happy with – but what if she never fully got her strength back? She could have died. Even Dolores wouldn't bounce back from this quickly. She needed Meg more than ever. 'She was attacked by a bear last week and was in Intensive Care for three days.'

'Jesus!' Hap exclaimed, looking genuinely shocked. 'Are you kidding?'

'Meg was there,' Ronnie said.

'You were there?' Hap repeated, looking ever more astonished. 'And now you're . . . you're here? Looking like that?'

Like what? Meg wondered, immediately regretting letting Ronnie do her make-up, wishing she'd never brought the subject up. She didn't care what Dolores said – it was no laughing matter. It wasn't *fine* just because they'd survived.

'But how are you not freaking out?'

'It didn't go for me,' she said with a calm she wasn't feeling. She was remembering the sight of the bear on its hind legs again, Lucy curled up on the ground . . .

Ronnie squeezed her arm proudly. 'No. Meg sprayed it. She forced it to back off. She saved Dolores's life.'

'You sprayed the bear?' Hap chuckled, shaking his head. 'Maybe you should go into bodyguarding instead.'

Even Meg chuckled at that. 'Now there's a thought.' She flexed a bicep, her arm looking pathetically weedy.

'Maybe not,' he winced, continuing the joke, his eyes steady upon her.

Meg felt another jolt of electricity again, not quite able to understand it. He wasn't anything like Mitch, he wasn't her type. And yet . . . there was an undercurrent, she couldn't deny it.

Jack smiled, watching the japes like a tolerant father. 'Listen, we've got reservations for dinner downstairs in the Pretzel Bar. It's got live music and they do great food . . . you up for joining us, or have you got to go on elsewhere?'

Ronnie bit her lip but deferred to Meg with an arched eyebrow. What could Meg possibly do but agree? Ronnie was almost aglow with excitement and delight.

'Sure,' Meg shrugged. 'I'm so hungry. I could eat a—'

'Bear?' Hap asked, as they stood up.

They walked back inside, Ronnie and Jack just ahead, Jack saying something quietly in Ronnie's ear that made her look up at him with a happy smile. Meg smiled at the sight of them, feeling hopeful – her little sister had never been one for boyfriends, she'd always been too busy studying, her sights set on distant horizons that the small-town boys back home couldn't see; and now, of course, there was never time. It made total sense she should date a doctor.

Meg put her hand on the rail as they got to the top of the stairs.

'Be careful here, the steps are steep,' Hap said, gently putting his hand on her waist.

Meg immediately stiffened as she began to climb down the steps, her heart racing faster than if she was running up them. The restaurant was on the next floor down and she could hear the music thump as they rounded the corner, the vibrations of the bass travelling through the walls.

She was on the last step, Ronnie and Jack already standing by the door of the bar, when she felt his hand drop down to the curve of her bum and ever so slightly squeeze.

She gave an audible gasp and Ronnie turned instantly. 'What's wrong?'

'The budgie!' Meg cried.

Ronnie blinked at her, open-mouthed. 'What?'

'We forgot to feed the budgie!'

Jack turned to Ronnie. 'You've got a *budgie*?'

'Uh . . . yes . . . yes . . .' Ronnie replied, her eyes never leaving her sister, an entire conversation passing between them in silence before she suddenly turned to Jack with an apologetic shrug. 'I'm so sorry, we'd better call a rain check – we left her out of the cage too. We should head back or she'll be tearing up the apartment . . .'

'Really?' Jack looked gutted.

'Yes, uh . . . fearsome temper,' Ronnie said regretfully, Jack and Hap looking at them both in amazement as Meg grabbed her by the hand and pulled her away, bounding into the street, her arm already outstretched for a cab.

Ronnie followed after in silence, knowing there was nothing to be done. The code word had been activated and a deal was a deal.

Date night was over.

Chapter Twenty

Sunday 30 July 2017

'Listen, there's nothing to be embarrassed about,' Ronnie said, spreading an avocado on her toast and drizzling it with chilli oil.

Meg watched, mesmerized that this was what people ate for breakfast here. Whatever happened to cereal or pancakes and waffles? 'Ron, I leapt like a freaking salmon,' she moaned, reliving the mortification again and again. She had barely slept, her brain trying to process what her body had done, as she tossed and turned. What was wrong with her? So he'd touched her backside? No, grazed it. So what? She wasn't ten! And as for . . . Oh, God. *'We forgot to feed the freaking budgie?'* Who said that? Who? *Who?*

Ronnie pulled a sympathetic face. 'You've just got to try to think of it as a compliment that he's attracted to you. After all, you are going to have to get used to the idea that guys like you, regardless of whether you choose to act on it.'

But Meg just groaned. Her phone beeped with a new email and she clicked on it uninterestedly. Another Gap sale? Lucy wanting to know if Ronnie had made her cry yet . . . ?

'So listen, what do you want to do about today? Are we going to go out on the boat?'

Meg stared at the email, her heart accelerating to a gallop as she saw who it was from. She had a delayed reaction of at least five seconds before she heard what Ronnie had said and looked up in surprise. 'Jack's boat?'

Ronnie shrugged. 'He's texted, reiterating the offer about joining them, but listen, it's no biggie to me. I don't want you to feel awkward. I'm only mentioning it 'cause I need to get back to him.' She took in Meg's face – sort of frozen. 'But . . . you know what? I'll just say we've got plans.'

Meg watched her, knowing that her sister was protesting too much. 'But you really like him.'

Ronnie's gaze flickered up to hers and then back down again. 'I can see him any time. I'll see him at work when I get back. We can grab a coffee maybe.'

'Grab a coffee? Instead of lounging around on his boat? I don't think so.'

Ronnie leaned in. 'Look, it would mean you coming too.'

'I realize that. It's fine.'

Ronnie looked surprised. 'It is?'

'Absolutely. I over-reacted last night. You were right. I have to get used to . . .'

'Men?'

'Exactly,' Meg murmured, her eyes falling back to the email on her screen.

From: Jonas Solberg
Subject: Hello from the other side

Hey there, Dog-Dog-Ellie,
     So, as you may have heard, it wasn't exactly the re-entry

we wanted but I guess it's true what they say about coming back to Earth with a bump. The bad news is that gravity and I are not friends right now. Even just typing this is taking more strength than I can fathom. On the bright side, it should only be for a few days. Well, weeks maybe. Remember how I said I was looking forward to walking again? I take it back. The soles of my feet are so tender, I'm having to wear Crocs to get around. Really not a good look. It's as well only astronauts and scientists are seeing me right now. (Although did you see my Kazakh return outfit? Hoping not.)

How was Toronto? Did you sip martinis at Soho House?

I'm now stuck at Houston being tested around the clock so all and any news of the outside world is welcomed! Arms too feeble to type more. Write back.

J.

PS Joke to follow. Sorry.

'I still can't believe this is a lake and not a sea,' Meg said, her eyes on the distant horizon as they walked down the boardwalks of the Outer Harbour Marina together, each carrying a tote – Meg's contained rolled-up towels and a change of swimwear; Ronnie's had a bottle of wine, some olives, pastrami, crackers and a selection of dips.

Sunlight winked on the still water, as bright as pennies, as darting as fishes, the chandlery rigging reels clanking like tin cups in the breeze. Both Jack and Hap were already there, Jack bare-chested and wearing navy shorts as he wound in the mainsail, prompting Ronnie to whistle under her breath at the sight of his toned physique.

'I bet he saw you coming and he's doing that on purpose,' Meg whispered.

'Yeah? Who cares? Hold me back!' she whispered excitedly, shooting Meg a mischievous look.

Meg rolled her eyes and groaned but in truth, she was happy to see her sister falling for someone at last. Nervously, she watched Hap, who was checking the bow ropes were clear, pulling them out of the water with a pole. He had his back to them and was wearing jeans (rolled up, natch) and a grey T-shirt and looking rather less metrosexual than last night.

The boat was bigger than she had anticipated. Jack's modesty had led her to imagine it was just big enough to buzz about in the bay, but this was a six-metre motorized sailing boat with a navy hull and turquoise pencil line, although it looked fairly old, the paintwork dull, and she supposed it had been bought as a refurbishment project.

'*Balm*, huh?' Ronnie called out, reciting the boat's name. 'I'm guessing that's a deliberate antidote to "trauma"?'

Jack turned and smiled at the sight of her and Meg thought that if he had seen them coming, then he was a good actor. 'Exactly! I told you it's my escape,' he said, ducking under the boom and jogging carefully over the deck to them. 'I'm glad you could come,' he said to them both, hands on hips, but his eyes returning to Ronnie.

'Well, we're glad too,' Ronnie replied after a pause.

'Good morning!' Hap called, coming to join them. 'How are you?'

'Great,' Meg nodded shyly, feeling his eyes upon her. It didn't matter what excuses they'd used to make their escape last night, he knew perfectly well that she had bolted the moment he'd touched her backside.

'How's the budgie?'

Meg froze as she realized she and Ronnie hadn't agreed a story in advance.

'Dead.'

She turned in astonishment to find Ronnie pulling a sad face.

'You're kidding?' Jack asked.

Ronnie shook her head. 'Flew into a window and broke her neck.'

'Oh, my God. I'm so sorry,' Jack sympathized.

Meg had to keep from laughing. Did budgies even have necks?

'But at least it was quick,' Ronnie said gravely. 'It's something to know that she didn't suffer.'

'Sure,' Jack nodded, looking handsome and so earnest as he stood there, hands still on hips. 'Well, I'm glad you're not so upset you didn't come out here.'

'Oh, hey, we're doctors. Death's just an everyday part of life for us, right?' Ronnie said lightly, dismissing the non-existent, now-dead budgie from all their minds.

Meg stole a glance at Hap, but he was already looking at her and the expression in his eyes told her that he wasn't buying the story for a second.

'Well, here, let me take the bags,' Jack said, reaching out for them. The girls swung them into his grasp and Hap held his hand out to take them by the arm as they stepped on board. He held Meg's arm a fraction longer than she thought was necessary and as she looked up at him, she felt that jolt again that she'd felt last night when their eyes had met.

She pulled away quickly, eyes down, as she followed Ronnie down to the cabin to stow their bags. If he thought something was going to happen between them, that this was a date between *them*, he was wrong. She was going to have to make that patently clear.

'I guess we do have to do this sooner or later, right?' Ronnie giggled, pulling off her T-shirt and shorts to reveal her tiny black triangle bikini with neon trim.

Meg took a deep breath and pulled off her own top and shorts – she was in one of Ronnie's spare bikinis, an Aztec-print, blue-and-white bandeau style, after Ronnie had deemed her navy racing swimsuit too 'Victorian'.

'Hey!' Jack said, his smile widening as they reappeared, scantily clad. 'Let's cast off then.'

'Can we do anything to help?' Ronnie asked casually. 'We're not complete strangers to boat life.'

'No?' Jack asked, throwing the rope onto the boardwalk as Hap untethered the bow line.

'Our dad took us sailing a few times when we were little,' Ronnie said. 'I may even be able to remember my bosun knots,' she grinned.

'Now that's just a challenge to my authority!' Jack cried, clambering across the deck and jumping down by the wheel, beside Ronnie. She gave a small yelp of delight. 'I don't believe this, Hap – we've not even left harbour and already there's mutiny!'

Hap grinned as he made his way to the stern as well, his eyes lingering on Meg. 'I have a feeling we're going to need to keep our wits about us, Jack,' he quipped as the engines puttered softly beneath the water, propelling them away from the moorings with the wind in their hair – smiles on all their faces.

The bay was deep, so deep they couldn't see the bottom, although the depth reader was saying it was sixteen metres.

Balm bobbed gently on the water's surface, only the wake from occasional boats further out in the lake rocking them every now and then.

They had eaten all the food – in addition to Ronnie and Meg's offering of dips, Hap and Jack had brought chicken drumsticks and a 'very metrosexual' salad with at least three different types of seeds in, that Meg hoped had been made by Hap – could he be *less* her type? – as well as a six-pack of beers.

'Well, I'm with you on the whole "living the dream" thing. I'm not sure a Sunday could be more perfect than this,' Ronnie sighed from her position lying on her back on the cabin roof.

'No? Not even a pfannenstiel incision laparotomy?' Jack teased, watching the way her stomach rose and fell with her breath. Meg knew this because she was watching him watch her sister.

Ronnie sucked in through her teeth, conflicted. 'Oh, that's not fair!' she cried and the two of them fell into laughter again. The creation of their very own in-jokes had already begun.

Hap looked over at Meg. 'Doctor humour,' he muttered with a sardonic expression. He was sitting on the captain's chair, one foot up on the controls, and Meg had been trying very hard not to notice the blond hairs on his legs. Mitch's had been dark and she'd always liked how masculine they'd looked, perhaps because they were so completely the opposite of her own.

'So listen, I've been thinking about you,' he said.

Meg's head jerked up. He'd what? Why? In her peripheral vision, she saw Ronnie's attention was caught too.

'About your design portfolio, I mean,' he added, but that

look in his eyes that he seemed to get when he looked at her . . . she felt like he was testing her, provoking her, trying to establish how easily she startled – to which he now surely knew the answer was 'very'. 'I've got a friend who works for Kate Spade. You know her? The handbag and acc—'

'I live in Banff, not Billericay. Of course I know who Kate Spade is.'

He nodded, amused by her prickliness. 'Well, they're looking to do a rebrand – everything from the store fronts to the tissue paper to the purse linings. It's a big gig.'

Meg stared at him, her stomach feeling empty, in spite of the huge lunch she'd just devoured. (She didn't know what was going on with her appetite. Since getting here, she'd been ravenous, as though her body had woken up to the fact that she'd been eating at a subsistence level for four months.)

'Anyway, I think you'd have a great shot at it. After you . . . uh, *left* last night –' he made his gaze more pointed, bringing them both back to that moment, the one that had made her run – 'I went back to my hotel and looked at the Titch boards in more detail. I mean, I was obsessed with the Crush series but I didn't really know your other stuff.' He looked impressed. 'You should definitely speak to her.'

'But . . . but they're in New York and I'm in Alberta.' Panic wrapped around her like a comforting cardigan – familiar and well-used.

His eyes danced. 'You've heard of planes, right?'

She laughed and looked away, feeling foolish.

'Listen, it's still early days – they'd want to see your portfolio first. But they'd fly you in if things got serious. Or they could do video-conferencing. You don't necessarily have to be in the same room as them to fulfil the brief.'

Ronnie, Meg noticed suddenly, was sitting bolt upright. 'Oh, my God, this is amazing. Meg! You've got to go for it.'

Did she? Did she really? It had been one thing designing the boards for the boys. They'd given her the vaguest of briefs – 'something cool' – and left her to it. It was no brief at all, in fact. Carte blanche. Free rein. That was a very different thing from taking a world-famous brand that all the chic, rich Park Avenue people knew and loved and . . . and completely redesigning it! What did she know about style? She was the girl who wore Patagonia T-shirts and the closest she came to a heel was on a welly boot.

'Hap, she's in!' Ronnie said, answering for her. 'Don't let her fret her way out of it. She'll always find a reason to push it away. Put her name forward.'

Hap looked pleased. 'I'm glad you said that. I suspected as much myself so I emailed my contact this morning.' He looked back at Meg. 'They should be in touch with you sometime in the next few weeks – just for a preliminary chat.'

'Oh, my God, you didn't!' Meg wailed, her hands pulling down on her cheeks.

But everybody laughed – as though her anxiety was amusing and already entirely predictable to this new-found group of four.

'Last one in does the washing-up!' Ronnie cried suddenly, running towards the side and launching herself into the water with a perfect dive. Jack, lying on the stern deck, was in barely a moment later.

Meg gasped – forgetting all about her panic for a moment – as she saw it was between her and Hap and she scrambled up onto her feet. Hap, already sitting upright, lost his advantage in that he had to swerve round the main mast, giving Meg just enough time to grab the giant inflatable ring from the side as she took a flying leap. Her feet made contact with the water only a split second before Hap's, both of them surfacing with gasps as Ronnie and Jack declared her the winner.

'Ha!' she crowed, pleased to have got an advantage over him for once, wriggling into the inflatable so that her legs, arms and head lolled over the sides. She gave a heavy sigh as she allowed her body to lie heavily and limply; she'd been so tense since getting on the boat, worried that as things intensified between Ronnie and Jack, Hap might take it as a cue to make *his* move.

Well, she'd put him straight if he so much as—

Hap swam slowly over, his nose and mouth submerged below the water so that only his eyes – glittering, full of predatory intent – were visible.

Oh, God.

Meg couldn't help it. She squealed as he ducked underwater, unable to see where he was as she wriggled about in the ring, looking for him. A pinch on her bottom two seconds later pinpointed his whereabouts exactly.

When he surfaced, her mouth was still open with surprise. He laughed again. 'You're very easy to shock.'

She closed her mouth, not sure what to say but aware that she looked daft. She glanced at him, away again, at him, away again. She didn't trust him, wasn't quite sure what he was going to do next. Her heart was racketing along at full pelt.

He drifted over to her, holding onto the side of the inflatable and pulling himself up slightly, his eyeline straight at her breasts, although he had the decency to look her in the eye. 'Tell me – there's something I really have to know.' His voice was low, as though he was asking her for a secret.

She swallowed, aware that his fingers were mere centimetres from her thighs, skin on skin. 'What?' Her voice was barely more than a croak.

A moment passed as he held her gaze, both of them bobbing lightly on the lake's surface, the hot sun already drying her stomach and his shoulders, beads of water travelling on brown skin.

He smiled wickedly. 'Where, in God's name, is Billericay?'

Chapter Twenty-one

Monday 31 July 2017

It was a date. It didn't matter what Ronnie or even Hap had said – 'You gotta eat, don't you?' – him coming over to take her to lunch was a date. Ronnie had been called into the hospital at first light, her pager vibrating so loudly on the mezzanine floor that Meg had incorporated the sound into her dream as chainsaws. Something bad had happened – a train had been derailed and there were multiple casualties, with all doctors in the immediate vicinity recalled to help, even those on annual leave.

Ronnie had been deeply apologetic as she hopped around on one foot, trying to pull on her trousers and scrape her hair back into a ponytail, as Meg watched from the sofa-bed, feeling glad that Dolores never called her in the middle of the night.

'Look, it's not your fault,' Meg had reassured her, but inside she felt daunted. What was she going to do here all day? Her first instinct was to see if she could rebook her flight, due for tomorrow, to this afternoon. But then Hap had called – no doubt alerted by Jack, via Ronnie, that she was at a loose end – and now lunch was happening and Ronnie wasn't here to vet what she should wear. She wasn't here to vet him and make sure he didn't make any moves that would send Meg flying back to Alberta without the need for a plane. Because this was all too soon; far too soon. She'd gone for the drinks at Soho House and the day on the boat purely to chaperone her little sister. But now she was the one needing chaperoning. Somehow, without intending it, without wanting it, she was going on a date, going through the motions of dressing for another man when her head and heart still throbbed to the beat of Mitch's name.

He buzzed on the dot of eleven, just as she was staring at her outfit in the mirror for the umpteenth time. Was there anything about it that Ronnie would object to? She was wearing the white boot-cuts Ronnie had worn on Friday night (because if they were good enough for Ronnie . . .), a pair of Stan Smith sneakers found down the side of the sofa (which meant they must have been worn recently, a sign that they were acceptable too), and a plain black T-shirt (because it was a black T-shirt, so how bad could it be?).

'Hi,' he grinned as she stepped out of the apartment building a few minutes later, her face half-hidden behind an enormous pair of Audrey Hepburn-style shades she'd found in the desk, all the better for avoiding eye contact. He was leaning against a black Mercedes AMG and looking 'full urban' again, wearing skinny dark jeans, no socks, moccasins, a pale blue shirt and a navy blazer. She gave an inward sigh of relief that he had reverted to type. The type that wasn't 'her type'. The type she could resist. 'You look beautiful.'

She almost asked, *'Do I?'* but that would be to open up a moment between them. Instead she stared at the car. She knew nothing about cars but a Buick this was not. 'This is yours?'

He nodded.

'And you drove it here all the way from BC?'

'Well, wouldn't you?' he smiled, opening the door for her. 'Besides, I make a lot of stops en route, visiting clients. Are you happy to have the roof down or would you prefer it up?' he asked, his eyes flitting to her high ponytail.

'Down's fine.' She'd never been in a car like this before – sleek, expensive, as beautiful as it was powerful. In Banff you drove cars that could cope – cope with the terrain, the weather, the elks (their truck had been badly dented last year by two rutting elks that had wandered too close to town).

Hap climbed into his side and switched on the ignition. Meg felt the power surge beneath her, barely restrained, and she felt a quiver of nerves and excitement arrow through her.

'You ready?' he asked, somehow still pinning her gaze even behind the shades.

'Born ready,' she nodded with a sudden flash of courage and then instantly regretting that she didn't regret it.

He glanced at her, a grin on his lips. 'My kind of girl,' he winked, pulling away with a squeal of rubber.

The journey was wild, the wind whipping her hair as they sped along the highway, David Bowie blaring from the speakers, and by the time they'd arrived at their destination – 'a small beauty spot', he'd said – she felt as exhilarated as if she'd run here herself. He was right – it was worth driving cross-country in that car. It was worth *moving to Canada* in order to drive cross-country in that car.

Two hours later and she was soaked.

'Can you believe *one fifth* of the world's entire fresh water volume is falling here?' Hap shouted, his face becoming steadily wet from the mist.

'Yes!' she shouted back, barely able to hear herself over the roar. 'Right this second, I really, really can!'

He laughed, tugging the hood of her pink waterproof poncho forward and tucking a damp tendril behind her ear. She looked quickly back at the view, telling herself it was a kind gesture, a friendly one – much like driving all the way out to Niagara for lunch.

The boat was moving towards the horseshoe falls on the Canadian side – the larger of the two falls. The US falls were supposedly louder on account of the rocks at the bottom, although it felt hard to believe that anything could be louder than this right now; it was like standing beside a jumbo jet. She tightened her grip on the handrail as the boat ferried closer, her eyes steady on the monumental cascades in front of them, the mist billowing like silk skirts so that the sky, land and the thousands of observers looking down at them were obscured from view as they moved through pockets of varying thickness. The water was rougher here as they got to within seventy metres of the base of the falls and Hap stood behind her, his arms either side of hers.

'Keep steady,' he murmured.

She didn't need to be told twice, holding herself as still and small as she could so that her body didn't touch his, not daring to turn and look at him – they would have been nose to nose, eye to eye, mouth to mouth – the rustle of their waterproofs close to her ear as the boat rocked.

She inadvertently closed her eyes, her body instinctively remembering how it had felt to be held by a man – Mitch's warmth, his solidity. It had been so long now . . . Hap was barely five centimetres behind her and in spite of her best efforts, every so often the rock of the boat meant her back was pressed to his chest, her head at his shoulder. He didn't move either.

Within a few minutes, they had passed by and the intimacy of the moment was lost as the mist cleared suddenly and the world peered back in on them from the barriers above, cameras snapping. Hap stepped back as though aware of their stares but she didn't move in any way, terrified she'd betray herself, instead keeping her eyes transfixed on the falls.

When they got off the boat half an hour later, he held out his hand to help her off the gangplank, but unlike yesterday he continued holding it and for a few moments, she pretended this was normal. But Mitch's memory was snapping at their heels as they walked and eventually she felt obliged to discreetly slip it from his grasp.

He glanced at her but said nothing, and they made their way to the restaurant he'd booked for lunch. They chatted but never talked, Meg barely stopping to draw breath as she kept the conversation on safe ground – asking him about the climate required for growing ice wines and the eye-watering cost of insurance for his car, telling him about the growing problem of wolf packs approaching people and how the parks were asking for the public's help in 'keeping them wild'. And in the car on the way back home, the wind did all the work for her, whisking their voices away before they could reach each other's ears and it wasn't until they hit the city that they could talk easily again.

Meg felt her nerves spike, knowing that 'goodbye' was coming.

'So I got a call back from my friend at Kate Spade this morning. They're definitely interested,' Hap said as they stopped at some lights, his arms straight on the steering wheel. 'She said she's going to show it to her boss today or tomorrow, and hopefully give you a call.'

'I don't know what to say,' Meg murmured, feeling awed that she was in the running for such a prestigious project when she didn't even have her own business, hadn't pitched for it. 'It was so kind of you to put me forward for it.'

'I'm not sure kind's the word.' The light changed to green and he pressed on the accelerator. 'You were on my mind.'

Meg stared at him but he kept his eyes on the road and she took the opportunity to study his profile. She couldn't help herself. Everything about him was slick, even his designer stubble. He was good-looking and funny, well-informed and easy-going, with an ability to say one thing with his mouth and entirely another with his eyes.

'When are you heading back to BC?' she asked, when he glanced across at her, catching her staring.

'Wednesday.' He shot a glance at her. 'You? Still tomorrow?'

'Yeah.' Why still? Did he . . . did he think she'd have changed her flight? For him?

She bit her lip and leaned away from him slightly, resting her arm on the passenger-side door, the wind buffeting her face. She was grateful for the protection of the sunglasses, in every way.

Her phone buzzed and she looked at the screen. Ronnie.

'K?' it read.

Meg arched an eyebrow, knowing this was city-speak for 'Are you OK?' City people were too busy to actually speak. 'OK' was just too long.

'Ronnie?' he asked.

'Yeah, she's still at the hospital.'

'Surprise, surprise. Although Jack's there too so they're probably not incentivized to leave . . .' He let the intimation hang in the air and Meg knew she had to say it, tell him now that nothing was going to happen between the two of *them*.

'Look, Hap, it's been really nice of you to do this for me today. I want you to know that I really appreciate it.'

He glanced across at her, hearing the tone in her voice. 'There's nothing else I'd have rather done with my day,' he said simply, pulling up outside an apartment block she recognized – pretty much the only one she recognized in the city. Really? They were here already?

He slung his arm over the back of the seat and smiled at her.

'It's just that, you and me . . .' Her voice trailed off.

'Yes?' His eyes were searching for hers behind the lenses.

'I mean, if you thought something was going to happen between us . . .'

He cracked another of his knowing grins.

'Yes?'

'It's not that I don't like you, I really do, I've loved getting to know you this weekend. It's just that I . . . I see you as a friend.'

'A friend?'

'Uh-huh. You're really funny and interesting and good-looking—'

'But?'

She pulled a sorry face. 'You're just not my type.'

He looked surprised. And then amused. 'So what is your type?'

'I don't know,' she said defensively.

'Well, you must do if you know that I'm not it.'

She shrugged. 'Dark, maybe? . . . More outdoorsy.'

'*I'm* outdoorsy. I've had the roof down the whole way.'

She laughed at the jest, relieved he'd taken it well, that they could still be friends.

'Well, I'm sorry to hear that. I must have been imagining it then,' he murmured.

Her smile faded. 'Imagining what?'

He leaned over and pulled off her sunglasses, exposing her to the full wattage of the current that ran between them. She held her breath as his eyes roamed her face, taking in the minute changes in her eyes and cheeks that spoke a truth she wouldn't utter.

'That.'

His eyes fell to her lips and she knew he was going to kiss her – that the kiss would be good and she would get lost in it, and then he would become the man between her and Mitch and that would never change, the fact only becoming truer with time that Mitch was gone for ever and she was spiralling further away from him every time the sun set. Despair and desire converged in a swirling maelstrom deep inside her heart. She wanted this man, she knew she needed to move on. But . . . not yet. She couldn't—

'There's no future in it, Hap,' she whispered as he drew closer still.

'I'm not interested in the future – or the past. Only right now, that's all that's real.'

Was he right? Did she agree with that? Wasn't she shaped by her past? Surely those years with Mitch had helped make her the woman she was now, sitting in front of him?

But then his lips were upon hers and ready or not, the moment she'd dreaded and craved – the one she had always known would have to happen some day, the one she'd sensed at her back on Saturday – it was here and it was irresistible.

And as she gave herself up to it, all the tears she had yet to cry were stalled with kisses, her despair overwritten, if only for a moment, with this new fleeting joy. And somewhere deep inside, she felt a door close and a lock turn.

Chapter Twenty-two

Tuesday 1 August 2017

'You've got to stop crying,' Ronnie smiled, wiping Meg's tears away as a couple walked past them, wheeling their suitcases, concerned expressions on their faces. 'People will think I'm breaking up with you!'

Meg half-laughed, half-sobbed again. 'I know, I'm sorry, I just . . .' she hiccupped.

'It's been a big few days,' Ronnie said knowingly, pulling her in for another hug.

Meg nodded into her shoulder, trying to quell the sobs. 'I never thought that when I came out here—'

Ronnie pulled back to look at her. 'I know. But it was good for you, even if it doesn't feel like that right now. It was never going to be easy but you pushed yourself forward this weekend, you broke the pain barrier.'

Meg gave her a shocked look. Falling into bed with Hap had been the opposite of painful – it had been hungry and raw and desperate, and then it had been coy and naughty and playful, and then it had been soft and slow and tender . . .

Ronnie laughed, reading her fluently. 'I'm talking about progress – it isn't always easy, nor is it linear. I see it all the time with my patients – two steps forward, three back. Today's the three-steps-back bit. But tomorrow . . . ? You won't regret it, I promise you that.'

'You don't think?' Meg sniffed.

'I know. Hey, trust me, I'm a doctor.'

Meg laughed, sniffing and wiping her cheeks dry again. 'Did you tell him about Mitch?' Ronnie asked.

Meg shook her head, staring at her trainered feet. 'No, but I think he'd worked out there was something.'

'He probably thinks you're divorced or something.'

'Single mother, six kids,' Meg sniffed.

They both laughed again, knowing they were running out of time. The weekend had sped past at warp speed and now it was over. Tuesday morning, back to business. Ronnie's shift started at lunch.

Meg inhaled deeply and looked back at her little sister, younger by eighteen months, wiser by a lifetime. Their mother had always called her an old soul and it was true. 'I'm going to miss you.'

This time it was Ronnie's eyes that welled up. 'I'm going to miss you too.'

Meg reached for her hand and swung it lightly from side to side, like she used to when they were little. 'The absolute worst thing about coming here and having such an amazing time is having to leave you again.'

'So then move here.' Ronnie said it simply, as though it was just like it had been when she'd relocated six years ago. 'The city likes you.'

'I like the city,' Meg shrugged, giving a little laugh. 'I never thought I'd say that but I actually do . . . Dolores will be *delighted* to hear she's been proved right again.' She rolled her eyes. 'I'll definitely come and visit more often.'

'And I'll come back too. To tell you the truth, I really miss the silence.'

'And the stars?'

'And the stars,' Ronnie nodded. 'And the freaking elks walking down the middle of Banff Avenue every night!'

They both laughed, hugging each other hard and long.

'Are you seeing Jack tonight?' Meg asked, finally pulling back and getting her boarding card out of her pocket.

'He's cooking me dinner.'

'Wow.'

'Hmmm, I'm not so sure. He mentioned something about roast toast.'

Meg laughed. 'Well, we wouldn't want him being *too* perfect.' She picked up her weekend bag. 'Love you, sis.'

'Love you.'

She hoicked her bag strap onto her shoulder and turned away, walking towards the departures hall where the tide of people was converging to a point.

'Meg!'

Meg turned.

'Think about what I said, OK? Just think about it.'

From: Jonas Solberg

I get it. You want the joke. Or perhaps you're still in Toronto, living the high life.

Either way, I'm missing your crazy shouts-outs to space already, so here you are:

'What happened to the astronaut who stepped on chewing gum?'

'He got stuck in Orbit.'

I know, not my finest hour. But I do have the

small excuse of battling gravity at the moment.
Now send me one back.
J.

'Well, hello there, stranger!'

Badger – who'd been snoring on the front step – was awake and bounding across the yard in a nanosecond, whining happily as Meg laughingly kissed the top of his head and made a fuss of him.

Lucy, who'd been unpegging the laundry, stopped dead at the sight of Meg striding towards her, the shirt she was holding falling from her hands. Meg had only been gone for a long weekend but it might as well have been a year, or a lifetime – was that really her? She was wearing clothes that had most definitely *not* come from Dolores's store, she had put her hair back in a ponytail that somehow looked more catwalk than gym-bunny because of the way she'd wrapped her own hair around the band, and she was smiling – beaming, in fact – in a way that Lucy hadn't seen . . . well, since that day when she'd had her final dress fitting and was still anticipating the beginning of her Happy Ever After.

Meg threw her arms around her. 'Oh, I missed you!' she gushed, enveloping Lucy in a cloud of expensive-smelling shampoo as Badger ran happy circles around them both.

'Stranger's right! Look at you!' Lucy exclaimed, pulling back to get a better look. 'What the hell happened? Did they clone you out there? And *how* tiny is your ass in those jeans?'

Meg giggled, waving away the compliment. 'Oh, it's just because Ronnie gave me some of her stuff. Her apartment's really small and she's got *way* too many pairs of jeans, so—' She shrugged.

Lucy turned her around on the spot. 'How much did they cost? You can tell they're expensive from the way they fit.'

'Really?' Meg asked. 'Jeez, I have no idea.'

Lucy looked at her friend's pert derrière jealously. 'It's not fair. I was on at Tuck for ages to get me a pair but . . .' She shrugged, bringing her hands to rest on her belly. 'What's the point now?'

Meg looked down at her bump with amazement. 'I swear to God it's grown just since I was gone!'

'Tell me about it,' Lucy groaned, pushing her hips forward to take some of the strain off her back. She had finally hit the stage where her bump was unmistakably baby – strangers smiled at her with kindly expressions when she passed, the supermarket clerks insisted on taking her groceries to the car and she loved it. She felt special. She felt *seen*.

'Are you tired? Here, let me finish that for you,' Meg said, dropping her bag to the ground and beginning to unpeg the rest of the clothes.

Lucy sank onto the plastic chair by the door and watched her, still marvelling at the transformation. The sun was sinking fast, its rays dazzling her from behind the hotel roofline and she had to shade her eyes. 'So then, tell me all about it – what was it like? Noisy? Dirty? Too many people about?'

Lucy realized too late that her big maternity over-bump knickers were hanging on the line, but Meg unclipped them without seeming to notice.

'No, actually. I mean, yes, of course, all those things, but also . . .' She wrinkled her nose, her eyes bright. 'Kind of great.'

'*Great?* The Big Smoke? Everything you said you never wanted?'

Meg glanced across at her, still beaming. 'We did so many great things. I went to Niagara! I mean, oh, my God! Have you ever been?'

Lucy shook her head, already feeling worn out by Meg's new energy level.

'You've *got* to go. And SUP boarding, you know, when you stand on the board and paddle? You'd love it. We should go down to Vermilion Lake and—'

'Ha, you think?' Lucy scoffed, hugging her belly. 'My balance is shot to hell. I can barely stand on one leg to get my pants on. I don't fancy my chances on a surfboard.'

Meg chuckled as she unpegged the final item – a pair of maternity jeans that looked, to Lucy's eye, as though they'd fit Texas – and picked up the basket. 'Shall I make us a coffee? I'm dying of thirst. I've come straight off the coach,' she said, heading inside.

'Sure.' Lucy went to hoist herself out of the chair again, but Meg told her to stay put. 'So how's Ronnie?' Lucy called into the kitchen, using the special voice they always reserved for talking about Meg's snooty sister.

'Ron? She's great,' Meg said, speaking over her shoulder as she reached up for the cups from the top shelf and managing to look even more long-legged than she already did. 'We had such a great time together. We really talked, you know?'

'*Really?*'

Meg cradled the mugs in her palms and leaned against the counter. 'I don't know *why* it felt so different being with her – maybe because we were on her patch? I didn't . . . I didn't feel like she was judging me, I guess.' She shrugged, pushing herself to standing again. 'I just . . . I actually feel like I've got my sister back.'

'Well, that's great,' Lucy said flatly, turning away and looking up at the mountains.

'*And* she's got herself a new man.'

Lucy spun back on her seat. 'No way! I thought she only lived to work?'

'Nope,' Meg said, smacking her lips together as though she was savouring the word, and walking to the fridge for the milk.

'Jesus, there goes my bet that she'd die a virgin.'

Meg chuckled. 'Don't!'

'Well, tell me about him,' Lucy said with an impatient sigh. 'Do we approve?'

'Entirely. He's gorgeous. Thirty-one I think? Called Jack. He's a doctor at the same hospital. Saves lives by day and then walks his elderly neighbour's dog at the weekends.' She rolled her eyes. 'He's perfect and certainly perfect for her. They're smitten with each other.'

'Wow.' Lucy swallowed, feeling a drop of bile in the back of her throat. She stretched; heartburn was beginning to become a problem, just as the nausea was starting to settle.

'We went out on his boat on the lake on Sunday too. It was so cool.'

Lucy jerked in surprise. He had a boat too? 'Wasn't that awkward, just the three of you? I'd have felt such a gooseberry.'

There was a small pause and Lucy peered into the darkness of the kitchen, wondering if Meg had heard her and watching as she poured the boiling water, her back looking narrow and her shoulder blades prominent beneath her new, silky, designer T-shirt.

'There you go,' Meg smiled, turning and coming back outside, handing her the mug.

Meg sat on the step beside her, resting against the wall and smiling at Badger as he sat on her feet as though trying to stop her from leaving again.

'So what else? Niagara, paddle-boarding, sailing . . . ?'

Meg inhaled deeply. 'Uh . . . so, sunbathing in the park, a bit of clothes shopping, mooching in bookshops, brunches . . . Oh! And we had drinks at Soho House!'

Lucy's eyes narrowed. 'What? Like in *Sex and the City*?'

'Exactly! They've got one in Toronto.'

'But I thought that was a private club?'

'It is, but Jack's got a friend who's a member there.'

'A friend?'

Meg shrugged dismissively, closing her eyes and angling her face up as she always did to catch the last of the day's rays. 'Anyway, enough about me, how's everything been here? Badger been good?'

'No trouble.'

'I just popped in on Dolores.'

She was staying in the hotel, where Barbara could look after her easily as the doctors had put her in charge of Dolores's medication schedule. 'Yeah? How did she seem to you?'

Meg opened her eyes and looked up at Lucy, the bright sunlight carving shadows into her hollow cheeks. 'Weaker. Older. Frailer.'

'I know,' Lucy tutted. 'And she's in complete denial, of course. Thinks she can go straight back to how things were before, like any normal seventy-three-year-old woman who's played fisticuffs with a bear. She's driving Mom nuts.'

Meg gave a shiver as she remembered it in vivid technicolour. Going to the city so soon afterwards – where the most problematic wildlife was racoons raiding the bins –

had helped to dim the trauma of the attack, but being back here, smelling the drift of pines on the breeze, hearing the silence, seeing this big sky . . . She remembered how it had felt to look straight into the bear's eyes. It had felt like falling into a bottomless crevasse. It had felt like the end.

'But don't worry, Mom's on it. She won't leave the room till Dolores has cleared her plate.'

'I've been so worried about her. I didn't want to leave her at all but she insisted I go.'

'Well, it looks like she was right. You seem . . . refreshed? Rejuvenated?' She arched an eyebrow. 'Which one do I mean?'

Meg shrugged. 'No idea. Right now all I feel is tired. Three and a half hours on the plane and two hours back from Calgary . . . ugh. I'm no traveller, that's for sure. It's a bath and early to bed for me tonight.' She tipped her head back and looked up into the sky again. 'Oh, but I missed seeing this, though,' she sighed, her eyes lazily tracking a plane that threaded through the clouds like a needle. 'In Toronto, with all those high-rises, you just saw it in little parcels and portions and chunks.'

'Well, at least there's something we do better,' Lucy said, unable to keep the testiness out of her voice.

Meg looked across at her and reached out a hand to squeeze hers. 'And of course I missed *you* guys like mad. How are you and the bub? No further problems I hope . . . ?'

Lucy shook her head. 'No, we're all good. We got away scot-free, it seems.'

'That baby's a lucky charm,' Meg smiled. 'And how's Tuck?'

Lucy nodded, unable to keep from rolling her eyes. 'You know Tuck . . .'

'What's he doing?'

'What do you think?' Lucy groaned, anticipating another lonely night. 'The submissions deadline is Friday. Ever since he changed the theme of the film, he's been behind—'

'Changed the theme? What do you mean?'

'Didn't I tell you?' Lucy asked with a sigh. 'Oh, yes. As if running the company on his own isn't enough, now he's decided to change the film altogether. It's quite unbelievable how many reasons he has for *not* coming home.'

Meg frowned. 'Change it how?'

'Your guess is as good as mine. He won't tell me.' Lucy shrugged. 'Honestly, though, you'd think he was working for Attenborough the amount of hours he's put in on it.'

'Well, I guess it's good that he wants to get it right.' Meg's voice was muted and they were both quiet for a moment.

'I think he can't bear to finish it, that's the thing,' Lucy murmured. 'When he's in the studio, I think it's like Mitch is still there – he can see his face, hear his voice. But once this one's done, there'll never be . . .' She swallowed hard. 'There'll never be any more films of the two of them. The snow will be here before we know it but there won't be any more camping trips, no more films. Once he finishes this one, that's it, it's really over.'

Meg was staring at the ridge line, a wisp of clouds curling off the top. Her jaw was set but her eyes were sad and Lucy could see that fizzing brightness she'd brought back from the big city dissipating like bubbles in the surf. Meg looked over at her, then away again, as though she couldn't maintain eye contact.

Lucy shifted on her seat, sensing something.

'I met a guy out there.' Meg said the words so quietly, at

first Lucy wasn't sure she'd heard correctly, Meg's eyes trained firmly on Badger who was staring up at her lovingly, her feet still trapped beneath his warm, heavy body.

'*What?*' Lucy gasped, feeling that she might fall off the chair.

'I slept with him.' This time Meg looked straight at her as she said it, as though daring Lucy to disbelieve her.

Lucy's mouth gawped open as the words rebounded around and around in her head and yet still made no sense.

'His name is Hap—' When she saw Lucy's expression at that, she added quickly, 'It's a nickname. His real name is . . .' She frowned. 'Actually, I don't remember it but everyone calls him Hap. His surname is Hazard, so . . . haphazard?'

Lucy could only stare at her.

'Anyway, he's Jack's friend, the one who got us into Soho House. He's the sales director for an ice wine company in BC,' she continued, looking more and more nervous. 'He's nice.'

Meg swallowed and looked away, ruffling Badger's head – he had come up to sitting again, alerted by the change of tone in her voice – before looking back at her again. 'Can you say something? Please?'

But Lucy couldn't find the words.

'I thought you'd be pleased for me.'

'Pleased?' Lucy almost choked on the word. It was like a stone in her throat.

'Yes. Ronnie said it was the best thing to do. She said it had to happen sooner or later and that it was better sooner.'

'Oh, she said that, did she?' Lucy asked, sarcasm dripping from every word. 'Because she's the expert in love as well as everything else? She knows what it feels like to lose the most important person in her life, does she?'

Meg swallowed, knowing perfectly well she already did – they were orphans, after all – but not wanting to go there. 'She didn't mean it like that.'

'No? You swan off for a weekend in the city and become, like, this whole other person and just hook up with some smooth wine guy?' Lucy said disbelievingly. 'The Meg I know wouldn't do that! What about Mitch?'

Meg flinched and Lucy thought it was as though she'd been shot every time his name was said.

'It's been four months, Meg! Four! That's *nothing*. Don't you think he deserved a little more respect than that?' Lucy asked angrily.

Tears filled Meg's eyes and Lucy watched as she inhaled slowly, as though the very air was like razorblades. Four months was nothing. No time. And he was gone now till the end of time. 'He's not coming back,' Meg said quietly, her voice wobbling.

'No. But don't forget him too quick, will you?'

Meg was on her feet at that, poor Badger almost leaping into the air. 'How could you say that to me? You, of all people? You know how much I loved him.'

'We all loved him!'

'*So?*' Meg cried. 'It still doesn't compare! *I* was going to be his wife! *I* was going to have his babies, *I* was going to share his life,' Meg cried. 'Not you. Not Tuck. He was *mine*. I'm the one who lost everything! I know you and Tuck loved him, Lucy – but I loved him most!'

'Well, now, it doesn't seem like it, does it?' Lucy asked, sitting rigidly in her chair, watching as Meg trembled, her arms and legs like bicycle spokes, her eyes too big for her face, fat tears sliding down her cheeks like raindrops on a window.

'I-I thought . . .' Meg's chest filled up with air, huge heaving sobs rolling upwards, coming out in judders. 'I th-thought y-you'd understand.'

But Lucy folded her arms, aware of the way they sat ridiculously atop her bump and they stared at one another, the sun glinting off Meg's head like a polished halo.

A minute passed in silence, a world crashed between them.

'Come on, Badger,' Meg mumbled finally, picking up her bag and turning away. Badger immediately, unquestioningly trotted at Meg's feet, not turning back once to look at her, Lucy, the person who had fed, watered, exercised and protected him for four days. But then, did she expect any better? Wasn't it always the case, Meg came first?

Lucy watched them cross the courtyard, Meg's shoulders several inches higher than they should have been, before turning out of sight. Lucy stared at the spot where they weren't for a long time, her body immobile but feeling everything that she so successfully kept hidden from sight beginning to shift. She wasn't like Meg; she couldn't wear her emotions, couldn't show off her victimhood.

But she was alone now. There was no one here; there hardly ever was. And as the sun finally dipped behind the mountains, casting her into shadow, her tears came too, every bit as hot and every bit as raw.

Wednesday 9 August 2017
From: Jonas Solberg

Meg? Are you there?

Chapter Twenty-three

Monday 23 October 2017

'Brrrr,' Meg shivered, pushing the door closed with her bottom and trapping the outside out. She could barely see over the boxes stacked in her arms, her chin holding them in place. 'It's freezing out there. It won't be long now till the snow comes. Did you see the clouds over Rundle?'

She stopped as she bent her knees in a deep squat and dropped the boxes – the new-season snow boots – carefully in a tower on the floor, beside the other eight stacks. They'd all need to be barcoded and priced and then arranged by style number and then size, out back. She was going to be so busy today. 'I bet—'

She stopped talking as she caught sight of Dolores's expression. Even sitting in a chair with a tartan blanket on her lap – doctor's orders – she looked fearsome. 'You just missed a call, missy.'

Her breath caught. Jonas? 'Oh?'

'Steven Pritchard at Kate Spade?'

Meg swallowed. Oh, God. She had all but put that out of her mind. Lucy's words during their fight all those weeks ago had struck bone and she'd taken a conscious step back from everything Toronto had promised – carefree youth, a career, romance, smashed avocadoes . . . Because Lucy had been right – what had she been thinking, imagining that the way to move on from Mitch was with another man? Imagining she could land a job like that? Her brief flash of self-belief had been nothing but a momentary lapse into madness and she had stepped back from everyone and everything. She hadn't returned the texts sent by Hap, the emails sent by Jonas, or the messages left by Kate Spade's office on her landline, hoping they'd get the hint sooner or later. Clearly, for the lot of them, it was going to be later. 'Look – it isn't what you think, OK? I didn't approach them. *I* didn't even want to be involved. Someone else put my name forward a while ago. It's nothing.'

'How is it nothing? They're saying they want you to fly to New York to meet them. Something about a redesign?'

Meg shook her head and looked away, feeling as though a weight was pressing down on her chest. 'I'll call them back. I'll tell them I'm not interested.'

'You're too late. I already told them,' Dolores said, not blinking once. 'That you're going.'

It was a moment before Meg realized what she'd said. *'What?'*

'They've booked you a flight for Wednesday of next week and they're going to put you up in some fancy-pants hotel overnight.'

'Dolores! What did you do that for?' Meg shrieked.

'Because you wouldn't! You're so determined to come back here and just . . . fester. I don't know what's happened to you, girl? When you got off the coach from Toronto, you were like one of those Disney cartoon animals – all bright eyes and a bushy tail. You were telling me how you were going to start this . . . *boarding* thing on the lakes every day and start travelling more, go and see Ronnie for long week-ends . . . But I don't know what it is with you, you step back into this town and it's like your lights go out. And all that ambition, all those plans to do something with your life, they just fall away.'

Meg steadied her breath, remembering still all too vividly, word for word, the fight with Lucy. 'Dolores, I know you're only trying to do what's best but I don't know how many more times I can say it. I'm happy here. I love working with you—'

'Pfffft,' Dolores scoffed.

'I do!'

Dolores stared at her, long and hard. 'You know you mean the world to me, Meg,' she said, watching her closely.

'I know,' Meg said quietly.

'And I hope it wouldn't disrespect your own dear mother if I said you're the daughter I never had. But if you're not careful, one day you're going to turn around and realize you've become me! Stuck in this town, wasting your life. And I don't want that for you.'

'But what if I do?'

'Don't be so ridiculous,' the older woman said, pursing her lips together.

Meg sighed and punched the keyboard irritably, bringing up her emails. There was one from Jonas – another one. She'd lost count of how many he'd written now and she wished he'd stop – she hadn't replied, not once, since he'd landed. She couldn't explain it. She didn't know why it felt different to correspond with him now he was back on the planet – perhaps space had been the necessary distance she'd needed to feel able to talk honestly and intimately with a person she'd never met. But now that she'd seen his face, now that he was back, now that meeting up was a *possibility* . . . Now that Lucy had spoken the brutal truth . . .

Her eyes scanned the message quickly. It was brief, and to the point, almost as though he'd known she'd be reading it in the middle of an argument.

Dog-Dog-Ellie,

   In one your first emails, you asked what I missed about being on Earth.

   But do you know what I miss, now, about being in space?

   Talking to you.

   J.

Meg felt a cold wind blow through her – fear and panic intermingling. What did it mean? Was it a goodbye? Was he reaching out or giving up?

She turned her back and stared at the towers of shoeboxes, desperate to do something, anything that might stop the black feeling of desolation that was beginning to spread through her. She reached for the barcode scanner kept under the till, and started scanning.

Dolores, watching her agitation, tipped her head to the side. 'When are you going to tell me what happened with Lucy?'

'Nothing's happened with Lucy,' she mumbled.

'Do you think I'm blind? She hasn't been round here once in all the time you've been back. All the cookies are still in the jar, for one thing!' She folded her hands over her lap. 'What did she say to you? Come on, out with it – although I think I can probably imagine.'

Meg winced, knowing full well she really couldn't. What would Dolores think if she knew Meg had moved on to another man so quickly? She'd be as disgusted as Lucy had been. More so, probably. 'I really would rather not talk about it right now.'

Dolores watched her, her handsome face softening as she watched Meg point and beep with studied intensity. 'I've never known you two to go so long without speaking. She's your best friend.'

'Was,' Meg said hotly. 'Friends don't . . . they don't . . .' But she couldn't get the words out, couldn't bear to remember how it had felt to be accused of betraying Mitch, to be moved down the line and demoted in the long queue of those who had loved him most, because she had tried to take a step forwards.

'Look, I know she can be . . . prickly, but it's been a tough pregnancy and the baby's due in just over a month. She needs you.'

'She's got Tuck,' Meg muttered, although they all knew that was scant consolation indeed. How many times had she seen his car still parked outside the Banff Centre editing studios when she'd been driving through town late at night, the only one left in the lot as he locked himself inside a soundproofed room with a film that was fast becoming a paean to lost lives – his own, as well as Mitch's?

She changed the subject, not wanting to dwell on what kind of husband Lucy was saddled with; at least she had one. 'What's the name of that person who called? I'll ring back and tell them to cancel the ticket.'

A beat pulsed. 'I don't remember.'

Meg arched an eyebrow. 'Well, can you at least give me the number?'

Dolores shook her head. 'I didn't think to take it.' She tapped her head. 'My mind isn't what it was, you know.'

'Yeah, right,' Meg muttered with a sigh. 'If you think I believe that for one second—'

'What can I say?' Dolores shrugged stubbornly, rearranging the rug around her legs. 'Ask the doctors. I'm an old woman.'

Tuesday 31 October 2017

Meg stood in the empty room, looking around with aching arms and a stiff neck, her dungarees on and her hair held back with a torn-up shirt. If she didn't know otherwise, she'd have thought the bears had got into the cabin, it looked so wrecked; the curtains were off the windows, the rugs pulled up and the paint-splattered floors ready for sanding. Most of the furniture she owned was piled in a heap on the grass with a tarp pulled tightly across it, and she had been sending nightly prayers to the weather gods not to send in either the rain or snow for at least another two days. And she was getting away with it – just; although it was hardly the time of year to decide to redecorate, she hadn't been up to doing this before now. Her instinct had been to preserve every last atom of the life she'd shared with Mitch, to make a museum of their home, to mummify the past. But with the Kate Spade interview looming ever larger on her horizon – she was flying out to New York tomorrow – and since Dolores had sabotaged her every attempt to duck, dive, weave and bob away from this opportunity, she'd been forced to acknowledge the fact that actually, she was really rather excited. She'd been designing non-stop for almost a week now, having taken time off at Dolores's urgings to put together a book to show the Kate Spade people, and now she could hardly stop. Ideas were everywhere, inspiration in every glance, and the fizz she'd felt in Toronto was back again. She wanted to create, to play, to indulge, to be free – and Lucy's righteous anger was becoming more and more distant as the silence between them continued to spread like blood in the snow.

Occasionally it reared its ugly head, usually in the evenings when she was sitting alone up here with just Badger for company and she was besieged by memories of Mitch at every turn. Before this week, the only solution she'd been able to think of had been to leave here, to just walk away from the home they'd shared, but that felt like defeat – and besides, Mitch would still be in her head wherever she went. No, what she needed was to find a way of living with the past and this, she had decided, was the answer. The cabin was still their home, but it had *her* mark on it now – Mitch would never have tolerated the dusky pink she'd put in the main bedroom (her first task, in the hope that she'd be able to sleep in there again, but to no avail) and he'd have moved back into town if he'd seen the Japanese cherry-blossom trompe l'œil she'd painted on the back wall of the bathroom. But it was this room, the spare room, that she was most thrilled with, that felt most *her*. She knew it was in here that she'd continue to sleep.

She walked around it slowly, her eyes trailing over the still-wet walls that were a chalky ice blue at the skirting boards, segueing upwards into an ever deeper and deeper indigo that turned midnight at the ceiling and was speckled with hand-painted stars and thousands of golden flecks thanks to a translucent glitter bicycle paint she'd found at the hardware store.

Slowly, feeling stiff, she got down on the floor, her bones hard on the unforgiving boards. Badger trotted over and lay down beside her, his head resting heavily on her tummy as she stared up at her home-made twilight sky. She could touch this one, kiss the stars if she wanted to; that had been the point – to bring Mitch back into reach again. But as she looked around at her very own *'long, delirious, burning blue'*, it wasn't Mitch who crowded her thoughts. This sky belonged to another.

It was four o'clock when Lucy walked through the revolving doors of the Homestead, one of the busiest periods of the day for the hotel. Barbara was at the reception desk, drawing on a town map for a Chinese couple and ringing in red pen – no doubt – Bob's Pizzeria (she and Bob were loosely an 'item'), her pearl necklace and perfectly coiffed hair setting the genteel tone for the establishment.

Lucy glanced across at the lounge as she made her way over, one protective hand on her bump as she negotiated past jutting elbows and sharp-cornered handbags. The fire in the imposing grey-stone fireplace was roaring, the red-patterned carpet wet with footprints, the chairs clustered in groups around it all filled with the tired bodies of the day's enthusiastic hikers back down from the mountains, now that the light was fading, and enjoying afternoon tea.

'You have a nice day now,' Barbara smiled, waving off the couple.

'Full house again?' Lucy murmured to her mother as she stepped behind the desk and opened the filing cabinet, looking for a stapler.

'I could have sold the rooms three times over,' Barbara murmured back. 'I can't remember the last time we had a pre-season like this. I haven't had to put up the offers card once.'

'Well, be grateful, whatever it's about.'

'What are you looking for?' Barbara frowned as Lucy crouched on her ankles and tried the other drawers, opening one accidentally against her mother's thigh. 'Ow!'

'The stapler. I've been doing last month's accounts.'

Barbara tutted and opened the front drawer, handing it to her.

'Thanks,' Lucy said, just as she realized she couldn't get back up again.

Barbara sighed and reached out a hand to pull her. 'Honestly, you're pregnant, not disabled.'

Lucy sighed too but didn't bother trying to defend herself as she was hoisted up. The truth was, she *was* enormous. She had sailed past the 'neat' stage, without so much as a pit stop, and with only four weeks to go, she felt ready to burst, her skin so tight she thought it might split; she could barely sleep, unable to get comfortable on her side – she'd always been a tummy sleeper – and even when she did drop off, she was then disturbed with having to get up several times in the night needing to make toilet trips. Tuck had moved into the spare room – still not a nursery, as he found excuse after excuse to put off decorating it – fed up with her new snoring problem too. The heartburn was almost constant, her back ached, her breasts had doubled in size . . . The entire pregnancy had felt like an endurance event and she just wanted this baby out now.

She held up the stapler wearily. 'Thanks. I'll catch you—'

'Wait,' Barbara said, sounding guilty. 'What are you doing for dinner tonight?'

Lucy looked confused. 'I hadn't thought about it. I'll probably just get a—'

'I mean, do you have any plans? Come over here. I've got a chicken pie ready. I don't like to think of you eating on your own over there.'

'Mom, it's fine,' Lucy muttered with a roll of her eyes.

'It's not fine. When's Tuck back from Toronto?'

'Next Monday. Mom, he's only just gone!'

'But I don't suppose you've made any plans to see anyone? Like—'

'I'm too wiped to socialize. All I want to do is sleep.'

Barbara frowned. 'You shouldn't be this exhausted. It isn't right.'

'Well, I'm obviously doing something wrong. No doubt you can advise me, in all your infinite wisdom,' she muttered sarcastically, putting a hand in the small of her back and pushing backwards, trying to stretch out her hips.

'I was being sympathetic, Lucy!' Barbara reached out an arm to her daughter. 'I'm worried about you, that's all. You haven't been yourself lately.'

Lucy pointed to her swollen stomach. 'Well, my body's been invaded by an alien, in case you hadn't noticed.'

'Darling, this is supposed to be a happy time for you. Instead, every time I see you, you seem so downhearted.' She tipped her head to the side. 'Why don't you try to make things up with Meg? Dolores tells me she's been very upset too.'

'Ha, hasn't looked like it to me,' Lucy said bitterly, remembering how she'd seen Meg coming out of the cinema on Wolf Street with Josie Wilson and Denise Lam – girls in their year at high school – last week.

'Well, did you hear she's going to New York tomorrow for a new job?'

'What?' Lucy's head whipped up.

'I don't mean she's moving there!' Barbara said quickly, catching sight of her daughter's aghast expression. 'But Dolores says she's in the running to redo the logo for some big designer. They want to meet her; apparently they've been very persistent.'

'Bully for her,' Lucy muttered, staring at her feet but barely able to see the tips of her toes.

'Lucy, you should be proud of her – she's beginning to do well. Didn't we always say she was talented? This is exactly what she needs to start getting her life back on track.'

Lucy felt her latent anger hit boiling point. 'Oh, trust me, her life is back on track, all right!'

Barbara looked taken aback. 'What does that mean?'

'You all think she's broken, like she's this delicate little doll, but she's not!' Lucy spat. 'She's not pining for Mitch! She's already moved on. It's onwards and upwards for her!'

'Lucy—!'

But she had already turned away, her cheeks hot with anger, betrayal, panic. No one else saw it. Mitch dying was Meg's get-out-of-jail-free card – or rather, get-out-of-Banff. Toronto had just been the beginning. Now it was New York. Where next? London? Berlin?

'Lucy!'

'Leave it, Mom. You don't know what you're talking about.'

'At least come for dinner,' Barbara called after her. 'Seven o'clock?'

Lucy didn't turn back – she didn't want her mother to see her tears – but she knew she'd be there. It was only just gone four and she was already starving.

*

Tuck watched the crowds as they spilled past the stand, some browsing disinterestedly, coffee in hand, and with no idea of who or what Titch was, others making beelines straight for him, high-fives ready as though he was the only reason they'd come.

Behind him, last year's film ran on a loop, the lights thrown from it cascading over him like a glitter ball. He and Mitch had had special suits made with coloured LED lights sewn along the seams and they'd planted coloured flares in the snow along their route which ignited as they wove their way past. Lucy and Meg had filmed them descending on the blackest night, the entire side of the mountain glowing a rainbow of colours, like an aurora borealis that had fallen to Earth.

He stretched, looking up at the arena ceiling and wishing he could see the sky. These fluorescent lights sapped his energy and he was already tired enough – he had crashed at the hotel last night, waking at three to find himself still dressed and on top of the covers, empty miniature bottles of whiskey scattered around him.

It was his first Snow Show without Mitch so he'd known it was going to be hard – but he hadn't reckoned on how boring it would be too, with no one to chat to or mess about with. And basic things like who'd man the stall when he needed to pee? He'd made the barest of small talk with the people on the stands either side of his, but it was scant pickings – one represented a Peruvian knitting cooperative and barely spoke English; the other was an avalanche safety specialist whose kit was near-identical to Mitch's that hadn't saved him. Tuck could barely bring himself to look at them.

He grabbed his iPad and looked again at the new orders.

Twenty-eight boutiques signed and this gig had only been going two days. They'd had a total of eighty-three last season and so far he'd signed with seven new stores. Everyone was going mad for Meg's graphics again. Last year she'd kept it minimal and used a 'flip-flop' paint, like the kind used on some top-marque sports cars, switching from magenta to orange, or blue to yellow with the merest ankle flex. The year before that, she'd used holograms on the top sheet and base. For this season, she'd been inspired by tattoos, going in hard with pen-and-ink detail, and using jewel colours that stopped just a tint short of neon. Tuck liked the snakeskin-effect background best – so had Mitch – and everyone who stopped at the stand kept reaching up to touch them. In short, they were the bomb and he was pretty sure he was going to go back home with many more clients than he'd arrived with.

A couple of guys who he'd seen doing the circuit came back again, looking up intently at the designs, and Tuck felt hopeful he'd get another order. They were dressed in dark jeans and half-zip jumpers; one of them had a beard. They looked as though they were trade.

'Hey there, can I help you with anything?' Tuck asked, putting the iPad back in his bag and wandering over.

'Looks like you're really doing something new here,' the bearded guy said, pointing to the small boards.

Tuck brought one down. 'Yeah. We set up eleven years ago with these babies, but as you can see, we've extended into the mainstream market too.' He indicated the regular-sized snowboards.

'Demand?'

'Had to. People were callin' for it. They loved what they

could do on these and wanted us to give 'em so back-country shredding sticks too.' He brought down one of the bigger boards and flipped it over so they could see just how great Meg's graphics looked scaled up too. 'These are on point for when you're getting serious air. Did you see our limited-edition Slayer series a couple of years back?'

'Sure heard about them,' the bearded guy said.

'They're hall of fame now, man. One of them comes up now, you're talking five, six thou.'

'Thought about reissuing them?'

'Hell, no,' Tuck laughed. 'Onwards.' He winked. 'It keeps resale values up too.'

He watched as they held the boards in their hands and turned them over with professional interest, scrutinizing them closely. 'We actually get some people buying them just to hang on their walls,' he continued. 'People who don't even board.' Tuck chuckled and scratched his head. 'Beats me, man, but there it is.'

'All the gear, huh?' The man laughed as his companion enquiringly slid his finger into the notch at the back of one of the bigger boards. 'And these swallow-tails—'

'Great for pow, man, gives you tons more response in the deep stuff. Only found it out by accident when I split a board and lost a chunk out riding one day with my buddy.' His smile faltered as he inadvertently brought Mitch back into the picture. 'We've put in for a patent for it. Just waiting to hear back.'

He saw the bearded guy look past him at the video screen. 'Cool film. That you?'

'Yep.' Tuck nodded as he jammed his hands in his jeans pockets and watched himself and Mitch tearing up the night, waking it up with colours that usually only bloomed under the sun. 'We're using the R170s you're holding there. Waisted, camber, notch tail.'

'Not to mention these shit-hot graphics,' the second man said, his eyes on the screen too. 'Do you do this as promo?'

'Sorta. We make two films a year – one's a snowboard film, the other's bikes in the summer – and submit them for the Banff Film Festival. That's where we're from, so it makes sense to get involved.' He shrugged.

'Ever won?'

'Not yet, though we've been shortlisted for Best Mountain category three times now.'

'I like that. "Not *yet*",' the bearded man said, his eyes still on the screen.

'That's last year's film. This year's festival is kicking off in a few weeks.'

'And you've got something in?'

He paused a moment, as though checking his voice would hold. 'That's right.'

'So, what – you're going for the prize money?'

Tuck scoffed at the idea. $4,000? 'Nuh, it wouldn't keep us in beers. The aim is to get selected for the worldwide tour. Forty countries, four hundred thousand visitors.'

The unbearded guy looked impressed. 'Those are good numbers.'

'And all we gotta pay is our time for the filming and the submission fee,' Tuck grinned, feeling proud of Mitch's canny marketing idea. 'It's an amazing vehicle for enhancing visibility and growing our brand awareness.'

'I imagine that must be going well for you, especially since the win at Aspen.'

Tuck's grin grew and his chest puffed up proudly. 'You know about that?'

'Sure. It's our job to know.'

'Man, our orders are up twenty-seven per cent on the back of it and it's been *insane* here – everyone wants to know about us now.' It wasn't entirely true. They were doing well but things were building progressively – as Mitch had forecast – and they needed their luck to continue. More pros, more wins, more films, more tours, more orders . . . More graft. More of this shit. Standing in windowless trade centres. Working alone in an attic . . .

'And what, is it just you running the outfit? You got a team behind you?' the bearded guy asked, looking closely at the ply layers.

Tuck looked back at them, his smile frozen now on his face. Mitch wasn't here. He should be here. 'Just me, man,' he said finally. 'Say, where's your store anyway? You didn't say.'

The bearded guy put down the board. 'We don't have one.'

No store? In a flash, Tuck felt his stupidity, his pride, trip him up. He'd been assuming they were retailers looking to stock the brand but instead they were competitors? And here he'd been, running his mouth off, telling them about their unique marketing strategies that Mitch had devised, the patents they had pending . . . He grabbed the boards angrily, whisking them away from him.

'Fuck, man! And I've been—' He felt the red mist descend. He was so stupid. So fuckin' stupid. This was why Mitch always took the lead at these things; he knew how to smell a rat. 'Where the fuck you from?'

The bearded man looked nonplussed as he reached into his jeans and pulled out a card. Tuck felt his stomach drop as he caught sight of the name on it. The biggest in the business.

The bearded guy smiled. 'Know somewhere we can talk?'

Chapter Twenty-four

Wednesday 1 November 2017

'Ron, I can't talk!' Meg panted, running through the main room with the wheelie bag unzipped. 'I've got a flight to catch, remember?'

'Oh, shit, that's *today*?'

'Yes!'

Ronnie gave an excited squeal and Meg could hear her clapping her hands together too. 'What you wearing?'

'My black suit.'

There was a short pause. 'The boot-leg one?'

Meg got to the bedroom and dropped the bag on the bed. She had hesitated about wearing it too, but only because the last time she'd worn it, they'd buried Mitch. But what choice did she have? She didn't have another one or anything remotely businesslike in her wardrobe. 'Yes! Why?'

'I'd reconsider.'

'I can't!' Meg wailed. 'This is it, this is all I've got. There's nothing else that's remotely right for a . . . Oh, God, a meeting with a fashion company in New York.' She sank onto the edge of the bed, her head in her hands. 'What am I doing? This is a joke. I can't go there.'

'Of course you can!' Ronnie said fiercely. 'It's not about what you're wearing, anyway.'

'Are you kidding? Of course it is! Why would they trust my style if I can't even dress for the interview properly?'

'There's nothing wrong with that suit.'

'But you just said—'

'Ignore me. The suit is great. The suit is black. It's New York – that's all it has to be.'

'What? Black?'

'Exactly. Just look like an angel of death and they'll love you. More to the point, have you got your portfolio ready?'

Meg got up and walked back through to the main room. 'You could say that.' She looked around despairingly – papers were strewn over every surface, her draft desk tilted up in the corner from where she had spent every evening and most of the nights for the past week, trying to come up with ideas. She still wasn't sure whether she'd got anything yet, or whether she was even supposed to? Perhaps they wanted to meet her *before* briefing her? That was Dolores's view but Meg hadn't been able to stop herself from trying out ideas, playing with designs, motifs, colours . . .

She'd spent hours at the public library photocopying early drafts and photos of the designs she'd drawn for Titch over the years. Of course, she could have asked Tuck for access to the archives and old stock but notwithstanding the fact that she still felt unable to look him in the eye, she didn't want it getting back to Lucy about this. Her? Going to New York for a job opportunity? She could only imagine the response that would prompt.

'Oh, hey, wait!' Ronnie cried suddenly. 'The black jeans I gave you.'

'What about them?'

'Wear those.'

Meg gasped. 'I can't wear *jeans* to a job interview.'

Ronnie sighed. 'Look, I realize this is an alien concept to you but most jeans now cost more than a suit. The days of wearing them only at the weekends are long gone. And this is a fashion company you're seeing, remember. You could wear a bin bag just so long as you can accessorize it properly.'

'But what about the suit?' Meg asked, looking at her black suit on the bed. It had a fair amount of shine to it.

'Ditch the suit. Burn it. It's a crime against fashion.'

'You just said—'

'I was being kind. You know, supportive sister?'

Meg grimaced, running back to the spare room – she hadn't been able to bring herself to move back into the main bedroom – hurriedly pulling clothes out of drawers and looking for the jeans. 'I don't know where they are,' she mumbled. 'What time is it?'

'Ten to eleven.'

'Oh God,' she wailed. 'I've *got* to leave here by eleven at the latest.'

'Loadsa time.' Ronnie's grin was audible. 'And excuse me, but why don't you know where they are? Don't tell me you haven't been wearing them.'

'I haven't had time,' Meg replied in panic.

'You haven't had time to wear a pair of jeans?' Ronnie shrieked. 'Don't you know how good your backside looks in those jeans? Have you any idea how much they cost?'

'Sorry,' Meg muttered, knowing the real reason she'd discarded them – they reminded her of the day of the fight with Lucy, of the weekend in Toronto which belonged to another sort of life, but not hers.

'Give them back if you're not going to wear—'

'Oh, got them!' Meg said, spotting them balled up under the desk. She reached for them, her gaze coming to rest on the radio rig. It had been months now since she'd used it. Ever since Jonas had landed, there had seemed to be no point. She didn't want to speak to just anyone. Only him.

She missed him, far more than she had anticipated – she missed her friend in the sky, her light in the dark – he was now earthed again, lost in the masses, moving amidst the seven billion people who shared this planet.

He'd stopped emailing now. Finally. He'd got the point after three months of silence. She'd been surprised at how long it had taken for him to get the message – at first wondering if her Wi-Fi was down, then his as he embarked on the publicity tour, visiting colleges, schools, societies and speaking at conferences, which was the next step after landing, debriefs and reacclimatization. In effect, the expedition had become a 'space roadshow' and though her silence had persisted, one quick Google search and she'd been able to keep track of his movements, clicking on YouTube uploads of press conferences (he'd been right, the very first one, with them dressed in Kazakh national dress, had been a peach) but her favourite was the one of him visiting a school of elementary-grade children – how they went to the loo in space had been their most pressing question, as it had been Lucy's. It was how she'd discovered he was going to be speaking at a public discussion in New York this weekend.

They were going to be in the same city. Together.

She had the advantage – she could sit there anonymously because she was still faceless to him, of course. She could be in the same room and he would never know. She could listen to his experiences without a time delay or static getting in the way; she could watch his face and see his mannerisms as he talked. It had even crossed her mind that he might talk about her and that night he'd become caught up in an emergency on Earth . . . And so the possibility had taken root. It was an idea that wouldn't quite go away. She didn't dare to meet him, but that was different from listening to him – wasn't it? She had been dithering and fretting about it for weeks. If only the gods could give her a sign as to what to do!

She realized suddenly that Ronnie was still talking to her. 'Huh? What?'

'What are you doing?'

'I – I dropped the phone. So how's Jack?' she asked, rolling the jeans into a ball and stuffing them into her bag. 'Oh, shit, wait – what should I wear with them?'

'White T-shirt or shirt. And plain white, I mean, no frickin' mountaineering companies on the front. And plimsolls. White as you can get 'em.'

'Really?' Meg asked, sceptically picking up a pair of her beloved Stan Smiths and a Gap shirt.

'Trust me.'

Meg did trust her, so in they went. 'Jack?' she prompted, zipping up the bag.

'So Jack's good.' Meg heard her sister take a deep breath. 'In fact, it's why I called. We're moving in together.'

'Holy crap!' Meg exclaimed, falling still. 'Are you sure? I mean, it's a bit soon, isn't it? What's it been? Three months?'

'I know, but you remember that thing you told me about you and Mitch? When you know—'

'You know,' Meg sighed. 'Wow. Well, I can't believe it . . . I'm so pleased for you.' And she was. She felt a glow of happiness for her sister that she too would get to feel what

Meg had been telling her about for all these years. How strange, she thought, that their lives were beginning to pivot – Meg's towards a possible career; Ronnie's towards love. Was the world correcting itself? Had they been on the wrong paths?

'But listen, we've got a bit of time off and thought we'd come up for a week or so. Can we stay with you?'

'Of course!' Meg said, flattered they'd want to. As much as she loved the little cabin, the deafening silence from Lucy and the cabin's non-stop solitude were beginning to get to her and she had found she was spending more and more time with Dolores after work, before making the lonely trek back up here. 'When were you thinking?'

'Is next week any good for you? The film festival's on and Jack's a pretty keen climber.'

'He'll be spoilt rotten then. I'll get tickets to some of the events, shall I?'

'Fantastic.' Ronnie sounded pleased. 'And listen, you really go for it in New York, OK, sis? This opportunity, it could be once-in-a-lifetime – it could be your sliding-doors moment when you step into the life you really want. And before you say it, that is *not* a diss on Banff,' she added quickly.

Meg smiled. She knew that now – she knew that Ronnie wasn't looking down on her, only looking out for her.

'And call me when you get back. I want to hear every last detail – down to what perfume they're wearing, you hear me?'

'Loud and clear.' Over and out. Copy that. Jonas Solberg . . .

They hung up in a flurry of blown kisses, Meg dropping the phone on the bed and swearing viciously under her breath as she caught sight of the time. She needed to get herself and Badger down the mountain and Badger dropped off with Dolores in time for her to catch the 12 p.m. bus to Calgary.

She ran back to the kitchen and checked the window was shut, the back door locked . . . her ears straining as they picked up the sound of an engine revving up the mountain, and then, moments later, gurgling to a stop outside.

'What the—?'

Meg ran out, coming to an astonished stop on the porch as she saw Lucy sitting astride Tuck's quad bike.

'Oh, my God, what are you doing on that thing?' she cried angrily, hardly able to believe she was lecturing Lucy about quad-bike safety. She knew perfectly well Lucy could handle one of those machines as well as she could, but the risks were always high – no seat belt, no roll cage, no windscreen, the gradients up here steep – and to have driven it, alone and heavily pregnant . . . ? One mistake and both she and the baby could have been killed. 'Lucy?'

She noticed Lucy's pallor – she looked peaky, a film of sweat on her face even though it was a crisp day, the first leaves beginning to curl on the bough.

'I thought . . . we should . . . talk.'

Meg frowned. Lucy's speech was patchy, her breath coming in small pants. 'Lucy, are you OK? You don't look so good.'

'I'm . . . fine,' Lucy murmured, swinging one leg over the seat and clambering gracelessly down, her face crumpling with pain suddenly, her hand clutching her belly as her feet touched the ground.

'Oh, my God, what's going on?' Meg gasped, running over to her and clutching her by the elbow. But even as she asked the question, she saw the dark stain on Lucy's jeans and understood. 'Your waters have broken,' she whispered, feeling a trickle of fear ripple down her spine. 'Oh, Lucy, the baby's coming.'

'Where *are* they?' Meg cried as she stood at the window, staring down the slope. 'It's been forty minutes already.'

Lucy moaned again and Meg went running back towards the bedroom. She had managed to get her onto the bed – her and Mitch's old one; the spare room she was now using was too much of a tip to get to the bed – and had propped her up with every pillow in the house. She had put a bucket of water on the floor for dipping towels to mop her friend's brow.

Meg didn't like the look of Lucy's colour as she came back into the room. She looked bloodless and the contractions seemed to be coming far too fast, with only a minute or two between them now. Lucy was struggling with the pain and was currently on all fours, her forearms gripping the brass bedstead as she moaned, frantically circling her hips.

'What can I do? Tell me what I can do?' Meg asked desperately. She was all out of ideas. She had called the paramedics, called Barbara, called Tuck – constantly, but he was at that Ski and Snow Show in Toronto, and Meg knew from experience of trying to get hold of Mitch in previous years that there was no cell reception inside the exhibition hall.

She raked her fingers through her hair, feeling helpless as she watched the pain wrack Lucy's body, her face contorted in a silent scream.

'Here, hold me, hold my arm,' she said, rushing forward

as she saw the way Lucy's hands blanched white as the contraction took hold.

Lucy, who couldn't open her eyes, grappled for her and Meg caught hold of her just as the contraction seemed to hit its peak and she let out a scream that sent Badger diving for cover in the furthest part of the cabin.

Meg thought she was going to faint from the pain in her arm, half convinced Lucy was trying to break the bone but she didn't say anything – whatever she felt, it was clear Lucy felt it a thousand-fold.

'Just count slowly,' she managed to say. 'One . . . two . . . three . . . four . . .' And then Lucy's grip loosened suddenly and her entire body fell slack, her great belly swaying almost to her knees as she dropped her head down, exhausted, onto her forearms.

'Are you comfortable?' Meg asked anxiously. 'Would another position be better?'

Lucy shook her head. 'Tuck,' she whispered.

'He's coming. He'll be here soon,' Meg lied. When was he likely to pick up the messages? The show went on till 6 p.m. tonight, EST.

'Tuck.'

'Yes, he's coming. He'll be here.'

'I've got to push!' Lucy said suddenly, tensing again as though an electrical current was coursing through her.

'What? No! No! Don't push, Lucy! It's too soon. The doctor's . . .' Oh, God, the doctor wasn't here. 'Just hold on. Don't push.'

'I've got to!' Lucy grimaced, her neck stretching as she faced the ceiling, like a wolf howling to the moon. 'I can't . . . stop.'

Meg wanted to cry. This baby was going to die. This baby

was going to die, just like Mitch had, because she lived in this godforsaken, unreachable place, where there was no help, no safety . . .

'Give me my arm back. Lucy. Give me my arm,' Meg pleaded, trying to make herself heard as Lucy withdrew inside herself again. 'If you're going to push, we need to get your jeans off and get you turned over . . . Give me my arm, Lucy.' She prised Lucy's fingers, one by one, off her forearm, rubbing her skin tenderly and wondering exactly how she was going to turn her friend, who was gripping the bed and clearly didn't want to be turned.

She reached down and slid the elasticated jeans down to Lucy's knees, blanching as she saw a couple of old, but bad, bruises on her thighs. She needed to get Lucy into a better position.

'Lucy, lean against me,' she said authoritatively. 'Put your weight onto me.'

'No,' Lucy moaned.

'Yes. If you're going to push, we don't want the baby to drop, do we?'

'No,' Lucy moaned but not in agreement to her question. She still didn't want to move.

'I need you to lie back for me, can you do that? Lie back.'

Lucy moaned again, tears streaking down her cheeks. 'I can't do it.'

'Yes, you can. You can do this, Lucy,' Meg said in her most confident voice. Lucy needed someone to trust right now. Even if Meg couldn't do this right, she could at least try to assuage her friend's fear. 'I'll look after you, I promise. Just trust me.'

Lucy opened her eyes, a film of fear drawn across them. 'Help me.'

'I will. Just hold my shoulders.'

Lucy gripped her hard, bruising her skin almost immediately, but Meg didn't flinch; instead she managed to get Lucy to lie back on the pillows, her knees up. She drew a sheet over her legs and reaching underneath, managed to pull off her jeans and knickers.

She ran to the bathroom and washed her hands with soap again, knowing she'd need to be scrupulously clean, and then grabbed the last remaining towels from the cupboard. If this baby did come before the doctor, they'd need to keep it warm, that much was obvious.

Lucy screamed again and Meg, taking one last frantic look out of the window – please God! Where were they? – ran back into the bedroom.

'It's coming!' Lucy cried, her face as red now as it had been white earlier, her fingers gripping the sheets. 'I . . . can't stop . . . it.'

Meg stood rooted to the spot for a moment, realizing this was it. There was no one else here to help them. The paramedics weren't going to make it in time. She was going to have to deliver this baby.

'Meg!' The scream was like a war-cry, deathly.

'Yes, I'm here, I'm here,' she gasped, running forwards and sitting at the end of the bed. What should she do? She didn't know the first thing about babies, only what they'd shown on *Grey's Anatomy*, but there was no time to think, to dither. Lucy's body tensed again, her hips lifting off the bed as a moan began to build, coming from deep within her core. She sounded like an animal.

'OK, Lucy, next time you feel the urge to push, go with it, OK?' Meg, seeing how her hair was plastered with sweat to her temples, reached for the towel in the bucket and mopped her face and brow again. 'How are you feeling?'

Lucy's reply was a cry that concertinaed her body as she folded inwards – her face, her stomach. Meg looked beneath the sheet and gasped.

'Oh, God, Lucy, I can see it! The baby's head is coming. Keep pushing!'

Lucy cried again, her hands twisting the sheet as she gripped harder, as though trying to stay anchored to the bed. 'I can't.'

'You can! Just push, Lucy!'

Lucy strained again, her face becoming berry-red as she tried and tried, but after a few seconds, the tension left her body like a shadow slipping away.

'You're doing brilliantly,' Meg said urgently, her arms outstretched under the sheet and trying not to panic that the baby's head was now out and resting on her hands – could it breathe? Was the cord being squashed?

But a moment later, Lucy tensed again.

'That's it. Now *push*,' Meg ordered. 'Push, Lucy. Push.'

Lucy strained and pushed and panted and then, with a pitch Meg would never forget, screamed.

'Yes! You're doing it!' Meg cried as she felt the baby propelled towards her, the shoulders coming free and then the rest of the body slipping silkily into her outstretched arms.

'Oh, my God,' Meg sobbed as Lucy dropped her head back on the pillows, gasping for breath, crying, exhausted. She pulled the baby to her, away and out from under the tented sheet. Was it breathing? It looked bluer than she'd expected, its hands and feet tightly scrunched, eyes opaque-looking . . . Was this right? Was she supposed to do something now? Why wasn't it crying? Wasn't it supposed to cry? Babies were always crying, weren't they?

The baby's sudden wail startled her. Oh, thank God.

'My baby, my baby,' Lucy moaned, her head lolling back on the pillow as she panted, trying to recover. 'What is it?'

Meg realized she hadn't even checked. She looked down at the child in her arms – wrinkled skin that was a mottled blueish colour turning pinker with every lungful of air, fingers as slender and tiny as matches, a head of dark, almost-black hair, and quite the most enormous pair of testicles!

'It's a boy!' she cried, laughing and sobbing simultaneously as she handed him over to Lucy with trembling arms.

'A boy?' Lucy repeated, her eyes filling with tears as she gazed down in wonderment at her son's face for the first time.

Meg covered them both with the softest towel and then sat back down at the bottom of the bed, watching as Lucy held out her little finger and the baby instinctively grasped it. She pulled the sheet down to protect her friend's modesty too, wondering again at the bruises she saw there. She was going to have some pretty impressive ones of her own tomorrow, she thought, stroking her arms gently.

'He's so beautiful,' Lucy whispered, tears streaming now. 'I can't believe I made him.'

'He's perfect,' Meg smiled, having to wipe back her own tears as the stress of the previous hour caught up with her. They still hadn't cut the cord. Was that OK? She thought she'd read somewhere that it was good to leave it, for a bit anyway. Lucy was too enraptured with her son to think of anything else now but Meg was still worried she hadn't done everything right or fully. She glanced out of the window again. 'Have you thought of a name yet?'

Lucy bit her lip. 'No. Tuck didn't want to "jinx" anything by talking about the baby before he was born.'

'I guess that's fair enough,' Meg smiled, thinking nothing of the sort. But it wouldn't help Lucy to air that opinion now.

'I can't believe we did it,' Lucy whispered, looking up at her with a softness Meg hadn't seen for months. When had they all become so hard-bitten? 'I was so frightened.'

'But you did it.'

'*We* did it,' Lucy said, reaching for her hand. 'I've missed you. I'm sorry.'

'I missed you too—' Meg smiled, turning her head as she saw Badger trot to the door, ears up. He was her alarm system, always hearing things before she did, and she jumped up. 'Oh, please say that's the doctor,' she gasped, running to the window just as a paramedic jumped off a quad bike and began running up the grass with his medical kit. Barbara – being driven by a stern-looking Dolores – was on another quad, cresting the hill just moments later. Poor Barbara looked stricken as she lurched up the grass.

'They're here!' Meg cried, beaming at Lucy and running to open the door. The paramedic already had his hand raised to knock and Meg just pointed to the back bedroom where Lucy and the baby were resting.

'It's OK, she's OK,' she called out, standing at the top of the porch steps and not wanting Barbara to worry for another moment. 'She's fine. They both are.'

'She's had the baby?' Barbara gasped, stumbling to a horrified stop, her hands on her knees. Dolores, still not recovered to her full strength, walked with slow dignity behind her up the slope, her trusty Nordic walking pole in one hand.

Meg nodded. 'And they're both doing well.'

Barbara laid a hand across her chest as though trying to still her heart as she began walking again. 'What . . . What did she have?' she panted. 'Boy or girl?'

'Why don't you come and see for yourself?' Meg smiled, standing back to let her pass.

Dolores came and stood with her on the porch, staring at her closely for a moment, reading the tension in her face. 'And are you OK? That must have been a scare for you.'

Meg shrugged and nodded, hiding her face in Dolores's shoulder as she reached for a hug, all the anxiety and pressure allowed to come out now. She wept quietly for a few moments before pulling back, feeling silly. 'I don't know why I'm crying. It . . . it was amazing,' she hiccupped, wiping her cheeks dry.

'I bet *you* were amazing,' Dolores said, rubbing her back.

'What took them so long? I've been calling for an hour.'

'They had to get transport arranged. We had to rustle up some quad bikes from the Search and Rescue unit, and obviously there's nowhere for a helicopter to land up here. Besides, I think they thought they had more time. That really was a very quick birth.'

'You know Lucy,' Meg shrugged. 'She never did mess about.'

Dolores chuckled. 'Come on then, I'd better take a look. Barbara's first moments as a grandmother . . . ?' She tutted and rolled her eyes. 'God help us all. It's all we're ever going to hear of now.'

They walked back inside together and Meg looked with fresh eyes at her chaotic little cabin, where papers were strewn across the main room, clothes across the spare room and towels across the bedroom, Lucy and her newborn son nuzzling contentedly in bed as the paramedic clamped the cord and Barbara fussed. And sitting in the corner by the door, she saw her own suitcase full of clothes – a plane in Calgary taking off without her, an office door in New York slamming shut, a seat in a conference hall remaining empty as an astronaut talked about living in space . . .

As signs went, this one was pretty unequivocal. She had asked for a sign and her question had been answered – she wasn't going anywhere. She was staying here.

The gods had spoken.

Chapter Twenty-five

Monday 6 November 2017

He was perfect. Ten little fingers, ten little toes; button nose; baby-seal eyes; a cry like a newborn lamb . . . Lucy had never known love like this before. He was hers. Totally and completely hers and no one could ever take him away from her. He was her reward for all the sickness and sleeplessness, the swellings and strange pains that had afflicted her throughout the pregnancy.

It all made sense now. Even coming almost a month early, he'd weighed in at 4.3kg and the paramedic had said she'd 'dodged a bullet' not having to deliver him at full term – he would have been almost 5kg, he'd guessed. It had made her mother sheepish too – all those waspish comments about her size and gargantuan appetite when, all along, she'd been growing this delicious, bouncing butter-ball of a boy. Of course she'd been hungry! Of course she'd been tired! Of course she'd been big!

She sighed, resting her cheek on her arm as she watched him sleep. He was five days old but already his cheeks were rounded and plump, his scrawny little thighs beginning to fill out. He startled a lot – Moro reflex, they called it; particularly strong in boys, apparently – so she liked swaddling him in a blanket, his little pointed chin dipping into the V where it criss-crossed over. It helped to settle him and she liked how solid it made him feel in her arms, like a bag of sugar rather than a flailing mass of limbs as he rooted for the breast.

He was feeding well – she was a natural! – but he wasn't sleeping great on account of her difficulty burping him. Her mother had been a revelation on this topic, showing off some complicated positions to help settle him but whilst they seemed to work fine in the day, they weren't so success-ful in the middle of the night, although possibly that was because she was worried his crying would wake the hotel guests across the courtyard and she gave up sooner. But the pattern seemed to have been set – she'd feed him for forty-five minutes, wind him for another thirty and then would only get ten, fifteen minutes' sleep before he was hungry again – and it was beginning to take its toll. She thought she could probably sleep standing up. The idea of sleeping for more than forty minutes at a stretch had suddenly become the greatest luxury she could imagine . . . Those were the times she wanted Tuck back. If they could just have tag-teamed, she might not feel so desperately exhausted . . .

But she knew she had to be strong now. Stronger than she'd ever been. This baby had opened her eyes only min-utes after opening his own and when Tuck – on being told his son had come early – had said he couldn't leave Toronto early (with 'no cover', he'd said, he couldn't risk losing winning accounts for the coming season) she had seen with crystal clarity how things had to be. How could he not have moved heaven and earth to see his child? Everyone had been astounded – even Dolores, who wasn't prone to senti-mentality.

No. He would never be a good enough father for her child and she knew now that at some level, she'd understood it from the moment she'd seen the line on the pregnancy stick – maybe they both had – his restlessness and persistent refusal to face up to fatherhood, even in spite of his best intentions. Several times, he had raised his game – after the Room 32 incident, and following the bear attack. But he could never sustain it, always falling back into his old habits within days . . . maybe they had both been aware that this clock ticking down in the background would be detonating *them*.

But it was done. There was no turning back. She had grown in more ways than just the physical and she was a mother now. Once upon a time, Tuck had been the sun that shone in her sky but he'd been eclipsed – she had a new sun now. A newborn son.

No one else knew of her decision yet. Not her mother. Not Meg. But yesterday afternoon, when Barbara had taken the baby for a stroll down Banff Avenue – ostensibly to give her a rest and him some air (but really to show him off to everyone) – Lucy had packed a case of his stuff and driven to the Titch store. Mitch always used to sleep over there on a mattress in the eaves whenever he was too late or too drunk to get back up to the cabin, and now Tuck could stay there too until he got himself sorted.

She hadn't yet decided on her cover story or whether even to use one. The truth was ugly but Tuck had made it easy for her in some ways, this latest no-show just another example of what she had to endure – his cheating on her, drinking too much, not coming home . . . But if that wasn't enough, then there were always the bruises. Enough people had seen them over the years, although only one person had ever seen the truth. Just one. That was how good she was at hiding it.

Lightly, she stroked her baby's cheek. He was what she'd been waiting for, he was the strength she needed to make the break and start afresh. Perhaps the way everything had happened hadn't been accidental at all; it had been fate . . .

The sudden sound of the kitchen door slamming shut – making the baby startle in his sleep – made her jump. He was back? Hadn't it crossed his mind that perhaps his new-born son was sleeping and he couldn't blow in and out of the house now like a teenager?

Of course not, and that action alone told her he was still the same man he'd been six months ago, a year, ten years ago. He wasn't a father. How could he be when he was still a boy himself? He was never going to change. Throughout the entire pregnancy she'd waited for him to join her on this path – after Mitch's death, after the bear attack, after she and Meg had fallen out and she'd barely spoken to another soul apart from him and her mother. But he was as fixed as the Pole Star; the man he was now was the man he would always be. She might once have taken comfort in that, construed it as constancy, but their lives had changed in the time it had taken her to grow this baby. She had to leave him.

He was standing there now, gazing at her from the doorway, looking indecently handsome in his jeans and navy parka, blond hair dazzling under the light. He'd always been too handsome for his own good and it had spoilt him – bringing pleasures he hadn't had to earn.

She pulled the belt tighter on her dressing gown (she hadn't got dressed today; if she couldn't stay in her pyjamas with her newborn, when could she?) and watched the change on his face as he saw the baby, swaddled tight and dreaming, on the bed beside her – physical proof at last of what had just been an abstract concept to him up to now, her pregnancy little more than an affront to his desires.

'Holy fuck,' he whispered, tiptoeing over.

He reached a hand to touch him but her arm shot out, stopping him. 'Don't wake him. He's just finished feeding.'

Tuck looked at her, apprehension in his eyes, and nodded. 'You look whacked.'

That was the first thing he said to her on becoming a mother? 'Thanks.'

He didn't seem to notice her sarcasm, instead tilting his head to the side and trying to get a better look at his son's face. 'Does he look like me?'

'He doesn't look like anyone yet.'

'I reckon he's got my nose,' he murmured, carefully lying flat on the mattress – boots and all – his face just centimetres from the baby's.

Lucy didn't need to look between Tuck's once-broken nose and the baby's snub one to know he had nothing of the sort. 'Mmm.'

He chuckled softly, looking up at her. 'I always think most babies look like pugs but he's cute, right?'

She sighed. 'Well, I think so, but clearly I'm biased.'

'He's big too. He's gonna take after his papa.'

Lucy nodded but she wasn't bemused or charmed by this belated show of affection. He was five days old already. How could Tuck not have come back before now? 'He wasn't as big five days ago. He's put on a hundred grams since then.'

She couldn't keep the tint of sourness from her voice

and Tuck heard it this time, pushing himself back up to sitting, the baby between them. 'Listen, honey, I'm so sorry I couldn't get back before now.' His voice was a low murmur.

'Oh, no, I get it,' she replied flatly. 'You can't let something like becoming a father get in the way of work.'

Tuck looked surprised, then hurt. 'No, you don't understand—'

'Oh, I think I do.' The vein of steel in her voice caught his attention and she watched as the realization dawned on his face as to how much trouble he was in with her. But it was still more than he knew. He had no idea of what was about to happen to him.

Tuck blinked at her. 'Sweetheart, believe me – our lives changed out there.'

'No, Tuck, they changed *here*,' she whispered. 'I had a baby. On my own.'

He frowned. 'I though you said Meg was with you?'

'Without a doctor, is what I meant!' she hissed. 'We were on our own in that godforsaken cabin. Anything could have happened and you were thirty-five hundred kilometres away, selling snowboards.'

'Hey, that is not fair! You weren't due for another month—!' he shot back angrily, raising his voice.

'Shh!' she hushed him furiously as the baby startled again.

Tuck withdrew, physically pulling in his arms and legs as though he was worried he might accidentally hurt the baby in some way, looking anxious as his son twitched and jerked his legs, his mouth beginning to open and root.

'I never would have gone if I'd known the baby was coming,' Tuck whispered.

'But you didn't come back when he did.'

'I told you! Things happened out there.'

She rolled her eyes. He just didn't get it. It didn't matter if he'd quadrupled their number of stockists for the coming season; they could have survived another year on the existing contracts. He should have been here. She'd needed him to prove to her the kind of father he could be; she had needed evidence that things had changed, that she could trust him. But he'd failed. He'd fallen at every hurdle and he was out of time. She couldn't – wouldn't – wait for him any longer. She had to put her baby first now.

But how did she say those words, *'I'm leaving you'*?

He reached across the bed for her hand. 'Look, I get why you're pissed. Honestly I do. And if things had worked out any way different, I'd have been straight back here. But there's something I really need to tell you.'

She inhaled sharply, summoning her courage. 'Yeah? 'Cause there's something I need to tell you too.'

He looked a little surprised. 'OK. You first?'

She shook her head. 'No. You. I insist.' Once she'd said *her* words, there'd be nothing left to say.

He looked straight at her and she felt those blue eyes lock around her heart like a clamp, holding her in place the way they always did, stopping her from leaving, giving her hope when she thought there was none. 'I sold the company.' The words smoked in the air like flares in a night sky. 'Well, in principle,' he added quickly. 'Obviously it's not just my decision to make but . . . it's an amazing offer.'

At first she couldn't reply. She couldn't form the shapes to make words, she couldn't push the air from her lungs.

'What?' she managed, finally.

'Nordica made an approach on the second day. I've been

in meetings with them ever since.' He grinned delightedly, his eyes electric. *'That* was why I couldn't leave, baby.'

It wasn't a joke? He'd *sold* Titch?

'Ask me how much,' he said, enjoying the stunned expression on her face.

It was another moment before she physically could. 'How much?'

His smile stretched across his face and she realized she hadn't seen him as happy as that, not once, in the last seven and a half months. 'Seven million dollars.'

He got up from the bed and walked round to her side, pulling her up by the hands so that she was standing toe to toe with him, his hands on her waist. Her stomach was still swollen – in truth she still looked pregnant – but for once she didn't care. 'I did it, baby. I did it for us.'

'Seven million dollars?' she whispered. They would never need to worry again.

He beamed wider, his excitement growing. 'Say it again! I don't think I'll ever get bored of hearing it.'

'This isn't a joke?'

'Luce, do you *really* think I'd have missed the first few days of my son's life for anything less than seven million dollars? I was too scared to leave until we'd got the details sorted out. I kept thinking it would just go up in smoke, turn out to be some crazy-ass dream,' he said, bending his knees so that he was eye level with her. 'It almost killed me not being able to tell you, but I wanted to see your face. I wanted to see *this*,' he said, clasping her face in his hands.

He kissed her and she let him. In fact, she kissed him back. She'd missed him. *Seven million dollars?*

'Oh, Tuck,' she whispered, looking up at him. 'I can't believe it.'

'It changes everything, don't you see?'

She caught her breath. 'Everything?'

'Everything, baby. We can get out of this shithole, buy someplace new—'

'Someplace bigger?'

'Much bigger. And without your mom spying from the windows.' He kissed her again and this time she snaked her arms around his neck, holding him closer. The physical side of things had always been good between them. Too good. Too much.

He kissed the tip of her nose. 'What was the thing you wanted to tell me?'

She swallowed, looking back at him, then shook her head. 'Nothing.'

'Really?'

'Really,' she smiled. 'It's not important.'

Wednesday 8 November 2015

Tuck was more nervous than he thought he'd be. In the intervening months since Mitch had died, they hadn't spent one moment alone together and he knew that was deliberate on Meg's part. In the past, he'd found her easy company – a ready smile, good sense of humour, loyal and pretty fearless on a board herself. How could he not have liked her? It was practically written in the stars; the two people in the world *he* loved most, loved *her*. And yeah, she was attractive too, he wouldn't deny it. She had a great body but she didn't flaunt it, which only made her the more intriguing as far as he was concerned, but she was Mitch's girl,

Lucy's best friend. Perhaps without those connections, something might have happened once, but there was no chance of it now – not just because he was married or she was a widow, but because she blamed him for Mitch's death. She'd never said the words out loud – she was too generous, too loyal to Lucy to do that – but he saw it in her eyes every time she looked at him.

It was why he'd gone out of his way to keep a low profile around her – not coming home early on the nights Lucy said Meg was stopping in for dinner, making sure not to walk past the window of Dolores's store, pulling his baseball cap lower and pretending not to see her if he passed her at the movies.

And she did the same, he knew – he'd seen her double back on herself in the reflection of the meat counter at the supermarket, driving past without waving on the nights he worked late at the studio. It was a game they were both pretending not to play and they were very good at it, for no one suspected the gaping great hole that flapped in the tight weave of their friendship – Lucy hadn't picked up on it, or Dolores; not even Barbara, who watched him like a hawk.

But he couldn't avoid this. Lucy had been resolute that *he* had to tell Meg, saying it was still too early for her to be up and leaving the house, the baby was still so small, the temperatures had started to plunge. It was true that snow was in the air, the sky lowering itself onto the mountaintops in readiness for the first heavy fall of the season, but that wasn't it – he knew she just didn't want to be the one to tell Meg the news. Because there was no way she was going to take it well, no matter how logically Lucy argued it.

It wasn't like Tuck even agreed with it himself. It didn't

sit well with him – on the contrary, in fact – but there'd been no arguing on it for once: the deed was already done, Lucy's signature was already dry on the dotted line.

He wrung his hands together, feeling how chapped and rough the knuckles felt in his palms. Still, once Meg heard the good news he had to share with her about the Nordica offer, he was confident she'd come round about this.

'Hey.'

He looked up. Meg was standing by the bar beside him, looking willowy in her plaid shirt and black dungarees, her hair held back in a loose braid. He twisted slightly on his stool. 'Meg, hey. Thanks for coming.'

She pulled out the stool next to him.

'Fancy a beer?' he asked, holding up his own bottle.

She shrugged and sat down, smiling opaquely and nodding to a few of the other locals.

'So how've you been?' he asked. 'It's been a while.'

'I know, right?' she replied, without answering him, and he felt his nerves spike again.

'Another two,' he said to Jeff, the bartender who'd been working here since Mitch and Tuck had tried sneaking in, underage, all those years ago.

'How's Lucy doing?' she asked, eyes everywhere but on him.

'Great. Really good,' he nodded. 'She's an amazing mother already – I mean, a real natural. It blows my mind just watching her with him.'

Meg shrugged. 'You should have seen her during the birth. Most women would have freaked but she kept so calm.'

Tuck snuck a sidelong look at her, trying to tell whether the remark was a jibe for the fact that he hadn't been there, but Meg was watching Jeff, her body language relaxed. 'I don't know how to thank you for what you did that day. I'm not sure I could've done it.'

Meg looked at him, doubt in her face too. Instead she shrugged. 'Instinct kicks in.'

Jeff brought over the beers and set them down on mats. Meg gripped hers, the tips of her fingers white as they pressed the glass, and he saw she was more nervous – or stressed – than she wanted to let on.

'I'll swing by after this – see how she's getting on and have a sneaky cuddle with the little man.'

'You'll be lucky,' Tuck grinned. '*I've* barely held him yet. He's always either feeding or sleeping.'

'Really?' Meg looked surprised. 'I guess I've been lucky with my timings then. I've had lots of cuddles with him.'

'She's probably scared I'm going to drop him,' Tuck joked after a pause.

'Probably.' Meg took a swig of the beer and glanced round the bar. It was surprisingly busy for a Wednesday afternoon, another small group of tourists walking in. 'Looks like everything's getting into full swing for the festival kick-off on Friday.'

'Yeah.'

She looked at him again without making eye contact. 'Are you nervous?'

'About the film?' He shrugged but looked into his beer. 'What will be, will be, I guess. It's out of my hands now.' His fingers played with the foil on the bottle's neck. In truth, he could hardly sleep. That film had been his lifeline in the immediate aftermath of Mitch's death; he had poured everything he had into it and if it didn't make the cut . . . he knew he'd never be able to better it. 'Are you going to go to the screening?'

'I'm not sure yet.' It was her turn to stare at her beer. 'Maybe.'

He hesitated, and then said, 'Me either.'

'*You're* not sure? But all that time you spent on it? Months.'

He gave a hopeless shrug. 'It'll be different. In the editing suite, I could make myself believe he was right there beside me. But on the big screen, all those strangers watching . . .' He sighed, cutting himself off. How could he tell her he was terrified it would feel like saying goodbye?

They sat in silence for a few minutes and Tuck could feel Mitch's presence between them, like a balloon being inflated in the space between their arms until finally it touched them both and their thoughts merged, putting voice to her blame, his guilt.

He wanted to say it – tell her how sorry he was for ever picking up the goddam phone that day. If he'd only waited. Or left it till later; if only he'd gone home instead of to Bill's – but her silence bristled like a wary animal, its hackles up, and he moved his thoughts away again.

'So, what's up?' she asked, inhaling deeply as she looked down at the beer mat and holding her breath for a moment. Tuck was reminded of an octopus he'd seen out diving once – it puffed itself up and made itself look bigger when it felt vulnerable or under attack. 'What did you want to talk to me about?'

'There's something I have to tell you.'

She frowned. 'Sounds ominous.'

'It's not,' he said quickly. 'But we thought you should hear it first. From us.'

'"Us"? You mean you and Lucy?'

He nodded and grabbed another swig of beer, just as someone came and stood by the bar behind her to place an order. Tuck regretted choosing here to meet – this was the wrong place to tell her after all. It was too public.

'Well, go on,' she prompted as he lapsed into silence. 'What is it?'

'Before I do, I want you to know the decision was made for the very best of reasons.'

She blinked. 'OK, now I'm really worried.'

He inhaled deeply, his gaze catching hold, for once, of her elusive hazel-green eyes. They were so clear, like a sky after the rain, washed clean, and he saw at once in them all the pain and sorrow, hurt and loss she'd endured. She was far lovelier than she knew.

'We've chosen the name for the baby.'

'Oh, my God, is that all?' she asked, visibly deflating, one hand over her heart. 'I thought you were going to—'

He watched as she stopped in her tracks. Understood.

'No.' She stiffened, her hand falling away from her beer, her face draining of colour. She rose from the bar stool in a single fluid motion.

He reached a hand out to catch her wrist but she pulled it away before he could touch her. 'Meg, it was Lucy's idea. She feels it's a fitting way to remember and honour him.'

'*Honour* him?' Meg repeated, beginning to tremble, the amber flecks in her eyes sparking like fire. 'Where's the honour in naming your son after the man you sent to his death?'

Tuck flinched as the words poured over him. They were the ones he'd been expecting ever since that fateful dawn knock at the door but still they burned, excoriating his flesh.

He hung his head.

'What do you expect me to say to this?' Meg spat. 'Do you really think I'm going to call him by that name? Must I have what I've lost thrown in my face, day after day, by the very people who stole him from me?'

'Meg, listen to me—'

'No! *You* listen.' Her face was up to his suddenly. 'He is *not* having Mitch's name. You change it, you understand me? This is not remembrance. It's not honour. It's torment. *You* are the reason why he's dead. You don't get to feel better about what you did by paying lip service to his memory. You don't! I won't let you do this.'

His mouth opened but it was another moment before the words would come out. 'It's too late. She's already registered the birth. Lucy's signed the birth certificate.'

Meg stared at him, her entire body trembling. 'No.'

'I'm sorry,' he whispered. Tears were filling his eyes but he didn't even care who saw. She was right in what she was saying. It was because of him that his friend was dead; he could never make amends, never make it right. Not with a film, not with a name.

Meg's hand connected hard against his cheek, the slap carrying over the music and making every person in the room stare. Tuck knew what they were all thinking – lovers' quarrel.

'If I could change it, I would. All of it.'

Meg stared at him, nodding, agreeing. 'So would I. It should have been you that night. *You* should have died, not him,' she hissed. 'You were right, what you said at the funeral – you never will be half the man he was. You're a deadbeat, Tuck, just a waste of space. You clung to his coat-tails, desperate to keep up while he took you on the ride of your life. And now he's gone and you're lost, you're nothing without him . . .' She stared down at him, desolation in her eyes, all the fight leaving her suddenly. 'Why couldn't it have been you?' she whispered, a single tear on her cheek like a dewdrop on a rose.

She turned on her heel and left, Tuck watching her go, her handprint like a tattoo on his face and marking out his shame. He hadn't even had the chance to tell her the *really* life-changing news.

He looked around the bar and in its unnatural stillness and quietude, saw the way everyone was looking at him, looking down on him. He turned back in his seat, his eyes on the upended liquor bottles on the other side of the bar. It was the only way out he knew . . .

'Get me a Scotch, Jeff, no rocks,' he mumbled. 'And make it a double.'

Chapter Twenty-six

Thursday 9 November 2017

'I can't actually believe he's using the outdoor shower,' Meg smiled, thoroughly bemused as she tucked the blanket tighter around her legs and looked out from the porch. The first snow of the year had fallen overnight and though it hadn't yet settled on the slopes, the mountain crags and peaks were sugar-dusted. 'Mitch always did that too.'

'Typical city boy,' Ronnie grinned. 'He's *communing* with nature.'

'I bet he won't be communing for long when he hears the wolves,' Meg chuckled, taking another sip of her beer.

Ronnie laughed too, her eyes on the thick rafts of cloud that floored their privileged vista and muffled the town's lights below. Behind them, inside the cabin, the stove threw out a golden light. The night sky was already stirring, stars beginning to peep from their hiding places and speckle the overarching black. Badger was at their feet, his head on his paws, although Meg knew he would have preferred to be sitting by the drowsy heat of the fire.

Meg turned her head to the side to look at her sister. She wore an expression now which underpinned all others. Meg thought it was peace. It was how she used to feel with

Mitch, that in spite of all the adversities they might face, the world made sense. 'So, have you chosen yet? His place or yours?'

'Actually, neither. We're going to buy somewhere new together.'

Meg arched an eyebrow, but didn't rush to reply. She didn't want to appear sceptical. 'Joint mortgage?' she asked carefully. The inheritances they'd received from their parents' estate had been enough to put Ronnie through medical school and place a down payment on her flat; for Meg, it had bought them this cabin (built on the land Mitch had inherited from his grandfather) and secured the Titch office and store in town. But Meg was aware Ronnie couldn't afford to put herself in an unequal financial arrangement.

'Fifty-fifty,' Ronnie smiled, reading her exactly. 'Don't worry, he's a good guy.'

'Oh yes, I know tha—'

'He's the One.'

'Oh, Ron, do you really think so?'

Ronnie nodded. 'I know it hasn't even been four months, but I knew it when he kissed me hello at Soho House that night. It felt like coming home. Like *"Oh, there you are."* . . . I guess I never knew that home could be a person and not necessarily a place,' she sighed. Before suddenly catching herself: 'Oh, God, Meg, I'm so sorry, that was tactless.'

'No! Don't be crazy. I couldn't be happier for you.'

Ronnie smiled but she still looked awkward as she stared out over the floor of white tufted cloud below their feet. 'Don't you ever get lonely up here? It's so beautiful but there must be times, surely, when—'

'I crave lights, noise, action?' Meg nodded. 'Sure. Especially once the snow comes in properly.' Her chest tightened at the thought of the landscape whitening again, dread following her like a shadow. The snows had been melting by the time she'd returned to the cabin after Mitch's death – the trees had shaken off their white jackets, grass studding the acres of white ground, water rushing busily in the streams – so that the horror of that night had seemed to belong to another place, another country entirely. But with the return of the snow proper would come the memories of that night; she would become isolated and confined again, the cabin almost impossible to get to, the massive vaulted sky her companion far more than the twinkling lights on the valley floor as it was increasingly lost from sight by clouds. Yes. She often felt impossibly lonely. Especially now Jonas – her guardian angel in the sky – was no longer up there, doing laps as she worked and slept, looking out for her.

'You know, Hap still asks after you.'

Meg froze at the mention of his name. 'Well, he shouldn't.'

'I don't mean he's being intense about it. He knows what it was. He just enquires, that's all. He really liked you.'

Meg nodded. 'Good. I liked him.'

Ronnie shifted position, angling her knees towards Meg, her cheek resting on the back of the chair. 'Anyway, that's just a by-the-by. What I really want to talk about is New York. How did it go?' She leaned in closer towards Meg. 'They loved you, right? Offered you the job on the spot?'

Meg blinked. 'You really don't pick up your messages, do you?'

'Messages?'

'I called you. Last week. Telling you what happened?' Ronnie's face fell. 'You didn't get it?'

Meg sighed. 'I didn't get the plane, Ron!'

'*What?*' Ronnie shrieked. 'Why the hell not?'

'Lucy had—'

'Oh, Lucy, of course! Why am I not surprised? Of course it was Lucy!'

'It was hardly her fault,' Meg said defensively. 'She went into early labour.'

Ronnie blinked back at her, stupefied.

'Exactly. She was almost a month early. Hardly a scenario she would have chosen.'

A small silence bloomed. 'Is the baby okay?' Ronnie had the grace to look sheepish.

'Yes. Fine.'

'What did she get? Pink or blue?'

'Blue.'

Ronnie smiled. 'Name?'

'They haven't chosen one yet,' Meg replied, stiffly. She couldn't bring herself to talk about it with anyone yet, least of all Ronnie – her sister would fly to her defence, she knew, but that wouldn't make her feel any better about it.

Ronnie frowned, deep in thought. 'So . . . I still don't get it. Why did Lucy going into labour early mean you missed your flight?'

'Because she was up here when her waters broke.'

'But it only takes twenty-five minutes to get up here from town. She must have known she was in labour before she left?'

'She said she thought they were those false labour pains. What are they called?'

'Braxton Hicks.'

'Yes, those. But her waters broke on the quad bike on the way up.'

'She drove a *quad bike*? *Pregnant*?' Ronnie echoed.

'I know! I know! That's exactly what I said.'

'So why didn't she go back into town again?'

'The contractions came on fast. It all happened really quickly. There was no way she could get back on the quad. I called for the paramedics, thinking they could bring her down on a blood wagon, but they took almost an hour to get here, trying to find a quad bike to get up here themselves.'

'Jesus, Meg! This place is too remote. I know you love—'

'I know, I know,' Meg said quietly.

Ronnie sighed and took another swig of her beer. 'Well I can't believe she made that journey, even with what she thought were Braxton Hicks.'

'We'd had a fight and she'd heard I was leaving so—'

'So she came up to stop you?'

'No,' Meg said patiently. 'She came up to clear the air between us before I went. Look, she made a bad judgement call. She delivered early, Ron. There was no way she could have known it was going to happen – Tuck was in Toronto, and let's face it, the last place you'd want to deliver a baby, without any kind of medical support, would be up here.'

Ronnie tutted and shook her head but she couldn't deny the logic. No expectant mother would have willingly put herself in that position. Her fingers drummed the glass bottle lightly. 'So what was this fight about then?'

'Huh?'

The sound of running water had stopped now, and the plumes of steam that kept wafting around the side of the cabin were dissipating.

'The one she had to come and clear the air about. You never mentioned you'd fallen out.'

'It wasn't a big deal,' Meg mumbled.

'So tell me then.'

Meg's shoulders slumped. She knew Ronnie wasn't going to let this go; she was like a sniffer dog, always able to track the scent of blood. 'I told her about Hap and she got angry. She said I'd betrayed Mitch.'

There was a long, stunned silence.

'Are you kidding me?' Ronnie asked, her voice dangerously low. '*She* stood in judgement of *you* for what she thinks you've done to *Mitch*? Who the hell does she think she is?'

'She was just being protective. Look, I get it, I do. We were a foursome for a really long time. I'm not the only one who's having to adapt to him being gone. Everything's changed now. It all feels different.'

But Ronnie shook her hands in the air, dismissing Meg's protestations. 'No, wait – I can't believe this. So you're telling me, she can go ahead and have a baby and be with her husband and live a happy life? *She's* allowed to move on, but you're not? You've got to stay in aspic the rest of your freaking life because you were once engaged to her husband's best friend?'

'That's not what I meant,' Meg flinched.

'God, don't you get it, Meg? Can't you see what she's doing to you? She's making you feel guilty, stopping you from getting on with your life, because she's *jealous* of you! She's so terrified you're going to go on to something bigger and better and leave her behind. Don't you see it? She's always desperately trying to keep you down.'

'Lucy is not jealous of me! Don't be so ridiculous,' Meg scoffed. 'She's got everything she ever wanted – Tuck, a baby. One day they'll have the Homestead, Titch is going well . . . And then take a look at *my* life! What could she possibly want that *I've* got? Badger?'

The loyal dog raised his head at the mention of his name, ears up and a little whine in his throat.

'No, it's OK, boy,' Meg murmured, dropping a hand down to stroke his muzzle.

'I can't believe you don't see it,' Ronnie said, shaking her head sadly. 'She's toxic, Meg. She's no good for you. I know you've been friends a long time and you think I'm jealous of her because she took you away from me, but I'm so *not*,' she said, her hands pressed to her chest. 'You're too close to see it.'

Meg groaned exasperatedly. 'Just be honest, Ron, you've *never* liked her. But can't you see how painful, how difficult, it is for me that my sister and best friend hate each other?'

Ronnie stared at her for a long moment, her eyes making tiny side-to-side movements as though trying to peer into Meg's mind, before she turned back in her chair, her eyes on the slowly rising moon. 'Fine. I don't want us to fight,' Ronnie said quietly. 'I've been so looking forward to this.'

'Me too.' Meg reached her hand out, already regretting her outburst. 'Look, I know it was probably a shock to hear that New York didn't happen. It was terrible timing! But you've got to be philosophical about these things. I never went looking for that job. It kind of landed in my lap from nowhere and then . . . it just got taken away again. Both events were kind of out of my control. I have to accept that perhaps it wasn't meant to be.'

'It was just such a great opportunity for you,' Ronnie sighed. 'I feel so strongly that there's something more for you than this.' She squeezed Meg's hand tightly. 'And I'm not saying this isn't beautiful, because it is. It's one of the most special places on the planet. But you're not *living* here. You're just . . . existing. If anything, it feels like you've gone backwards. When we said goodbye at the airport, you felt like a different person to the one I'd picked up there a few days earlier. You were so energized. I really felt you got it, you know?'

'And I did! I do.'

'So . . . ? What happened?'

Meg fell quiet and drank from her beer again. How could she say that Lucy had happened? Lucy's protectiveness over Mitch . . . Lucy's baby coming early . . . None of it was necessarily Lucy's fault – she wouldn't have any idea of the impact those encounters had had on Meg's life – but to put voice to it would be to fan the flames of Ronnie's jealousy theory. 'Well, it's too damned cold to risk falling in the lakes at this time of year, for one thing,' she said lightly instead. 'I'll pick up the SUP boarding in the spring, thanks, if it's all the same.'

Ronnie arched an eyebrow quizzically but didn't press the matter. 'Fair enough.'

Just then, Jack walked through, looking quite the lumber-jack in Timberland boots, jeans tucked into woollen socks, a plaid shirt and cable-knit sweater.

'Oooh, my handsome logger,' Ronnie grinned, reaching her arms out to him as he went over to her for a kiss.

'Enjoy your outdoor shower?' Meg smiled, handing him a beer from under her chair.

'It was incredible.' He looked across at Ronnie and held out a hand, pulling her to standing. 'We should get one in the new place.'

'Yeah, because the neighbours would just love that!' she

laughed, as he sat down in her chair and pulled her back onto his lap.

Meg smiled, watching them, knowing she'd been like that once too.

'I can't believe you don't use it,' he said, looking back at Meg.

'I work to a basic rule – no outdoor showers if there's snow on the ground.'

'But—'

He was about to point out the luscious green grass on the lower slopes but she beat him to it, pointing to the frosted mountaintops on the other side of the valley. 'Snow on the ground. No negotiating.'

Jack grinned. 'So, the film festival kicks off tomorrow night?'

'Yep, highlight of our town calendar. Every hotel is booked.'

'Well, I bet nowhere compares to this. Seriously, this place is stunning,' Jack said, his eyes on the tented sky that was now richly studded with stars. 'You ever thought about renting it out?'

Meg shrugged. 'That was the original plan when we were building it but . . . we fell in love with it up here. It felt like our corner of the world and no one else's.'

'Don't blame you. I'd keep this all for myself too,' Jack smiled.

'Well, you're welcome any time you like,' Meg said. 'Ron said you're big on climbing?'

'It's my great love – aside from your sister,' he said, squeezing Ronnie's waist.

'Well, tomorrow there's a flashback screening – you know, of films they've shown in previous years and then after that there's a kick-off party in the Square and then on at Bill's. But then on Saturday, they're screening the Opening Weekend films. There should be plenty of mountain action to get you itching to put on your crampons.'

'Crampons? You know your stuff.'

'Well, of course. I do work in a mountain rental store, remember.' She didn't dare glimpse Ronnie's face as she said this, though she wasn't ashamed of the fact. 'I am so going to have to introduce you to Dolores while you're here. She'll love you. She's obsessed with the mountains too. She doesn't have blood running through her veins, she has granite.'

'Ha! Ain't that the truth,' Ronnie chuckled.

'I can't wait. And who goes to the party? All the towns-folk? Am I going to be the token outsider?'

'Far from it. People come from all over the world – film producers, explorers, photographers, athletes, you name it. Anyone who loves the big outdoors, basically. It's a riot.'

Jack frowned. 'We should have asked Hap along. It's not like he's that far from here and I bet he'd—'

'No!' Meg said, too quickly. She smiled nervously, well able to imagine him speeding over the mountains in his souped-up car, shades on and designer jeans. 'I just mean, it's too late, that's all. Everything's sold out.'

'Oh. That's a shame.'

Meg nodded, keeping the smile on her face. But there would be no double dates this time.

Chapter Twenty-seven

Friday 10 November 2017

Lucy stood at the window, jiggling Baby Mitch on her shoulder. She'd fed him for over an hour, burped him for half that again, but still she couldn't get him to settle. Every time she thought he was asleep and she laid him down, he woke screaming four minutes later. She was exhausted. It had been exactly like this yesterday and all night too, and her arms were leaden and stiff from the weight of constantly carrying him.

'Sleep, please sleep,' she whispered desperately, rubbing her cheek against his soft-furred head.

Across the courtyard, she could see the lights on in every single one of the hotel rooms, almost all of them getting ready for the kick-off party in the square in a few hours. There was no chance of Lucy being able to get out for it; she couldn't take a newborn (and a premature one at that) out into a heaving mass of revelling strangers. Besides, she didn't have the energy. Barbara had been so run off her feet she hadn't even been able to do her usual pop-in at lunch to allow Lucy a quick sleep, and even Tuck – who was notoriously hands-off with the running of the hotel – had been drafted in first thing to help with getting all nine of the fires flaming; they had awoken to an unexpectedly hard frost and the hotel's rather aged central heating meant roaring fires were needed for more than just decoration.

Lucy had thought he'd just be out for the hour or so it took to sweep the ash and snap the kindling and set the logs, but that had been hours ago and she hadn't even glimpsed him since – and she'd spent most of the day standing by this window.

Still, it wouldn't always be like this, she told herself, desperate to believe it. As soon as the contracts were delivered (expected next week) and Tuck had a chance to tell Meg the good news – they were both certain she'd jump at the chance to be financially secure; why wouldn't she? The business had never interested her beyond the design side – they could start planning the rest of their lives. And first on the list would be looking for somewhere new to live; somewhere where she'd have a better view than those goddam bins and the back of a hotel. She could maybe get a nanny, or at least a night nurse, although she still couldn't believe that was a job – that someone was prepared to sit up through the night with another woman's screaming baby. If she was honest, it was all she could manage to do it for her own. She loved her son; she loved him desperately, but *how* did people do this? Take the baby out of the equation and it was just a year-long round of torture, plain and simple. How did they never talk about how back-breakingly awful it was? Was it deliberately kept as a secret to stop from putting other women off? She hadn't planned this baby but if she'd had any idea how hard it would all be . . . the pregnancy, these early weeks. She felt battered and broken down. Everything was such a struggle. Why couldn't she be cut some slack, just for once?

Tuck was trying hard again. He'd changed a few diapers, walked around with the baby strapped to his chest when she'd attempted to get on with other household duties that needed attending to – like the washing and ironing – but he too often got it wrong, putting the diaper on backwards once and leaving the baby unattended on the changing table when he'd run out of talc and had to get more from the bathroom. She couldn't trust him to get it right.

Lucy leaned against the wall, staring out at the courtyard that felt increasingly like a prison yard. She felt as though the world was closing down, folding inwards on itself like a collapsible box. In the past week, she had left the bungalow only twice (once to drive Tuck's belongings to the studio, and then again to pick them up before he noticed) and she'd barely seen another soul. Apart from Barbara crossing the courtyard a couple of times a day, and Dolores stopping in once or twice, she'd had hardly any visitors. Lots of cards, yes, balloons, gifts . . . But precious few people had actually come over to hold the baby for her or make her a coffee whilst she bemoaned the utter lack of sleep, her close-to-exploding boobs, the almost constant bleeding 'down there' as Barbara put it. And Meg . . . well, she was stonewalling her now, seemingly sulking about their choice of name and ignoring Lucy's friendly texts suggesting coffee.

The sound of the hotel fire-door slamming made her look up and she watched with relief as she saw Tuck jogging across the courtyard. Her heart skipped at the sight of him. She wouldn't be alone now. He could help. She could sit down and straighten her arms, maybe close her eyes . . .

But as his hands reached for the door knob, a small movement in the upper corner of her eye made her look up again, just in time to see the lace curtain drop back down at one of the hotel windows.

She froze, oblivious to Tuck's wave as he saw her standing there.

'Hey!' he panted a moment later, slamming this door shut too, although at least this time he had the grace to wince, remembering his error that second too late.

But Lucy didn't notice. Heart pounding, cheeks pinched, she was already counting in the number of windows from the corner to the window where the curtain was still fluttering slightly. Sixth window in, third floor . . . Room 36 then?

'How's he been?' Tuck asked, coming over to her and crouching down to stroke his son's cheek.

Lucy turned away from him and walked over to the phone, awkwardly – with only one hand free – setting it down on the side table and punching in the numbers.

She could feel Tuck's puzzled stare on her back.

'Here, let me take him,' Tuck said, taking the baby from her before she could tighten her grip. She watched apprehensively as he positioned him on his shoulder, still handling his baby as though he was made of glass.

'The Homestead, hello?' The sound of the voice on the other end of the phone startled her. She turned away again.

'Oh, hi, Linda. Is Mom there?'

'Hey, Lucy. She's just in the kitchen. Want me to get her? Is the baby OK?'

'No, no, it's fine. I mean, the baby's fine, I don't need to speak to her. Could you just check the register and tell me who's booked into Room 36, please?'

Linda sounded surprised but Lucy could hear the sound of a keyboard being tapped. 'Sure.'

345

Tuck frowned. 'Luce? What's going on?'

But Lucy wouldn't look at him, instead turning her back and staring up at the ceiling, one hand on her hip. If he was cheating on her again . . . She closed her eyes. God help her, she would leave him this time. She would just go and to hell with waiting for those contracts to be signed. She'd fight for her half in court if she had to.

'Hi, Lucy? . . . Yes, it's a Mr and Mrs Hughes from Denver. Repeat guests. They came last year for the festival too.'

Lucy bit her lip. Mr and Mrs Hughes? Yes, Lucy remembered them; they had come last year. Every year since Mr Hughes had retired, in fact. They were in their mid-seventies; she knew Mrs Hughes walked with a stick. 'Great, thanks, Linda.' She hung up and turned back to face Tuck.

'Lucy? Wanna tell me what's going on?' Tuck was staring at her, the baby somehow, expertly, positioned on its tummy across his arm in the 'Tiger in the Tree' position that Barbara had demonstrated the other day. And of course, the baby was now fast asleep.

She gave a wan smile, trying to come up with an excuse. She'd been so sure. 'I . . .' Her mind blanked.

'You what?' His eyes narrowed. 'Why did you want to know who's in that room?'

'I . . .' Still she couldn't answer. He'd been gone all day. The hotel was full. She'd been on her own with a crying baby. Didn't it make sense that he wouldn't want to come back here? That any other woman would look better, be more inviting, than her right now?

She looked back at him and he saw it all in her eyes.

'Oh, what? . . . *Jesus*, Lucy,' he hissed, looking away, rocking the baby gently from side to side.

'I'm sorry!' she pleaded. 'But you've been out all day. I-I thought you were going to come straight back here.'

'They're flat out over there,' he said angrily, jerking his head towards the window. 'Your mom's running on empty, trying to get everything done in half the time so she can get over here to help you. If you must know, after I'd finished helping out there, I went over to the store to do some paperwork, then to the lawyer's, before going back to help your mom because the freezer's packed in.'

'Oh.'

She watched him – so handsome, rocking a baby she hadn't been able to settle all day, making it look so easy suddenly, and she had to resist the temptation to take baby Mitch from him. What was wrong with her? All day she'd felt so claustrophobic, trapped, unable to get away from him, but now that they were physically separated, she felt curiously weightless without him, as though she might just float up and drift far away from here, a balloon without string that no one could catch.

She bit her lip, hating that she needed to ask this, needed to know. 'Did you see anyone today?'

Tuck blinked. Anyone?

'No, I didn't,' he sighed, knowing exactly who she meant. 'Look, Lucy, she's just gonna need some time, OK? We knew it was going to be a shock for her.'

'But I don't understand why she doesn't see it in the spirit in which it's intended?' Lucy cried. 'I haven't seen her for four days, Tuck. Four days!'

Tuck turned away, looking almost guilty.

'You have told me everything, haven't you?' Lucy asked desperately. 'There isn't something else I don't know about?'

347

'Of course not. Like what? I told her, she got upset, said she wouldn't call him that name and left.' He shrugged. 'End of. It was . . . embarrassing and it was painful. But she'll come round. Just give her some space.'

Lucy stared at him. She sensed his own ambivalence about it too. Still. He hadn't once called the baby Mitch either, instead calling him Titch.

'And you don't like his name, either. I know you don't . . .' Then, when he didn't say anything to contradict her: 'I thought she'd be pleased. I thought you all would.'

She heard the whine in her own voice, saw something seem to snap inside him.

'Did you? *Really*, Lucy?' Tuck asked, an incredulous expression on his face.

'Of course! Why else would I have done it?'

'I don't know,' he shrugged. 'I really don't. You made that decision all on your own, without once asking me. What, was it punishment for not coming back?'

'No!' she cried.

'What then? What made you think you could make such a crucial decision all on your own, without talking to either me or Meg about it?'

'Why would I have talked to Meg about it? It has nothing to do with her!'

'It has everything to do with her. You made sure of that when you chose to call our son by her dead husband's name.'

'He wasn't her husband.'

'By a week! Are you gonna pretend their relationship meant less because he died before they could get married? They were engaged! They'd been together since forever! Of course it's gonna hurt her hearing you call our son by his name!' Tuck stared at her like she'd gone mad . . . Had she? She was so dog-tired, she wasn't even sure any more.

'Jesus, Lucy,' he cried. 'I do not get why this is going over your head. Is it the baby blues, is that it? Why are you making this all about you, when it's not? You can't act as though what you've done doesn't have consequences. But we can't change it now so we're all just going to have to get our heads round it. And *you* – you're just going to have to be patient while we do, OK? It's that simple.'

His shoulders slumped as she started to cry. 'Look, Meg will forgive you. She always does.'

'*Always does?* What does that mean?'

'It means that you've hurt her, Lucy. I know you didn't mean to – I know your intentions were good but for Chrissakes, wake up to what you've done!' His voice softened as he saw her expression. 'She'll come round when she's ready.'

'But what if she doesn't?' she asked, her voice small.

He looked at her for a long time. 'Then we'll have lost her too.'

'Good knife skills,' Jack said, staring at an impressive life-size ice carving of a brown bear. It was standing on its hind legs, paws up, teeth bared.

'Said the surgeon to the sculptor,' Ronnie smiled, resting her head on his arm.

Meg clapped her hands together to keep warm, her eyes on the bear. 'Mmm. Well, it's rather too lifelike for my liking,' she said, her eyes on one of the particularly sharp claws. 'If we're going to linger over impressive knife skills, I'd prefer we did it admiring the slightly less life-threatening elk over there.' She nodded her head towards the equally giant carving of the herbivore on the other side of the street. 'Shall we?'

They continued walking, Ronnie and Jack hand in hand, the three of them trying to carve a course through the multi-coloured pom-pom-hatted crowds, the sound of a band playing further down the street drifting to their ears. Meg wasn't sure she'd ever seen the town this busy before. The festival had been going for over forty years now and she and Ronnie had always come down here with their parents – in fact, her father used to offer fly-fishing workshops during the week it ran – but it was the opening-night party that held the most treasured memories for Meg, as though the carnival had come to their remote mountain town. Every year the film festival attracted bigger crowds and flashier sponsors but this year's had to be the most impressive yet. There couldn't be an empty bed in the whole town.

Certainly the Homestead was at capacity and she glanced in through its arched windows as they passed by. The fires were roaring, as ever, people sitting in the lounge chairs, looking cosy and pink-cheeked as they drank coffees and read the papers, Barbara's staff looking run off their feet as they rushed to and fro with trays.

Meg looked away again, feeling bad that she hadn't been over in the past few days. She knew Lucy needed her – the texts were coming almost hourly, sometimes in the middle of the night – and she could feel Lucy's longing for her to drop in and make a coffee, hold the baby and shoot the breeze. The day of the birth had given them both a glimpse of how things used to be between them – trusting and selfless and supportive – and Meg had allowed herself to believe their friendship was restored again; but that moment had been but a shooting star, briefly bathing in light a ship that was sailing out of sight on dark waters. They were estranged once more; *this* was the new normal now and she just couldn't bring herself to see any of them – not Lucy, not Tuck, not even the baby.

Meg was trying to understand why she'd done it – this idea of remembrance, honouring his memory – but she couldn't. Lucy kept blurring the boundaries of their friendship, as though they all had an equal status to one another within their four – but how could that be? They were two couples with two friendships, but it wouldn't occur to Meg to treat Tuck as on a par with Mitch, so why should Lucy? It wasn't right. It wasn't *appropriate*.

'Hey, do you like marshmallows?' Ronnie asked Jack, immediately steering him towards a huge fire pit with a cluster of young families standing around it.

'I guess I do,' Jack grinned as she placed a wooden skewer in his hand.

'This was always our favourite bit,' Ronnie said, handing one to Meg too.

Meg smiled, placing a pink marshmallow on the end of her stick and holding it out over the fire. 'My sister likes her marshmallows flambéed,' Meg said. 'Watch. Perhaps call the fire service.'

Sure enough, Ronnie was holding hers straight into the flames, the marshmallow blistering and swelling, blackening rapidly. 'The moment before the point of utter collapse is what's she's aiming for,' Meg continued, watching as Ronnie withdrew hers that moment too late and it collapsed onto the grill in a runny dribble. 'Yeah . . . it can get messy.'

'Oh!' Ronnie pouted. 'I'm out of practice.'

'So, total annihilation is what we're aiming for,' Jack

murmured, sticking his marshmallow stick into the flames. 'Let's see if I can do it.'

Meg preferred hers lightly toasted and as she ate one and skewered another, enjoying the warmth of the fire, she looked out, down the street. It was a winter wonderland now. The snow, after its tentative start yesterday, had come down hard overnight and they had awoken to deep drifts, Jack having to do more than just look the part now as Ronnie had handed him a shovel before breakfast and asked him to clear a path to the snowmobile shed. He'd seemingly loved it as he'd no sooner done that than he'd chopped up some logs too, for which a grateful Meg had rewarded him with extra eggs and sausages.

The Christmas lights weren't yet up in the town, but the stores and houses looked so pretty with their softly topped roofs rising like soufflés, the windows beginning to slant in the bottom corners as the snow built up on the sills. There were already snowmen in some of the gardens and the pavements were becoming streaked with the tracks of sledges pulling tired children.

Meg scanned the crowd for familiar faces, finding plenty. She saw Barbara and Bob walking arm in arm together down the street; Josie and Denise heading towards Bill's – they'd never been particularly close friends at school but since her relationship with Lucy had become strained in the past few months, she'd hung out with them more. It was never going to be more than a friendship of convenience, though, and when they'd texted her earlier, asking if she wanted to meet up for the rodeo-riding contest, Meg had been more than a little relieved to bow out under the pretext of hosting her sister and boyfriend for the week.

A child walked past with a balloon dog bumping against

his bobble hat; two teenage girls, their cheeks smacked bright pink, walked past giggling, their hands wrapped around hot chocolates to go; a group was gathering around a fire-juggler just a few yards away, some of them stamping their feet against the cold. One man turned, looking about him with a smile. He was wearing a black beanie and thickly padded down jacket zipped up to his chin, so there wasn't much of him to see – but still, Meg froze.

She blinked, watching as he laughed at something a woman said as she was dragged past by her Newfoundland pulling on its lead.

No. It couldn't be him. Why would he be here?

His gaze alighted on her momentarily and she froze again – she recognized him exactly from his photo and the footage she'd seen on TV and all those YouTube videos. Would he see the recognition in her face? Would he guess, *sense*, who she was? But one of his companions turned and said something in his ear and as he looked away, forgetting her, she felt a sharp stab of disappointment, of hurt.

She watched as he laughed at his companion's comment and nodded, saying something back. If she could just hear his voice, be absolutely sure . . .

'Meg?'

Huh? She felt something touch her arm and whirled round sharply, almost colliding with Ronnie, who had come round the fire pit and was now standing beside her.

'Hey!' Ronnie laughed, a slightly strained smile on her face. 'We've been calling you for like a minute. You were miles away.'

'I—' Meg faltered as she saw the reason they'd been calling her. Lucy and Tuck were standing with them, the baby strapped to Lucy's chest in a baby carrier.

'Hey,' Lucy nodded, looking nervous. Tuck was staring into the crowd – whether diplomatically or because he didn't want to set eyes on her, she wasn't sure. Had he told Lucy what she'd done – slapping him? What she'd said – wishing he'd died?

Meg felt her chest tighten as her gaze fell to the baby, his arms and legs dangling heavily, his cheek pressed against Lucy's chest, dark eyes blinking. He'd grown so much already! He was becoming a little person, a proper baby boy. Another Mitch.

No!

She turned away quickly. She couldn't do this. Not here.

'Meg, please!' Lucy called out, desperation in her voice, as she began walking away. 'Meg!'

Directly ahead the man in the black hat whirled round, his eyes scanning the crowd like a parent looking for a lost child. They settled on her this time as she froze once again, in front of him.

A slow smile of disbelief crossed his face as he took two steps towards her and she heard that voice that she knew so well and had missed so much. *'Meg?'*

Who was this guy and why was he looking at Meg like that?

Lucy had caught up with her but Meg didn't appear to notice. She was staring at the man with an expression that was sort of in between pleasure and pain.

Lucy looked back at him. He was good-looking in an intellectual kind of way and quite tall – way taller than Mitch, about the same as Tuck. He didn't look that sporty although he had on all the best kit. Lucy took a guess – he was some city-type film producer who fancied trying his hand at adventure films.

So, how did Meg know him? Because she clearly did.

The penny dropped with considerable force. *The guy from Toronto?* He'd come all the way out here? Had Meg invited him? Oh, God. A bullet of nausea lodged in her throat as the thought came to her – had Meg been seeing him all this time?

'Who's this?' Lucy asked tersely, not bothering to dress up her hostility.

Meg blinked, as though roused by the sharpness in Lucy's tone, and Lucy thought she saw a wariness in her eyes now. 'Lucy, this is Jonas Solberg.'

Jonas? Lucy mused. The name was familiar.

'Hi,' Jonas said, dragging his eyes from Meg and holding out a hand, before catching sight of baby Mitch and bending down to the baby's eye level, gently stroking his tiny, curled gloved palm. 'Wow, so small! How old is he?'

He had a soft trace of an accent, she thought. 'Nine days.'

'And you brought him out in the snow?'

'He's plenty warm,' Lucy replied defensively.

'Of course. I didn't mean to imply he wasn't,' Jonas smiled easily. 'What's his name?'

Lucy, her gaze sliding to Meg, watched her stiffen. 'Mitch.'

'Mi—?' Jonas began, before immediately looking back at Meg too. She had turned her face away, her lips pressed tightly together as though stopping tears from falling, her feelings on the issue perfectly clear and making Lucy look like a monster. 'Oh.'

Lucy saw, as Jonas looked back at her now – his expression still mild – that he understood exactly the friction between them, and it was clear to her which one of them he sided with. She turned round to look for Tuck, to feel his hand in hers as she endured this silent opprobrium, but he was still standing by the fire pit, chatting awkwardly with Ronnie and her boyfriend, all of them looking over frequently.

'Tuck!' she barked.

He turned reluctantly and she waved him over. He obliged, the others following too.

'Hey. Tuck,' Tuck said, offering his hand to Jonas as though the fact that he was standing with Meg was all the evidence he needed that he was friend, and not foe.

'Jonas.'

Ronnie gasped, pressing a hand to her chest. 'Oh, God, you're the astronaut!' she exclaimed loudly. She was always so loud, Lucy thought, and several people turned to stare – the word 'astronaut' seeming to stand out of all the other conversations being had. Jonas looked embarrassed.

'The same.'

Lucy felt a rush of irritation that she hadn't placed his name sooner. She knew she had heard it before!

'We've heard *so* much about you,' Ronnie gushed. She always gushed too, Lucy thought. 'Oh, my God, Meg and I watched your landing *live*. It was terrifying.'

'Yeah, tell me about it,' he grinned. 'So I'm guessing you must be . . . Ronnie?'

'How did you know?' Ronnie asked, amazed, looking at him like he'd just done a magic trick.

'Well, Meg talked about you a lot; plus you look alike.'

Had Meg talked about *her* to him, Lucy wondered, instantly jealous.

'Yeah? You think?' Ronnie grinned, grabbing Meg by the

arm and squeezing it excitedly, pressing her cheek next to her sister's so he could see them side by side. 'Our eyes are different but apart from that, people often used to think we were twins growing up, didn't they?'

Ronnie had directed the question at Meg but Meg didn't seem able to answer. She just nodded, still looking very shocked.

'I can't believe you're here. How come you're here?' Ronnie looked at Meg. 'Did you *know* he was coming? You never said!'

Ronnie was talking in a gabble now, getting way too excited, and Lucy gave an impatient groan. Poor Meg couldn't get a word in edgeways, even if she wanted to.

'Actually, I'm presenting a prize at the festival,' Jonas said, his eyes on Meg. 'But I was going to try to make contact . . . I mean, I was hoping I'd get to see you but I wasn't sure if . . .' His voice trailed off and Lucy wondered if Meg had fought with him too.

Why was Meg being so quiet? She'd done nothing but talk about the guy when he'd been in space.

'I'm Jack, by the way,' Ronnie's boyfriend said, reaching an arm over her shoulder, and they shook hands.

'Oh, I'm sorry,' Ronnie laughed. 'I was so wrapped up in the excitement of meeting you that I completely forgot . . .' She patted Jack's chest affectionately. 'Jack's my boyfriend.'

'Got it,' Jonas smiled, looking back at Meg again; but Lucy could see that every time he looked at her, his expression became more apprehensive. Perhaps this wasn't the welcome he'd envisaged? She and Tuck, Ronnie and Jack had all been way more welcoming than Meg had.

'Hey, why don't we get out of the cold and warm up

somewhere?' Ronnie suggested. 'Are you free, Jonas, or have you got to be somewhere?'

'Uh, no, I'm being looked after by a festival rep but I'm sure he'll have a lot more fun without me hanging on.' As he said this, a guy came over to him, an enquiring smile on his face. 'Talk of the devil.'

'Are these the friends you said you were looking for?' the man asked him.

Jonas looked at Meg again before answering. 'Yeah. Do you mind if I—'

'Hey, have fun,' the guy said, simultaneously slapping his shoulder and shaking his hand. 'That's what this week's all about. I'm glad you found them. I'll give you a call tomorrow, OK?'

Jonas turned back to them. 'Well,' he shrugged, clapping his hands and looking a little nervous now that he'd cut himself loose, his eyes back on Meg. 'Shall we go for that drink?'

Chapter Twenty-eight

'It's so weird. You don't look at all like I thought you would.' Jonas looked down at her as they shuffled in the snow towards Wild Bill's, where the kick-off party was continuing. Her red bobble hat was pulled down over her ears so that her long dark hair flapped at her neck in the breeze, snowflakes settling on her shoulders.

'No?' Meg asked shyly. 'How did you think I'd look?'

'I don't know – shorter, maybe? Lighter hair? Shorter hair? Heavier?'

'Are you saying my voice sounds fat?' she laughed and he noticed how her face lifted as she smiled. When he'd first caught the drift of her name in the square and seen her, she'd caught his eyes because of how desolate she'd looked amongst the crowd, the light in her eyes dimmed as though something inside her had been shut down. She had been trying to leave, that much was apparent, and he wondered if it had been something to do with her friend Lucy; there was an evident tension between them, Lucy's eyes constantly resting on Meg, whilst Meg's stayed on the ground. Was it something to do with the baby's name? He remembered Meg's expression when he'd innocently asked and it had been a visible relief for all when Lucy and her husband had decided against coming on to the after-party. ('No place for a newborn,' Tuck had said despondently.)

But Meg's smile was like the striking of a match, that sudden spark of ignition enlivening her face, and he couldn't help but smile back. 'Well, how did you think I'd look?' he asked.

'Bald. Five foot tall. Walk with a limp. Hook for a hand.'

It was his turn to laugh. 'Ah, no, that's Sergei. You must have confused us.' He looked across at her. 'Although your sister said you watched the landing, so you did see me before? Perhaps you had the advantage just now.'

She shrugged and he thought she looked a little embarrassed. 'You looked very different back then.'

'I felt very different.' He rolled his eyes.

'Was it hard, reacclimatizing?'

'Worse than I expected. The nausea was extreme. And once they got us back to base, I literally slept for fifteen hours solid and didn't move once, not even a finger. They said they had to keep coming in to check on me and make sure I hadn't died!'

They had reached the bar, a short queue bottle-necking at the bottom of the steps that led to the entrance. They looked back to find Ronnie and Jack had lagged behind a little. Deliberately?

Jonas looked across at her again, still trying to tally her face to her voice. He could remember her so clearly from that first night, her voice thrown into the void like a brittle bone, panic shaking her core. 'I can't believe we ran into each other like that just now,' he said. 'What are the chances?'

'I guess smaller than the chances of meeting the way we first did.'

'That's true!' he agreed. 'We must be destined to keep meeting against the odds.'

He had intended it as a quip but it must have been the wrong thing to say for she looked away suddenly.

'I would have called you up, you know. That was my intention. I wouldn't have just come here and left without saying hello.' She glanced up at him then and he tilted his head, watching her. 'Would that have been OK, if I had?'

'Of course.'

'Only, when you stopped writing, I wasn't sure if . . .' He looked at her, pulled an apologetic-funny face. 'Was it something I said?'

He waited, wanting an answer. The way she had just cut off contact so abruptly . . .

'Of course not.'

'I mean, I couldn't work it out. I thought something must have happened to you, Meg. Something bad.' And when she looked back at him, uncomprehending of the devastation he'd felt at her sudden departure from his life: 'I didn't know if you were dead or alive.'

'You thought I'd *died*?' She looked shocked.

'Well yeah! I didn't know what to think! It was so abrupt. One minute we're sharing jokes, the next minute . . . you were gone.'

She shook her head, staring down at the ground as she scuffed the snow with her foot. 'I'm sorry. I just . . .' She trailed off.

'You just what?'

'I just kind of assumed that you'd lose interest in talking to me once you were back here. I'm hardly the most fascinating pen pal to have. Let's face it, there was *way* more upside for me than for you. You're an astronaut, for God's sake!' She gave another of her embarrassed smiles. 'I guess I just didn't want you to feel obligated in some way.'

'Obligated? Why would I feel that?'

'Well, because of the way we met. The circumstances . . .'

He realized suddenly what she meant. 'You mean you think I was only in contact with you out of *pity*?'

She swallowed. 'I dunno. Maybe.'

He looked down at her, his mouth already open to tell her she couldn't have been more wrong – that maybe it had started out that way but it had changed so much, so quickly; they'd been friends, hadn't they? – but Ronnie and Jack bowled up.

'Do we need tickets?' Jack asked.

'It's OK, I already bought some,' Meg said, pulling her hand out of her pocket and holding up three.

Jack frowned. 'But what about Jonas? We're one short. Unless you've already got one?' Jack looked at him and Jonas had to shake his head in reply.

'It's fine. Bill's a friend,' Ronnie said, patting Jack's arm. 'We're not in the city now, you know.'

She was right. They got to the bottom of the steps and climbed, the guy taking tickets by the door at the top waving them through without even asking to see theirs. 'Hey, Meg,' he winked, tipping his uniform Stetson at her.

'Hey, Jon.' She spoke over her shoulder as they walked in. 'His dad's our dentist.'

The first floor saloon was already becoming crowded, which was really saying something as it was a big space. There were numerous seating areas – booths in the windows, stools by the 360-degree bar which was positioned centrally in the room and dramatically lit with blue lights – and a mechanical rodeo bull in one large cordoned-off area.

Meg seemed to keep her head down as they passed, as though avoiding people.

Jack motioned for them to grab a table whilst he went to the bar. Music was pumping and Jonas felt the bass throb through his boots, his eyes squinting automatically at the flashing strobe lights.

Meg noticed, putting a hand towards his arm but not quite touching. 'Are you OK?'

He nodded. 'Yeah, sorry . . . it's just one of the hangovers from space, that's all. Radiation exposure.'

Meg pulled out her chair, shooting him an alarmed look. 'Radiation?'

'It's nothing serious. In fact, it's quite common in astronauts. Down here, the atmosphere and magnetic field mean we're protected but in space, the high-energy particles from the cosmic rays just make direct hits on the optic nerves. It's all right, it just means I see flashing lights in my furthest peripheral vision when I close my eyes, that's all.' He pulled a face as they sat down, watching as Meg took off her bobble hat, her dark hair falling free around her face. He grinned, unable to believe his luck that he'd found her again. 'It's brilliant, really – I get to have a disco in my head, *all the time.*'

'Are there any long-term effects on your eyesight?' Ronnie asked, looking fascinated as she placed one hand on top of the other on the table and leaned in.

'Well, eyesight definitely does degrade but there's no evidence of increased rates of cancer or cataracts.' Jonas remembered Meg telling him her sister was a doctor.

Ronnie grinned and joshed Meg with her elbow. 'I still can't believe you literally bumped into this guy *in space*. A real-life astronaut.'

Jonas looked at Meg again. He was fairly used to the reaction his job engendered. 'Well, you could be an astronaut,' he said to Ronnie.

'*Me?*' Ronnie spluttered.

'Why not? It's basically a laboratory in the sky. Plenty of astronauts have medical backgrounds. Just do your space training for a few years and you're good to go.'

Ronnie laughed. 'That easy, huh?'

'Exactly,' he grinned, even though his post-graduate degree and several years in the Norwegian Air Force as a jet-fighter pilot had been merely the minimum entry requirements for the basic astronaut programme; after beating over ten thousand applicants, he'd then had to complete that two-year course and qualify for a further three years' training on mission-specific material. On average, it took most successful applicants eight years until their first space flight; he'd done it in six.

'So what were you, before you became an astronaut?' Ronnie asked.

'I was a fighter pilot in the Royal Norwegian Air Force.'

Ronnie frowned. 'How *old* are you?'

'Thirty-three.'

'How can you have done all that by thirty-three? I mean, isn't that really young to have already been in space? I always think of astronauts as being, like, proper grown-ups.'

'So you think I'm not a proper grown-up?' Jonas grinned, bemused.

'You know what I mean,' Ronnie grinned. 'Forties.'

He nodded. 'I am pretty young to have done an expedition already.' He glanced across at Meg. She was sitting to his left, her head resting in her left hand, watching him. He liked how it made him feel, to have her attention.

'So that was your first then?' Ronnie pressed.

He nodded, bringing his focus back to her again.

'And when are you going up next?'

Jonas smiled. He liked Ronnie's directness, her evident intellect and enquiring curiosity. 'There's no guarantee I will. But it would be another few years at least.'

'And you want to?'

Jonas glanced at Meg again, trying to draw her into the conversation. 'Yes. Although only if your sister promises to write. I don't know which were funnier – her jokes or her call signs.'

Meg narrowed her eyes and stuck out her tongue – 'Oh, ha, ha' – just as Jack came back with the drinks on a tray and set them down. 'Beer OK?' he asked, handing the first one to Jonas.

'Great.'

'Bet it tastes even better than before, doesn't it?' Jack asked, serving the girls too.

'Like you wouldn't believe. Everything tastes of cardboard up there.'

Jack held up his bottle as he sat down and joined them. 'Well, cheers – to new friends and new frontiers.'

'Cheers!' the others said, clinking their bottles together.

'Or as we say in Norway – *Skål*,' Jonas added.

'*Skål!*' they all said again.

'So where are you from?' Jack asked.

'A small village called Stavanger, five hundred and fifty kilometres south-west of Oslo. It's pretty similar to here really – mountains, lakes . . .' He shrugged.

'Did you see it from the ISS?'

'I did. I sent the photographs to my mother for her birthday.'

'Oh, my God,' Ronnie breathed, dead impressed. 'Ha! Beat that, people!'

Jonas smiled at Ronnie, liking her more and more.

'And did you see here? I mean, did you look, specifically?'

'Yes, I . . .' He glanced at Meg. 'Once Meg and I became friends, I made a point of looking down whenever I knew we were in range.'

'Did you take any photos?' Ronnie asked, getting excited.

'Of course.' He took in Ronnie and Jack's wide eyes; even Meg appeared to be holding her breath. 'Would you like to see?'

'You've got them here?'

'Sure. I can get them off my cloud.'

Ronnie gave an excited squeak as Jonas fiddled with his phone, Jack squeezing her knee and kissing her affectionately on the temple, one arm slung languidly over her shoulder.

'There's a few of Banff, actually.' He put his phone on the table and watched as the three of them huddled together, heads touching as they swiped. 'I made a little folder especially, in case I got to meet you – I wondered if you might be interested,' he said to Meg and she smiled.

'So that's . . .' Ronnie asked.

Jonas leaned forward, identifying the image. It had been taken in the morning, a thin veil of clouds like a haze between photographer and subject, the topography more like a crumpled piece of paper, the land beneath a rich, lush, verdant green, only the sharp shadowing betraying that it was actually a mountain range. 'This isn't the best one. It was pretty cloudy that day – but you can make out the Vermilion Lakes, see the way this one hooks?'

'Oh, yeah!' Ronnie said. 'I didn't realize it was so angled.'

'There's the ski area.'

'Wow.'

Jonas glanced at Meg. She was rapt, her hair tucked behind one ear, her brownish-green eyes moving slowly as she appeared to take in every detail.

'The Rockies look like ripples,' she murmured, her eyes meeting his briefly. 'And the town, it's just a dot.'

'Well, this one was taken at a particularly high elevation. There are others that were closer. You can see more of the town . . . see, here.' He swiped to the next photo. It was taken significantly closer to Earth, the individual parcels of land on the valley floor differently coloured and creating a kind of geometric patchwork effect. There was no telltale curve of the Earth in the corner of this image; in fact, it could almost have been taken from a plane and the fat scudding clouds looked like pillows or cotton-wool balls or even sheep, their shadows on the Earth so dark and distinct.

'Is that Mount Rundle?' Jack asked, peering closer.

'It is.'

The next image had been taken at night and it looked almost as though the sky had fallen to Earth, with several clusters of blazing light constellations and all around them, the pitch black of a night sea.

'So you're here,' Jonas murmured, orientating himself as he stared at it too. 'There's Calgary to the right, Vancouver just in shot to the bottom left there.'

'And we're – what?' Ronnie asked, squinting hard. 'That teeny smattering of lights?'

Jonas nodded.

But Meg shook her head. 'We're so insignificant. It's like

we're barely a presence. No one would ever know we're here.'

'I knew.'

Meg glanced at him and he saw it again in her eyes: that guarded look.

Jack flicked to the next photo and Ronnie gave an audible gasp. 'What the—?'

'Whoa, holy shit,' Jack murmured. 'Mother Nature's killin' it there.'

Meg and Jonas looked back down at the phone and Jonas winced. He had forgotten this one was in here, not sure whether Meg would want to see it, although he had stared at the picture many times. The image had been taken at a high elevation and at dawn, that first chink of sunlight like a brass skin being peeled over the Earth's white flesh. But it wasn't the extraordinary light that had elicited Ronnie's shock, nor the polar uniformity of the all-white landscape, but the thick cloud swirl that spun in the very centre of the image, like a ballerina's netted tutu. The sheer power of the storm – a Category 5 – was visible even from this far above; at its furthermost edges, the clouds seemed friable and tattered, but as it pirouetted and tightened into a coil, the striations were as clearly defined as meringue whites and almost traceable with one's finger, with a small articulated 'lid' in the centre.

'Where was I?' Meg's voice was quiet and he knew she hadn't needed to clock the date in the bottom-right corner to understand what she was seeing.

Jonas hesitated, before leaning forward and pointing to the part of the storm where the cloud was most dense, like towels being tumbled.

Meg looked back at him, aghast, and he could put *that*

face now to the voice he knew. He felt a rush of protectiveness towards her again; he instinctively wanted to grab her
hand and hold it, to put his arm around her shoulder and
lead her away from the horror. But he couldn't do that. She
was his friend, but still a stranger.

It had been no *footless hall of air* that night, Meg realized,
staring at the photo – that sky had killed Mitch as surely as
if it had been shooting arrows instead of snowflakes from
the clouds.

'You OK, sis?' She looked up to see Ronnie's arm reaching across the table towards her.

'Of course.' She nodded too, for good measure.

'I'm sorry, I should have realized—' Jonas took his phone
back.

'Really. I'm OK.'

Jonas glanced at her but she could see her reassurances
sounded false to his ear too and there was a heavy silence
as everyone simultaneously drank their beer. They watched
a girl get up on the rodeo bull, her hair beginning to fly as
it rotated and dipped, going faster and faster.

Meg knew it was her fault, ruining the party mood;
nearly nine months on and she couldn't hide the devastation of her loss. She drew a deep breath, trying to pull
herself together. She was a terrible hostess.

'So what are your plans for this week?' she asked with
staged brightness.

Jonas shrugged in his easy way. 'I'll go with the flow. My
only commitment is handing out a special prize on Awards
Night.'

'Well, there's so much to do, you'll love it,' she said with
forced cheer.

'Yeah? What kind of things?'

Meg considered. 'Well, Tuck and—' She stopped herself. She had automatically gone to say Mitch's name. She took another breath. 'Tuck loves going to the film-making workshops. They get these really experienced adventure-film producers and they go through editing and camera work, narrative, cinematography, script-writing . . . I think they even get a chance to pitch documentary ideas to *National Geographic*.' She smiled. 'Oh, my goodness, I bet they'd love to hear from *you*.'

Jonas looked intrigued. 'Well, I did do quite a lot of filming on board. Time-lapse photography too.'

'Well, then you should go! Check it out.' Meg's eyes brightened and she saw him smile, as though her smile was infectious.

'Perhaps I will. And if Tuck's doing it too . . . He seemed nice.'

Tuck. The thought of *him* deflated her again. There was no doubt he'd been friendly to Jonas – friendlier than Lucy, in fact – but then putting on the charm had never been Tuck's problem.

'What other things do they do?' Jonas was watching her still, his eyes steady upon her.

'Uh . . . loads of film screenings. Oh! And you can actually go on a training session with some of the sponsors' athletes if you want. I think it's North Face who host it.'

'What kind of training?' Jack asked. 'I don't think I'd fancy doing pull-ups with a professional mountaineer.'

Everyone chuckled.

'Run and hike? I think that's it,' Meg mused.

Jonas nodded. 'Sounds interesting. I'd love to get out and see the scenery while I'm here.'

'Are you big on skiing?' Ronnie asked.

'Yes. But more of the cross-country sort.'

'I've never done that,' Meg said. 'I can't imagine skiing without a slope.'

'Yeah. When gravity gets fun,' he smiled and she thought how piercing his eyes were – inquisitive, insightful, probing. She felt as though he could see right to the heart of her. 'Cross-country's a different vibe altogether – I'll teach you if you like.'

'Oh, no,' she protested. 'I couldn't let y—'

'Why not? You'd get to show me around and I'd get to show you how to cross-country ski.'

'I've got to work.' The town was packed and with most of the visitors choosing to ski by day and attend the screenings by night, Dolores had already had to call in extra cover for shifts.

'I'll cover for you.'

Ronnie looked almost as surprised as Meg at the words that had just come out of her mouth – Jack looked at her in astonishment. Ronnie covered Jack's hand with her own and looked at him. 'It's fine. You can go to that workshop you wanted to go to and I'll cover for Meg. It's only for a day.'

'But—' Meg protested, looking from Ronnie to Jack and back again.

'No buts. You should go. You definitely should.' Ronnie shot her a meaningful look although what the meaning was supposed to be, Meg wasn't sure.

'Well great, that's really generous of you,' Jonas said, drinking his beer, his eyes back on Meg again.

Ronnie looked back at Jonas again. 'How long are you here for?'

'Just over a week. I have to fly to Washington on Sunday for a series of lectures.'

'Is that for your tour?' Meg asked.

'Yes, but it's almost finished now. A couple more weeks up to Christmas and then I'm done and I can take a bit of time off.'

'You must be so shattered,' Meg sympathized. She couldn't imagine the reserves it must take to train and train, then spend six months in space, six weeks adjusting to gravity again and then going out on an international tour. What had *she* done in that time? (Although she supposed surviving a bear attack and delivering a baby was a notch above her usual accomplishment levels.)

'Are you going home for Christmas?' Ronnie asked.

'Yes.' He sighed. 'And I can't wait. I haven't been back to Norway for over two years.'

'Your family must be so excited.'

'I certainly hope so,' Jonas grinned. 'I can't wait to see them.'

Meg was surprised. 'You mean you haven't seen them yet, since landing?'

He shook his head. 'Only on a screen. It was too difficult to get away with the little ones. My youngest brothers are still at school.'

Ronnie's eyebrows shot up. 'School? How many brothers do you have?'

'Three.'

'Wow. Three brothers,' Ronnie echoed.

'And two sisters.'

'*Two sisters?* You mean, there's six of you?'

'I'm the eldest,' he nodded.

'God, talk about boots to fill,' Meg murmured. She had a hard enough time having a doctor for a sister.

'Oh, my God, that's insane,' Ronnie grinned, slapping the table. 'Six kids.' She pointed a warning finger at Jack. 'No ideas.'

Jack held his hands up, but he was grinning wildly and reached over in the next instant, hugging her tightly around the shoulders and kissing her cheek.

Meg felt embarrassed as Ronnie turned to kiss Jack properly; Jonas looked across at Meg, his eyes resting on hers for a moment, and she felt her stomach contract. She couldn't believe he was here.

'So, I've got a joke,' he said in a low, confiding voice.

She relaxed, a smile escaping her already. 'Oh, yes?' She arched an eyebrow. 'I sincerely hope it's better than your last effort,' she deadpanned. 'This needs to be good.'

'It is. I've had plenty of time to think about it.'

Meg placed both hands around the base of her almost-empty beer bottle, hearing the chide in his voice. 'Go on then.'

He dropped his head and leaned in to her slightly. 'What should you do if you see a green alien?'

Meg chewed her lip, trying to think of the punchline, aware that Jonas was watching her and hoping for exactly the opposite. But after a few moments, she had to concede defeat. 'I don't know. What should you do if you see a green alien?'

Jonas left a dramatic pause. 'Wait until it's ripe.'

She didn't want to give in but she couldn't hold down the smile. 'Oh, my God,' she laughed.

'It's great, right? The best one.'

'It's terrible!'

'How?' Jonas gasped, but laughing too. 'How can it be terrible if you're laughing? I win!'

'No!' she shook her head, still laughing, wishing she could stop.

'Yes!' Jonas said triumphantly. 'It's the best. I made you laugh.'

She sighed, her laughter subsiding finally into chuckles. 'Fine. It was vaguely amusing.'

'Vague—?' Jonas gasped again, pulling a face of mock-outrage as he picked up his beer and went to finish it – only to find it already was. 'I'm going to get another round in and whilst I do that, you can see if you can top that joke.'

'Fine,' Meg grinned.

'Fine,' he quipped back.

Meg didn't notice Ronnie and Jack watching them. She was too busy staring at his back as he disappeared into the crowd, this man who had seen, achieved and done more than any other person in the room – the state, the country, almost the planet – and yet seemed more grounded than any of them. He was everything he'd been in space – attentive, patient, kind, wise – but so much more than that too. In the flesh (the very handsome flesh), his gaze was direct and unflinching, his laugh low and easy, his hands large but smooth . . . It was precisely why she'd wanted to cut off contact. It was their anonymity to one another that had made it so easy to talk – no judgements possible. As she sat right here beside him, however, he was no longer a voice in the dark, but a man.

He wasn't just the faceless floating figure of a thousand comic books and adventure films – he was a man from a large family and a small town; a man who had walked in space but loved traversing mountains; who was cleverer than anyone she knew but laughed at the daftest jokes. He wasn't just a disembodied voice, but flesh and blood and gorgeous. He'd been up there but now he was down here. He'd come to find her and she could no longer pretend he was a stranger; he was her friend.

This thing was real.

Chapter Twenty-nine

Monday 13 November 2017

'Hey, it's Tuck, right?' Jonas asked, extending a hand to the good-looking blond guy he remembered meeting briefly in the square. 'I'm Jonas Solberg, Meg's fr—'

'The astronaut!' Tuck said, brightening and shaking his hand firmly.

Jonas automatically dipped his head as people turned and stared, not quite sure if they'd heard correctly. He nodded vaguely. 'Meg said you'd probably be here.' He cast a casual glance around the room. It was populated almost entirely by men, and most of them were classified further by their shaggy haircuts, weather-worn tans and performance-logoed clothes. 'Apparently this workshop's good?'

'Oh, man, it's the nuts. Are you into film-making?'

'I'm interested in the idea of it. I've got a lot of footage.'

'I bet!' Tuck pointed to a bearded guy in a red fleece gilet and walking trousers at the front of the hall, standing by the whiteboard. 'That there's the guy you need to talk to by the time this thing ends. He's a commissioning editor at *National Geographic* and it would blow his mind to know you were here.'

'What kind of films do you do?' Jonas asked, changing the subject from himself.

'Snow-based mainly. Me and Mitch have—' He caught himself and stopped dead, a strained smile on his face as he corrected himself. 'We *had* a snowboard company together.' He hesitated. 'I mean, the company's still going, just not with . . .'

'Sure,' Jonas nodded, seeing how Tuck was tangling himself in knots. 'What's it called?'

'Titch. Have you heard of it?'

Jonas shook his head apologetically.

'No? Well, you soon will. We started in small trick boards and now we're pushing into the main market. We've had a run of luck with some big-name riders winning on our styles so there's . . . it's going well, put it that way.' His eyes sparkled excitedly. 'Anyway, Mitch had this big idea that we should submit a film to this gig every year – he thought it was the perfect marketing tool for the boards. We're not trying to win – although that would be nice – but to get on the world tour. They select like ten, fifteen films from the shortlist and go on this big road trip. Forty countries, man! And almost all the people buying tickets to it are our bang-on market.'

'It's a great idea. Have you ever made the cut?'

'Twice. And I'm really gunning for this year too.' He shook his head sombrely. 'Man, I put everything I got into this year's submission. If this film don't make it, nothing will.' He paused, as though speaking required strength, the light in his eyes seeming to fade. But then in the next instant, he suddenly switched back on again, as though remembering Jonas was still standing there. 'But Mitch was right, it really works – we see a thirty-nine per cent spike in sales in the six months after each tour. Why pay for advertising when we can build brand recognition and loyalty this way? Plus it means we can continue to do what we've always done – go ride the mountains, make a film out of it, build the brand – all in one . . .'

'It sounds like Mitch had a head for business.'

'And thrills, man. *Nothin'* scared him. He was fearless,' Tuck said, with mannerisms better suited to a teenage boy. Jonas watched as Tuck's face dropped again and thought it was like watching him running through trees – for some moments, the memories bathed him in sunlight; for others, he receded into the shade. Who was this guy who had cast such a long shadow over them all – Meg, Tuck, even Lucy giving her baby his name? They'd only been talking for a few minutes but Tuck struck him as the most lost person he'd ever met, living on past glories.

'I'm really sorry. From everything I've heard, he sounded like a great guy.'

'Yeah.'

They were silent a moment, Jonas having to step out of the way to let a few people past to their seats. The auditorium was two-thirds full and the bearded man at the front was taking a sip of water, a sure sign he was getting ready to begin.

'Anyways,' Tuck said, trying to rally. 'That's why I'm here. Every year I try to learn a bit more and perfect the craft.'

'So you said you've got a film in for this year?'

'Yeah. I'm nervous, man.'

'Well, I wish you luck with it. I hope it's you I'm presenting the award to on Sunday night.'

Tuck's eyes widened. 'Are you a judge?'

'Sadly not. I'm here in an honorary capacity only.'

'Shame,' Tuck grinned. 'I was about to shamelessly bribe you, bro – unlimited beers at Bill's, the phone number of three very hot sisters . . .'

They laughed, just as the lights dimmed and the logo of the film festival suddenly came up on the giant screen.

'Can we sit here?' Jonas asked, gesturing to the empty seats behind them.

'Yeah, anywhere, man,' Tuck said, taking the one beside him.

They sat down together as the bearded guy cleared his throat and introduced himself.

Tuck leaned in slightly. 'Hey, you wanna go to lunch after this?' he whispered.

Jonas smiled, feeling somehow as though he was back in high school. 'Yeah. You're on.'

'I think I've seen planets smaller than that pizza,' Jonas said as Tuck's order was set down before him.

Tuck laughed and patted his stomach, able to feel the ridges of his muscles beneath his fingers. 'What can I say? I'm a man of big appetites.'

Jonas grinned as his peppercorn steak and fries were set in front of him. 'Well, that was really interesting. I'm glad I went.'

Tuck leaned in on his elbows. 'I learn something new every time. Just when I think I've got it all, they blow me sideways with some new piece of editing software or a camera technique. I always come away wanting more. Swear to God, if they ran it as a college course, I'd be there like a shot.'

'Sounds like you're really serious about the filming gig. More so than the snowboards?'

Tuck sighed, holding up a pizza slice and pulling it away so that the cheese stretched into elastic strings. 'I can't pretend it hasn't felt different without Mitch.' He shook his head, dropping his hand back down to the plate, the cheese strings slack again. 'Nothing's the same, man.'

It was several moments before he realized Jonas had stopped chewing and was watching him with a concerned expression; that he had lapsed into a desolate silence.

'But—' He rallied, forcing a smile. 'We all gotta deal with our shit, right? It'll get better. It's already getting better. I'm a father now.'

'I saw! How old?'

'Twelve days now,' Tuck said, his mouth full. 'Although ask Lucy and she'll give you the answer right down to the minutes.'

Jonas grinned. 'And are you enjoying it? Fatherhood, I mean.'

Tuck rolled his eyes. 'Well, I'm not sure "enjoying" is the word. Those broken nights are *brutal*, man. They are way harder than I thought they were gonna be.' He shrugged. 'But he's got a way of kind of reeling you in, that little guy. Sometimes, before I get home after a day in the office or the store or the studio, I kinda stop outside the door and just feel like "Jeez". I'm so wiped, you know? But then I walk in and see him and . . .' He shrugged again, making a clucking sound with his tongue. 'I'm a sucker. He kills me.' He pulled apart another slice. 'You got kids?'

'No.'

Tuck grinned. 'That's kind of a shame. You almost want a kid just so he can say, "My daddy's an astronaut!"'

'I guess,' Jonas said, laughing at the backwards logic.

'How about a woman? You married?'

'Nope. The training's pretty intense once you're selected for an expedition so even if I did meet someone, it wouldn't really be fair to get involved and then . . . well, leave the planet.'

Tuck guffawed with laughter, smacking his stomach again. 'It puts a whole other complexion on travelling for work, that's for sure!'

'Exactly.'

They ate.

'And Meg?' Tuck watched Jonas's expression as he asked the question, pulling off his sweatshirt. Surprise was all he saw before his sight was blocked, his T-shirt riding up and inadvertently showing off his six-pack. 'What are your intentions?'

'What do you mean?' Jonas asked, his fork hovering in mid-air.

'Well, I was just wondering whether there was anything more between the two of you,' Tuck said. 'She talked about you a lot.'

'Talked? Past tense?'

'Yeah, not so much recently, although she and Lucy haven't been getting on lately so who knows what she's been talking about? Maybe she's talking to other people.'

Jonas hesitated. 'Is that because . . . Don't take this the wrong way, but is that because of the baby's name?'

Tuck's shoulders slumped. 'That obvious?'

'Well, when I asked the baby's name and your wife said "Mitch", she looked pretty stressed. I just wondered . . .' He shrugged, resuming eating again.

Tuck dropped the piece of pizza he was holding and

wiped his fingers on the paper napkin. 'And you know what? I don't even blame her. I'd feel exactly the same.' He hesitated. 'Hell, I *do* feel the same, but what's done is done. Lucy registered it and there's nothing I can do about it.'

'She named your child without consulting you on it?' Jonas's shock was evident, breaking through even his formal European politeness.

'Pretty much.' Tuck flicked his eyes up to his dining companion. 'But then that's Lucy all over. Nothing stops her. Once she makes her mind up about something, she's like a human dynamo. Force of nature.' He rolled his eyes. 'It was one of the things I liked most about her when we got together so I guess I can hardly very well complain about it now.'

'But that must be hard for you, to hear Mitch's name over and over. Or is it not? Perhaps it makes it easier in a way, desensitizes it?'

'No, man, it sucks. I jump every time I hear it.' Tuck shook his head bitterly, eyeing his pizza with remarkably little gusto.

'And so now Meg's avoiding Lucy?'

'Like the plague. She hasn't been over once since we told her and she was the one who delivered the baby.'

'Sorry? Meg delivered the baby?' Jonas echoed in disbelief.

Tuck chuckled at his expression. 'She sure did. Baby came early and they were up at the cabin together. The paramedics couldn't get there in time.'

'So she had to deal with a medical emergency on her own?'

'Yep. It just seems to be one disaster after another up there. We keep trying to get her to move into town but she won't have any of it.' He picked up the next piece of pizza and looked at it lethargically. The dough was limp in his hand, the cheese beginning to thicken and congeal as it cooled. 'Anyway, they've fallen out again and so now I've got Lucy crying all the time and I don't know what to tell her. How can I say it'll all be all right? The more days go past, the less likely it looks.' He grimaced. 'You know what I think? I think Meg's had enough. She's moving on and that means *my* life is gonna be hell.'

'Can't you talk to her, on Lucy's behalf?'

Tuck gave a dismissive snort. 'Hell, no. I'm the last person she wants to talk to.'

'Why?'

Tuck caught Jonas's gaze briefly, before he looked away again. 'I'm just persona non grata, that's all.'

'So she's upset with you *and* Lucy?'

Tuck nodded. 'And the way I see it, she's right to be. I don't blame her for feeling that way about any of it.' He set down the unwanted pizza slice and picked up his beer. 'Funny, isn't it, how you think some things are gonna be for ever but then they're . . . pulled apart and dismantled in the blink of an eye?' He looked around the restaurant, at the familiar faces at almost every table. 'I thought I'd got my life all set up. I thought we'd made the template for how things were gonna be for the next sixty years. Work was going great, me and Mitch best buddies since third grade. And then—' He clicked his fingers. 'Everything changed, *we* changed, and nothing's what I thought it would be – not my friends, not my marri—' He stopped abruptly. 'Shit. Listen to me. You got me rambling on like you're a shrink and I'm a wacko!'

Jonas smiled. 'I'm genuinely interested.'

But Tuck shook his head and frowned at his beer with a funny expression. 'They put some sort of truth serum in here?' he asked, back to being the clown.

Jonas laughed and they moved on to the ice-hockey league, Tuck pleased to find Jonas was well informed on the sport, having avidly followed the Norwegian league all his life, even when in space.

By the time they parted an hour later, Tuck felt unburdened. He had been joking about the whole 'shrink' thing but there was no doubt Jonas was easy to talk to. He was a good listener – so good, in fact, that it was only when Tuck stopped at the bungalow front door, hearing the baby's cries coming from the other side, that he realized his question – what exactly were his intentions with Meg? – had gone unanswered.

Chapter Thirty

Wednesday 15 November 2017

'Oh, my goodness, old-school!' Meg laughed, seeing how far the ski tips extended past the front of her boots – boots that were so soft she could wiggle her toes in them. They reminded her of old-fashioned leather ice-skating boots, only with the blade removed.

'Now raise up,' Jonas instructed, bending over and looking closely at the bindings as she lifted onto her tiptoes, her heel coming completely free of the back of the ski. 'Good.' He straightened up and smiled. 'You ready?'

Meg inhaled deeply and nodded. 'How hard can it be, right? We're just going to glide.'

She looked ahead of them, the ski tracks already pre-set, four deep grooves running in tandem away from them on the flat, towards the trees. It had snowed heavily – almost continuously, in fact – for the past few days, forcing them to abandon this plan yesterday, and they had spent the day at screenings and drinking coffee instead, sharing popcorn in the dark and talking non-stop in the bright; after their initially hesitant start, they had fallen into a gallop, their face-to-face conversations as animated as their faceless emails had been. So when this morning they had woken to a sky that was rinsed clear, the trees listing slightly beneath the fresh weight, sporadic showers of snowflakes sprinkling to the ground every time a squirrel scampered along a bough, they had been packed and ready by nine. Badger was already a dark dot in the distance, nose to the ground, tail flapping like a pennant as he tried to track a snowshoe hare that had a good 100-metre head start on him.

They set off, Jonas looking sleek in his all-black skins – insulated leggings with special muscular compression pads, a soft-shell jacket, gloves and a beanie. Perhaps it was because his outfit was so stark against the all-white landscape, but it somehow served to define him more sharply, making his light eyes glitter, his pale skin flushed in the biting temperatures, the soft brush of stubble glinting in the sunlight like iron shavings – and Meg remembered again why she had cut off contact. That face was distracting; she'd known it when she'd seen him for the first time on TV in Toronto.

He moved rhythmically and powerfully, the extra-long poles (which came almost to chest height when stuck straight in the ground) stabbing the snow in clean, alternate movements as his skis glided along. Meg caught the rhythm quickly. As an accomplished Alpine skier and snowboarder herself, she understood how to move on snow, although it was an odd sensation having such freedom of movement in the foot.

They poled and glided at a good speed, the car park receding behind them quickly as they moved towards the trees. Occasionally, Jonas told her to delay transferring her weight or to bend more into the push-off, but mostly they enjoyed the silence. It was an easy peace, both of them used – she supposed – to solitude and quietness; her at the cabin, him on his rocket. (She knew the ISS wasn't actually a rocket, but it amused her to think of it in those terms.)

The mountains looked down on them from all sides, only the steepest cliffs still a stubborn, grey granite. Animal tracks decorated the virgin snow, most of which she recognized as she poled past, faithfully following the tracks like a train and keeping her intrusion into this beautiful natural playground at a minimum.

'Do you like it here?' she asked him, glancing over and seeing how his eyes roamed the space as though trying to absorb the view into his body.

'It's exactly what I hoped it would be.'

'How's it different to your mountains and valleys?'

He looked around him as he skied. 'The mountains here are higher, with more forests. Ours are a lot more barren but we have more grazing pastures.'

'That's specific,' she smiled, hearing how the birdsong changed as they moved into the trees, shadows stippling the ground so that sunlight fell on them in staccato bursts now. The gradient began to climb a little and she felt the first twinges of burn in her thighs. Jonas had studied the route after she'd emailed it over and had advised her to 'carbload' at dinner the night before – Ronnie had said afterwards who couldn't love a man who insisted you eat pasta? – because if they wanted to enjoy the fun of going down the slopes, they were going to have to pay on the way up first. Personally, this was why Meg was such a big fan of chairlifts.

The snowfall had been dispersed and irregular in the forest, the higher trees distorting where the snow fell so that some of the smaller, younger saplings were almost bare, others overloaded with bulbous snow growths that deformed and bent their shapes.

'You know, this is pretty easy,' Meg quipped, keeping pace easily as they moved in deeper and the silence loudened.

He looked over at her, a bemused smile on his lips. 'I'm glad you think so. Tell me if you still think that when we get past the bridge.'

'OK,' she replied with a nonchalant toss of her head, but these skis were a good thirty centimetres longer than any she had ever used before for downhill skiing and she wasn't sure she'd fare quite so well out of the tracks.

'Do you ski a lot?' he asked, his breathing a little laboured, his cheeks really pinking up.

'Usually. Not this year, though.'

'Because of Mitch?'

Meg looked over at him but his gaze was dead ahead. 'Yes, probably.'

'Are you scared of being caught up in an avalanche?'

'No, nothing like that,' she said, shaking her head. 'It's just . . . the memories, more than anything. Pretty much everywhere here has a story or adventure attached to it.'

'Tuck was telling me how you all used to go on expeditions together and stay in the mountain huts . . .'

What else had Tuck said, she wondered? 'Well, it wasn't like we did that *all* the time. He was probably exaggerating. Tuck's prone to that.'

Jonas glanced at her, raised an eyebrow. 'Yeah?'

'Yeah.'

'So does here have memories for you?' he asked, meaning this valley, these woods.

'No. Because it's on the flat, we never came this way.'

'Well, good, then. So today we can make a new story.'

She looked over at him. He was smiling at her – easy-going, languid. 'Do you do this in Norway?' she asked.

'All the time. Sometimes it's the only way to get about. If there's a heavy fall and they don't clear the road . . . I often used to ski to school when I was younger.'

'What you need is a snowmobile. I've got one for getting to the cabin. It's so steep where I live, it's the only way up in the winter. If you go by day you can get the chairlift up to the top and ski back down, which is pretty fun, but not that great if I've got shopping to carry or whatever. And after dark when the lift's shut . . .' She shrugged.

'I would love to see this cabin of yours.'

'It isn't anything fancy,' she said quickly.

'I'd be disappointed if it was. Fancy isn't really the point of a mountain cabin, is it?'

'No, I guess not,' she smiled, feeling relieved. Then feeling shy. 'Well, then you should come for dinner while you're here. If you want. I mean, it's a bit crowded with Ronnie and Jack staying—'

'You say crowded, I say cosy. I lived on a space station, remember.'

She smiled. 'So what do you like to eat?'

'Well, I'm really into Samoan flavours at the moment . . .' He looked over at her aghast expression and laughed. 'Relax. I'm messing with you. I spent six months eating freeze-dried food from packets. I love everything. There is literally nothing I will not try.'

'Nothing?'

'Try me.'

'Scotch bonnet stir-fry?'

He laughed but gave a lackadaisical shrug. 'It wasn't quite what I had in mind, but absolutely.'

She narrowed her eyes, wickedly, trying to think of another. 'Puffer fish sashimi?'

'Why not?'

It was her turn to laugh. 'You're mad.'

'Quite possibly.'

'So what did you pack for our picnic then? Because I'm starving.'

'We've only been going for forty-five minutes!'

'I know. I'm a nightmare. Always hungry at the wrong times.'

'I'll bear that in mind,' he said, glancing over at her. 'Well, I went traditional. I thought if we were skiing in the Nordic style, we should eat and drink that way too. So we have pickled herrings, *lefsa*—'

'*Lefsa?*'

'They're like potato pancakes. *Agurksalat* – cucumber salad, basically – and *snarøl*.' He saw her blank expression. 'It's a drink made from lemon, sugar, yeast and an alcohol-free malt called *vørterøl*.'

'OK,' Meg said slowly. 'I haven't heard of a single one of those. Except for the fish.'

'Not scared, are you?'

'Never . . .' she grinned, sensing a challenge. 'Oh, look at that!'

They had emerged from the trees onto an open pasture, the snow spreading away from them like a carved woodcut. 'It's so beautiful.'

'*Sastrugi*,' Jonas said, following her eye line.

'What?'

'That's what it's called – the ripples and ridges that are formed by the wind. It's called *sastrugi*.'

'How do you know that?'

'Just picked it up somewhere,' he shrugged.

She shook her head. 'Is there anything you *don't* know?' In the course of the journey, she'd already ascertained that he had flown for the Norwegian air force, was a black belt in karate, spoke five languages (Norwegian, English, Spanish, German – and Russian, which was compulsory for astronauts) and was considering – on account of his crackshot shooting skills and love for cross-country – taking up biathlons now that he had more spare time. 'Oh! See the eagle?' she asked, pointing it out, wheeling high above them.

He looked up. 'I love eagles.'

'Don't tell me, you can speak eagle too.'

He tapped her on the legs with his ski pole. 'Hey.'

'What?' she laughed. 'It wouldn't surprise me. You're like Superman.'

'Hardly.'

'No? Give me one flaw then.'

'Hmmmm . . . I guess my colleagues would tell you it's that I always think I'm right.' He looked bemused by the exercise. 'That or I'm too frank. I tend to just speak my mind.'

'And your mother? What would she say?'

'*My mother?*' he chuckled.

'Oh, yes. You can tell a lot about a man by his relationship with his mother.'

He considered that. 'Well, then I think she'd say that I'm too driven.'

'How do you mean?'

'I'm single-minded to the point of obsession. When I want something, I go after it and don't stop till I get it.'

Meg swallowed. 'But isn't that a good thing?'

'It depends what I'm going after. Up till now it's been my career, which has meant having to give up, or go without other things.'

'You mean, like friends?'

'And relationships. It's hard to ask someone to wait for you whilst you leave the planet for six months.'

She looked dead ahead. 'I'm sure the right girl would,' she murmured, trying to keep her tone light.

They fell silent for a moment, gliding through the crystal quiet. 'OK,' she said then, 'so you've got your flaws. You're gobby and opinionated and ruthless—'

'Hey!'

She chuckled. 'Now give me one vulnerability that makes you merely human.'

He considered for a moment. 'Well, there's one big one.'

'Tell me.'

'I'm scared of heights.'

Meg was delighted. 'You're kidding me.'

'I'm not. Terrified of them, in fact.'

'You're scared of heights so you became an astronaut?'

'Well, I wouldn't say that was why I became one. I became an astronaut *in spite* of it.'

'But that's like . . . being a doctor who's scared of blood.'

'Or a vet who's allergic to cats,' he agreed.

'Or . . . Or a vegetarian pig farmer!' she cried.

Jonas grinned. 'Or a teacher who hates kids.'

'A claustrophobic lift engineer!'

Jonas arched an eyebrow at her slightly random simile and she giggled.

'I just don't get it. You're scared of heights and yet you chose a job that would mean you had to go to the highest heights of all.'

'Yeah, I'm sick like that.'

She laughed. 'But how can you do that? I mean, how do you make yourself do it?'

He looked across at her, his eyes dancing at her amusement. 'Because I fully believe that we have to push past our fears. It is highly unlikely that height itself is ever going to harm me – but my fear of it could seriously damage my life. We have to live before we die.'

'That sounds like a title for a Bond film.'

'I do consult for them.'

'Stop it!' Meg laughed.

He chuckled. 'OK. So now you tell me your flaw.'

'Ha! Where to begin?' she groaned. 'There isn't just one, you know. There's a *huge* list,' she said, drawing out the word.

'No, there's just one. There's always just one.' He looked straight at her. 'What's the one thing that's stopping you from living before you die, Meg Saunders?'

She stared at him, all her amusement and levity deserting her in a flash. Did she even need to say it?

They shushed through the snow, their skis flattening the ice crystals, their breath rhythmic and paired without any conscious twinning on their parts.

She glanced across and saw he was looking up into the sky. More than looking – searching.

'Do you watch for them, every time you look at the sky?' she asked, panting lightly.

He smiled, like a child caught with his hand in the cookie jar. 'Yes. I can't help it. Do you?'

'Yes.' She smiled back. 'Are you going to go back up there?'

'I don't know. It's not guaranteed.'

'Do you want to?'

He was quiet for a moment. 'If you'd asked me six months ago I'd have said yes, no question. I beat over ten thousand applicants and spent years in specialist training to get up there, and I'd have stayed for as long as they'd have let me.'

'But now?'

He looked straight ahead. 'Things are different. I'm different.'

'You mean because you've already been up there now? Been there, done that?'

He glanced across at her. 'Something like that.'

They skied in silence for a hundred metres. 'How about you?' he asked. 'What's next for you? Are you going to carry on designing for Titch?'

'How did you know about that?' she asked in surprise. She knew she'd never brought it up with him.

'Tuck told me. He said you're really good. That some of your designs have become collector's pieces.'

She was silent for a moment, wishing Tuck would keep quiet. 'No. That feels . . . done. I did it for Mitch. It wouldn't be the same any more.'

'I understand. But couldn't you take your skills and apply them to different products?'

'Well, I did think about it, but . . .' She wrinkled her nose, tossing the idea – and conversation – away.

'What? Why not?'

'Let's just say things didn't work out . . .'

'Why not?' he pressed.

'You don't get tact, do you?' she smiled. 'OK, fine. A job opportunity came up in New York.'

'Doing what?'

'It was a redesign for a big designer. I don't know – my name got put forward, they knew about me through the boards and so somehow, I got invited for interview.'

'So far, so brilliant. So what happened?'

'Lucy had the baby early.'

'Oh, Tuck told me about that.'

Meg felt another rush of irritation at Tuck's blabber-mouth nature. Was there anything he hadn't told Jonas about her?

'You actually delivered the baby yourself?'

'Had to. But it meant I missed the flight helping her.'

He frowned. 'But why didn't you just call them and go out on the next flight?'

She rolled her eyes. 'Oh, no. I took it as a *pretty big* sign from the universe that I wasn't supposed to go to New York.'

'*Really?*' Jonas sounded baffled.

'What? You don't think it was?'

'Well, I think there's another way of looking at it.'

'Which is?'

'That you got to do for Lucy what you couldn't for Mitch . . . You got to save her.' His tone was gentle but his eyes direct as he glanced over at her and she sensed he never shrank back from facing the truth. 'Maybe it was the universe squaring off that particular circle.'

Meg stopped poling, gliding to a stop within seconds,

and it was a few moments before Jonas realized she had fallen behind. He stopped too and turned.

'Are you OK?' he called back, leaning on his pole.

She stared back at him, her breath coming heavily. In the distance, she saw Badger come back into view, a growing dark speck on the white horizon, and she knew the hare must have made its escape. 'I never . . . thought . . . of it . . . that way . . .' she panted.

He pushed himself backwards along the tracks again, stopping beside her. 'Well, hey, what do I know? It's just a thought.'

She blinked, looking at him. 'But it's a nice thought . . . A really nice thought.'

He smiled, the corners of his eyes crinkling slightly, and she felt something inside her relax at the sight of him. She remembered something Ronnie had said once about how she felt full of sharp corners and hard angles when she came back here, never quite fitting in, and for the first time, Meg realized that was how she felt all of the time too, always trying to fit into other people's moulds . . . But he didn't judge her or try to force her to be bigger than she felt; he didn't make her feel small or guilty or stupid. He made her feel soft and languid, witty and clever, interesting, beautiful, brave. She remembered how she'd debated whether to see him talk in New York that weekend, if she could hide out in the crowd. Instead, they were here, the two of them alone in the Canadian wilderness, no hiding possible.

'You know . . .' she said, trying to get her breath back. 'You were in New York the same weekend I was supposed to be there.'

He looked surprised. 'I was?'

'Yeah. You were speaking at the public lectures for the Space Grant Consortium.'

He arched an eyebrow, was quiet for a moment. 'And you know that because . . . ?'

She laughed. 'I was cyber-stalking you.'

He grinned, his eyes dancing with amusement. 'So let me get this straight – you were completely stonewalling my emails, but stalking me online?'

She chuckled. 'Something like that.'

'*Why?*' he laughed. 'Why the hell didn't you just write back to me? It drove me half mad not knowing if something had happened to you, or if it was something I'd done.'

'Well, you'd landed is what you'd done.'

'Wasn't that a good thing?' he asked, baffled.

'No. It made you real.' The words were out before she could edit or filter or stop them and as he looked at her, she felt the space between them fill with heat.

'So you're saying you *didn't* want to meet me?'

She bit her lip and shook her head. 'Shy.'

'Shy,' he repeated, watching her closely. 'So if you had been in New York, would you have come to see me?'

'I would have come to see you, but you wouldn't have seen me.'

He frowned at her riddles. 'You mean you'd have hidden? Seriously?'

'Yes, but it didn't matter in the end because the universe conspired against it and I didn't end up going at all,' she said quickly.

'Oh, I see, so it was the *universe* stopping you from seeing me?' he asked, his voice wry.

'Exactly,' she chuckled.

'So then I've gone against the laws of the universe coming here to find you?'

'You didn't come here to find me,' she protested. 'You're handing out an award.'

He stared back at her, his tracks only twenty centimetres from hers, his body twisted to face her. 'Meg, I came back from *space* to find you.'

In the silence that followed, she could hear the tiny crackle of snowflakes shifting on the ground, the whisper of the breeze shaking the trees. His gaze fell to her mouth and before she could react, he had leaned over and kissed her, his hands still on the poles, his feet still planted in the tracks so that only their lips met. Lips and hearts.

He pulled back after a few moments and she looked into his pale eyes.

'I came all this way to find you and now I hear I've got the universe on my tail,' he murmured, his eyes on her mouth. 'Should I be worried?'

She swallowed, wanting him to kiss her again. 'I think we both should.'

She pulled a sickie the next day – not that Dolores, who was busier than she'd ever been, seemed to care; she'd never sounded happier to hear from Meg holding her nose as she bemoaned the sudden cold that had afflicted her overnight – and they drove higher up into the mountains to Lake Louise, an hour away.

Meg drove as Jonas took charge of the music selection, unwrapping and popping toffees into her mouth every few kilometres. The scenery was predictably spectacular, the mountains now freshly dipped in their winter colours, although the famously jade waters of the lake were hidden beneath a duvet of fresh powder and wouldn't be seen again for another five months. The snow had been pushed back in one large area, revealing the thick ice and creating a skating rink. There were a couple of teams playing ice hockey, with goals set up at either end in one part, and others were curling; but they had just skated – Jonas was very good, having grown up doing exactly this in Norway, but they still held hands as though one of them needed to balance. They tried to do pirouettes – him kissing her when she fell over, her kissing him when he pulled off a spin; they raced each other, with a kiss as the prize, and when he'd chased her around the huge ice-sculpted castle she'd let him catch her, too eager to give him his reward.

But it wasn't enough. It hadn't been enough the previous night when she'd dropped him back at his hotel with just a kiss (rather a long, involved one, admittedly) and she was fast running out of self-control. She didn't care about skating and he didn't give a damn about seeing the sights. They both knew what they really wanted and by the time they'd driven home again after lunch, they'd almost given up talking altogether; the desire and frustration beginning to be overwhelming, with his body pressed against hers, her hands upon him, every chance they got. The original idea for the afternoon had been for her to introduce him to snowboarding, the way he'd introduced her to cross-country skiing, but that would mean staying on the pistes and they could only get to the cabin by riding over back-country. And when she'd asked if he'd like to see the cabin . . . they both knew what she was really asking.

They were lip-locked all the way up on the chairlift, a snowboard strapped to her foot, skis clipped to his, their cheeks pink with the cold even though their bodies felt hot.

And when they got to the top, they skied and boarded straight off the piste, in their jeans, Meg leading the way effortlessly through the trees, her hair flying in loose plaits behind her – she'd never had Tuck or Mitch's daredevil recklessness but she could get down anything, in any weather condition, with considerable style.

It wasn't a long run to the cabin, just a technical one, but Jonas was both a good skier and a desperate man and they were there in fifteen minutes.

'Wow,' he exclaimed, clipping off his skis, his eyes on the little cabin. It looked especially pretty under the fresh snow-fall, only animal tracks by the bottom of the steps betraying any signs of life. 'It's so cute.'

'It is. It is cute,' she repeated breathlessly as she sat on the step, her eyes on him as she unbuckled her foot from the board harness, quite sure she was going to perish from sexual desperation. 'Do you want the tour?'

'Uh, yeah . . . sure,' he said, sticking his poles in the ground and coming over to her in three strides, just as she got her foot free. She stood up, eyes fixed to his, and he scooped her into his arms, kissing her again as he carried her towards the door.

It was unlocked.

'You don't lock it?' he murmured, stepping into the hall, kissing her neck, her cheek . . .

'Don't need to. The bears haven't got opposable thumbs,' she whispered.

His laugh vibrated against her and he let go of her legs so that she was standing again. They were in the hallway, one door to their left, one straight ahead and two to their right.

'So – main room and kitchen, bathroom, guest room, my

room,' she said quickly, nodding her head towards the various doors.

'Great tour,' he grinned, his eyes not taking in anything but her, his hands sliding down her arms and making her shiver. He held her hips, pulling her closer to him. Their bodies were touching from the tips of their noses to their toes. 'Which is your room?' he asked, kissing her face.

'There,' she whispered, her eyes shut, pointing to his right.

'Let's go there then,' he said, his lips still upon hers as he walked her backwards towards the doorway.

He pulled his jumper over his head, his T-shirt riding up with the movement to expose a flash of toned stomach. Then the T-shirt went too and he was in just his jeans.

She lifted her arms up and he pulled her jumper over her head, taking the T-shirt with it – deliberately, she sensed – so that she was in just her bra. He took one of her plaits and cocked an eyebrow, twirling it playfully between his fingers.

She laughed.

Jonas's eyes travelled down the length of her, the desperation of a few moments ago suddenly quelled now that they were here; they could take their time. He brushed the backs of his fingers up her tummy, between her breasts, cupping her head against the palm of his hand. 'You are so beautiful,' he murmured.

She stared up at him, her hand on his chest; she saw him finally take in their surroundings, the room they were standing in, the night sky painted on the ceiling, the radio equipment on the desk. 'Oh. Yes, that's . . .' Her voice faded out.

He looked back at her. 'It's strange seeing it at last. I imagined you were in a shed or hut.'

'No . . . This used to be the study.'

He nodded, his eyes back on the radio rig. 'It's incredible to think that's how we started.'

'I know.'

He looked at her again and she saw that the urgency had come back. Without saying another word, he lifted her and she wrapped her legs around his waist, kissing him deeply as he carried her to the bed. They sank down in a tangle of limbs, skin upon skin at last, back in the place where they'd first met – under the stars.

Chapter Thirty-one

Friday 17 November 2017

'What time is it?' Meg asked in a panicky voice, her hands sheathed in the oven gloves and an apron on, her hair pulled back in a high ponytail. Steam was escaping from the lidded saucepans on the hobs and her skin was as flushed as if she'd been in a sauna.

'Relax. It's ten to,' Ronnie said from her curled-up spot on the sofa. 'And he won't be early. No one's ever early.'

'Shit,' Meg muttered, turning a circle on the spot, wondering what to do next. She needed to peel the potatoes and finish making the topping for the cobbler, but she hadn't even put her make-up on yet and she was still in her dressing gown from her shower.

'You should get dressed first,' Ronnie called through helpfully, as though reading her mind.

'Yes, right. Clothes,' Meg muttered, pulling off the oven gloves and darting towards the back bedroom, just as the door was opened suddenly and an arctic blast chilled her bare legs.

Jack grinned apologetically as he came through with yet another haul of logs. 'Sorry!' he said, unable to close the door behind him without setting down the log bag.

Meg ran to the door to shut it, desperate to keep the cold air out, and was startled to see a dark figure coming up the steps.

'Hey,' Jonas said, stopping as he saw her standing there, a bottle of wine in his hand.

'You're early,' she whispered, the hem of her short dressing gown flapping at her bare legs as the wind gusted suddenly, blowing snow at his back.

He stepped onto the porch, his hands reaching for her, eyes glittering. 'Sorry. I just couldn't wait.'

He leaned down to kiss her and she felt herself sink into him, her arms automatically snaking up around his neck. She felt exactly the same way. The past ten hours had been exquisite torture as he'd been corralled by the festival organizers into fulfilling his official duties – a press conference, a lecture and Q&A session – and every minute without him had dragged. She'd spent her day at work – having made a 'miraculous recovery', Dolores had observed – with her eyes glued to the street hoping to catch a glimpse of him, even though she knew he was stuck in private screenings of the category-winning films. But now he was here again and the agony of separation was instantly forgotten, his arms around her, his mouth upon her . . .

'Meg! Did you shut the door or what?' Ronnie yelled from the next room.

Meg sprang away from him, breathless, desperate. 'Y-Yes!' she called, stepping back so that he could come in.

Jonas grinned, stepping towards her again, his eyes never leaving her, reaching down for another kiss.

'Jonas is here,' she called again as they broke away for air.

'Wow! Prompt much?' Ronnie yelled back, eliciting a chuckle from Jonas. He pulled off his hat, snowflakes still caught on his hair and light stubble, the fur trim of his parka.

'Did you get up OK?' Meg asked, in a deliberately 'normal' voice for Ronnie and Jack to overhear. But her eyes were on his mouth again and all she wanted to do was kiss him. So she did.

'Great. The snowmobile started up first time and those red ribbons tied round the trees are brilliant. You can see them so easily,' he replied in an equally 'normal', slightly-too-loud voice. She had left the snowmobile down in the lock-up for him to use, having taken the chairlift up and skied down to the cabin herself earlier in the afternoon.

He kissed her again.

'It's such a nightmare trying to give people directions otherwise,' she replied, having to resist the urge to laugh between kisses.

'I can imagine. Well, it really works,' he said loudly, kissing her again. 'Good markers.' Kiss. 'Great system.' More kisses . . .

'Are you coming in or what?' Ronnie yelled. 'We're not having the dinner party out in the hall, you know!'

Jonas chuckled, kissing Meg one last time before unzipping his coat and shrugging it off. She reached to take it from him, hanging it on one of the hooks on the wall and thinking how good he looked in his half-zip navy sweater and jeans. She saw him properly take in the sight of her dressing gown and hockey socks under her apron, scruffy hair . . .

He was kissing her again. Oh, God, why did she have to have Ronnie and Jack staying with her? She loved having them of course, but ugh . . . *timing*!

They pulled apart just a split second before Jack appeared

round the doorway with the empty log sack. 'Hey! You made it up here OK then?'

He and Jonas shook hands, looking pleased to see each other. 'Yes. What an incredible location. I literally didn't see another soul.'

'I know, right?' Jack looked at Meg. 'Where is your nearest neighbour?'

'There's no one on this side of the mountain. We're officially in the nature reserve here. We've only got this spot because it belonged to Mitch's grandfather before they created the reserve.'

'What kind of "nature" are we talking about?' Jonas asked, bending down to unlace his boots, which were caked in snow that was rapidly melting and beginning to puddle on the floor.

'Oh, cougars, wolves, bears . . . You know, all the cuddly, cute animals,' Meg quipped.

'Let me just put this bag back in the log store,' Jack said, heading for the door again. 'Then I'll open some wine.'

'Come on, I'll give you the grand tour – all five seconds of it,' Meg said loudly for the benefit of her sister and stopping at the doorway of the first bedroom – her old one, which Ronnie and Jack had been staying in and was now more like an archaeological dig, with detritus and strewn clothes everywhere. 'The guest room. What can I say? My sister is a pig.'

'I heard that!' Ronnie called, still not moving off her spot on the sofa.

'And then, this is my room.' She couldn't keep the smile off her mouth as he arched an eyebrow and kissed her again. No one knew he'd been up here already, that he'd slept in this room, in that bed with her last night; that they'd had breakfast together, that she'd driven down with him on the snowmobile this morning with her arms wrapped around his waist; that they'd succumbed to each other again in the jeep in the tiny lock-up before he'd had to drive into town . . .

Hearing Jack's boots on the porch steps, they pulled apart again and wandered into the main room.

'Don't mind her,' Meg grinned as she passed her sprawled-out sister. 'She's depressed about going back tomorrow.'

Jack chuckled as he followed in after them. 'She's decided, after years of medical training, that actually being a lady of leisure suits her.'

'I don't *want* to go back to work,' Ronnie moaned, dramatically flinging an arm over her face for a moment before huffing and finally getting up.

'Me either,' Jonas said, kissing her on the cheek.

'When are *you* going?' Ronnie asked him.

He glanced at Meg. 'I'm flying to Washington on Sunday morning.'

Ronnie looked over at Meg – did she suspect something? – and Meg suddenly felt obliged to say something. 'Well, at least you'll get to see who wins the festival,' she said with false cheer, as if that was the main reason for his presence here.

'Yes.'

Ronnie's eyebrows shot up at the silence that lingered and wriggled and stretched. 'Well, why don't we have some wine and you can *get dressed*,' she said pointedly to her sister. 'Unless this is actually a sleepover party and we're all going to do our nails?'

'Yes. OK. Good plan,' Meg nodded, shooting Jonas another look before darting from the room.

She grabbed the clothes she'd left lying on the bed earlier and dressed in record time – Ronnie's black jeans and a slim-fit cream jumper, pulling her hair down and brushing it through quickly. There didn't seem to be much point in putting make-up on, not now he'd arrived and had already seen her; besides, she could hear them all laughing next door and she wanted to get back out there. She took one quick look in the mirror – did she look OK? She didn't want to *dress up* – everyone was in jeans and jumpers and socks – but then again, she'd invited him over for dinner; he'd brought wine. She had to make some effort. She wanted to look good for him.

Jonas straightened up with a knowing look as she came to the door and smiled in.

'That was quick!' Jack exclaimed, before looking over at Ronnie. 'Learn from your big sister.'

Ronnie stuck out her tongue at him and Jonas laughed. 'Meg does that too.'

'Does she?' Ronnie asked, but with a particular note in her voice, an eyebrow hitched again as she looked across at Meg. 'You are a very observant man, Jonas Solberg.'

'Oh, shit! The pudding!' Meg gasped suddenly, running through to the kitchen and resuming her panic of a few minutes earlier. Grabbing the cobbler topping from the fridge and squeezing a lemon into a bowl of water, she began peeling and slicing the apples, dunking them in the lemon water before they could brown. The kitchen bar where she was working looked back into the main room, so she could still see and hear everything, but she felt cut off in her separate quarter and like an eavesdropper as she listened to Jack continue to grill Jonas – as he had at every encounter – about astronaut life.

'So, stream of consciousness, OK? I want one-word answers. What was the single best thing about being in space?' Jack was asking.

Jonas glanced over at her in bemusement. 'The view.'

'And the single best thing about being back on Earth?'

'The weather – wind, rain, sun, snow. It all feels incredible.' Badger had gone to sit by him, conveniently positioning his head just under Jonas's hand, and Jonas fondled his ears.

Meg smiled, as Jack continued his interrogations. With the apples all cored, peeled and sliced, she arranged them in the buttered dish, sprinkled over the topping and set it aside. Then, pouring water into a pan and grabbing the peeler again, she began de-skinning the potatoes at speed.

'I just realized you don't have a drink,' Jonas said, wandering over a few minutes later. 'Where are the glasses?'

She pointed with the knife. 'Thank you. It's thirsty work, all this chopping.'

'Can I help?' Jonas asked, pouring her some wine and placing the glass down in front of her, his hand sliding down her bottom and squeezing lightly.

'Oh, no, please, sit, relax,' she said loudly again, in case Ronnie was listening. 'Enjoy. This'll only take a—'

'I know, but if they say a problem shared is a problem halved –' he said, opening the drawer and pulling out a small paring knife – 'I reckon the same must be true of potatoes.'

She stepped along so that he had room to join her and they stood side by side, peeling the potatoes together, facing back into the main room. Jack and Ronnie were huddled together on the sofa, looking at something in a magazine, Badger stretched out and snoring in front of the fire. Snow dashed past the windows, lit up by the outdoor light, and the blue-hued cold was in contrast to the rich honeyed light of the cabin. The fire was at full roar now and the rich textures and tones of the reindeer-skin rugs, sheepskins thrown over the chairs and the ruby-red curtains, embroidered with white pin dots, rendered the little home to its fullest glory. The smell of pie wafting from the oven wasn't bad either. Meg couldn't remember the last time she'd felt this happy.

'I love this place,' Jonas said, dropping each potato into the saucepan in front of them. 'I totally see why you wouldn't want to leave here.'

'Thank you. Although you might not think that when I tell you there's no Wi-Fi and the TV reception is dodgy.'

He looked back at her, that look on his face again. 'Well, there are other things to do.'

Her stomach flipped; she wasn't sure how she was supposed to get through dinner.

Ronnie glanced over, curious at their quiet industry, and Jonas cleared his throat. 'Do you ever worry about the wildlife getting too close?' he asked, in a louder voice.

'Not really. We've got locks on the bins and we keep a gun loaded, just in case.' She bit her lip as she realized she'd use the plural 'we'. As though Mitch was still here.

If Jonas noticed, he didn't show it. 'But what if you're outside, or on the snowmobile?'

'There's a gun that fires blanks in the seat compartment and I never go anywhere without pepper spray. Especially after what happened in July.'

He put down his knife and squeezed her hand in silence. She'd seen from his expression how horrified he'd been when she'd told him in detail about the bear attack, earlier in the week.

'Good. Take no chances.' He winked at her, making her stomach do flips again. 'We've got a universe on our tail, remember.'

'Would it be wrong to have thirds?' Ronnie asked, but she was already pushing her bowl back towards Meg. 'When did you learn to cook like that?'

'Oh, you know, when I wasn't at med school,' Meg replied with a wink.

'Ouch!' Jack grinned as Ronnie laughingly stuck out her tongue.

'Yeah, well, if I had to choose between being able to do a laparotomy and that cobbler I'd definitely choose—'

'The cobbler!' Jack finished for her.

'Exactly,' Ronnie chuckled. 'Gimme more.'

Jonas watched as Meg spooned out another round of extra helpings, even though they'd all had seconds. She looked enquiringly at him but he shook his head lightly.

Forty-eight hours from now, he was going to be at a dinner in a hotel in DC with an elite bunch of scientists, and this night was going to feel more distant to him than he'd ever felt in space. The banter, the fire, the food, her laugh, this tiny cabin . . . this tiny cabin where it had all begun . . . The golden light almost made him feel he could dip the night in gold and preserve it for ever.

Part of him wished now he'd never come. It would have been best to leave things as they were – the silence that she had begun between them just spinning out into eternity, like the very space that had brought them together. Because how was this supposed to work? Her life was here. Her life was this. How could he ask her to give it up – these roots, this home – for the life of a nomad, trailing from country to country to space to country . . . ?

But it was already too late. When Jack had asked him those questions earlier, wanting stream-of-conscious responses, he had had to work to ensure he gave him nothing of the sort.

'What was the best thing about being in space?' Her. *'The view.'*

'What's the best thing about being back on Earth?' Her. *'The weather.'*

Jonas sighed lightly and reached forward for his drink, seeing how Meg's gaze kept fluttering over to him and then away again like a butterfly that couldn't be caught, checking he was OK, that he was having a good time . . . He watched her as she listened to the others, seeing how she blushed whenever he caught her gaze.

He knew that he was screwed.

'Well, if the graphic design's not going to work out, you could always go into catering,' Ronnie was saying.

Jonas tuned back in. 'I think it'll work out.'

'Do you?' Meg asked, looking both surprised and touched by his certainty.

Ronnie leaned in to the table and reached for the bottle of wine – their third. 'Well, not if Lucy has anything to do with it. She has an incredible knack for stuffing things up for my sister.'

'No, she doesn't,' Meg said warningly.

But Ronnie wasn't deterred. Wine had made her fearless. 'Have you met Lucy yet?'

Jonas's eyes slide over to Meg. 'Just the once.'

'And what were your impressions of her? Be honest.'

'Well, as I said, I only met her the once and that was briefly,' he replied tactfully.

'I know. But your *gut* response.'

He sighed. 'Unhappy. Insecure. Angry.'

'Thank you! My assessment exactly,' Ronnie said triumphantly.

'Ron,' Jack murmured, catching sight of Meg's expression.

'Well, if she is all those things, it's because that's how Tuck makes her feel,' Meg replied with defiance.

'Tuck?' Ronnie repeated. 'Lucy's behaviour is Tuck's fault?'

'Yes. He's a terrible husband and an even worse father. She worships the ground he walks on but it was the biggest mistake of her life marrying that man.'

'Because . . . ?' Jonas asked.

Meg looked at him in astonishment, as though his question implied scepticism of her words. 'Because he cheats on her. Yes, he does,' she said quickly as Ronnie's mouth dropped open too. 'There, I've said it. He's always been a player and marriage hasn't slowed him down. Everyone knows it but no one will talk about it. Poor Lucy's always treading on eggshells, freaking out every time he's late home. She's a nervous wreck and it's all his fault.'

'That's odd,' said Jonas. 'It isn't the impression I had of him at all.'

Meg frowned, looking baffled by his comments. 'You've barely met him.'

'Well, I know but . . .' He shrugged. 'We did the workshop and had lunch together the other day.'

Meg looked gobsmacked. 'So because you had *lunch* that

makes you an expert on him, does it? Even though I've known him eleven years?'

'Not at all. Look, I admit I barely know the guy, but sometimes we can be too close to people to see them objectively, that's all.'

Meg's mouth opened further and Jonas could tell he'd said too much – been too frank when everyone had had too much to drink. 'So now you're saying you think I'm blind to my oldest and best friends' characters?'

Jonas paused, hating that they were seemingly now on opposing sides of an argument. He shook his head. 'No, I . . . No.'

'No, you're not saying that?' Meg persisted, refusing to let it drop.

He smiled, trying to defuse the situation and wondering how this had escalated so quickly. Was this assassination of Tuck's character just her being protective of Lucy, or was there more to it? He remembered Tuck's own comments about Meg hating him – although he'd refused to be drawn on why, he was clearly right. Otherwise why would Jonas's own defence of the guy have upset her so much? 'Look, does it really matter what I think?'

'Yes! It matters hugely,' she blustered, her cheeks hot but she couldn't meet his eyes as she fiddled with a napkin instead. 'I want to know why you would take his side over mine.'

'But I don't.'

'Clearly you do,' she argued, her eyes bright, her colour rising.

Jonas looked for a moment, his own arm slung over the table in front of him, hers on the other side. Her hand was trembling, he noticed, and all he wanted to do was reach out and take it in his. But he couldn't. Not in front of the others. They'd all had far too much wine.

'Look, when I was in training at the ESA, we were taught to see what was really there, not what we assumed would be there. It's like that sentence: "The cat sat on the the the mat." Eighty-two per cent of people don't pick up on the second "the" because they expect there to be only one, so the brain rejects what is anomalous and processes the information according to what is expected to be there.'

She frowned. '*Meaning . . . ?*'

'Meaning, that if Tuck or Lucy don't behave in a way that corresponds to your perceptions of them, then you process only what does correspond and reject any evidence to the contrary.'

There was a long silence, Meg looking back at him with a look of having been betrayed that physically pained him. 'But that's just theoretic—'

'No,' she said quietly, looking down at the table and beginning to stack everyone's bowls. 'If this is what the ESA is teaching then it must be right. It's scientific fact. I'm sure Tuck would be over the moon to know what a cheerleader he's got in you.'

Jonas watched as she got up from the table and placed the dirty dishes in the sink, her back rigid, her shoulders too high to her ears.

He slumped back in his seat as across the table, Ronnie – looking sheepish now – mouthed, '*Sorry.*' But the damage had already been done.

They'd just had their first fight.

Chapter Thirty-two

Saturday 18 November 2017

It was a pale dawn, as though the sun was sleepy too. Meg shivered in her favourite chair on the porch, the sheepskins and blankets tucked tightly around her, and Badger – over-sized though he was – curled across her feet. It was a rare treat but on such a cold morning as this . . .

The snow had stopped falling sometime around five and the landscape was more beautiful than ever, the mountains' sharp crests softened into rounded hillocks, the valley floor tucked tight and white like a sheet; streaks of red were painting a sky which had billowed upwards and stayed there; trees had become monuments – decorated frosted pillars with the interplay of snow and leaf like the fretwork of an intricate lace . . . Meg stared into the void, the moon still visible, a fingernail in the sky.

Twenty-four hours and he'd be gone.

A week ago everything had been fine. She'd been fine – finer than she'd been for a long time. He'd been a voice in the dark, a page on a screen, an idea of a person, and now he'd ruined it. Ruined her. Because in that week, it was as though her world had shifted, so that although she had the same life, the same view – *this* view – she had a new perspective. He had reminded her what it was like to have a friend, a lover, someone to talk to, confide in, laugh with . . . even fight with.

She dropped her gaze as she remembered last night again, how awkward she'd made it for him when he was leaving – her smile fake, her body stiff as she waved him off. She'd seen the confusion in his eyes, known he hadn't understood what had just happened, oblivious to the fact that he'd just walked through a minefield. Of course, he couldn't know what Tuck really was or what he'd done. Infidelity to her friend was the very least of it.

But that wasn't Jonas's fault—

A creak made her jump.

Ronnie, wrapped in about ten layers of Jack's clothes, it seemed, crept onto the porch and gave an apologetic smile. Another one. 'Hey.'

'Hey.' Her voice was short and she looked away again.

'Room for a little one?' Ronnie asked, walking to the side of the swing chair and sliding herself next to her sister. She carefully shuffled her feet beneath Badger's slumbering body. 'Oooh, he's warm.'

'Mmmm.'

Ronnie snuck a sideways glance at her. 'Meg . . .'

'I know.'

'But I really am.'

'I know.'

'I never should have started on that topic.'

'I *know*,' Meg said pointedly, shooting her a stern look, before looking back out to sky again.

They sat in silence for a bit.

'Listen, Meg, I just want to say . . .' Ronnie began, sounding uncharacteristically hesitant.

'It's better if you don't.'

'No. I wasn't meaning about last night.'

Meg arched an eyebrow. 'What then?'

'I was going to say, don't put any store by those things Lucy said – about Hap, I mean. I'm not having a go at her,' she said quickly, defensively. 'But she's got no right to make you feel guilty for wanting to be happy again.'

'You've told me that before.'

'I know! Because it's true, especially . . .' She hesitated again.

'Yes?' Meg asked impatiently.

'Especially because, I do feel – and so does Jack – we both think it . . . that Jonas makes you happy— Wait!' she said, seeing how Meg instinctively turned away.

'Ron,' Meg said, stopping her. 'I appreciate you saying this. Really I do. But he's going to be gone from here this time tomorrow – he's flying to DC and then on to New York and then after that, back to the ESA headquarters in Cologne, and then God knows where, before he will finally go back to Norway for Christmas. And *I* . . . I will still be here. OK?' She shook her head. 'I know what you're saying but there's no point in it; there's no way forward from this. Pen pals is as good as we're gonna get.'

Ronnie slumped under the dead weight of her words. 'There's always a way if you want there to be.'

Meg snorted. 'Since when did you get to be such an optimist?'

'Since I fell in love, that's when. You're only living half a life if you're living without love.'

Meg felt suddenly exhausted by her little sister's impassioned conviction. Talk about the zeal of the converted . . . From the moment she'd put her relationship with Mitch before art college, she had had nothing but grief for choosing love over a career, but now that Ronnie had bitten from the apple, love was the answer? 'Look, I've *had* my love, Ron. I've been where you are. I was a week from getting married and then he died. I'm sorry that I can't just *move on* from that.'

'I know how much you loved Mitch. He was a great guy, and you were a brilliant couple. But just do me a favour, OK? Don't idolize the man. Don't turn him in death into something he never was in life.' Meg's mouth parted but Ronnie carried on. 'He wasn't perfect, because no one is. But try to remember that as well as all the good times – and there were loads, I know – you guys also used to argue a lot. He drove you mad when he'd stay in town with Tuck and not tell you till he was too drunk to stand, or when he drank the juice from the carton – and he could be a right grumpy bugger.' She blinked, looking both fierce and frightened at the same time. 'All I'm saying is, just keep the balance, OK? Because if you hold him up as this shining beacon of perfect love, no one else will ever be able to compete. And that would be a real shame because Jonas is brilliant.'

Meg was quiet for a very long time, the words spinning round in her head as she tried to keep the tears from coming. Her gaze was on the distant sky again. It seemed curiously empty now, without him in it. 'Saying goodbye never gets any easier, does it?'

Ronnie watched her. 'No,' she murmured. 'It never does.'

He could see her through the glass. She was chatting to a little girl as she fitted her for ski boots, laughing at something the child said.

Jonas pushed the door open, seeing how she froze as she looked up and saw him coming through, her smile fixed on her face but seeping from her eyes.

'Hi . . .' she began, and he could tell from her tone what she was going to say. *'It's not a good time.'*

'I'll just browse,' he said quickly, turning his back to inspect the rows of skis and boots, gloves, hats, goggles . . . Badger, who must have been snoozing somewhere, trotted over on hearing his voice and gave a low whine for a cuddle, his tail thumping on the floor as Jonas obliged.

The little girl's voice was sing-song to his ear as he picked up a ski mask. It was top-spec, with a built-in camera and infrared capability. He replaced it and wandered over to the helmets, listening all the while to her conversation – hearing the kindness in her voice as she asked if the heel slipped or if the little girl could wiggle her toes, marvelled at *how tall* she was for her age as she measured for poles, gave her a free lollipop for being so patient when they'd tried on thirteen different helmets.

Eventually, to his relief and Meg's discomfort, the girl and her mother left; Jonas turned to face her as he heard the bell jingle above the door. Meg was standing by the till, trying to look occupied, her mouth pulled into a flat line.

He didn't hesitate. There was no time. 'Meg, I'm sorry.'

'You have nothing—'

'Yes, I do. It was tactless of me to suggest that a scientific theory could ever best what you've learned from years of friendship.' He watched her blink, saw the tension in her chest as she took only half-breaths, her gaze flighty as her hands sought to busy themselves, settling finally on fiddling with a paper clip on the counter.

She shook her head. 'I'd had too much to drink. Besides, you were probably right. I'm not Tuck's biggest fan right now.'

Right now? But Jonas didn't push it. Frankly, he didn't care who thought what about Tuck right now. Nineteen hours from now he would be gone – gone from here, gone from her. That was all that was in his head.

'But if he is sleeping around, then he is a shit.' He saw Meg's surprise at his language, a hint of a smile come to her eyes. 'And that would explain why Lucy is angry and in-secure and depressed.' He shrugged. 'So you were right. I was wrong.' He grinned. 'Astronauts know everything about space and nothing at all about the human race. Everyone knows that. Why do you think we're always looking for Martians?'

'That sounds like one of your jokes,' she muttered, but a smile escaped her – it was only a tiny one, but it was still like the sun emerging from behind clouds.

'Have brunch with me,' he said, walking towards her.

But her smile faltered and she looked away, the moment gone again. There was something else.

The jangling bell of the door behind him signalled new customers and his spirits sank. Dammit! He turned to find an older woman coming in. She was wearing a trapper hat, a beaten-up puffa jacket and a beautifully old pair of chestnut-brown hiking boots with decades-old tide marks on the leather. She looked at Jonas with a clear, concise gaze, her brown skin deeply lined and yet firm at the jaw, her short, straight haircut of the DIY variety.

He turned. 'Dolores,' he smiled. He had somehow missed her all week – any time he'd stopped by the store to see or pick up Meg, she'd been out.

'Jonas,' she replied in recognition, walking over to him and assessing him with a frank scrutiny, much like a farmer in the market for a bull. She put a hand to his cheek and nodded. 'So you are flesh and blood after all.'

'I am.' He stood still as she looked at him in the way that only his mother had ever looked at him – seeing him fully, in the round, and accepting everything she saw.

'Sorry – have you two met already?' Meg interrupted.

Dolores dropped her hand and turned to Meg, unzipping her jacket. 'No. But who else could he be? One look and you can see he's a man who stepped off the world because he wanted a better view.'

Meg looked at him, as though trying to see him through Dolores's eyes. But that was impossible. Too much had happened between them already for either to see the other clearly.

'So, what are you kids up to today?' Dolores asked, walking out back and hanging up her coat.

'I was just trying to convince Meg to have brunch with me,' Jonas said, leaning over and calling slightly so that Dolores could hear. He sensed he had an ally in her.

'But as I was just about to explain,' Meg said in a too-patient voice, her eyes on him, 'I've got to work.'

'Nonsense,' Dolores said dismissively, walking back through. 'You go.'

'Dolores, really, it's been insane all morning – I've barely stopped. And the eleven a.m. from Calgary has just pulled up. As soon as all those people have checked in, they're going to be straight over here, wanting—'

'I said, you go. I'll deal with it.'

'Dolores, *no.*'

'Megan, *yes*,' Dolores said firmly.

Meg inhaled deeply, casting an anxious glance between her and Jonas. 'I'm not hungry.' She seemed to be shooting Dolores some sort of meaningful look.

Dolores looked back at Jonas. He shrugged his eyebrows, feeling increasingly awkward. It was patently obvious Meg didn't want to eat with him. She turned back to Meg again. 'Fine. You're fired.'

Meg gasped. '*What?*'

'You heard me. Go.' Dolores crossed her arms over her chest.

'What? No!' she half-laughed, half-cried.

'I'll call the police on you if you don't.'

'Dolores! You can't . . . you can't do that!' Meg cried, watching as Dolores disappeared out the back again and returned a moment later with her bag and coat.

'On the contrary, I should have done it years ago. Your performance has been below par for months now. You've been getting sloppy with the customers recently and you over-ordered on the Oakley account so now I've got to find a way of shifting three hundred pairs of four-hundred-dollar sunglasses.'

'But—'

'No, leave the dog with me. You can collect him on your way back.' Dolores was pushing Meg towards the door. 'Go. Just go.'

'But—'

Meg stumbled out into the street, looking back into the store with an expression of utter shock and disbelief. 'I did *not* over-order the Oakleys,' she cried, throwing her arms out.

'Chicken, you are without doubt the worst assistant manager I've ever had.'

'I'm the *only* assistant manager you've ever had!'

'That's all well and good, but I should have done this years ago. It's only my affection for you that stopped me. Now don't make a fuss – it's vulgar and my mind is made up.' Dolores turned away from her.

'What the *hell* . . . ?' Meg asked, aghast; she looked as though she was about to burst into tears.

Dolores handed the bag and coat over to Jonas, her back to Meg. 'Blueberry crêpes at Melissa's Missteak,' she murmured. 'And she likes her coffee with hot cream,' she whispered – sending him off with a wink.

Chapter Thirty-three

The lights were too bright, that was the problem. That was why he wouldn't sleep. They needed low-wattage bulbs fitted. Or dimmers. Or maybe wall lights instead of these strip things that made her feel as though she was in an interrogation room. No wonder he was crying. She felt like it herself.

Lucy paced, her hands pulling at her hair as the baby continued to scream in his cot in the next room. The book said to let him cry for exactly ten minutes before she went in so she mustn't go in before then. She mustn't or it wouldn't work. He wouldn't learn and all this . . . all this torment for both of them as he screamed till his lungs must surely be bleeding, it would all have been for nothing.

What time was it? How long it had been now? She ran to the kitchen and stared at the clock. Five forty-two. Six minutes.

She remembered the screening was at six. Tuck had said he'd be back for it. He'd said he wouldn't be late. Not today. He'd be here any moment. She could do this. She could last.

The baby's crying was less in here – he was two rooms away now – and she put the kettle on, praying for the roiling sound to drown him out further. She paced at the window, her hands on her hips as she kept her eyes on the arch, waiting for the nose of the truck to appear.

It had been snowing since lunchtime and there was a good thirty centimetres of new fall, judging by the tops of the bins. But that was no excuse.

None of them had any excuse for not coming here, not helping, leaving her here on her own with a screaming baby. She'd heard all about Meg's exciting week with the astronaut from Tuck, and of course from her mother, via Dolores. Nordic skiing and picnics! Films and popcorn! Dinner parties and wine! She was living the high life, quite the girl about town now, relishing her freedom, her independence, her single status . . .

Lucy wiped a tear away angrily as the water in the kettle boiled loudly, decisively drowning out the baby. No, she wouldn't cry. Not over her. Lucy knew she'd been a loyal friend to her; whatever mistakes she'd made in the past, she'd done her best to make up for them in those first, darkest weeks when Meg hadn't even been capable of blowing her own nose. She'd looked after her, fed her, sat with her . . . she'd even gone to find Meg at the cabin and apologize, even though the stomach pains she'd been having all that day had been getting worse; even though it was Meg who'd been in the wrong, sleeping with that guy like it was no big deal. No, Lucy knew she'd done her best to try to clear the air between them and get them back to where they always used to be; and for a few hours, for a couple of days, she'd thought she'd done it. They'd felt close again, bonded by an incredible, life-affirming experience. So for Meg to throw her over because she *disapproved* of Lucy's choice of baby name?

Lucy felt the resentment simmer her blood. It was unfair

and unjust, but her reward was coming. Her life was about to change beyond recognition and she wouldn't be the one left holding the baby on her own any more. If living well was the best revenge, she intended to turn her life around three-sixty. The contracts, several days late from the lawyers due to some fine print that Tuck said had to be clarified, were due any day and then everyone would know about their good fortune. Instead of 'poor Lucy', they would stare at her with admiration and envy; they'd be getting a new house – a better one than this dump – and she'd get a personal trainer, a sexy new wardrobe to incentivize her to lose the baby weight and remind Tuck that he used to love her.

She slapped the tears away again, pulling hard on the skin so that livid red finger marks tracked her cheeks.

The kettle had boiled, the rush and torrent of the rolling water beginning to subside again and the baby's screams grew in pitch once more. Hurriedly, she poured the water out of the kettle and refilled it with cold water from the tap, switching it on and waiting again . . . waiting for the relief. Why was it so hard, listening to him scream? Why did he sleep through the night when Tuck was there to help, but when she was alone with him in the day . . . ? Didn't he love her? Hadn't he bonded with her the way she had with him? Was she destined to always repeat this cycle – loving more than she was loved?

She felt that distinctive tingle in her breasts and looked down, seeing two milky blooms spreading across her T-shirt.

'Dammit,' she spat, feeling the tears come again as she pulled the T-shirt away from herself. But it was too late and Tuck was due back any minute . . . She didn't want him to see her like this. She hadn't washed her hair in a week, her nails were bitten to the quick and she hadn't had a wax since before the birth. Things were bad enough between them as it was. The baby had changed nothing, not really. Tuck had tried for the first few days, offering to hold the baby, but he'd given up after she constantly rejected his offers, feeling like every time he succeeded, she'd failed; and of course he couldn't feed the baby until she introduced bottles, so now he was already back to drinking too much again, coming in late, and he wasn't even trying to have sex with her, which could only mean one thing.

She ran into the bedroom, pulling the T-shirt off over her head and unclasping the sodden bra. She let it fall to the ground and opened the drawer, reaching for a fresh one. She had run out of breast pads but Tuck had bought more yesterday on his way home, as she'd asked, the plastic bag still sitting in the corner of the bedroom where he'd dropped it before having to turn on his heel and help out her mother with some goddam broken-down appliance in the hotel. She went over and pulled out the box, freezing as she saw that he'd also bought a biking magazine, some fresh mints and a pack of condoms.

But it wasn't that which stopped her breath. Slowly she reached in and pulled out the letter discreetly slipped in at the back, her heart beginning to pound at double time as she saw the name written on the front in black ink.

Meg.

It was a change in her eyes that was always the first sign. Then her voice – lower. Slower.

In the next room, the baby was screaming, as he always was when Tuck got back at this time. It was one of the reasons he delayed coming home . . . He'd tried suggesting she should give the bottles a go, that perhaps the baby wasn't getting enough milk and was hungry, but she always took this as an insult, a slur on her maternal capabilities, so he'd stopped. He'd stopped pretty much everything. She got angry if he stayed in, for 'getting under her feet'; angry if he stayed out; angry if he got the baby to sleep when she hadn't; angry if he tried to reach out to her in bed and then even angrier when he didn't.

'Hey,' he said warily, putting his keys down on the counter and watching the way she stood, so still, by the door to the bedroom, something in her hand. Could she tell he'd been drinking? He'd got wise recently, switching from beer to vodka; it meant his breath didn't give him away. 'Want me to go in to him?'

She ignored his question. 'What the fuck is this?'

His eyes flickered down to what he could see now was a letter, the letter he'd picked up only yesterday and had intended to hide. But Barbara had called almost as soon as he stepped in the door – she must have been looking from the window again, her timing was so spot on – and he'd had to cross the courtyard almost immediately to help with a dripping tap.

He fell still himself. 'I was going to talk to you about it.'

'Yeah? When? *After* you got her to sign it?' she asked, her voice dripping with sarcasm.

'Look, Luce, I've been thinking—'

Lucy laughed, a hard, bitter sound that clanged like a dropped bell. 'The hell you have. You don't *think*. You just do, Tuck. You're led by your stomach and your dick.' She sneered. 'And the goddam bottle. Where have you just come from, huh? Bill's? Or were you drinking on your own in the office again?'

He stared at her, debating whether to just pick up the keys and get the hell out of here. She was spoiling for a fight and he would lose. He had to. It was the only way to make it stop.

He took a deep breath. 'Look, you've had a bad day. You're exhausted. Why don't I just get the baby to stop crying—'

'Mitch! His name is Mitch! He is not the Baby! Or Titch!' Lucy screamed. 'Why do you *never* call him by his name?'

'OK, OK,' Tuck said calmly, trying not to blanch at the word. 'I'll settle Mitch and then we can talk about this calmly . . . Shall I run you a bath?'

Lucy looked at him like he was insane. 'You're giving away all our money and you think I want a freaking bath?' she hollered, so loudly that for a moment she even drowned out the baby.

He blinked, a sudden wave of nausea surging from his stomach, her yelling making his head throb, the lights in this godforsaken bungalow too bright. 'Not all of it. Just my share.'

'*Your* share? You mean half of your share? Because you realize that's what I'm entitled to, right? Fifty per cent of yours is mine and I'*m* not giving any money away.'

'OK,' he agreed quickly. 'But even at that, a quarter share is still a very significant amount of money. More than we need.'

'Why?' she yelled, her face puce and distorted with rage.

Tuck knew his calm only inflamed her anger but he had no other option. They couldn't both lose control. He tried to steady his breathing, to not be drawn into matching her heat. 'Let's just sit dow—'

'I don't want to sit! I want to know why! Why are you doing this to us?'

His shoulders sagged. 'Because I have to. It's the only way I can make amends.'

'By giving her – what, seventy-five per cent of the value of the company? It's bad enough that she's getting Mitch's share!'

'She's his *widow*,' Tuck said, disgusted by his wife's ugly greed.

'They weren't married!'

Tuck blinked, finding it hard to believe Lucy was actually arguing this again. 'Apart from the fact that they were a *week* away from being married –' he couldn't quite keep the bitter sarcasm from his voice – 'they had lived together as man and wife for over three years. In common law that means she's got the same rights.' He held out his hands, softening his tone. 'Lucy, come on – surely you can see it's the right thing to do?'

'No, it's not! Your responsibility is to *us*, your family,' she cried, slapping herself so hard on the chest it left angry marks on the skin. He looked at them, wondering if they would bruise.

He looked back at her. 'Mitch was my family. I'm not going to betray his memory on top of everything else I've done.'

Lucy straightened up. 'Everything else?' she sneered and a silence expanded between them.

'It's my fault he's dead.' He heard the strain in his own voice. Couldn't she see he was near breaking point?

Evidently not. 'Do you know what? I've had enough of this self-pitying fucking depression,' she sneered. 'It's been months! When are you going to get over yourself, Tuck? You didn't *do* anything wrong.'

'I should never have called him.'

Lucy planted her hands on her hips. 'It was his decision to go out looking for them. *His.*'

'I know! But I am not blameless – I told him, knowing he'd go out looking for them, because I knew it was what I would do. Meg hates me, Lucy! She can't even look at me. As far as she's concerned, I'm as responsible for killing him as if I'd buried him myself!'

'So? Why do you care what she thinks?'

'Because I know she's right. I can't live with myself.' His voice cracked, tears springing to his eyes as suddenly as if they'd been poked. He turned away.

'So this is your answer, is it? You're going to try to *buy* her forgiveness?'

'No! It's because I don't want to do it any more! OK?' Tuck yelled, losing control as suddenly as if a wire in him had been snapped, everything suddenly becoming jerky and loose. Spasmodic. 'I'm done! I want out. I don't want to spend every fucking day being confronted with me and Mitch on a film together, his face on a poster. There's not a single thing about that company that doesn't remind me of him and the way we used to be. And I miss him, Lucy! I miss him so bad, some days I don't even want to get out of bed, I don't want to speak—'

He ran out of breath, staring back at her, pleading with her to understand. Didn't she get that it was why he couldn't even go to the screening tonight? Why he'd choose oblivion in a bottle over dancing with ghosts? But as he saw the contempt spread on her face, construing his fraternal love as weakness, he knew he'd been right never to admit to all those evenings and overnights spent on the mattress in the studio, drinking himself into a stupor as he watched film after film of them both – young, free, alive. It was actually easier to let her pretend he'd been with other women, though in fact he'd cheated only twice since Mitch had died.

Could he say 'only', like that was a good thing? An achievement? But then compared to how he'd been before, it was. He'd never wanted to hurt her, he'd just settled down too young. He knew that now and he'd known it then – he'd tried telling her too, but she'd refused to let him go and then Mitch had died, then she'd told him about the baby . . . And now they were trapped, inexorably linked to one another even as they were spiralling towards certain doom, like a fighter plane that had been shot out of the sky and was blazing in the blue before plunging to a fiery death.

He sagged, slumping against the wall as though he'd been physically depleted, the room spinning. 'Lucy, we can't—'

His very tone was enough. She knew what he was going to say next. But as the paperweight came hurtling through the air, he also knew she wouldn't let him say it.

Chapter Thirty-four

The screening room was packed, heads bobbing all the way down the rows, the ambient noise level of chatter ridiculously loud.

Jonas came back with the popcorn, the two seats beside Meg still empty.

'Have you tried calling them?' he asked, handing Meg her portion and sitting down on her far side.

'No. There's no reception in here.' She looked down the row again and Jonas could see she was conflicted about whether or not she actually wanted Lucy and Tuck to show. The longer the silence grew between the two girls, the louder it became.

'Are you OK?' he asked, watching as she fidgeted. Her mood had been changeable all day. In some moments, he glimpsed what had burned between them last night – saw the longing in her eyes, sensed her instinct to reach out and take his hand – but in the next, the shutters would come down and he knew it was because he was leaving; they were running out of time before they'd had a chance to begin, the hours slipping away from them with no clear resolution in sight. Because it wasn't enough to want each other. They belonged to different worlds and this time tomorrow, he would be gone from here – in another country, another city, another time zone.

And now, as if that wasn't enough, they were both about to come face to face with Mitch, this almost-mythical man who still dominated all their lives, even his. Ten minutes from now, he was going to be moving in front of them on that giant screen – all but alive – and Jonas wasn't convinced she would get through it.

Jonas stared at her profile in the dim light, seeing how her mouth was pulled down at the edges. It was six o'clock already and after this final round of films – the Short Film, Mountain category – there would be a brief hiatus, the awards, bed and then he'd be gone . . .

'There they are!'

They both looked up, startled, to see two older women making their way across to them, all the other visitors having to angle their knees awkwardly to let them pass.

Jonas recognized Dolores, of course, but he didn't know the glamorous ash-blonde woman behind her in a pale turquoise twinset, ropes of pearls swinging at her chest. They made an incongruous couple, with Dolores in her almost brutally mannish clothes.

'How are you, chick, had a fun day?' Dolores asked, winking at Jonas as she sank into the chair beside Meg and kissed her on the temple.

'You know, you could have just told me to have the day off rather than pretending to fire me,' Meg said, still cross.

'Oh, I wasn't pretending.'

'*What?*'

'No, my love. If you will not fly the nest, then I shall have to push you.'

'But . . . but you can't do that, Dolores!'

'I already did.'

Meg stared at her, all her anger dissipating and a forlorn look creeping onto her face. 'But what am I going to do?'

'Precisely,' Dolores smiled, patting her hand. 'Now you'll have the time, and impetus, to figure it out. No more hiding behind my skirts.'

Meg pouted. 'You've never worn a skirt.'

'Thank *God*!' Dolores said with a laugh.

'You must be Jonas,' the blonde woman said, reaching over the others to shake his hand. 'I'm Barbara, Lucy's mother.'

'Oh, Barbara, yes, I've heard a lot about you. It's a pleasure to meet you at last.'

Barbara smiled, seeming delighted that she had been the topic of conversation, jogging Dolores with her elbow as she took her seat. 'Have you enjoyed your stay with us?'

'Very much.' Too much.

Barbara tutted. 'Everybody says that. All my guests.' She held her hands up. 'It's a very special place to live.'

'Absolutely.'

'And are you going up into space again soon?' she asked, as though it was like catching a bus.

'There are no immediate plans to return, no.'

'It must get terribly lonely up there,' she suggested, eyes narrowed and shaking her head slightly.

'Well, I guess I got lucky with my pen pal here,' he replied lightly, as though that was all Meg was.

'Isn't she a peach? We love our Meg.'

Jonas glanced across at her. 'Yes.'

Meg wouldn't look at him. 'Where's Tuck and Lucy?' she asked.

'Not coming,' Dolores replied. 'Lucy's with the baby and

436

Tuck's . . . well, we don't know where he is, do we?' she asked Barbara.

Barbara shook her head. 'Although I think we can all make an educated guess,' she said, lips pursed together disapprovingly.

Meg bit her lip. 'He did say he might not come.'

'Well, it's very brave of you to be here,' Dolores said quietly, patting her hand again.

'Thank heavens *you've* known better than to find solace in the bottom of a bottle,' Barbara said admiringly.

'Are you OK?' Dolores asked, concern shining in her eyes.

Meg nodded but didn't reply. Jonas didn't think she looked OK. She was pale and her body language had become more and more closed.

The lights flickered on the screen suddenly, the festival logo flashing up, and everyone fell into an expectant hush as the film official made a short speech about the Best Short Mountain Film category and the high calibre of entries this year.

One after the other, they rolled. Stories about people free-climbing rock towers in the American national parks, a paraglider soaring off mountaintops and skipping with the chute in the air, guys in wingsuits scooting past cliff faces with death-defying audacity, another daredevil mountain-biking up a mountain – from beach to sky-touching ridge – with skills that would scarcely be possible on two legs, much less two wheels.

Some of the films were only a few minutes long, others almost twenty minutes in length but for every one, Jonas felt transfixed, awed. They showed he wasn't the only one doing remarkable things; every single one of these film-makers was making sure they lived before they died.

He glanced over at Meg as the screen went black and the next film was readied to play. She was as still as if she'd been cast from marble and he wondered, if he were to touch her hand, whether she would feel as cold.

Snow Dog ran across the screen in bold titles.

'Oh, God,' he heard her murmur as Tuck's name came up next, and Jonas held his own breath as he prepared to come face to face with what – or rather, who – she had lost.

The opening scene was a dawn shot of the sun slowly peeping from behind a jagged ridge. There was no doubt, from the steep terrain, that this was remote back-country and snow blanketed the ground in deadly deep drifts, not a footstep or blown twig marring its pristine white perfection. The camera cut to a tiny hut, two red enamel cups on a chunky wooden counter, steam rising from the open neck of a thermos flask. And then a large black dog – Badger – was seen from behind, jumping excitedly into the snow, which was as soft as foam as it sank up to his belly; he had to move in a front-back rocking motion to get through the powder, his tail leaving snake-trails on the surface behind him. And then he turned, his muzzle white from a quick exploratory burrow in the snow, those ginger eyebrows so distinctive . . .

Jonas tensed as a snowboarder – his face obscured by reflective goggles and an oversized orange jacket which had the hood up and was zipped to his nose – was shown beginning to climb a treacherous peak. His snowboard was strapped to the backpack he was wearing, Badger leaping around him in excited circles, the boarder's hand reaching out every so often to pat the dog affectionately on the head. Who was it, Jonas wondered impatiently: Mitch or Tuck?

As if in answer Meg, beside him, sank lower in the chair, her hand over her mouth.

Jonas felt his own anxiety build as the film cut to the boarder throwing the board down, strapping in his feet and without even a pause, tipping himself over a sheer vertical drop, snow flying in huge arcs as he cut left, then right, his hand trailing in the snow alongside as the mountain reared up to him, standing as upright as any man. And all the while, Badger rocking and leaping, never far behind, a dark shadow on the all-white surface as the streak of orange charged ahead without hesitation. Sometimes the camera was uphill of the two of them, sometimes down, and both Mitch and Badger got equal airplay – but Tuck was never seen.

Jonas watched, conflicted, as he saw just how brilliant Mitch had been, able to glimpse the marrow of the man through his sport – bold, fearless, arrogant, reckless, coura-geous ... He'd been tall and powerful, just as much an athlete as the businessman Tuck had told him about.

Jonas strained to glimpse his face, to see the eyes which had once reflected Meg's love. But he was hidden behind photochromatic lenses that tinted like a rainbow, remaining an enigma, as out of reach to him as to Meg.

Time-lapse technique showed the sun tracking the sky, a sky Jonas was personally acquainted with, cutting from the exhilaration of the downhill sweep to the pain of the uphill climb.

The music that played in the background was evocative and free, stirring feelings in Jonas that he was already strug-gling to contain. He didn't just want to live a life with these pitches – the grit of endeavour, the bliss of achievement – for he had already been there and done that: all those years of training for six months in space. Yes, it had been everything he'd been drilled and educated to expect, but he needed more now. He needed to share these experiences. This life.

And for a moment, he had thought, sensed, Meg was the one—

Suddenly, the sky was amber, the snow growing grey, and the camera cut to Mitch, pulling off the goggles at last. The day was done and so was he. He was laughing, his dark hair floppy and wild, his skin windburned with ridiculous goggle marks round the eyes. The sun glinted onto his handsome face, as though the sunbeams were seeking out him alone and he closed his eyes, face tilted up, arms outstretched as he fell back in the snow. A plume exploded upwards, Badger scurrying onto his stomach, head down and body curled, trying to bury into him for cuddles, his tail wagging every bit as hard as it had when they'd set out. The final shot lingered on them both inert in the snow, bodies spent but spirits soaring. A man and his dog and a mountain. A lesson in how to live, how to love.

The image faded to white, as though the snow was claiming them.

In memory of Mitchell Sullivan, 1989–2017.

The words, in bold, brutal black, drew a collective gasp of horror and disbelief from the crowd, as though they were asking, '*How could someone that alive, be dead?*'

But that wasn't what had made Jonas startle. He stared at the screen for several long moments, trying to process it, look for other possibilities . . . But there were none that made sense, only a terrible truth.

He turned his head and saw what he expected to see –

Meg as low in the chair as she could get, tears skimming down her cheeks as she struggled for breath.

His hand reached for hers and he pressed it hard to his lips. He would never tell her. Because he clearly saw now what she'd lost. Because he clearly saw now she was lost to him. Because he knew he couldn't beat a ghost.

'She needs some air,' Dolores was saying, her voice sounding far away, as though she was speaking through a wall or from underwater.

'Move, please. I said move . . .' Barbara was saying imperiously, jostling people out of their way as arms around Meg held her up, guided her through the crowds. Faces were a blur, conversation indistinct . . .

The cold air outside was like a slap, shocking her, bringing her back to herself. It was snowing heavily again, the evening air a dancing whirling white, and Barbara was wrapping Meg's coat around her shoulders, popping closed the fasteners even though her arms were hugging her torso, the empty sleeves hanging limp by her sides.

'How are you feeling?' Jonas asked her and she blinked at him, feeling sorrier than ever as she saw the sadness – recognition – in his eyes. The film had been more than a homage, more than a tribute; it had been a love letter, a celebration of everything that had defined Mitch, a man who had lost his life helping others. Ronnie had been wrong. He had been perfect.

'I need to see Tuck.'

'Are you sure that's wise?' Barbara asked, pulling the hood of Meg's coat over her head now and beginning to rub Meg's shoulders warm, as though she was a toddler in the playground. 'Your feelings are very raw. Perhaps—'

'I want to thank him.'

'Oh.' Barbara looked surprised. 'Well, that's different.' She looked at Dolores. 'Do you want to drive? I shouldn't have had that sherry in the foyer.'

'I did warn you,' Dolores muttered, holding out her hands for the keys.

Meg was helped into the car, the street lights refracted into a million stars by the snowflakes spreading and melting on the glass. Jonas, beside her, was silent but she couldn't offer any words of consolation. They both knew their strange, tentative fledgling relationship had reached its end.

But it wasn't Jonas she could think about right now, or even Mitch. It was Tuck. And it wasn't just 'Thank you' she wanted to say to him, but 'Sorry'.

Chapter Thirty-five

'We don't have long, remember,' Barbara said, striding ahead through the hotel's crowded lobby. The Homestead was the unofficial HQ of the festival, with many of the luminaries of the adventure-film world staying there for the duration, and those who weren't already at the hall for the screenings were milling here over drinks instead, and preparing to leave for the awards show shortly.

Meg drifted after her, with Jonas and Dolores flanking her as though she needed protection, watching detachedly as Barbara nodded greetings to those guests she knew by name or had booked in personally. Meg would have preferred if they'd parked out the back – she couldn't wait another minute to make this long-overdue apology; she felt sick as she remembered the things she'd said, how harsh and unforgiving she'd been – but Barbara had forgotten her glasses and wanted them for the awards show, so it had just been altogether easier to park on the street and walk through.

'How are you feeling now?' Dolores asked, peering round as they walked to get a better look at her face.

'Fine.'

'Mmhmm,' Dolores nodded, before casting a sceptical look at Jonas and mouthing, *'Pale.'*

'Just wait here. I'm certain I had them last in the office,' Barbara said, scooting around the reception desk and disappearing into the back room.

'Do you want to sit down?' Dolores enquired.

'I said I'm fine.'

'You don't look fine, chicken.'

Barbara came back out only a moment later, the glasses swinging on a chain at her bosom. 'Right! At last!' she huffed, rolling her eyes. 'I *knew* I'd had them doing the linen invoices earlier but that daft girl Linda put a whole heap of papers on top of them. Honestly, I don't know why I haven't fired her already. She's more trouble than she's worth. Come along then. Let's go and congratulate my son-in-law for once. It's not often he's in the good books.'

'Oh, Mrs Wakefield!' a woman called after Barbara, who was already heading towards the fire exit that led onto the courtyard.

Barbara turned with a low groan. 'Oh, God, what now?' she said under her breath as a woman in her early fifties, wearing a berry-coloured roll-neck jumper and jeans, rushed over.

'Mrs Wakefield,' the woman panted, reaching her. 'I'm so glad to have caught you. We thought we might miss you. I'm Beth. Beth Stedman? We stayed with you last March. My husband Paul and son Cory—?'

'Of course!' Barbara said quickly, cutting her off, but Meg's head had whipped round at the mention of those names. She would never forget them. How could she? 'How could I forget?' Barbara replied with a cool smile, straightening up to her full height. 'Are you staying with us again? I don't recall seeing your names—'

'Sadly not, we couldn't get a room. You're so busy!' Beth

laughed, placing a hand over her chest. 'And this trip was all rather last-minute. Cory's been having a little trouble moving on from that terrible fright we had when we stayed here last and we thought that coming to the festival and celebrating all the many positives of the mountains might help give him some closure.'

Terrible fright? Meg felt frozen to the spot.

'And have you enjoyed it?' Barbara asked impatiently.

'Oh, yes, very much. Isn't it incredible to see what some people can do?'

'Isn't it,' Barbara agreed. 'Well, it's lovely seeing you but if you'll excuse me, I'm afraid I have to—'

'Oh! But I just wanted to reiterate our great thanks to you once again. There hasn't been a day gone by when we haven't given thanks for such a lucky escape. What you did for us that day—'

'It was nothing,' Barbara said briskly, her eyes flitting onto Meg and away again.

'Oh, but it wasn't. You opened the kitchens specially to have a hot meal ready for us, you'd run the baths in readiness, your lovely daughter even arranged to have the beds warmed, I remember . . . Of course, a hot-water bottle can't counteract the effects of exposure, but it was the thought that counted and we were so grateful. They saved Cory's fingers, you know. Did you hear? It was touch and go for a while; it went terribly black and—'

Someone's hand settled on her shoulder – Dolores's – but Meg barely felt it. She was back there, in the horror, his face freshly imprinted in her mind again: Mitch setting out to his death, searching in a blizzard for people who were already back here enjoying a hot meal and a bath . . .

'Excuse me, won't you? I'm afraid I'm late for an appointment,' Barbara said, her smile gone now as she took Meg by the arm and steered her towards the fire door, leaving the woman looking after her, mouth agape.

They crossed the courtyard in hurried silence, Barbara muttering under her breath about '*that damned family*'. The lights were on inside the bungalow and Lucy was visible through the window.

Barbara stopped walking abruptly at the sight of her. Lucy was crying, her face red and swollen, angry weals across the front of her chest. She was walking backwards away from Tuck, shaking her head as he approached, his hands angrily splayed like cacti, hard and spiky, his head hidden by the low blind.

Barbara gave a horrified gasp and ran the small distance, bursting in without knocking. 'Don't you touch her!' she screamed, just as Meg, Dolores and Jonas got to the doorway too.

Tuck, surprised, turned around and Meg's hands flew to her mouth as she saw the blood pouring from a deep gash on the bridge of his nose.

'Mom,' Lucy faltered, her gaze scanning their small assembled group. She looked terrified, exhausted, ragged. Barbara pushed through to her, almost tripping on something on the floor and she turned to see what it was – a small bronze paperweight.

Barbara looked, white-faced, from her daughter to Tuck. 'Oh, my God, what have you done?'

'He was coming at me!' Lucy cried. 'It was the first thing I could find!' Her face crumpled and she hid it in her hands, rolling sobs making her shoulders heave. 'I panicked. I was so frightened.'

Barbara was rooted to the spot with horror.

Meg – remembering in a rush all those strange scratches and bruises – covered her mouth with her hands, feeling ashamed. 'Oh, Lucy,' she cried. 'I'm *so* sorry. I never knew. I should have known.' She glared at Tuck, hardly able to believe she'd been taken in by the film. It had been an exercise in indulgence, a panegyric to his drunken, wallowing self-pity.

Tuck, swaying slightly – though whether that was from the booze or the blow, she wasn't sure – stared back at her, blood cascading down his face and neck, soaking his T-shirt. He seemed dazed and from the corner of her eye, she saw Jonas move to the sink and soak a towel in cold water. Without saying a word, he pulled out a chair, pushed Tuck firmly into it and started to clean his face.

'Where's the ice?' Jonas asked, looking between Meg and Dolores.

'Here,' Dolores said, snapping into action and walking across to the fridge, filling a glass with ice from the dispenser. She took a few cubes, wrapped them in a tea towel and handed the parcel to Jonas who persuaded Tuck to tip his head back. They watched as the ice pack quickly staunched the blood flow and the tension in the room slackened a degree as Tuck looked less like an extra in a horror film.

'Where's the baby?' Meg asked Lucy in a quiet voice.

Lucy stared at her for a moment and Meg knew that was the moment she should have called him by his name – that name – but even now she couldn't. 'In his cot, sleeping. Finally.'

'Have you called the police?'

Lucy's eyes widened, fear flooding them again. 'Wha—? No! No!'

'There's nothing to be afraid of,' Meg said, walking over to her as Barbara continued her wide-eyed stare, her mouth parted in a silent, continual gasp. 'He can't hurt you any more . . . But we need to call the police.'

'No!' Lucy repeated, staring at Tuck as though willing him – even now – to charm his way out of this, find a way to explain that this wasn't what it looked like.

Meg looked on sadly, seeing how even now her friend was trying to hide the truth, to protect the man she loved.

Tuck was still sitting on the chair, his legs splayed straight in front as though they'd been broken, Jonas lightly pressing the ice pack to his nose. Tuck was staring at a distant spot on the wall. He looked dazed, defeated. Drunk. Meg wasn't even sure he could hear them.

She felt a curl of disgust. Had she ever really known him, called him her friend? How could *he* ever have laid a claim to Mitch's friendship? He was a forlorn excuse for a man – pathetic, weak, a bully and a coward, beating up a woman half his size, the mother of his newborn child. It wasn't enough that he had to humiliate her, playing around with other women – he had to beat her too?

In a flash, everything was explained, Ronnie proved right yet again – was it any wonder Lucy had been so clingy with her? Never wanting her to leave, always trying to meet up, desperately trying to please Tuck and stay on his good side, keep herself attractive. Even using Mitch's name – had she been trying to give her baby a name to grow into, the name of a role model who was a hundredfold the man his own father would ever be?

'Th-this is a private matter,' Lucy said to her, to the room, her eyes wide and imploring them all. 'There's no need for anyone else to become involved in this.'

'But don't you see? For as long as you stay quiet, you protect him. You *enable* him to carry on doing this to you,' Meg cried. 'You have to speak out. This has to stop.'

'Meg's right, it does have to stop,' Barbara murmured and Meg glanced over, grateful for the backup.

But it wasn't Lucy Barbara was talking to.

Meg jolted as she watched Barbara walk across to Tuck and crouch beside him, her eyes sad upon his as he slowly swivelled his head to look at her. 'It's gone on long enough, wouldn't you say?' Barbara said quietly, resting her hand on Tuck's forearm.

'Barbara?' Meg croaked, seeing Dolores's stunned expression in her peripheral vision.

But Barbara wouldn't take her eyes off her son-in-law. 'This is my fault. I should have realized what was going on. But I got things the wrong way round. I had my suspicions but I thought that if history was going to repeat itself, she would marry a man just like her father . . . I thought she'd be like me. Not *him.*'

There was a long moment of silence, Dolores's mouth dropping open in astonishment as she digested what her friend was saying. 'You're saying *Lucy's* the one using her fists?'

Barbara squeezed Tuck's forearm apologetically.

'Mom! He's ninety kilos, for Chrissakes!' Lucy cried.

But Tuck had shifted, stirred, hunching forward on the chair, his elbows on his knees, his head dropped as though trying to hide his face away. And Meg knew what she was seeing. Shame. Tuck was a jock, a man's man, an athlete. He would rather have been called a wife beater than wife beaten. His pride wouldn't have allowed Barbara's assertion to stand – not unless it was true.

'No!' Meg cried, unable to believe it. She recalled how he often had minor injuries – burn marks on the backs of his hands, scratches, bruises; he'd broken his hand that time they'd come back from a camping trip in Jasper – but they were easily explained, surely? He was a physical man, always on a board or a bike. 'It's simply not possible. There's no way *she* could hurt *him*.'

'It's more common than people realize,' Barbara said in a flat tone. 'Before Roger did the honourable thing and quit town, I saw a counsellor and she told me domestic abuse can take many forms. You don't have to be big to be a bully; you don't even need to hit – emotional control can be enough. Very often, the bigger the man, the more afraid he is of protecting himself for fear of hurting her.'

There was another silence, everyone trying to understand how the truth couldn't be the most plausible, the most obvious explanation. Meg felt the room spin, her chest compress. She felt sick, looking over at the person she'd once thought was as close as a sister. But she was a monster. A stranger.

'He's lying,' Lucy gasped, seeing Meg's disgust. 'You've all seen the bruises on me yourselves. You were always asking about them. Meg, you remember!'

'Yes. I do.' Meg felt drugged, confused, trying to make sense of this interpretation – which one fit the history she remembered?

'Then most likely they're defensive injuries,' Barbara said quietly. 'When someone flies at you in a rage, you're going to protect yourself, even if you don't want to fight.'

'This is bullshit!' Lucy roared suddenly, grabbing the

nearest thing to hand – a beer bottle – and throwing it with all her force across the room. It shattered against the wall just a metre away from Dolores's head and a sudden silence rained down on them all, for in that moment, they all saw it, the full force of her rage.

Barbara's hands flew to her mouth as tears flooded her eyes. The truth confirmed, once and for all.

Meg felt as though she couldn't breathe. Lucy – breathless – had locked stares with her and was watching as certainty dawned in Meg's mind, seeming to grow in size as Meg felt herself shrink. 'Oh, my God, Lucy, what have you done?' she whispered.

'Me?' Lucy repeated and Meg could see from the curl in her lip, the deadness in her eyes, that a line had been crossed, a tether snapped. 'What have I done? . . . What about you? What have *you* done? Where have *you* been? When I've needed a friend . . . when *he's* come home late after his whoring – and that's when he comes home at all – where were you?'

Meg blinked, dismayed. What did this have to do with her?

'You're not my friend,' Lucy sneered, her mouth curling up. 'You've never been my friend.'

'That's not tr—'

'Not like Mitch.'

'What?'

'*He* was my friend. *He* noticed me. He bothered to see what was going on, to ask if everything was OK. But not you. Oh, no, not you . . . with your wedding-dress fittings and your cute little cabin-building and your being *so busy* in the store with Dolores . . . you never noticed that my *entire life was fucked*!' she screamed. 'You couldn't see past the end of your pretty little nose!'

'Lucy—' she breathed, feeling sick, feeling frightened.

'Because it's always got to be about you, hasn't it? No one's ever huddling around me checking *I'm* OK, or checking whether *I'm* happy! No one's ever saying I should be doing more with *my* life instead of living in this dump, working for my own goddam mother. No one even sees me. I'm invisible to all of you. And one wrong move and you all just turn your back on me so easily, like I don't matter. I'm only ever one step away from being abandoned altogether.'

Meg shook her head. 'That's not true—'

'No? So what've the last ten days been about then?'

'You know what.'

There was a pause, Lucy trembling all over with barely suppressed rage. 'You've got some nerve, do you know that? Acting like you have complete jurisdiction over him – his name, all our memories. You've spent the past eight months drifting about like what you had was so perfect – and now you're standing here, looking at me and him and you're *pitying* us. You think we're pathetic but you two were no better. All these months you've been mourning your perfect little relationship when you've got no idea how deluded you are!'

'I don't know what—'

'—I'm talking about?' Lucy finished for her. 'Don't you? Well, what about how quickly you got over him with that guy in Toronto!'

Meg recoiled as though she'd been hit, noticing how Jonas's head whipped round to see if it was true, and Meg knew that Lucy had dropped that little bombshell just for him.

'Lucy! That's enough!' Dolores said sharply.

But Lucy didn't stop. She wouldn't now. 'That's not love. You couldn't have done that if you'd truly loved him. *I* wouldn't have done that to him.'

Meg turned to go, feeling hot tears rushing to her eyes. 'I'm not going to stand here and listen to—'

'Fuck!' Tuck's voice was like a gunshot in the room, stilling even Lucy. He had risen to his feet, his eyes suddenly focused, Jonas left standing beside him with the bloodied ice pack in his hands. 'You were in love with him!'

'No.' The word dropped from her lips like a cigarette butt. Careless. Inconsequential.

'Yes. That's why you called our baby his name! It had nothing to do with honouring him at all.'

Lucy sighed, looking suddenly bored. 'You don't get it, do you? You were the only one I ever loved. The only one I ever wanted. But you ruined it. You killed us because you couldn't keep it in your pants!'

Tuck stared down at her. 'And who could blame me? You're a crazy bitch! You beat me when I'm sleeping and then want to fuck? Who can live like that? Why wouldn't I drink? Why wouldn't I look elsewhere?' His mouth twisted. 'But here's a news flash – I don't love you, Lucy. I hate you. I've been trying to leave you for months, but you *won't let me go!*'

Meg felt the hatred spin round the room with their words – *'crazy bitch'* . . . *'hate'* . . . Lucy was trembling, her eyes bulging, adrenalin making her shake as she slipped into survival mode – fight or flight, and Lucy was a fighter.

'Hate me? You don't hate me!' she jeered. 'You're obsessed with me. I'm the best thing that ever happened to you. You'd be nothing without me.'

He shook his head sadly. 'Maybe once. You want to know why I hate you now? Because you're the one who fucked up the night Mitch died. It was only half the truth when I told you I blame myself for Mitch's death; the fact is, I blame you and I'll never forgive you for it. I can hardly bear to even look at you.'

'*You* blame *me?*' she laughed, the response chilling in its inappropriateness.

'You let me call him when they were already back!'

'But I didn't know that.'

'How could you *not* know? They were staying in your fucking hotel!'

'Yes, and as *soon* as I knew they were back, I told you. But it was too late. You'd already done it, made the call. Because you just couldn't wait for the actual professionals to do their jobs. Oh no! You had to be the have-a-go hero, and if not you, then Mitch.' She shook her head. 'This is all on you, baby. This is about *your* guilt, *your* feelings. You screwed up sending Mitch out there, you sent him to his death, and now you're nothing without him. Nothing but a drunk.'

Meg looked over at Tuck, hearing the echoes of her own accusations thrown at him that evening in the bar, seeing how his face accepted the truth in both their words. He looked like his own ghost – cowed, spectral, beaten by her words as much as her fists, just as Barbara had said. How long had the two of them been living like this?

Lucy watched him, unsteady on his feet, like a boxer after a blow to the head. 'Christ, you really are an incredibly stupid man,' she sneered. 'Why did I think the sex would ever be enough? Marrying you was the worst fucking mistake of my life.'

She had won. Tuck slumped, staggering towards the counter to lean on it, the wound on his nose beginning to bleed again as his blood pressure soared.

'Actually, no.'

Everyone looked surprised as Jonas stepped further into the room – into the ring – his eyes on Lucy, his voice so cool it was like liquid nitrogen, immediately freezing the air temperature.

'What?' Lucy sneered, hatred in her eyes for this stranger, this interloper, this unwanted man who had dared to break and enter into their closed world without her invitation. 'What did you say?'

'It wasn't marrying Tuck that was the worst mistake of your life.'

'What would you know about me? Or my life?' She looked quickly at Meg. 'What has she told you?'

'Meg hasn't said anything.' He glanced across at her, apology in his eyes, and Meg felt the fibres in her muscles stiffen. She had never seen Jonas like this before. Up till now, his calmness, his intellect, had been passive, tolerant and wise, but here in this moment, it felt menacing, like having a shark swim beneath them. 'In fact, I'm pretty sure she doesn't know. But your greatest mistake is in front of all of us, there for anyone to see. I saw it for myself just now.'

Meg watched as Lucy's high colour drained away, and she suddenly appeared to be on the back foot.

'Saw what, Jonas?' Dolores asked.

Jonas didn't take his gaze off Lucy. 'The resemblance.'

'What?' Barbara whispered. 'What resemblance? Who . . . ?'

The baby began to cry again, disturbed no doubt by their raised voices, the tension in the bungalow making the air crackle and split. Jonas turned his head in the direction of the baby's cries before looking back at them all, his eyes coming to rest sadly on Meg.

Her lips parted as she realized, her hands flying to her mouth. 'No—'

In that moment when the film had stopped on the frame of Mitch's face, his goggles off at last, he had seen the likeness so clearly he'd been astounded no one else had. He'd seen the baby in the square only for a few minutes that first night, but even then it had struck him – a brown-eyed baby born to two blue-eyed parents. Of course it was possible. They might both be carriers of the recessive blue allele, and eye colour could change over time. But the baby's name, Lucy's dominance, her jealousy of Meg, Tuck's faltering swagger . . . ? Even without the baby, he'd drawn a worrying conclusion about the friendship dynamic. There was a certain logic to what was going on.

Barbara folded over, dissolving into tears, and Dolores rushed across to put an arm round her. Jonas wasn't sure Meg had heard, or understood. She hadn't moved at all – not an expression had flitted over her face, not a finger had twitched, not a foot stepped back; she even appeared to be holding her breath . . . Jonas went over to her, half expecting her to pass out.

'Meg,' he murmured, as from the corner of his eye he saw Tuck sink to the ground, as felled and deathly pale as if he'd been struck with an axe; it was another question answered. On the way over here, as he had turned the discovery over in his mind, he had wondered whether Tuck had – on some level – known the truth. That day they'd done the film workshop together and had lunch, he'd seemed like a man looking for a new purpose – desperately applying himself to the tough business of adventure film-making – his friendly smile overwriting a palpable desperation. He wasn't yet thirty and yet his prime had already been and gone – a handsome guy whose looks were beginning to fade, drinking too much and finding reasons not to go home. On some molecular level, had he known he was raising another man's child? His best friend's? But now, as he watched Tuck's shoulders begin to heave, his face hidden in his hands, Jonas could see in the starkest of terms that he hadn't.

But it was another moment before he realized Tuck wasn't crying. He peered closer, just as Tuck dropped his hands away and unfurled like a bud, throwing his head back as he laughed.

Everyone stilled as Tuck grew in the room, lifting first one leg and planting the foot flat on the ground, then the other, until he was standing, head still tipped back, his arms stretching outwards like the Christ the Redeemer statue in Rio.

'Stop it!' Lucy yelled, as he continued to laugh, beginning to turn on the spot. 'What are you doing? *Stop it!*' She ran at him, her fists pounding and flailing at his chest but he just grabbed them as easily as if she were a child and held them away from him, her skin blanching where he squeezed. 'You're hurting me,' she whimpered.

'Good.'

No one did anything, not even Barbara. They all just watched as Tuck – battle-bloodied, his face already bruising, eyes bloodshot, the deep gash across the bridge of his nose beginning to cake – stared down at her with a contempt that made Lucy fall into silence, disbelief and then despair crossing her face as she saw where they were now. The end of the road. 'No . . .'

'Thank you.'

She was wrong-footed again. *'What?'*

'You've given me exactly what I wanted. I'm free again.'

'Tuck . . .' she whispered desperately, her features beginning to crumple. 'Wait . . .'

But he released his grip on her with almost violent dismissal, breaking the cycle of make-up/break-up for the final time. He reached for an envelope that had been lying, unnoticed, in a corner on the floor, and held it out to Meg. Her name was on it. 'Take what's in the letter. I want it this way. I'm starting over.'

Meg, seemingly in a trance, couldn't even lift her hands and Jonas took it from him instead, his eyes coming straight back to Meg. He was worried about her. She was as pale as a snowy sky, her breathing too shallow as her body tried to keep up with her brain. He hadn't wanted her to know, hadn't wanted to have to be the one to say it – but Lucy had gone too far. She'd had to be stopped.

'Mitch . . . ?' Meg murmured.

Tuck took a sidestep, positioning himself in Meg's line of sight, forcing her to look up at him. 'Meg, he loved *you*. You remember that, OK? You were all he could ever think about. You guys weren't like me and her.' He was quiet for a moment, trying to gather his thoughts, process the revelation himself. His life, perhaps more than any other, had been changed most in the past few minutes. 'Whatever it was that happened between *them*, my guess is it was a one-time thing.'

'No—'

'Yes. When we spoke on the phone the night of the storm, he said there was something he needed to tell me, something he needed to tell me in person. I thought he wanted out of the business. We were supposed to meet at the studio the next afternoon but ... well.' He shrugged. They all knew what had happened then. 'Ever since then, it's been killing me not knowing what he wanted to say.' He paused again and as his knee-jerk first response of exhilaration began to subside, Jonas could see the devastation in his eyes. 'I guess now we do. I don't know why what happened between them, happened, but I do know Mitch loved us both, Meg. It was only a week till the wedding and he would've wanted a clean slate. He wouldn't have been prepared to live with lies.'

'Tuck, do you want us to call the police?' Dolores asked, her voice soft.

'No ... just want out of ... ew start ...' Tuck's voice drifted away from Meg's ear in fragments.

Mitch. Her mind kept snagging on him, as caught fast as silk on a nail. Something wasn't right, something was vying for her attention; it was something that woman had said in the hotel lobby, but what ... ? Meg tried to recall her words, her eyes on Barbara as she hugged Tuck.

And then it came to her – the one discrepancy that made the official story collapse like a house of cards. The lie exposed. The truth revealed.

'You opened the kitchens for them,' Meg said quietly, looking straight at Barbara.

Barbara turned, and seeing the comment was directed at her, looked baffled. 'Sorry?'

'The woman, the mother you spoke to just now—'

'Beth Stedman?'

'Yes, her. She said you opened the kitchens for them.'

459

'That's right. I put some soup on for them. I knew they'd need something hot to warm them up'.

Meg's eyes narrowed. 'And your first sitting is at seven. The kitchens open at five.' Meg had spent too many years with Lucy and her mother not to know the workings of the hotel intimately.

'Yes.'

Meg looked at Tuck. 'But you called Mitch at six.'

Tuck's face fell again. 'That's right. A couple of guys came into Bill's bitching about Search and Rescue not going out to look for them. As soon as I heard they were in Wilson's Gully, I took off and tried to get hold of Mitch. I thought you guys were coming down to town in the weather break that afternoon so I rang Lucy first to check where you were. But she said she hadn't seen you so then I tried the cabin.'

Meg remembered how they'd spent the day in bed, choosing to remain snowed in. If they'd only gone down to town that day instead, Mitch would still be alive, as unable to help those people as the rest of the town.

But that 'if only' was not a road she could follow. They'd taken the dead end and there was no changing the fact – Mitch was never coming back.

'So if the kitchens had to be opened especially – as the wife said they were – then the hikers had to have got back *before* five. Over an hour before you heard they'd even gone missing.'

Tuck's head dropped. 'Yeah.'

But Meg wasn't looking at him. She was looking at Lucy. 'But you just said to Tuck you didn't know they were back when he called.'

Lucy raised an eyebrow, surprised to be included in this conversation. 'Because I didn't.'

'No, *he* didn't. But you did. You had warmed the beds for them over an hour earlier – Beth Stedman said so.'

Lucy shook her head, denying the intimation, but Meg's gaze didn't falter. The truth was pressing into clarity at last, like a traveller emerging from the mist. 'You had the beds warmed for them *before* five o'clock, before the kitchens opened – a whole hour before Tuck heard and called, asking if you knew where we were.'

Tuck whitened. A silence spread. 'You deliberately let me call him? You *knew* those hikers were back?' he uttered, a glint of fear in his true-blue eyes. 'I thought you'd made an honest mistake, woman! I thought you'd just heard too late, like me!'

'I forgot!'

'Forgot?' Tuck cried. 'I phoned you to tell you those people were missing, that I was looking for Mitch to tell him, and you *forgot* to tell me that they were already safe and well in the hotel, drinking soup and having hot baths? You'd helped them! *You* had! That isn't forgetting! That's lying. That's deception. That's—'

It was sending a man to his death.

'Oh my god, Lucy,' Barbara quailed, her hands pressed to her mouth.

Meg felt the first hot tears begin to streak her cheeks because she understood it now. She not only knew what Lucy had done; she also knew why. Even if Mitch hadn't known about the baby – and he probably hadn't if Lucy had been only five weeks at the funeral – he'd have wanted a clear conscience before walking down the aisle. She remembered his restless agitation, those strangely tortured looks that had come into his eyes that final weekend together.

'He'd told you he was going to tell us, hadn't he?' she

asked, but the question was rhetorical. She knew exactly how Mitch had worked. Tuck knew too. *He wouldn't have been prepared to live with lies.*

'No—'

'Say it, then!' she roared. 'Tell me you didn't deliberately lie to Tuck. Tell me you didn't let Mitch die, just so you could keep your secret.'

But for once, Lucy was silent. She couldn't make any assurances of the sort.

Chapter Thirty-six

Sunday 24 December 2017

Meg watched Badger as he sat in the silver moon puddle, his nose tipped to the air as he sniffed at the scents drifting past in the evening breeze, the sky above him a marbled dance of green and red lights. Occasionally he indulged a prerogative to chase a squirrel back up a tree, or keep away the coyotes slinking past their boundary, but otherwise he was happy to sit on the steps, a far cry from the dynamic snow dog she'd seen on film that night, bounding through the snow with Mitch down near-vertical mountain slopes. He hadn't been that dog for quite some time and she doubted he ever would be again. The night of the avalanche hadn't just changed her destiny but his too and now his greatest contentment was sitting on these steps with her, watching the stars come out.

She still didn't know if she was doing the right thing, leaving him. It made her heart ache every time she thought about it.

Dolores came back out, the cocoa mugs steaming in her hands.

'There you are! I was beginning to think the racoons had got you,' Meg joked, reaching up and taking both cups, allowing Dolores to use her hands to settle herself in the low seat, before handing her drink back again.

'Well, I'm afraid I was rooted to the spot by the sight of the mess in your bedroom. I wasn't sure if I'd taken a wrong turn into a landfill.'

'Packing's not my forte,' Meg smiled as they both re-tucked their blankets tightly around themselves to keep off the winter chill.

'What a couple of old women we are,' Dolores sighed. 'Thank God we're finally getting rid of you. There might just be time for you to relearn how to act your age again.'

'You mean, going to biodynamic dawn raves and drinking algae?'

Dolores gave an appalled look. 'Is *that* what they do now?'

'No idea,' Meg shrugged and they both chuckled, letting the steam from their cups warm their faces.

'Have you gone back to Ronnie about that apartment?'

'Not yet.' Meg bit her lip. 'I know it looked amazing but . . . I just don't think I want to commit to anything immediately. It's not like I have to rush. Ron's said I can stay at hers for as long as I like – she's always at Jack's or sleeping over at the hospital anyway – so I'd rather get the feel of the city first and find my own hub. Plus I want to be sure I can afford it on my new salary.' She grinned wickedly. 'I never knew you were such a generous employer!'

'What can I say? You'd worked your way up to the top. It's back to the bottom of the ladder for you now, chicken.'

'Thanks to you,' Meg quipped, harking back to her sacking.

'You're welcome. I was fifty years on this earth before I

really got going. Darned if I was going to let you do the same.'

Meg reached over and took her hand, squeezing it in her own. 'I'm really going to miss you.'

'Can't say as I'll notice,' Dolores replied, doing her best to sound neutral. 'That damned dog's going to take up all my time, wanting walks and feeds and cuddles all the time.'

'I'm going to miss him so much too. I wish I could take him with me.'

'Well, you can't. He'd absolutely hate it, he's a mountain dog to the bone. Besides, the customers would have something to say if they didn't find him curled up in his corner.'

'I wish I could take you too.'

There was only the barest of hesitations. 'Same applies. I'm a mountain dog to my bones too.' But Meg saw the way the moonlight glittered off her unshed tears and smiled. Dolores never had been the soft and fluffy type and good-byes were the stuff of nightmares for her. Meg had already braced herself for Dolores giving her a handshake when the actual time came, two days from now.

'Well, I at least wish you'd stay here tonight. It's madness to be going back to town this late.'

'You know I'm far too old to sleep anywhere but in my own bed these days. I could die at any moment,' Dolores quipped.

'I doubt it,' Meg grinned. 'If a bear isn't going to finish you off, I don't know what will.'

'True. Perhaps I'm immortal, God help us all,' she chuckled. 'Martin Hughes is coming to collect me. I told him not to leave it too late or you'd have me washing up as well as packing up.'

It had certainly been a manic few weeks. Ever since That

Day, when she'd finally made the decision to leave, her life had become overrun with admin – clearing and inventorying every last towel, pan and fork left in the cabin for rental (Dolores was going to manage the bookings for her); flying to New York to meet at long last the Kate Spade team – now her first clients – who'd come back to her when the other candidates 'hadn't panned out'; registering her fledgling business; packing for her new life in the big city; sorting out the paperwork for Titch – in spite of Tuck's big-hearted offer, she had refused to take the cheque for his half of his share of the company; partly because it had been offered out of guilt and he had nothing to feel guilty for, but also because he'd need cash if he was going to go ahead with his big dream of making and producing adventure films. She wasn't the only one overhauling her life.

But now it was Christmas Eve and everything was set to go. The cabin was stripped back to its bones, her life with Mitch dismantled and segregated into little boxes. There was nothing left to do here. She was good to go.

Leave. Be gone. Depart. Fly.

Her eyes tracked a plane flashing in the sky and she wondered about the people on board, flying home for Christmas, making it with just hours or even minutes to spare. Families being reunited; homes filled. And yet hers was empty.

'It's so weird, don't you think?'

'What is?'

'The way everything's turned out. Putting the cabin up for rental was what we'd always planned – we'd never intended to live here ourselves and now that's what's happening . . . Even with work and that contract coming back to me, in spite of the fact I messed them around for the best part of five months. I was so sure, when I missed the plane that day, that—'

'You'd missed the boat?' Dolores quipped.

'Exactly. I was so sure the moment had gone.'

'Listen to me. I'm a firm believer that if something's intended for you, it'll keep coming back for you, no matter how long it takes.'

Meg looked across at Dolores – the comment felt pointed somehow – but she was watching the plane overhead too.

'I take it you've heard about Lucy?' Dolores asked in a sober tone.

Meg stilled at the mention of her name and she wondered how long it would take before the very thought of her didn't induce a physical reaction. The news of Lucy's admission to a clinic in Saskatoon for depression and anger management had been greeted with utter shock by the town when she'd left the day after the festival, but for the people who'd been in that room, it was the only solution they were prepared to accept: if Lucy would get help, Barbara would become the baby's guardian and the police would not be called.

Meg had struggled with the decision for weeks afterwards, longing for justice for Mitch on the one hand, knowing on the other that even if Lucy's guilt could be proved – and it was highly unlikely because Lucy hadn't directly told Mitch to go out in the storm; she had just stayed silent, a deliberate omission that had had fatal consequences – that child was Mitch's and he needed one of his parents in his life.

It had been a bitter truth to accept on so many levels – that there was a piece of Mitch in the world and he didn't belong to her; that Mitch had not only betrayed her but done so with her best friend – and some nights, as she lay alone, she had felt as though she couldn't breathe. Every pillar in her world had toppled, bringing the sky crashing down onto her head – Mitch's death was Lucy's fault; Lucy's child was Mitch's son; Lucy had been beating Tuck; her fiancé and best friend had been together – and it felt so unfair, so unjust that he wasn't here to answer to her, that he wasn't here to see the consequences of what he had done, nor of what it had done to *them*. He had shown her in concrete terms that he wasn't the perfect man she'd insisted on remembering after all. Ronnie had been right that day when she'd tried to tell her he'd been flawed and reckless, rash and immature at times; he'd made mistakes like any other person, most of which didn't matter, but that one really did.

She and Tuck had pieced together what must have happened. Tuck had told her how Mitch had seen his scratches and questioned him about them. At the time, Mitch had appeared to accept Tuck's explanation ('They were big fuckin' logs, man') but he must have confronted Lucy, and Lucy . . . ? Well, they knew how skilled a liar she really was; how she could turn a story around and paint herself as the victim, so that Mitch found his anger turn to regret; pity to desire. Even if he had gone to Lucy with the best of intentions, Mitch had hurt Meg more than he would ever know and though she had loved him, she could leave him now.

There was no hatred in her heart; she was leaving here with a light step. Everything was in order, even the financial arrangements for baby Titch (as he was now commonly known); she had allocated half of Mitch's share of the sale into a trust for him which could only be accessed by Barbara, with both Meg and Dolores's approval. Lucy would never be able to get her hands on it.

'They've diagnosed PTSD,' Dolores said.

Meg looked back at her sharply. 'You mean they're giving her an *excuse* for her behaviour?'

Dolores tried to look neutral. 'Apparently children who witness domestic abuse display the same changes to brain activity as front-line soldiers.'

Meg looked away again. 'Please don't ask me to feel sorry for her, Dolores.'

'I'm not.'

But the memories came anyway, from when she was sixteen and fresh from Kent, Lucy's smile in the chemistry class that day as Meg had almost set fire to her hair and the school on her very first day. Lucy had invited her back to the bungalow afterwards and introduced parents who had seemed perfect and completely unlike her own – settled and glamorous and prosperous with a fancy hotel. Meg had been smitten by them, loving their accents, their carpets, their car. Yet behind closed doors, what had Lucy been subjected to? What had she seen? *Learned?*

'It's Barbara I feel sorry for,' Dolores tutted. 'She said she used to watch over Tuck like a hawk, checking when he was coming in late, coming in drunk . . . So to find out *he* was the one who was standing in her shoes . . . She just can't forgive herself.'

'I can't believe I never even suspected . . .'

'Don't give yourself a hard time about it. Jed and I were friends with Roger and Barbara since we moved here in the seventies – we would have barbecues together, go to the movies – and she never let on to me, not once. Not back then, and not even after he's been gone all these years.' She tutted pitifully. 'I thought we knew all each other's secrets.

I thought we could blackmail each other to the day we died. Now I wonder if I ever really knew that family at all.'

Meg was quiet for a long time. Was life just a mirage, she wondered, when dearest friends were revealed as strangers? Not just her and Lucy, but Barbara and Dolores; over thirty years of secrets and lies . . . ? She slid her head to the side and looked across at Dolores. 'How did he see what we missed?'

Dolores arched an eyebrow. 'Jonas?'

Meg nodded, swallowing at the mention of his name. He had left the day after the festival without saying goodbye.

Dolores considered. 'Perspective. Distance can give you a clarity that's impossible when you're personally involved.'

Meg swallowed. That was exactly what he'd said, the night he'd defended Tuck, the night of their first argument.

'And let's face it, the man spent six months looking back down on Earth. If anyone's going to see the bigger picture, it's him.'

They both sank into another silence, watching as the green lights tripped up to yellow, the whole sky seeming to vibrate with electrical intensity.

'Have you heard from him?'

Meg swallowed, knowing Dolores was looking at her, but not wanting to meet her gaze. 'No.'

'He hasn't called? Emailed?'

'Well, would you? He couldn't get out of here fast enough.' She shook her head, staring at her tucked-up knees. 'He must have wondered what the hell he'd walked into.' Meg sighed, resting her cheek on the chair and giving Dolores a weary look. 'No, it's better this way. It's been a month. If he'd wanted to be in touch, he would have been by now.'

'Well, you said he was touring. Have you tried contacting him?'

Meg shot her a look. 'No.'

'Then maybe you should. A lot happened that night. What if he's giving you space? Perhaps he's waiting for you to make the first move.'

The sound of a throttle being choked on the steep pitch, just out of sight, heralded Martin's arrival and they both looked up.

'Bother, that'll be my ride,' Dolores said, briskly tossing aside the blanket and getting up as Badger gave an excited bark from his perch at the top of the steps. She disappeared into the cabin to get her coat, just as the single beam from the snowmobile poled up the snowy lawn towards the cabin.

'Well, now, doesn't this look pretty?' Martin called, turning off the engine and stomping up the deep snow with a smile which was only visible beneath his balaclava because of his raised cheeks. 'It's a regular gingerbread house. I've never seen it look like this before.'

'I'm glad you like it,' Meg replied, proud of how beautifully her little cabin twinkled in the trees. Gingerbread house was exactly right – every gable end, every window had been picked out in the pin lights which were left up all year round, but she hadn't felt like switching on till now.

'Are those your bags?' Martin asked, pointing to the two small suitcases at the top of the steps.

Meg nodded. 'That's them.'

He glanced up at her as he lifted them and carried them towards the trailer attached to the back of the snowmobile. 'For someone about to relocate her entire life, you sure pack light.'

'I've got everything I need,' she said simply.

Dolores stepped back out on the porch, buttoning her coat. 'Chilly tonight, Martin.'

'You're telling me,' he replied, holding out a hand to steady her as she came to the top of the steps. 'Especially with the wind chill. Have you got a scarf for your face?'

'Does this face look like it's scared of the cold?' Dolores scoffed, before turning to face Meg. 'Now you get down to us nice and early, you hear?'

'I will. I'm going to ski down before breakfast.'

Dolores smiled. 'Well, I imagine Badger will enjoy running through the snow with you.'

Meg hesitated, remembering Tuck's beautiful film of a man and his dog; a man and his dog and a mountain. 'Yes.'

'I'll have the coffee ready,' Dolores said, reaching over and hugging her hard. She pulled back, looking stern. 'But I want you to consider this overnight. It's something a wise woman once said: "Perhaps things fall apart so that better things can fall together."'

Huh?

Meg repeated it in her mind as Dolores winked at her. She took hold of Martin's hand as she descended the steps.

'Which wise woman?' Meg called after her.

Dolores, who was at the snowmobile now, looked back. 'Marilyn Monroe!'

'*Marilyn Monroe?*' Meg cried. She'd been expecting Sylvia Plath or Germaine Greer or at the very least, Angelina Jolie. 'Since when has she been considered wise?'

Martin turned on the ignition and the beam fell perfectly onto Meg on the porch, picking her out like a player on the stage. A moment later she was in darkness again as Martin turned the snowmobile and headed back down towards the trees, but Meg caught Dolores's cry before she was swept out of sight.

'Well, she jolly well ought to be!' Dolores called back with a laugh. 'I think she had a point, don't you?'

Meg stared up at the sky. The real one. Hers, in her bedroom, didn't flicker and shimmy and leap like this; she couldn't harness such vivid tones. This was more beautiful than anything inanimate could ever convey. She felt her spirit stir, her senses bloom as though it was showing her exactly how magical and unpredictable life can be and as she watched it play, she sensed this dance was a grand finale just for her. For better and worse, this sky had been her constant companion. It had taken Mitch away from her with its whirling blizzards and full-cheeked winds, but it had given to her too, bringing her Jonas as he circled high above her in looping ellipses, keeping watch over her little life in these big mountains.

Was Dolores right? Was he giving her space?

She was sure there was a joke in there somewhere, but if so, it was bad, even by their standards.

Their. The possessive pronoun. As though there was a 'them'. As though they already had a past.

Her fingers played with the diamond on her ring, as they always did, an unconscious, reassuring habit, like worrying with prayer beads. But the action jarred her mind to a halt today and she looked at her hand and that single white diamond – like a fallen star – which had been given with the promise of forever.

In the event, they'd had two years and eight months from the time he'd given her the ring – a long way short of forever. But how could she have another future when she was still wedded to the idea of this one?

She was still for a moment, then she got up, her blanket falling to her feet, and walked through the cabin into the bedroom. Pulling out the desk chair and taking it over to the wardrobe, she stood on it; her arms reached overheard as she went by feel rather than sight for a tiny hook she'd noticed when painting the room. She had painted over it without thought and its position in the far corner where the wardrobe stood meant it wasn't visible from the floor. It was several minutes before her fingers found it.

She pulled the engagement ring from her finger – with the past months' weight loss, it wasn't just her jeans that were too big – and it slid off without resistance. She stared at it one last time, letting the memories and all that could have been, wash over her. Then, with a single kiss, she stood on tiptoes and hung it on the little hook, the diamond hanging downwards like a newborn star in the night sky.

None of the strangers who stayed here from now on would ever see it, but perhaps one day, maybe thirty or so years from now, she could take it down and give it to the man who was named after his father.

She stepped down and put the chair back, clapped the dust off her hands and took a deep breath. For the man she'd once adored, it was her final act of love.

Jonas. She could almost believe he'd been a dream – something to sustain her when the nights had been their darkest, a voice from the sky like whispers on a pillow. But then he'd stepped into her world and become real. She closed her eyes at the thought of him again; she could see him so easily it was as though his image had been scorched onto her retinas, his kiss like a tattoo on her lips. He'd only been here for a week and yet he had seen them all more clearly than they had ever seen each other; he'd seen *her* with his quick, quiet looks, drawn her close with his private smiles, made her laugh with his goofy jokes.

After all the heartache, could something better really fall together?

He would be in Norway by now and she tried to imagine Stavanger as he'd described it – crooked white, weather-boarded houses with red ridged roofs and cobbled streets; tried to imagine him with his family, home at last.

Sleep wouldn't come but she didn't much care. She lay in bed, looking out at the cascading stars that had come out once the light display had ended, the fire still aglow in the stove opposite the foot of the bed. Badger was snoring . . . Her last night in the cabin was as comfortable as a sock, warm and snug around her. She could hardly believe this was it. The ending. Tomorrow she would ski to Dolores's for breakfast, before the two of them headed over to the Homestead for Christmas Day lunch with Barbara and baby Titch; after thirds of everything and too much sherry, no doubt, she would head to the airport on Boxing Day morning to fly to where Ronnie and Jack were waiting for her and her new life would begin.

She knew she could do it now; she could let go. The impossible was becoming real because she understood something she hadn't known before: her home wasn't these log walls or that puffing stove or even that amazing view. Yes, she'd lost Mitch and her parents here, but Banff would always be her home so long as she had Dolores; Toronto would be her new home because she had Ronnie there.

Home wasn't tied to a place, but to a person, to the feelings she got whenever she was with them . . . with *him* . . .

Her eye fell to the red dot just a few metres away. She still hadn't dismantled the radio rig yet, intending to make it the last thing she did before leaving tomorrow. She had told herself it was a security precaution – in the event of a freak storm tonight, she would need some way to communicate. But in her heart she knew she was unable to bring herself to close down once and for all the channel to another world, another life, another love.

She got up and went to sit at the desk by the window, Badger raising a dozy head at her alert, erect figure in the moonlight, before falling back into slumber again. Quickly, competently now, she switched the red light to green, watched the needles flicker and twitch, listened to the buzz of static fly into the room like a swarm of mosquitoes.

Heart pounding, she listened in, turning the dial by fractions whenever she picked up another transmission, looking for a clear channel. Finding one, she waited thirty seconds, forty . . . her heart beating fast, wanting to get on with it before she chickened out. There was only a minuscule chance that he would be on here; it was ridiculous to think he might be looking for her, as she was looking for him. But then again, hadn't the chances of their first contact been infinitesimally small? They'd gone against the laws of the universe to be together. He'd come back from space to find her.

Heady with excitement, she picked up the transmitter and pressed the 'speak' button.

'This is Victor X-ray Four Delta Delta Echo calling—'

She stopped short suddenly and dropped her head – feeling stupid, feeling despair. The last time they'd communicated via this, he'd been on the ISS. Now he was in Norway, he'd be on a new call sign, if he was on at all.

She felt the crashing disappointment bite. *'Shit!'*

'This is Lima Charlie Six Alpha Foxtrot, calling Volcano X-ray Four Dog Dog Ellie. That's no way to communicate on an open channel, do you copy, over?'

There was a pause. And then –

'Jonas?' Meg's voice careened down the transceiver. 'Oh, my God, is it you?' Her laugh sounded far away, further away than when he'd been in space – ironically, because it was.

He grinned. 'Hey, who else knows your special call sign? Or do you tell it to all the passing astronauts, over?'

She laughed again, sounding shyer now, and he could imagine her expression – could envisage that she probably had her hand over her mouth the way she did whenever she was surprised or embarrassed. 'Oh, my God. I can't believe you're on here.'

'I've been on here every night for the past month, over.'

'You have?'

'Copy that . . . Partly to check in with the guys still drawing circles in the sky . . . Mainly to see if you checked in, over.'

She sounded amazed. 'Really?'

'Yeah, I wondered if you might come on for a chat.'

'You did?' Even more amazed.

'Sure . . . over.'

'But I . . . I didn't even have your new call sign. What made you think I would check in?'

'I was banking on you not remembering that in time.' He

laughed softly, teasing her that he'd been proved right. 'Over.'

'Well, if you'd wanted to chat, you could have just emailed me!' she half laughed, half wailed.

'Yeah, for all the good that did me last time!' There was a pause and he felt his chest tighten. 'Besides, I thought I had better wait . . . When I left, things were—'

'I know,' she said quickly. 'But everything's better now. Over.'

He hesitated. 'Do you mean, "It's over" over – or "over"?" he asked, before adding, 'Over.'

Her laugh was infectious. 'I don't know! . . . All of them?' 'Yeah?'

'Yeah! I'm moving to Toronto in two days . . . got a new job.'

'No way! You mean Dolores hasn't relented and taken you back?'

'She's been as hard as nails,' Meg giggled. 'I've been forced into this! . . . Spade contract. I thought I'd lost . . . back again . . .' He made a minute adjustment of the dial. 'Step in the right direction. Hello? Jonas? Are you there? . . . Can you hear me? . . . Over.'

He was looking out beyond his window into the dark sky, the arctic light a deep indigo. Though he was a long way south of the Polar Nights in the north of the country, where the sun never rose at all for two months of the year, the day here would still be short – maybe six hours or so of sunlight. He was eight hours ahead of her but he knew her sky would still be looking like this right now. Forget the time difference, they had the same sky. They always had.

'So Toronto, huh?'

He heard her breathe a sigh of relief. 'Yeah.'

'I guess that's not so far from Quebec. Better than Banff anyway, over.'

'What's in Quebec?' Puzzlement speckled her voice.

He took a breath. It had been a gamble on his part, not knowing whether this was the right thing to do or, more to the point, what she'd want him to do. 'It's the headquarters for the Canadian Space Agency. I've landed a secondment there. I'm starting next month.'

There was a time delay, static crackling between them and making the needle on his dial flicker wildly. 'You're going to be working in Quebec?' she repeated in astonishment.

'That's right. About an hour and a half plane ride away.'

There was another silence.

'Well, I guess we should be grateful that it's an improvement on being on the wrong side of the atmosphere.'

He laughed, relief flooding his bones. 'It is. We're getting better.'

They were both silent for a moment at his use of 'we'. Them. Him and her.

'I guess this means you'll be able to see my new apartment then,' she said and he could tell from her voice that she was smiling.

'And you mine, over.'

'Hey, what time is it over there anyway?'

'Uh . . .' he checked his watch. 'Quarter to eight in the morning.'

'So then it's Christmas Day already for you.'

'It is.'

'Happy Christmas, Commander Solberg.'

He smiled. 'Happy Christmas to you too, Meg Saunders . . . I got you a present.'

She gasped. 'You did?'

'Well, if you count a joke as a gift.'

'Oh God, I should've *known*,' she groaned and he heard her laugh, all the way across the world. 'Go on then. Do your worst.'

He took a deep breath. 'Did you hear the one about the astronaut who spent six years training to go into space?'

'Go on.'

'He met a girl six weeks in and spent the rest of his time trying to get back down to her again.'

There was a small silence. And then, from the darkness, 'Yes,' she whispered, her smile carrying over in the dark. 'I heard about him.'

Epilogue

Wednesday 27 December 2017

The wheels of her suitcase bumped along the ground, the taxi driver passing her with a wave as he drove off and she steeled her nerve, knowing it was too late to back out now. In spite of the heavy sky that had been disgorging snow ever since she touched down, the roads had been cleared to reveal glistening cobbles and she reread the address she'd written on her inner wrist as she'd whiled the time away at the airport.

The town itself was big – the third largest in Norway, Jonas had told her – but his family's house was in the Old Town and it was pretty close to how she'd imagined it, although the distinctive red roofs were currently whited-out beneath deep drifts and the little lanes so narrow that the taxi driver wasn't even close to being able to get his car down them, and had had to drop her several streets away. Thick garlands of fir were strung up between the houses, lights twinkled at every window and door, and the giant Christmas tree in the town square was so densely latticed with fairy lights, it looked to have been trussed by silk spiders.

The streets were quiet – everyone still indoors with their

families – and as she listened to the rumble of her little wheels on the stone setts, she became acutely aware of her status here as an unexpected traveller. Below a pale moon that seemed ten times the size of the one she knew, she passed from the pools of one old-fashioned street light to the next, raising her head and smiling as a couple of children, no more than ten, ran past dragging a sledge behind them with a small terrier yapping excitedly as it raced to keep up.

She felt another pang of longing for Badger. He was settled with Dolores, she knew that, and he was used to Meg leaving him with her, but that hadn't made Meg feel any better when the time had come to leave. It turned out he was her home too.

She saw the street name she had been looking for and stopped. The lane was one of the narrowest yet, the white weatherboarded houses still looking crisp against the snow which, apart from the indents of footprints, lay deep and untouched, for the snow-clearing machines and gritters would be too big to get down there.

Pulling up her sleeve with her teeth to expose the address on her inner wrist, she checked the house number on her skin against those on the doors, and stepped into the deeper snow, having to lift her bag clear. It was awkward but her mind wasn't on that as she counted down the numbers. She was trying to remember what she'd rehearsed on the plane over – in fact, both planes. It had taken two flights and a six-hour stopover at Heathrow to get here, so she'd had plenty of time to think about it. But now that she was here, everything had gone blank.

She dropped the bag into the snow, panting slightly, as she stared at his door. One knock and this new life she'd come in search of would begin. She took a deep breath and raised her hand, but the sound of voices made her turn and she saw three silhouetted figures coming down the street, one taller than the others.

He stopped walking as he saw her standing there and she swallowed, wanting to laugh and cry all at once. And then he ran, dropping something off his shoulder into the snow, powder being kicked up by his feet as he closed the distance between them: space, a continent, this lane . . . There was nothing separating them any more and he swung her around, lifting her easily as he laughed. 'I can't believe you're here! You came all this way to see me?'

'I wanted to surprise you.' She grinned, looking down into his ice-clear eyes.

'You have!' He lowered her to the ground again, his gaze softening as he took in the sight of her properly. 'You always do.'

The two boys he'd been walking with reached them now, but stayed standing back slightly as though shy. Jonas turned to them, drawing them in closer with a scoop of his arm. 'Hey, this is Meg I was telling you about.'

Meg smiled, holding up one gloved hand in a timid wave. 'Hi.'

'Hi,' they said in accented voices, blinking back at her in unison like a pair of deer. They had ice skates strung over their shoulders, the older one carrying two pairs, and she looked back at Jonas, remembering the day they'd skated on Lake Louise, the day they'd got together.

Jonas reached for her hand and took it in his, squeezing it. 'These are my youngest brothers Matias and Kasper. Matias is fifteen and Kasper is eleven.'

'Oh, my goodness, you're both so tall!' she laughed in astonishment.

The boys looked as though they didn't know what to say to that, and both nodded politely; then a moment later, pushing open the door that was clearly on the latch, they ran into the house together, calling out something to 'Mamma' and 'Pappa' that made Jonas laugh. 'Well, your secret's out. Brace yourself for the welcoming party.' He pulled her in closer to him, pushing her hair back from her face. 'God, I missed you,' he murmured, clasping her face with his hands and kissing her.

'I missed you,' she smiled, entwining her arms behind his neck and kissing him back. 'I couldn't wait till Quebec.'

'Que—? Wait, I thought I was visiting you first?'

'You are.'

He frowned. 'But—'

She smiled. 'Well,' she sighed, stretching the word out teasingly. 'I figure Quebec is as good a base as Toronto. I haven't signed an apartment lease in Toronto yet and I can operate my business from anywhere.'

His mouth parted as he realized what she was telling him, relief and desire and so many other emotions swimming through his eyes. 'Ronnie will hate me for taking you away from her.'

'Ronnie *loves* you.'

'Why?'

'Because I do.'

He blinked, trailing the back of his hand down her cheek. 'Copy that. I love you too, Dog Dog Ellie.'

Acknowledgements

People often ask me how I think up the ideas for my books and my answer is a dull one – I read a lot and keep my ear to the ground in conversations – but the truth is I never know where the idea for the next book is going to come from; equally, once it's written, it can be hard to think back and dissemble the events and remember how it spun into shape from nothing. But the genesis of this particular book will always stay with me. It was a Saturday morning and I was prepping food for a dinner party that night, with Radio 4 on in the background. An astronaut called Dr Helen Sharman was being interviewed ahead of Major Tim Peake's launch into space the following week (in fact, Sharman was the first Briton to go into space, back in 1991; but that's another story) and Sharman mentioned in passing that she had been granted a ham radio license just for the duration of her expedition to the Mir Space Station; she went on to say that some astronauts had been known to strike up friendships with the ham radio enthusiasts who contacted them regularly. Well ... if ever there was a 'Eureka' moment! Could there be a more perfect way to have two characters meet? My mind went into overdrive and within the hour I had sketched out a plot. I wasn't sure if I was completely mad to try to write a love story when one of the characters wasn't even on the planet, but I was excited about the challenge from the offset and knew I had to give it my best shot.

I also didn't know, when I sat in the audience of the Banff Mountain Film Festival Tour, that the films I saw that night would become another well of inspiration for this story. Some of the films prompted scenes for the characters, such as *The Ridge* by Danny MacAskill, which inspired the mountain biking scene with Tuck in the woods, *Afterglow*, which is used as the backdrop film in the Toronto Snow Show scene, and the film made by Tuck of Mitch and Badger is directly based on the stunning short *Sun Dog* by The Shadow Campaign. You can find them all on YouTube and I really highly recommend checking them out – I have watched them numerous times since the festival; they are achingly beautiful and always leave me damp-eyed (and wishing I could ski better).

You'll be happy to hear that Badger, the dog, is real and living the good life in Cornwall with my great friends Sally, Ian, Mhairi and Muirne. His eyebrows really are a thing to behold.

My brother Andrew (whose eyebrows are also notable) was fantastic at giving me local colour – he worked in Banff as a ski lift operator during his gap year – and was particularly helpful with details of what Banff Avenue looks like after midnight when you're rolling out of a bar: it's all true about the elks wandering down the middle of the street in the moonlight too.

I'd like to thank Dan Wagstaff and all the team at PGC for taking this book to their hearts and doing such a fantastic job of getting it out to my Canadian readers. I hope my love for your beautiful country sings from the pages.

For everyone at Pan Macmillan: this is our eleventh book together and I am so proud of everything we've achieved. At the time of writing this, you are Publishers of the Year and you deserve to be: not only do you have the best staff – fresh, innovative, professional – but your support, enthusiasm and nurturing of emerging talent separates you from the pack. It's little wonder you are rewarded not just with chart-topping titles but loyalty too. My hearty thanks to Jeremy Trevathan, Wayne Brookes, James Annal, Jodie Mullish, Katie James, Anna Bond, Daniel Jenkins, Claire Gatzen, Phoebe Taylor; and to my copy-editor Mary Chamberlain and proofreader Camilla Rockwood, thank you – you should probably be paid danger money when it comes to untangling my manuscripts!

To my agent Amanda Preston and my editor Caroline Hogg, I'd like to thank you both for not freaking out when I first mentioned the words 'astronaut' and 'space' and 'ISS'. That you remained calm and trusted me to take those elements and turn them into a Karen Swan book was hugely appreciated. I think we pulled it off, don't you?

Finally, to my lovely big, noisy, slightly mad family –if we're going to name names, then here's a shout-out to Anders, Ollie, Will, Plum, Mum and Dad – I love you all. Over and out.

Prima DONNA

by
Karen Swan

Breaking the rules was what she liked best.
That was her sport.

Renegade, rebel, bad girl. Getting away with it.

Pia Soto is the sexy and glamorous prima ballerina,
the Brazilian bombshell who's shaking up the
ballet world with her outrageous behaviour.
She's wild and precocious, and she's a survivor.
She's determined that no man will ever control her
destiny. But ruthless financier Will Silk has Pia in
his sights, and has other ideas . . .

Sophie O'Farrell is Pia's hapless, gawky assistant,
the girl-next-door to Pia's prima donna, always either
falling in love with the wrong man or just falling over.
Sophie sets her own dreams aside to pick up the debris
in Pia's wake, but she's no angel. When a devastating
accident threatens to cut short Pia's illustrious career,
Sophie has to step out of the shadows and face up to
the demons in her own life.

Christmas at
TIFFANY'S
by
Karen Swan

Three cities, three seasons, one chance to find the life that fits.

Cassie settled down too young, marrying her first serious
boyfriend. Now, ten years later, she is betrayed and
broken. With her marriage in tatters and no career or
home of her own, she needs to work out where she
belongs in the world and who she really is.

So begins a year-long trial as Cassie leaves her sheltered
life in rural Scotland to stay with each of her best friends
in the most glamorous cities in the world: New York,
Paris and London. Exchanging grouse moor and mousy
hair for low-carb diets and high-end highlights, Cassie
tries on each city for size as she attempts to track down
the life she was supposed to have been leading, and with
it, the man who was supposed to love her all along.

The Perfect
PRESENT
by
Karen Swan

Memories are a gift . . .

Haunted by a past she can't escape, Laura Cunningham
desires nothing more than to keep her world small
and precise – her quiet relationship and growing
jewellery business are all she needs to get by. Until
the day when Rob Blake walks into her studio and
commissions a necklace that will tell his enigmatic
wife Cat's life in charms.

As Laura interviews Cat's family, friends and former
lovers, she steps out of her world and into theirs – a
charmed world where weekends are spent in Verbier
and the air is lavender-scented, where friends are wild,
extravagant and jealous, and a big love has to
compete with grand passions.

Hearts are opened, secrets revealed and as the necklace
begins to fill up with trinkets, Cat's intoxicating life
envelops Laura's own. By the time she has to identify the
final charm, Laura's metamorphosis is almost complete.
But the last story left to tell has the power to change all
of their lives forever, and Laura is forced to choose
between who she really is and who it is she wants to be.

Christmas at CLARIDGE'S

by
Karen Swan

The best presents can't be wrapped . . .

This was where her dreams drifted to if she didn't blot her nights out with drink; this was where her thoughts settled if she didn't fill her days with chat. She remembered this tiny, remote foreign village on a molecular level and the sight of it soaked into her like water into sand, because this was where her old life had ended and her new one had begun.

Portobello – home to the world-famous street market, Notting Hill Carnival and Clem Alderton. She's the queen of the scene, the girl everyone wants to be or be with. But beneath the morning-after make-up, Clem is keeping a secret, and when she goes too far one reckless night she endangers everything – her home, her job and even her adored brother's love.

Portofino – a place of wild beauty and old-school glamour. Clem has been here once before and vowed never to return. But when a handsome stranger asks Clem to restore a neglected villa, it seems like the answer to her problems – if she can just face up to her past.

Claridge's – at Christmas. Clem is back in London working on a special commission for London's grandest hotel. But is this really where her heart lies?

The
SUMMER
WITHOUT
YOU

by
Karen Swan

Everything will change . . .

Rowena Tipton isn't looking for a new life, just a new
adventure; something to while away the months as
her long-term boyfriend presses pause on their
relationship before they become engaged. But when a
chance encounter at a New York wedding leads to an
audition for a coveted house share in the Hamptons –
Manhattan's elite beach scene – suddenly a new life
is exactly what she's got.

Stretching before her is a summer with three eclectic
housemates, long days on white-sand ocean beaches and
parties on gilded tennis courts. But high rewards bring
high stakes and Rowena soon finds herself caught in the
crossfire of a vicious intimidation campaign. Alone for
the first time in her adult life, she has no one to turn to
but a stranger who is everything she doesn't want – but
possibly everything she needs.

Christmas in
THE SNOW
by
Karen Swan

In London, the snow is falling and Christmas is just
around the corner – but Allegra Fisher barely has time to
notice. She's pitching for the biggest deal of her career
and can't afford to fail. When she meets attractive
stranger Sam Kemp on the plane to the meeting,
she can't afford to lose her focus. But when Allegra
finds herself up against Sam for the bid, their passion
quickly turns sour.

In Zermatt in the Swiss Alps, a long-lost mountain hut is
discovered in the snow after sixty years. The last person
expecting to become involved is Allegra – she hasn't even
heard of the woman they found inside. It soon becomes
clear the two women are linked and, as she and her best
friend Isobel travel out to make sense of the mystery,
hearts thaw and dark secrets are uncovered . . .

Summer at
TIFFANY'S
by
Karen Swan

A wedding to plan. A wedding to stop.
What could go wrong?

Cassie loves Henry. Henry loves Cassie. With a Tiffany
ring on her finger, all that Cassie has left to do is plan the
wedding. It should be so simple but when Henry pushes
for a date, Cassie pulls back.

Henry's wild, young cousin, Gem, has no such hesitations
and is racing to the aisle at a sprint, determined to marry
in the Cornish church where her parents were wed. But
the family is set against it, and Cassie resolves to stop the
wedding from going ahead.

When Henry lands an expedition sailing the Pacific for
the summer, Cassie decamps to Cornwall, hoping to find
the peace of mind she needs to move forwards. But in the
dunes and coves of the northern Cornish coast, she soon
discovers that the past isn't finished with her yet.

Christmas on PRIMROSE HILL

by
Karen Swan

On Primrose Hill . . .

Twinkling lights brighten London's Primrose Hill as
Christmas nears – but for Nettie Watson, it's not parties
and presents that she wants.

Promises are made

For Nettie, Christmas only serves as a stark reminder
of the life she used to have . . . One day she made
a promise to never leave home, and so far she's
stayed true to her word.

Promises are broken

Under the glaring spotlight of the world's media, Nettie
is unexpectedly caught up in a twenty-first-century
storm . . . Her exploits have made her a global name and
attracted the attention of one of the world's most eligible
men – famous front man, Jamie Westlake. But now she
has his attention, does she want to keep it?

The Paris Secret

by
Karen Swan

Down a cobbled street in Paris, a long-forgotten
apartment is found. Thick with dust and secrets,
it is full of priceless artworks that have been
hidden away for decades.

When high-flying Fine Art Agent Flora Sykes is called in
to assess the collection, she is thrown into the very heart
of the glamorous Vermeil family – and into the path of
the terse and brooding Xavier.

Shying away from the instant attraction between them
and reeling from a devasting family shock back home,
Flora focuses on tracing the history of the paintings,
delving deep into the Vermeil family's past. But as she
moves between London and Paris, Vienna and Antibes,
she finds herself with more questions than answers.
Xavier seems intent on forcing her out, but just what is
he hiding? And will uncovering the truth heal the
past – or destroy her future?

It's time to relax with your next good book

THEWINDOWSEAT.CO.UK

If you've enjoyed this book, but don't know what to read next, then we can help. The Window Seat is a site that's all about making it easier to discover your next good book. We feature recommendations, behind-the-scenes tales from the world of publishing, creative writing tips, competitions, and, if we're honest, quite a lot of lists based on our favourite reads.

You'll find stories and features by authors including Lucinda Riley, Karen Swan, Diane Chamberlain, Jane Green, Lucy Diamond and many more. We showcase brand-new talent as well as classic favourites, so you'll never be stuck for what to read again.

We'd love to know what you think of the site, our books, and what you'd like us to feature, so do let us know.

 @panmacmillan.com

 facebook.com/panmacmillan

WWW.THEWINDOWSEAT.CO.UK

extracts reading groups
competitions books new
books discounts extracts extracts
competitions events
books
new extracts discounts events
events books reading groups
extracts discounts
new titles reading groups
interviews
events extracts extracts events
discounts books new
new books èvents events new
events new interviews new books extracts

www.panmacmillan.com
extracts events reading groups books
competitions books extracts new